THE BAD SHEPHERD

THE BAD SHEPHERD

J. A. Springs

All long journeys start with the first step.
Always for J.M.S. first.

Prelude

Shadows of Betrayal
In shadows deep where secrets roam,
A bad shepherd strays, far from home.
His flock betrayed, the trust undone,
As night descends, the tale begun.
A lone wolf's howl, a shepherd's flight,
Dark echoes in the pale moonlight.
The shepherd's path, a twisted track,
In the bad shepherd's wake, a wolfish pact.

1

Jack's swift finger switch on the radio dial silenced the deceptive promises of a 'light dusting' of snow. The actual scene outside his windshield betrayed the forecast, an unrelenting white haze that defied the reach of his windshield wipers. A cacophony of bad pop music spilled from the speakers, mirroring his foul mood. The weather was unequivocally harsh; in Jack's unassuming estimation, venturing out at four-thirty in the morning in thirty-below temperatures in what was touted as a gentle snowfall was sheer lunacy. He mused that even the Almighty might still be snuggled up in celestial warmth.

He peered through the windshield once more, his view limited to a mere thirty feet ahead—a pitiable distance given the so-called 'light' snowfall. He chuckled, though devoid of any amusement. The morning was off to a dire start. As a detective en route to a crime scene, he begrudgingly fulfilled his duty while yearning to trade places with God, enveloped in comfort and shelter.

But for the disused black-and-white police cars squandering taxpayer funds by idly running, Jack might have questioned his location. He eased his sedan behind the last parked police cruiser on the roadside, yet even in this stationary position, visibility remained a hazy veil.

Drawing his hat further down, he sought refuge from the relentless wind, determined to keep it securely in place. Popping up the collar of his trench coat, he couldn't help feeling like a walking cliché—an embodiment of the fedora-wearing, trench-coated stereotype. His sole desire was to ward off the chill, not to become a paperback caricature of a gumshoe detective. In the pre-dawn hours, snowflakes fluttered with just enough density to obscure his vision slightly, now

1

that he had abandoned the shelter of his car and wasn't inching forward at a cautious fifteen miles per hour.

The alternating flashes of red and blue emitted by the police cruisers cast an otherworldly hue on the surroundings, unequivocally affirming his precise alignment with the expected location, irrespective of his personal preferences.

In the face of the snow's determined efforts to thwart his observation, he surveyed the neighborhood's surroundings, seizing the sporadic gaps in the relentless downfall. Within these intermittent pauses, glimpses of the area unfolded before him. It was an enclave of affluence, a bastion of opulence where the only minorities present were the uniformed figures scattered across the crime scene. Jack was acutely aware that the homes here commanded staggering prices, reaching into the millions. A hefty sum for what essentially amounted to sticks of wood topped with shingles or stacks of bricks crowned by the same shingled roofing. Yet, Jack's indifference was palpable—he had no stake in this place.

Navigating the slush-coated street with cautious steps, Jack advanced carefully, determined not to grace the ground with an unintended encounter with his rear end, all while yearning to escape the frigid night. His eagerness to evade the cold, however, was laced with uncertainty about the scene awaiting him within the house. The moment he stepped inside, the chill might recede, but the harsh reality of the impending crime scene would envelop him.

As the police force's top-ranking detective, Jack held the coveted title of number one, a distinction that had recently become more of a burden than an honor. The weeks had blurred into a series of gruesome scenes, each more unsettling than the last. Faces distorted by violence had become an unwelcome tableau etched into his memory. It was a cycle he longed to escape, a wish that seemed to grow stronger with each new case.

His assignment to this particular murder scene carried a twofold purpose, the first revealed itself as he pulled up to the address—a tableau of suburban opulence. The second, a reason he knew all too well, lingered beneath the surface, a truth he had to confirm once he crossed the threshold. An unspoken weight accompanied him, a mixture of reluctance and duty. In his gut, he grappled with the knowledge that this was the job—the part that sucked, a truth he couldn't deny even if he tried.

Stepping into the house, the soft tap of his feet echoed a rhythm against the floor. Each tap was an attempt to rid his shoes of the snow they'd collected, an instinctual ritual to prevent muddying the crime scene. With meticulous precision, he brushed off the remaining stubborn snowflakes that clung to his jacket, delicate remnants of the world outside that were yet to melt. His breath escaped in a slow exhale, a moment of pause he claimed before delving into the next chapter of this grim narrative.

The tang of iron danced upon his taste buds, a peculiar sensation that prodded Jack's curiosity. His gaze swept the surroundings once more, seeking familiarity and a sense of orientation within the confines of the house. The swirling snowstorm outside had obscured the usual urban landmarks that would confirm the presence of a bustling metropolis. The time of day added little clarity to the scene; instead, it served as a conspirator in the atmospheric confusion. Guided by a flicker of recognition, he spotted one of his subordinates and navigated his way toward him.

Observing Jack's entrance, his subordinate met him with a sluggish shuffle. A pang of envy tugged at Jack's thoughts as he noticed the ease with which others embraced lethargy and ineptitude. He couldn't help but question, not for the first time nor the last, why he seemed to stand alone in a sea of duty and purpose. He sighed, mentally chiding the early hour for demanding his attention before his coffee.

Detective Skipple, Bob as he was known, sidled up to Jack, a stance that left Jack pondering whether his arrival signified a desire to share his findings from the crime scene or to jot down Jack's coffee order like a waiter. The man stood, a stoic sentinel by Jack's side, emanating an air of someone yearning to escape the present moment—a sentiment Jack could readily relate to. Bob's expression mirrored what Jack himself was feeling, a tacit acknowledgement of shared discontent.

Jack wrestled his way out of his jacket, determining to make productive use of his time while awaiting the mental gears of his colleague Bob to transition from idle to engaged. The process was undoubtedly slow, but eventually, Bob's cognitive engine roared to life—albeit in the realm of thoughts.

"Hey, Jack," Bob's greeting rolled out, perhaps a little reluctantly.

Leaving his jacket behind, Jack pivoted, his gaze alighting on a uniformed officer who seemed to blend into the background with an air of nonchalance. With a courteous nod, Jack surrendered his trench coat to the officer, requesting it be stowed away from the hubbub. The officer complied, ambling off with the garment in tow.

Returning his attention to Bob, Jack couldn't help but feel that his colleague's mental gears had slipped back into neutral. The perpetual cycle of frustration tugged at Jack's patience—why did he even bother sometimes? Suppressing his exasperation, Jack bided his time, a realization slowly dawning that any response from Bob was becoming an elusive mirage.

"Bob," Jack prodded again, his patience now subtly tinged with irritation, his gaze shifting steadily, "what transpired here? Any inkling yet?"

Bob's gaze was firmly rooted to the rich red carpet, his eyes veiled by a distant and vacant expression, his countenance eerily neutral. Jack felt as though he were a dentist grappling with the challenge of extracting teeth from a skittish chicken.

From Bob's perspective, Jack was the quintessential embodiment of a serious, by-the-book detective. Jack's meticulous attention to detail and analytical approach to solving cases were qualities that Bob admired on some level. However, they also left Bob feeling somewhat inadequate, as if he were constantly falling short of Jack's expectations. Jack's ability to piece together complex puzzles and his dedication to his work made Bob feel like he was always playing catch-up.

Bob's perception of Jack's demeanor was that of a stern, no-nonsense individual who took his job very seriously. Jack's intense focus on the cases they were working on created a sense of pressure that Bob struggled to meet. It was as if Jack's analytical mind was always a step ahead, leaving Bob feeling like he was stumbling in the dark. Jack's measured tone and his often reserved expressions made Bob wonder if he was ever truly satisfying his boss's standards.

After an elongated pause, Bob finally initiated a hesitant, faltering movement forward. Jack instinctively extended his hand, its firm grasp gently curbing Bob's progress. In that instant, it became palpably clear to Jack that something about this crime scene had rattled Bob profoundly.

Bob swiveled toward Jack, their eyes locking in a moment of shared connection. But what Jack encountered in Bob's gaze was a disconcerting trifecta—slack-jawed bewilderment, dazed distraction, and a blankness that resembled the aftermath of a mental blackout. It was as if Bob's metaphorical groceries were persistently eluding the top shelf where he sought to put them.

A series of blinks followed—one, two, and a third for good measure—before Bob tentatively began to string words together, an attempt to convey the shambles he had witnessed thus far.

"I'm at a loss, Jack. This mess defies explanation. You'll have to see it to understand," Bob eventually relinquished, his words coated with an audible layer of exhaustion.

Exhaustion coated his voice, a weariness cultivated over the years spent grappling with the inscrutable, striving to impose coherence upon the nonsensical. But this morning wasn't just another chapter in that enduring struggle. This was much more. The tableau Bob had encountered surpassed any semblance of his understanding. It lay beyond the grasp of his cognitive faculties, shrouded in a veil of incomprehensibility.

Bob's movement resumed, and Jack hesitated, uncertain whether this resurgence was a harbinger of clarity or a mere manifestation of his colleague's inner turmoil. Opting for acceptance, Jack relinquished his grip on Bob's arm, his hand sliding away like a wilted leaf. Bob was slowly but surely regaining a sense of direction, a ray of hope amid the confusion.

Jack couldn't recall ever seeing Bob in such a state—disoriented, shaken. Jack was well aware of the job's weight, its capacity to chisel away at one's resilience. The encounters it entailed were far removed from the ordinary. Such was the unwritten contract—deal with the cards dealt by the job, and hope fervently that, at day's end, you could leave its specters behind, confined to the office. Yet, certain cases, certain scenes, they clung tenaciously. They became part of you, entwining with your very being, insidiously altering your essence. It was an odor, an indelible taint, that no amount of washing could scrub away.

Bob led Jack deeper into the house, navigating past the opulent, sparsely inhabited living room—a space that felt more like a pristine exhibit than a lived-in environment. The ostentatious display of possessions conveyed an exaggerated abundance, an excessive material opulence designed to impress. Beyond the grand foyer, the living room extended into an expansive open-concept area.

This vast expanse seamlessly incorporated distinct zones for dining and family activities. The family area boasted a wood-burning fireplace, neatly stocked with firewood on the left-hand side of the hearth.

Two numbered placards rested on the floor, a stark contrast against the luxurious carpeting. These markers delineated spots of blood, stark reminders of violence that had shattered the elegance of the surroundings. Jack artfully maneuvered around them, approaching the midpoint between the dining and living areas—a relatively untouched space that seemed to serve as a provisional sanctuary within the burgeoning crime scene.

Amidst the tension, Jack's query echoed through the room. He pivoted slowly, his gaze probing the space as he sought answers from Bob, whose assistance was proving frustratingly elusive.

With a deep inhale, Bob began his response, a hint of trepidation echoing in his voice. "We're piecing it together, Jack. It's... well, it's unlike anything I've encountered before. Just give me a moment." The words left Bob's lips, accompanied by a pronounced swallow, revealing the magnitude of the scene's impact on even a seasoned detective like him.

The soft murmur of voices from the uniformed officers and forensic teams provided an ambient backdrop, infusing the space with an atmosphere reminiscent of a sacred sanctum or curated museum exhibit rather than a mere dwelling. The ambiance seemed to emanate from the very opulence of the surroundings, an unspoken agreement to tread lightly and preserve the solemnity of the scene.

Jack moved purposefully through the environment, his steps synchronized with Bob's as they advanced towards the rear of the house. By absorbing his surroundings, Jack assimilated a comprehensive understanding of the space's layout. As they traversed, his attention was drawn to the wood-burning fireplace where two forensics team members were meticulously photographing an item—a clear indicator of its significance. Further inside, near the heart of the house, two uniformed officers occupied the kitchen area. Their focused gazes were fixed upon an object on the floor, although the kitchen island obstructed Jack's view, leaving him in anticipation of what had captured their attention.

The notion that the backdoor might be ajar proved accurate as Jack's hunch found validation in the open entryway. The draft that crept inside sent a shiver down his spine, prompting a fleeting wish that he had retained his coat's warmth. Yet, that wish was preemptive. He would indeed experience the cold, but he wouldn't need to venture out into it. As he approached the backdoor, an unsettling sight unveiled itself before him—the body.

Positioned midway between the confines of the house and the external elements, the unfortunate victim straddled the threshold. Technically still within the shelter of the home, yet exposed to the biting cold, Jack found himself caught in the dissonance of the situation.

The aversion he harbored toward the frigid environment was growing more intense by the moment, underscored by this grim tableau that now embodied both life and death in a state of unsettling transition.

Amid the chill that enshrouded the scene, Jack's disdain for the cold deepened, recognizing that the low temperature could potentially tamper with the accuracy of the body's cooling process, inevitably skewing the determination of the time of death.

Jack's gaze settled on the lifeless form sprawled awkwardly, suspended between the indoor haven and the frigid outdoor expanse. An immediate disquiet took hold, as if his instincts were setting off muted alarms that he couldn't quite decipher. Bob, in his current state of assistance, was about as effective as a bucket with a gaping hole at retaining water. The nagging sensation that something was amiss gnawed at Jack's patience, and his frustration simmered with the unshakable awareness that the discrepancy should be glaringly evident.

The body's positioning, jutting partially out of the back door, bothered Jack on more than one level. Beyond the discomfort of facing the biting cold, he yearned for either the door to be sealed shut or the ambient temperature to be elevated. Yet, even in the midst of these tangible concerns, the uncanny detail he sought to discern remained elusive. In the recesses of his mind, a subtle process began, whereby the scene, fragment by fragment, was reassembled for his cognitive dissection.

The victim lay supine, facing upwards, one hand gripping the door handle. The once-pristine door was now marred by a sinister splattering of blood. Then, like a revelation, Bob's contribution finally held merit. In a moment that belied the disarray of the scene, Bob's words unfurled, carrying the weight of their insight.

"It appears the victim was attempting to escape through the back door when the killer intercepted them," Bob's observation cut through the enigma.

Jack felt a retort welling up within him, but he managed to quell it. In this intricate dance of investigation, silence could often be more productive than verbal sparring. Jack shifted his focus, opting for action over words, and knelt beside the body to conduct his own examination. The tableau before him bore the mark of a grim struggle, and he needed to extract every ounce of information it held. As Jack scrutinized the body, his trained eye dissected the telling details. The right arm, stretched out and fixed on the back door handle, painted a vivid picture of desperation. It was a pose that narrated a futile attempt at escape, a fleeting moment in time that now lay frozen in its tragedy. Blood had seeped beneath the victim, darkening as it congealed, etching a morbid chronicle of events.

Yet, like the elusive pieces of a puzzle that defied coherence, the solution to his vexation lingered just beyond his grasp. The seconds ticked by, each one a reminder of his persistent struggle to unravel the mystery that concealed itself within the scene.

"Bob," Jack started, his voice measured and deliberate. Amidst the whirlwind of unfolding events, he felt a pressing need to ensure utmost clarity in their communication. "Bob, where is the victim's head?" he inquired, his words taking on a cautious cadence. The gravity of the situation necessitated precision in his question.

The body was eerily incomplete, lacking both a head and the left arm up to the shoulder. Jack's gaze shifted from the unsettling sight before him, and he followed the telltale path of blood. It led him to the kitchen, where the two uniformed officers were stationed. Jack's gaze alternated between the floor and the officers, his curiosity piqued. A nonchalant shrug from one of the officers elicited a wry amusement from Jack, who had a hunch that he had stumbled upon the missing arm and shoulder.

Indeed, his deduction proved correct. Resting on the floor was the dismembered left arm, tightly gripping a substantial kitchen knife. The scene spoke of brutality, an image that was both gruesome and puzzling.

Amidst the disarray, Bob's voice cut through the air once more, prompting Jack's internal plea for silence. "Far as I can tell, the killer busted in through the front door," Bob stated matter-of-factly.

Jack cast a reflective glance back through the expanse of the house, his eyes fixing on the front door that held crucial evidence. He strolled over to the door, scrutinizing its construction. Crafted from robust materials, the door was a deceptive amalgamation of metal and wood. Its wooden veneer cloaked its true nature—a fortified barrier designed to deceive while securing. Despite its imposing façade, the deadbolt remained firmly engaged. Jack's attention shifted to the adjacent trim, where the frame had been forcibly breached, accompanied by a segment of the reinforced wall. He returned to Bob, absorbing the unfolding puzzle.

As Bob's voice resonated with an air of detachment, the pieces of the sinister puzzle slowly aligned. "The victim ran into the kitchen and got the knife and the killer... disarmed... him," Bob's words unfolded with a chilling clarity, maintaining the same deadpan tone that belied the gravity of the situation.

Amid the gravity of the situation, Jack's thoughts flitted momentarily to the inappropriateness of humor, and Bob's somber words only exacerbated the situation. The mentioning of 'disarmed' with a victim whose arm had been torn from its torso was somehow aptly fitting.

Jack knew that Bob's words lacked any hint of jest, making the situation even more chilling. The severity of the statement stripped it of any potential for levity, leaving no alternative manner in which Bob could have relayed the disturbing revelation. Inwardly, Jack was relieved that those engaged in the investigation refrained from finding amusement in the macabre disclosure. Inwardly, he implored Bob to cease speaking—first his silence, and now this, a stark contrast that disconcerted Jack profoundly.

"The victim got to the back door and the killer took his head clean off," Bob's unsettling summation of the grim scene fell heavily on Jack's ears.

He cast a sidelong glance at Bob and let out a weary sigh before firmly requesting, "Bob, enough."

Bob was aware of Jack's frustration with him. He sensed Jack's impatience with his lack of substantial contributions and the occasional inappropriate comments he made. Bob felt like he was constantly disappointing Jack, and this created a sense of unease whenever they interacted. He wished he could better meet Jack's expectations, but he couldn't shake the feeling that he was always falling short.

Amidst the disquieting puzzle before him, Jack assimilated the details with a searching gaze. The reconstruction of events formed within his mind, yet within this mental tableau, a glaring incongruity stood out—a gaping hole that left him with more queries than answers. The discord between the image he envisioned and the reality presented left him grappling with skepticism, a gnawing uncertainty that refused to be easily dismissed.

Jack gestured toward the imposing front door. "Bob, that door is no ordinary entrance. It would take SWAT and C4 explosives to breach it. This place is practically a fortress. And the back windows? Bulletproof glass with a security shutter above."

Amid the unsettling scene, Jack's intuition honed in on another concern. Leaving Bob by the left arm on the kitchen floor, Jack walked over to where the forensics team worked. He had a gut feeling that he would discover the missing head here. His intuition didn't fail him. He studied the severed head momentarily before rising and addressing Bob. At this juncture, Jack had realized that conversing with Bob was as productive as talking to a wall. His words served as a way for him to navigate through the labyrinthine thoughts swirling in his mind.

"Bob," Jack inquired, his tone laced with curiosity, "what do you reckon the killer used as a weapon?"

The hesitation in Bob's response was palpable, a clear indication that he was unprepared to offer even a speculative answer about the nature of the dismembering tool. Jack mentally excluded swords, knives, or any typical cutting implement from the possibilities. The violence and brutality of the act seemed to rule out a conventional edged weapon. The extent of the trauma inflicted on the victim was overwhelming, suggesting a frenzied attack that could hardly be explained by a mere blade. Though Jack's mind flirted with the idea of limbs being torn away, he couldn't allow himself to fully embrace the notion—it bordered on the implausible. Still, he had a hunch that Bob's thoughts were running along similar lines of skepticism and disbelief.

Jack resumed speaking, his words flowing with a cautious rhythm. He intended to guide himself through the maze of his thoughts, offering a verbal narrative of his deductions as he continued to analyze the perplexing scene before him. "Our perpetrator kicked in the front door and surprised the victim. The victim gets to the kitchen and grabs a knife. The perpetrator tears his arm off."

As he spoke, Jack moved deliberately through the house, his determination overriding the biting chill that surged in with each pass between the open portals of the front and back doors. "The victim, likely in a desperate bid to escape, goes to the backdoor to get away. The perpetrator, perhaps letting the victim believe he's about to elude capture, allows him to unlock and swing open the backdoor, and then the perpetrator knocks his head off"

Seeking Bob's input, Jack turned his gaze towards him. However, the hope for a valuable contribution seemed futile, considering Bob's un-helpfulness since Jack's arrival. The sense of it being a wasted endeavor nagged at Jack; it was as if his partner had become a mere bystander in their own investigation.

"The only thing around here strong enough to do that kind of damage to a person is a bear," said Jack as he looked at Bob to see what insight Bob might have been able to bring.

"Yeah, Jack," Bob's voice finally chimed in. "Sounds pretty spot-on to me. I was scratching my head over this one, thought I was losing it," Bob mused, his voice trailing off before he cleared his throat.

Bob's gaze roamed the scene, his eyes searching for any additional clues that might shed light on the enigma before them. In response, Jack let out a heavy sigh, bracing himself for the impending conversation.

"The bear theory would be convenient, Bob. Although not realistic in the least," Jack began, his tone tinged with frustration. As much as he might have preferred such an explanation, the facts didn't align. "Problem is, the front door. Take a look, that's a foot impression on the door."

Upon closer inspection, a visible indentation marred the door's surface, a result of the impact it had endured. A trained eye might discern the faint outline of an unusual impression embedded within the wood, an unsettling reminder of the strength that had been harnessed against it. It was a mark of power, a testament to the violent clash that had unfolded at this entrance.

In this juxtaposition of strength and vulnerability, the door's defiance was undeniable, yet the intrusion had also left its mark. It hinted at a force beyond the ordinary, a force that might have defied the door's expectations. The scene spoke of an enigma, of a power that dared to challenge even the most fortified of barriers, raising questions about what could wield such strength.

Jack's gaze shifted to Bob, his expression inviting any insight his partner might have to offer. Yet, as Jack waited, the realization settled in that Bob's mental engine wasn't just idling—it was entirely switched off.

"A bear can't explain the front door, plus we're in the middle of the city," Jack continued, his patience wearing thin. "And what about the method of the dismemberment? This wasn't done by a wild animal. This was deliberate."

Bob remained rooted in his spot, a perplexed expression clinging to his features. Jack's attempt to engage him seemed futile; it was as if the switch of understanding had been flipped off. Frustration gnawed at Jack as he observed Bob's vacant state. His jaw tightened and loosened. It was like a house fully lit but uninhabited, a meal simmering but no chef in sight, a car cruising without a driver. Use any metaphor you liked; Bob was embodying it. Jack's efforts felt wasted. Bob was dimmer than a crate of bricks, a flashlight stripped of both bulb and batteries—utterly fucking useless.

With a look around, Jack caught the eye of the uniformed officer he had handed his coat to earlier. Signaling to him, he requested his jacket back. As the officer returned it, Jack slipped the officer's flashlight off his belt, acknowledging the irony of needing illumination in more ways than one. With a curt gesture, Jack motioned for Bob to follow him as they navigated around the lifeless body and exited through the back door. Jack's intention was to scour the surroundings for any elusive clues that might help them salvage a modicum of sense from the bewildering chaos he had stumbled into. Riddles weren't Jack's preferred puzzle—ironic, considering his surname was Riddle. Cases without solutions irked him. Throughout his career as a detective, Jack had rarely encountered enigmas he couldn't unravel. He poured his heart into each investigation, leaving no stone unturned. His experience and skills had solidified his reputation as an exceptional detective, rendering him vigilant when it came to even the minutest of details.

But this current case defied his usual methods. No small particulars presented themselves; they eluded his grasp just as slippery as quicksilver. The two similar cases that had crossed his path hadn't offered any easy answers either. Their unsolved files rested ominously on his desk, glaring reminders of his limitations. There were no insignificant clues, nor were there apparent omissions. These cases, along with the one at hand, shared a chillingly distinct signature—a disturbing dismemberment method that baffled reason.

Jack's unease deepened as he pondered the meticulous depravity that connected the dots. The dismemberments had a unique quality that pointed unequivocally to the same twisted perpetrator. It was a calling card, a macabre signature imprinted on the scenes like a cruel seal.

For someone who prided himself on understanding the intricacies of his city, this was an affront he found intolerable. Jack's frustration grew with every piece that refused to align. The riddles were adding up, and they whispered of a deranged serial killer prowling the streets he had come to admire.

But the problem was that Jack's arsenal of clues was dangerously scant. He found himself ensnared in a massive, unsettling jigsaw puzzle with no reference picture and no certainty of where the next piece would fall. All he could feel was the gnawing inevitability of more victims in the wake of this ruthless predator's spree. It was a sinister game, and the odds seemed stacked against him.

Jack stepped out into the backyard, his flashlight sweeping over the landscape. He noticed that the metallic tang of blood had finally left his mouth, a relief brought by the crisp air that filled his lungs. The darkness was unbroken except for the faint moonlight that struggled through the falling snow, casting meek patches of illumination.

As Jack moved, the scent of the breeze cleansed the residual scent of blood from the atmosphere. The serenity of the night contradicted the brutality he had just witnessed within the walls of the house. He had no distinct objective in mind as he searched, an unsettling realization that he might be searching for a bear in the middle of the city. The flashlight played across the shrubs, briefly capturing what could have been a glint of eyes reflecting light. It might have been an animal, a mundane explanation, but uncertainty crept into Jack's mind. An inexplicable chill settled into his bones, not the kind induced by the cold, but the sort of bone-deep shiver one feels in the presence of fear.

The sensation urged Jack back into the house. The lingering fear was like an unwelcome guest that nestled within him, refusing to depart until the light and company pushed it away. He turned on his heels and re-entered the house, addressing Bob as he moved, his tone carrying a mix of exhaustion and determination. "Finish up here, Bob. Put the case file on my desk. I'll tackle it first thing tomorrow," Jack instructed, his voice trailing as he headed inside, eager to escape the darkness that seemed to harbor more than just the unknown.

"Alright, Jack," Bob responded, his tone trying to strike a balance between agreement and defensiveness, "I'll do my best to dig deeper. I know you've got high standards, and I don't want to let you down." Bob's words held a hint of self-consciousness, revealing his awareness of Jack's expectations. He tried to convey a willingness to improve and contribute more meaningfully to their investigations. Bob's outward demeanor was a mix of determination and a touch of insecurity, as he attempted to bridge the gap between his own capabilities and Jack's formidable skills.

Jack trudged back to his car, the chill of the night gnawing at him. He settled into the driver's seat, seeking refuge in the warmth of the car's heater against the biting cold. As he sat there, his mind circled back to the taste of iron in his mouth. A mixture of disgust and unease washed over him, and he made a mental note to brush his teeth immediately. Blood was a scent he loathed, an odor that lingered long after the immediate exposure had passed. He yearned for a hot cup of coffee to cleanse his palate and clear his senses.

The radio piped out lackluster pop tunes, mirroring Jack's foul mood. The early hour compounded his annoyance, and he knew the day ahead wouldn't bring much improvement. Despite his slow speed, visibility was still abysmal, yet Jack pressed on, navigating the treacherous road while remaining vigilant for reckless drivers who seemed immune to the dangers of snowy conditions. The goal was simple: reach his destination without incident.

His thoughts, however, lingered on the crime scene he had left behind. The violence he had encountered was already unsettling, but there was more to it that unsettled him deeply. The brutality required a level of strength that was chilling, but that wasn't the only puzzle piece that troubled him. The perpetrator's behavior baffled him. Allowing the victim to reach the back door, even taking the time to unlock it, hinted at a perverse kind of game. Jack questioned the motive. Why create such a scenario if the ultimate objective was murder?

The scene defied easy categorization. It wasn't a straightforward robbery homicide, as nothing else in the house bore the marks of a thief's intrusion. Jack's mind churned with these thoughts, his analytical nature wrestling with the puzzle that lay before him. The pieces didn't fit together neatly, and it left him with a deep sense of unease as he drove on through the snow-covered roads.

The oddity of the house nagged at Jack's thoughts. He hadn't thoroughly explored the entire property, but what he had seen raised his suspicions. A dwelling nestled within an upscale suburban neighborhood, yet fortified like a shelter—it was a paradox that didn't add up. Jack couldn't fathom what might be concealed within the walls, but he was fairly certain it wasn't just standard drywall, insulation, and wood. It stood to reason that even the walls themselves were reinforced, given the presence of that impenetrable metal door and bulletproof windows. The question that gnawed at him was: who was the victim trying to keep out? Had he known that his defenses would prove futile against an assailant capable of breaching such a fortress-like façade? The multitude of questions only seemed to multiply, while answers remained frustratingly elusive.

Jack's mind sifted through the details of the other two cases, attempting to draw connections. But the similarities weren't immediate; the victims hailed from disparate corners of the city. Their residences varied, each featuring some form of security measure that should have ensured their safety. Yet, the fact that those safeguards had failed begged a more profound query: what remained hidden that eluded comparison, and what subtle patterns might be lurking beneath the surface?

As Jack pondered these enigmas, he felt as though he were grappling with puzzle pieces that stubbornly refused to fit. The patterns he sought eluded him, the pieces resisting alignment. He recognized that he needed either a broader perspective—a larger puzzle—or more individual pieces to assemble the whole picture. Either way, he was well aware that such clarity would likely come at the cost of another crime scene, another unfortunate victim. The chilling prospect only deepened his determination to unravel the mysteries shrouding these unsettling cases.

Another victim was the last thing Jack desired. The thought of it hinted at an unforgivable lapse in his duty—a failure to prevent more tragedy. As he stared through the windshield, his gaze was drawn to a familiar glow emanating from a store's window, prompting a rare smile to touch his lips. Jack was about to succumb to the allure of cliché, yet he cared little for that label in this moment. With the car now parked and the engine running wastefully, he abandoned his official responsibilities. Shielded from the frigid outdoor air, he found respite in the comforting warmth of the store.

The neon beacon above the entrance blazed brightly enough to burn through the falling snow. It read 'Hot Donuts', and it captured Jack's attention with a magnetic pull. Surrendering to the pull, he stepped inside, escaping the cold that had seeped into his bones. A sense of ease settled over him as he claimed a seat, his order for two freshly glazed donuts and a coffee—lightly adorned with two creams and two sugars—soon placed before him. It was his solitary indulgence, the one luxury he allowed himself without hesitation. The two donuts, tenderly sweet, were but an added bonus to the main act—his cherished cup of coffee.

Donovan Pike's footsteps resounded through the vacant corridors, their echoes bouncing off the walls like a solitary symphony. The desolate halls stood in stark contrast to the usual hustle and bustle of populated spaces. He acknowledged the stationed guard with a nod—a gesture that spoke volumes, given the handful of personnel present. Their familiarity rendered formal identification unnecessary; Donovan's presence was its own validation.

The scarcity of authorized personnel contributed to the ease of Donovan's passage through the facility. The elevator controls beckoned, unguarded yet secure in their access. It was a testament to the exclusivity of the establishment. Donovan's identity was etched in the guards' memories, a mark of his significance.

Beyond the realm of visual recognition, the facility's security employed DNA-based metrics. This advanced authentication system ensured that only those authorized could breach its barriers. Such measures made redundant the need for physical identification checks. The sophisticated dance of electricity within fluorescent tubes above cast a flickering light, accompanied by a low hum that served as the acoustic backdrop to Donovan's purposeful strides.

The solitude amplified even the minutest sounds—the subtle friction of his fabric-clad legs brushing together was discernible in the quiet expanse. Donovan's entitlement extended across every stratum of the facility, an imperative borne of his role as the facility administrator. Every facet of its operation fell within his purview, demanding unrestricted access.

As Donovan navigated the corridors, his presence etched a trail of significance through the facility's very fabric. He was a seasoned veteran of his role, his tenure spanning decades. Ever since the inception of this subterranean complex some thirty years ago, he had been intricately intertwined with its growth—a silent witness to the patient transformation of raw materials into a functional stronghold. The very bricks and mortar of this underground labyrinth had solidified under his watchful eye.

In distant corners of the globe, similar enclaves existed, hidden in plain sight. To the fortunate few in the know, their existence was no secret. Locating these covert sanctuaries posed no challenge, nor did gaining access to their concealed entrances. Reserved for the exclusive use of a select few, these facilities offered both workspace and refuge.

The emptiness of the expansive chambers now stood in stark contrast to their potential vitality—a stark reminder that the bustling energy of personnel could surge forth at a moment's notice. The facilities, though currently vacant, possessed the latent capability to house a thriving population if circumstances demanded. Each facility, strategically positioned in various locales, adhered to a uniform blueprint, the blueprint of secrecy and function.

The nondescript exterior of the complex masked its true purpose, a facade that allowed it to blend effortlessly with its surroundings. Its accessibility throughout the day underscored its operational flexibility. From the inception of their construction, meticulous planning was a mandate—logistics needed to align seamlessly with the organic world around them. The directive was clear: these sanctuaries should remain both unobtrusive and inconspicuous, serving their clandestine function without raising any alarms.

Donovan traversed the intricate corridors of the facility, a journey that consumed about fifteen minutes. The duration held no sway over him; time's grip was tenuous in the face of the activities that commanded his attention. He allocated however many minutes it took for the tasks requiring his resources, allowing the passage of time to fall in line with the necessities at hand. The march of minutes held little dominion over him as long as his objectives, lofty and precise, were met or even surpassed. With an ancestral heritage of longevity, time yielded to his intentions. The architects of this complex—each and every one of them—shared the gift of extended lifespans. With such an advantage at their disposal, time assumed an entirely distinct significance.

The office space he eventually entered was pristine, marked only by a desk and chair. It radiated an almost ascetic simplicity, the stark white walls mirroring the sterile ambiance of the hallways he had traversed. Floors and ceilings maintained a symphony of minimalism, a harmonious continuity throughout the space. Seated behind the desk, Donovan's surroundings mirrored his demeanor—unadorned, pragmatic, and efficient.

Unlike the desks of those seeking a veneer of power, Donovan's held no familial photographs, no trinkets to distract from his responsibilities. The artifacts that often served as diversions from the rigors of high-stakes roles found no place here; functionality held sway over sentimentality. His fingers danced over the surface of the desk, activating a communications network. The technology at his disposal transcended the bounds of modernity, reaching a level of sophistication that was, in the present age, nothing short of extraterrestrial.

As the connection established itself, A holographic image of the person he wanted to speak with appeared from the surface of the desk. Its resolution made it seem as if a miniature version of the person were present. Donovan engaged him in dialogue with a purpose.

"Dr. Brundle, are we ready to proceed?" asked Donovan. It was a simple question and he received a simple reply in response that met the expectation that he had.

Donovan disconnected the communication channel and placed his palms, face down, onto the surface of his desk. His shoulders shook and he took a deep breath.

Donovan reflected on how he'd already lived several centuries and was likely to live more. While time was something he had no concern over, especially in the present, there was one thing he was still worried about. That was a time in the future where things would be entirely different than they were now. A future where many lives hung in the balance. He wondered to himself if he was ready for that. The future he envisioned loomed as an unyielding certainty, a landscape in which change seemed impossible. However, amidst the shadow of inevitability, a small glimmer of thought flickered within him.

But if I can alter it just a bit... he mused inwardly, his mind a landscape of contemplation. Within the confines of that seemingly predetermined future, he sought out the slivers of potential alteration, the avenues that held the promise of improvement.

Within that possibility lay the foundation of his actions—a fragile hope, a beacon of change, even if it came at a steep cost. Donovan clung to the belief that in the face of unchangeable inevitabilities, there existed a chance, however slim, to weave a thread of difference. A thread that, despite the sacrifices it demanded, could weave a tapestry of change that would ultimately be worth the struggle. In the midst of an unalterable destiny, his resolve was firmly rooted in the potential for meaningful transformation, and he faced the uncertain future with that tenacious hope guiding his path.

2

Jack was a creature of routine, always arriving at work a solid hour before his shift began. This pre-dawn ritual was his sanctuary, a time to hone his physical prowess in the station's basement gym. Here, he engaged in spirited boxing sessions with the younger members of the police force. It wasn't about proving himself anymore; Jack's aim was to remain in peak physical condition. The younger officers respected his dedication to this purpose, and the added incentive of sparring with a former heavyweight contender was a considerable bonus.

Back in his college days, Jack had navigated the boxing ring with prowess, even earning a shot at the Olympics during the infancy of his pugilistic career. A silver medal in his weight class marked his achievement, and upon his return from the Olympic stage, a professional boxing career seemed destined. However, that destiny remained unfulfilled. The lights of professional boxing never illuminated his path; he retired without ever landing a professional punch. This unexpected turn left spectators in the boxing world perplexed, having anticipated a remarkable career, complete with the coveted heavyweight belt.

Yet Jack's journey didn't halt there. Trading boxing gloves for a badge, he chose the path of law enforcement. Retirement from both the military and the ring led him to the police academy, where he excelled, emerging as the top graduate. Advancement through the ranks came steadily, culminating in his role as a detective. Within the police force, Jack's superior officers boiled down to the Deputy Chief and the Chief of police, resulting in a streamlined chain of command that suited him well.

However, there was one recurrent wrinkle in his career: his struggle with partners. Jack's inability to tolerate fools had proven a consistent obstacle. The partners he'd been assigned were often of the foolish variety—some too young, eager to wear their hearts on their sleeves rather than focus on the job, while others were the embodiment of lethargy, merely counting down the days to retirement from the comfort of their desk chairs. The former type of partner typically ended up on the wrong side of a bullet, prematurely ending their careers or lives and, oddly, taking their partners down with them.

The latter variety of partners exhibited an indolent approach to their responsibilities. A disdain for diligence often led them astray, leading to perilous situations due to their lack of attention to detail. Their carelessness indirectly implicated their partners, reinforcing Jack's skepticism toward collaboration. Incidentally, the latter variety too could also end up on the wrong side of a bullet.

The notion of playing catch with bullets didn't sit well with Jack. There was something unsettling about the sudden halt of a speeding projectile that stirred his aversion. His history was dotted with former partners who shared a common grievance about him: an incompatibility with what they often described as a bullheaded, stubborn, unreasonable, and unyielding—grade-A ass.

Jack mused on these reflections as he sat in the dimly lit gym, cooling down after his workout. He contemplated the intricate dance of personalities within the force, acknowledging that his quest for a compatible partner was an ongoing challenge—one he couldn't escape but had to confront head-on.

Jack ascended the building's floors, his movements deliberate and focused. He cast a glance toward the chief of police's office, aware of the value placed on his job performance. The chief appreciated Jack's ability to deliver results, prioritizing his efficacy over his flaws. Jack's qualities, both positive and negative, were acknowledged and accommodated, despite his reputation for working best alone. The loss of fourteen partners across his twenty-year career didn't hinder his standing, as long as he kept producing outcomes.

Marriage had never been a part of Jack's life; he was wedded to his profession. The job consumed him, leaving little room for anything else. Posters depicting workaholics could easily feature Jack's face, an emblem of dedication. While he wasn't tethered to his work every waking minute, it often seemed that way.

The gym had revitalized Jack, infusing him with renewed energy and alertness. After his invigorating session, he showered and shaved in the locker room before ascending to the upper floors. Walking past the Desk Sergeant, he exchanged a passing glance. She peered over her glasses at him, her gaze hinting at a message. With a nod of her head, she gestured toward the police chief's office, silently conveying that his presence was anticipated.

In response, Jack offered his signature smile, radiating charm. While he found the Desk Sergeant attractive, he recognized her unavailability. Her returned smile brightened his day, a consistent interaction that uplifted his spirits.

"I'm not falling for you, Jack," she teased, shaking her head affectionately. Although flattered by his attention, she maintained a level of distance, content with their amicable rapport.

"You know you love me, Mary," Jack responded with nonchalance, their banter emblematic of their comfortable camaraderie.

Navigating through the cluttered arrangement of desks, Jack adeptly threaded his way, an obstacle course seemingly designed to impede swift passage from one end of the building to the other. The malicious intent behind this layout stirred unpleasant thoughts within Jack. He mentally entertained the notion of meeting the mind behind this design with a solid punch to the back of their head. Fairness being his creed, he maintained the equal opportunity to deliver that punch regardless of the orchestrator's gender.

The journey to the Chief's office was an exercise in patience, a maze of incongruity that drew sighs of frustration from Jack. While he briefly contemplated the notion that the Chief himself had sanctioned this spatial nightmare, he dismissed the thought as rapidly as it had taken shape. Finally, he reached his destination, facing the Chief of Police's glass-walled office. The transparent confines of the room seemed to symbolize a mutual observation, where the Chief scrutinized the world beyond just as effortlessly as Jack surveyed the Chief within.

Gazing at the large, gold-lettered nameplate—'Eugene Ritter-Police Chief'—Jack's focus was momentarily absorbed by the designation. The blinds inside the office were raised, providing a clear view from the outside. With little ceremony, Jack pushed the door open and entered. The Chief had anticipated his arrival, rendering the absence of a formal announcement inconsequential.

Chief Ritter spared Jack a fleeting glance, his gaze rising above the mountain of paperwork that had engulfed his otherwise bare desk. This wordless acknowledgment served as both a nod and a welcome, a prelude to the business that awaited them.

"Have a seat, Jack," Chief Ritter mumbled, his voice a weary invitation.

Sinking his balding head into his hands, elbows planted firmly on the desk's surface, Chief Ritter was the image of a man worn by time and responsibility. In his late fifties, he bore the physical marks of his age—thinning hair, an overweight frame that hadn't ventured into the realm of morbid obesity, and an air of anticipation, as if his next heart attack loomed about half an hour overdue. A loosened shirt collar and an abandoned tie beside a stack of folders spoke of a chaotic morning, and Jack could only anticipate that the day's trajectory was far from favorable. The clock had just struck nine.

Eugene's broad shoulders rose and fell in a deep inhalation, a visible attempt to dislodge the weight of frustration clinging to him. The vein on the right side of his temple pulsated rhythmically—a telltale sign familiar to everyone on the force. It was Eugene's pressure gauge; when that vein throbbed, it was a precursor to his boiling point, a signal that his voice might soon rise above its ordinary pitch. As Jack analyzed the scene, he couldn't help but speculate that Chief Ritter's pending heart attack was a mere hour overdue, given his palpable stress. The chief resembled a man cornered by an unrelenting tide of anxieties, a glimmer of respite nowhere in sight.

This was a refrain Jack had heard countless times before—Chief Ritter's lamentations about the toll the job exacted on his health and the specter of an early demise. Unsurprisingly, medical professionals corroborated his self-assessment. Retirement was a desire that loomed large, yet remained unfulfilled. The Chief's resolve was firm: he wouldn't hang his hat until these unsolved murders were resolved. The saddle of responsibility was still his to bear, the weight of these cases bearing down without leads to follow.

Though Chief Ritter had directed Jack to a seat moments ago, the command seemed to evaporate from his mind, a fleeting memory. An absent wave now motioned for Jack to take his place, an unintentional pause to gather his own thoughts.

"I read through Detective Skipple's report. Do you have any additional insights?" Chief Ritter's voice carried a note of resignation, a tacit acknowledgment of Skipple's shortcomings in comparison to Jack. Inwardly, Chief Ritter acknowledged that even he might have struggled to match Jack's prowess when he was in Jack's shoes. His patience wore thin as he awaited Jack's response.

Jack hadn't yet taken his seat; he hovered over the chair, his intention clear but his body not quite committed to it. A last-minute decision diverted him from settling into the faux-covered seat. Instead, he opted to stand straight, leaning against the backrest. One question into the conversation, Jack surmised that brevity was on the agenda.

"Yeah," Jack began, his smile edged with mischief. "Skipple's not exactly the sharpest tool in the shed."

A frustrated groan escaped Chief Ritter, the tension evident in his voice. "We're all well aware of that. Get serious, Jack. Can you contribute anything worthwhile?"

Jack's grin faded, replaced with a more measured expression. "Honestly, probably not. At this point, boss, it's a repetition of the same pattern we've seen in the previous two cases."

Eugene heaved a sigh heavy with the weight of exasperation. Suppressing the urge to scream, he strangled out his words. "Do whatever it takes to crack this case, Jack. Sooner rather than later. Make it happen."

The chief's chair creaked as he shifted, his vein now dormant. Jack interpreted this as a sign that some of the stress had ebbed, yet he remained cautious. The day was young, and the city still had its share of undisclosed crimes, a defining aspect of police work—reactive by nature.

"I've got a deceased banker, an attorney, and a judge on my hands—the last one with connections to the mayor or deputy mayor, or god knows whoever else. The mayor, deputy mayor, even the damn principal at my daughter's school are on my ass about these cases. And now the Major's breathing down my neck, demanding answers I don't have," Chief Ritter lamented, his voice a mix of exhaustion and frustration.

He sighed once more, his eyes scanning the ceiling in search of solace. A dismissive wave signaled the end of the discussion, granting Jack the freedom to return to his duties. "Leave my office and get some work done," Eugene breathed out, a visible exhale to release pent-up tension.

As Jack turned to exit, a summons from the chief halted him. "Jack..." Eugene began, hesitation apparent in his voice, as if reconsidering his words. "Never mind. Just go." As Eugene watched Jack leave, he thought to himself, *be safe out there.*

The door shut behind Jack as he left, his thoughts untethered as he walked. This was the time his mind thrived, sifting through the intricate details and hidden patterns. Absentminded nods were directed at the uniformed officers and detectives he passed—seated, standing, engrossed in the morning's tasks. His team of plainclothes detectives received similar nods, though his focus lay elsewhere. Engrossed in his mental plan of attack for the case, Jack's attention wavered as he entered his own office.

Jack's inattention to detail was immediately evident as he entered his office, failing to notice that the door stood ajar. His focus was riveted on an unexpected sight that grabbed his attention and held it hostage. Twin shoulder holsters cradling matching MagSec handguns dangled conspicuously from his coat rack. A touch of bewilderment clawed at the edges of his consciousness, preventing swift reconciliation between the reality before him and the pattern his mind had anticipated.

Strategically positioned on the right upon entering, the coat rack shared its space with a petite table, upon which a faithful coffee machine rested—a constant companion through Jack's days. His desk occupied a corner against the far wall, its commanding presence greeting visitors as they crossed the threshold. Across from the desk, a modest couch was nestled against the wall that was on his left as he entered the room, forming a cozy seating area that seemed to have succumbed to a sudden vacancy.

Jack's gaze fixated on the couch, his instinct honed by years of detective work. There was no need for a sweeping search; the room's limited dimensions left little room for hidden corners, and the absence of anyone behind his desk was palpable. A wry smirk formed on his lips, amused by his own predictably astute observation. *This is why they call me a detective—I've got that 'detecting' down,* he mused silently and grimaced outwardly, his inner monologue echoing with an undercurrent of self-deprecation. A subsequent thought immediately followed, derailing his ego's momentum: *Well, even an imbecile could have cracked this one.* The uninvited image of Detective Bob Skipple's face intruded, unfairly shouldering the blame for Jack's current introspection.

Unexpectedly, Jack's office played host to an enigmatic guest, cocooned in slumber upon his couch. Young, yet bearing an undeniable allure, her presence elicited Jack's scrutiny, a deliberate examination guided by a sequence he was aware of. His head tilted back ever so slightly as he gave her a second look, a response so visceral he had to consciously restrain an exhaled sigh, acknowledging the impact of her appearance on his senses. She was a picture of comfort, feet nestled beside her, knees drawn close, hands supporting her head as it rested against the couch's backrest.

The object of Jack's attention was graced with raven-black hair that framed her face, its cascades lending her an air of mystery. Though partially obscured, her countenance remained visible enough for Jack to discern the faint pink flush gracing her high cheekbones and the rosy hue that graced her lips. Those lips, a delicate shade of rose, seemed slightly moist, their contours curving with a subtle hint of a smile.

Draped in a white, cotton button-up blouse, her rhythmic breathing orchestrated the barely perceptible rise and fall of her shoulders, a testament to the tranquility that enveloped her. A black skirt, extending to her knees, revealed a smooth expanse of legs that remained uninterrupted, her feet small and seemingly in harmony with the serenity of her repose.

As Jack's gaze lingered, his eyebrows furrowed in a bemused expression. His initial thought, swiftly dismissed, questioned who had allowed a child into his office. That notion dissolved as he comprehended the woman before him, a realization that dawned with a sense of intrigue.

Jack's estimation of her stature confirmed her petite nature, her frame suggesting she stood no more than five feet tall. He reasoned she likely weighed less than a hundred pounds, perhaps only reaching that mark with the addition of clothes and an imaginary brick in her pocket. A second glance only solidified his perception; he couldn't help but speculate whether he could lift her with a single hand.

His gaze meandered back to her face, and in that instant, their eyes locked. She had awakened, her gaze unflinching and fixated on him, ensnaring his attention like a moth drawn to a flame. There was a primal magnetism in that gaze, a sense of danger intertwined with allure. A moth, captivated by the blaze, could risk being consumed. When her eyes blinked, the spell was broken, the momentary enchantment shattered.

Jack grappled with his own mind, attempting to rationalize the intensity he had perceived in those eyes. In the wake of that profound connection, he convinced himself that any sense of peril he had sensed was merely a figment of his imagination, a transient trick of the light and his own restless thoughts. Jack believed that there was something uncanny about her eyes but he wrote it off as being an effect of the unusual greenish gold color that he saw there.

"You were staring there for a while," she remarked in a mild tone, coupled with a hint of disinterest. The way she spoke conveyed neither approval nor disapproval of his gaze, an attitude that struck a balance between those two poles. Still nestled in her relaxed recline, she hadn't shifted from the position she had been in during her nap.

"Huh," Jack stuttered, his reply an eloquent masterpiece of human communication. He deemed it an apt representation of his current state of bewildered surprise.

"I was wondering when you were going to come back up for air," she added, her lips curving into a slow smile that began to grace her features.

"What?" Jack's confusion was palpable, a thick haze of bewilderment that clouded his thoughts. Despite the perplexity that enveloped him, he recognized he was skillfully maintaining his status as a bumbling fool. To him, the conversation had veered off course from the start. He yearned to ascertain her identity and the purpose behind her presence in his office, but her initial comments had thrown him off balance.

"What did you say?" he queried, his grasp on coherence gradually returning.

"You were staring at my legs for a long time, so I was beginning to wonder when you were going to be coming up for air," she teased, her words laced with a playful undertone. A secretive and seductive smile began to take shape on her lips, unfurling like a hidden treasure slowly revealing itself.

"Oh... umm..." Jack's response trailed off, his flustered state evident as he struggled to regain his footing. He recognized that he had been thrown quite off guard, and he paused to gather both his composure and his thoughts. This, he surmised, was the first step he needed to take, considering he was standing there with his mouth agape.

With a determined effort, he managed to find his voice once more. "Who are you and why are you in my office—miss..." Jack prodded, seeking answers to the questions that had danced on the tip of his tongue since he entered the room.

She shifted her body, gracefully kicking her feet off the couch. Her hands dropped to her sides as she effortlessly transitioned to a standing position. Perched on the tips of her toes, she stretched her arms above her head in a languid motion, reminiscent of a contented cat stretching after a leisurely nap in the sun. The aura of an afternoon catnap clung to her, an illusion that could easily fool the world. An illusion that Jack felt might not be a lie.

Her hands waved gracefully in the air, inadvertently causing her blouse to ride up. Jack's eyes traced the exposed expanse of her midriff, revealing her smooth belly and the delicate dip of her belly button. A coy smile played upon her lips as she lowered her arms, smoothing down her blouse with an enchanting finesse. Her movements seemed to mirror the fluid grace of a feline, captivating Jack's attention as she glided toward him and then past him, a dance of both allure and intrigue.

Her capacity to disorient Jack was undeniable, a realization that settled firmly in his mind. He conceded that even on his own turf, she had managed to claim the higher ground. Despite her petite stature, he found himself looking upward at her, a position that left him feeling disarmed and off-kilter.

"Two creams and two sugars, right?" she inquired, her enigmatic smile persisting as a gentle laugh curled the corners of her mouth. A coffee decanter dangled gracefully over his coffee mug, poised to pour a fresh cup.

"Uh—yeah," Jack responded, surrender evident in his posture as his shoulders relaxed. He felt utterly bewildered, recognizing that she was capitalizing on his lack of equilibrium. His equilibrium was off-kilter, his thoughts tangled in a web of confusion spun by her presence. She was well aware of the impact she had, leaving him off balance.

Jack grappled with his frustration, knowing that she had effortlessly disrupted his routine. Yet, despite the frustration, there was something undeniably magnetic about her that made it challenging for him to sustain irritation for long. Her gravitational pull was too strong, drawing him into her orbit, a captivating force he couldn't easily resist.

She gracefully placed the coffee cup into his awaiting hands, a move he neither resisted nor could have resisted. His astonishment was palpable, his mouth slightly agape as he absorbed the unexpected turn of events. As if ensnared in a spell, Jack found himself temporarily bereft of coherent thought or action. The world seemed to stand still, and it was as if only she and the coffee cup mattered in that suspended moment.

Seemingly unperturbed by Jack's awestruck demeanor, she settled onto the couch, her posture relaxed as she crossed her legs at the ankles. With practiced patience, she gently blew on her own coffee, casting him a sidelong glance while concealing the burgeoning smile that played on her lips. Taking a sip from the cup, she masked her amusement behind the veil of her actions, all the while keenly observing Jack as he navigated the invisible currents she seemed to weave around him.

Her initial impression of Jack had been framed by the expressiveness of his warm brown eyes. Beneath the gruff exterior he donned like armor, she discerned a genuine kindness and caring nature that lay beneath. His dark chocolate skin exuded a sense of strength and resilience, and she couldn't help but admire the way his broad shoulders carried his presence. His close-cropped hair bore a sprinkling of gray, just enough to add a touch of distinction to his appearance. His casual dress shirt hugged his frame, revealing the underlying muscular physique that marked him as someone who took care of his body.

As Jack's astonishment slowly gave way to a more focused awareness, he felt a shift in the air—a subtle change in the dynamics between them. The power of her presence, combined with the enigmatic allure she exuded, was enough to turn the usually unflappable detective into a temporary whirlwind of thoughts and emotions. The room seemed to shrink, leaving only the two of them within its borders, caught in a dance of intrigue and curiosity.

"I'm Special Agent Atwood. Faye Atwood," she finally introduced herself, her words marking a slight shift in the atmosphere that she had seemed to weave within the confined space. With her introduction, the enchanting spell that had momentarily enveloped them appeared to disperse, and the veil of mystery lifted ever so slightly.

Jack found himself experiencing a wave of immediate relief, a sensation that escaped through an audible sigh. With Faye's revelation, a piece of the puzzle had fallen into place, reassuring him and bestowing upon him a sense of order he had momentarily feared lost. The world, it seemed, wasn't entirely chaotic. There was still a modicum of predictability to hold onto. The slender presence of this enigmatic woman, ethereal yet undeniably real, hadn't completely overturned his sense of stability. The universe, in its divine wisdom, had granted him a reprieve, reminding him that there was a cosmic balance overseeing the intricate affairs of mortals.

Jack covered the short distance to his desk, placing his coffee cup upon its firm surface. He allowed his head to droop slightly, a subtle movement aimed at shaking loose the cobwebs that Faye's entrance had blissfully woven into his mind. As he gently shook his head, a metaphorical act of ridding himself of the spell's lingering effects, he sensed clarity gradually returning.

With his mental faculties realigned, Jack was once again prepared to face Faye without feeling swept away by the current of her presence. The world, once deemed chaotic and unfathomable, had declared him insane, a verdict he vehemently refuted. Their dispute had reached a resolution—Jack had silenced the world's claims, redirecting his focus to what mattered at hand.

His gaze shifted, gradually bringing Faye back into his line of sight. Inwardly, Jack acknowledged the undeniable truth—Faye was unbelievably captivating. He admitted, if only to himself, that her presence had provided a momentary and not altogether unwelcome diversion from his routine. Yet, he reminded himself sternly, business called. The questions that lingered were too pressing to ignore, and he needed to unravel the mystery of this unanticipated intrusion into his life.

Determined and composed, Jack turned his full attention to Faye. She stood before him, a testament to the inexplicable forces that had woven their paths together. The tides of his thoughts had calmed, settling into a steady rhythm, as he faced her with a mix of curiosity and purpose. He recognized the woman before him as more than just an enigma; she was a puzzle he was eager to decipher. Jack wanted to know why this orphaned little waif had drifted into his office and interrupted his life.

"What can I do for you, Miss Atwood?" Jack inquired calmly.

"That's 'Special Agent' Atwood," she corrected with an air of nonchalance. "But you can call me Faye. I would prefer that," she added, her lips curving into an award-winning smile. Without a care in the world, she continued to sip her coffee, as if the mere act of being in his office was a leisurely endeavor.

Jack stood before her, dumbstruck yet again. Amid his clouded thoughts, a nagging sensation arose—the realization that she hadn't actually provided a response to his question. He mustered his thoughts and posed the question anew.

"Do you need something, Faye?"

Faye's response was swift and definitive. "Yes, Detective Riddle, I've been assigned as your partner."

"My what?" Jack exclaimed, his disbelief evident in his tone.

Faye's voice assumed a gentle cadence, every syllable pronounced with deliberate clarity. Each word she uttered was enunciated with precision, her emphasis leaving no room for misunderstanding. "I.

Am. Assigned. As. Your. Partner," she declared, punctuating each word as if etching the truth into the air between them.

Jack blinked, then blinked again, a sense of déjà vu washing over him. The word 'partner' reverberated in his mind, its meaning echoing through his consciousness.

"Hold up. Did you say 'partner'?" Jack sought clarification, grappling with the foreign concept that Faye's statement had introduced.

While the prospect of teaming up with a woman as captivating as Faye held certain allures, such as the constant presence of her beauty during duty hours, the idea of having a partner was an alien notion to Jack. This unfamiliar concept began to chip away at the comfort he found in his solitary existence, threatening to reshape his perspective of the world around him.

Once more, he blinked, grappling with his disbelief. For an instant, he almost believed he had indeed heard her say the word 'partner'. The realization that this petite woman, brimming with firepower and seemingly lacking the experience for a serious investigation, had declared them partners, took root in his mind.

Jack's gaze remained locked on Faye, absorbing her slow nod of affirmation—an acknowledgment of the new reality she had set in motion. This time, Jack didn't blink. Instead, he pushed away from the desk with determination, his footsteps quickening as he strode purposefully toward the office of the Police Chief.

Jack found himself halfway to his intended destination when the Desk Sergeant, the same one who had informed him earlier that the police chief wanted to see him, stopped him in his path. Her expression was far from accommodating, lacking any trace of a warmth this time. Serious and business like.

"He doesn't want to hear it. He said, 'no arguments, tell the 'ass' to deal with it,'" Mary conveyed, her tone both firm and matter-of-fact. She'd intervened, intercepting him before he could progress any further down the path he had set out on. Running interference, a formidable obstacle between him and his goal.

"But... he can't be serious," Jack retorted, a hint of disbelief lacing his words.

Mary's response was swift and decisive, punctuated by a file that she deftly slapped against Jack's chest. The impact wasn't forceful, yet it succeeded in capturing his attention and redirecting his focus away from the Chief's office door. He instinctively reached out to grasp the file as Mary released it into his hands.

"Transfer orders. Deal with it, Jack," Mary asserted, her tone carrying a mixture of sympathy and pragmatism. "This came from way above his pay grade, and now it's on your plate. He's passing the buck, so you're the lucky one," she added, a touch of empathy in her words. Having known Jack for an extended period, she was well aware of his idiosyncrasies and couldn't help but feel a twinge of compassion—for him and the potential partner who was about to be thrust into his world.

A sweet smile curved on Mary's lips as she turned to leave, leaving Jack to grapple with a sudden sense of unsteadiness. The ground beneath him seemed to shift, as if the world were conspiring to throw him off balance. It wasn't merely the pressure of solving three gruesome murders with scarce evidence and no viable leads that weighed on him now. The universe appeared to be toying with him, adding an unexpected twist to his already complicated circumstances. The prospect of babysitting an agent who, by all appearances, was fresh out of the academy was the last thing he wished to contend with.

The weight of his new task settled on his shoulders, a duty he had little choice but to accept. As he clutched the file in his hand, Jack couldn't help but reflect on the irony of the situation. He had always been the detective unearthing mysteries, yet now he found himself ensnared in a puzzle not of his own making. The task ahead promised to be as complex as any case he had encountered, but what weighed even heavier was the looming presence of a partner he hadn't asked for—a partner who might be just as challenging to decode as the enigmas he was accustomed to facing.

After a few minutes, Jack reentered his office, his demeanor akin to that of a dejected child burdened with unwelcome responsibilities. He carried a folder, containing Faye's transfer orders and her service information. With a heavy sigh, he dropped the file onto an already accumulated stack on his desk. His displeasure was palpable, casting a shadow over the room. Gazing in Faye's direction, he couldn't help but release a wearied breath, his frustration evident.

Recognizing the urgency of clarifying their working relationship from the outset, Jack felt compelled to establish certain boundaries, ensuring there were no misunderstandings about his expectations and the extent of assistance he required. As he began to address her, he adopted a tone that was meant to convey authority, attempting to position himself as a mentor, parent, or senior figure. This air of superiority was a conscious effort to assert dominance, even if it risked dampening her spirits on their very first day of collaboration. Jack believed that addressing these matters upfront would be more effective in the long run, rather than allowing misconceptions to fester.

"Look... kid," he commenced, his tone tinged with hesitancy, "I'm not sure what they told you to expect, but I'm not interested in playing nursemaid to some rookie fresh out of the academy. So, just do yourself a favor and stay out of my way, focusing on carrying out the tasks I assign."

Having voiced his initial concerns, Jack leaned back, awaiting Faye's response. While he braced himself for potential objections, he also harbored a sense of anticipation. He intended to lay down the groundwork for their partnership, ensuring they understood each other's roles and limitations, and striving to forge a functional working dynamic—albeit one that he hoped wouldn't last too long.

Faye responded to Jack's initial directive with a benign expression that held the power to silence him within mere seconds. Her gaze, unwavering and composed, conveyed a depth of maturity that contradicted her youthful appearance.

"Let's get a few things straight," she began, her tone measured yet carrying the weight of her words. "I might look like I'm barely twenty, but I'm thirty years old. I graduated from West Point in the top ten percent of my class. I trained at Quantico, worked with the DEA in the Panamanian jungle for a year straight, and then joined the NSA. So before you go spouting off terms like 'wet behind the ears rookie', you misogynistic, sexist, agist, ass, make sure you have your facts straight." Her words, while not overtly charged with anger, resonated with a clear sense of determination and a depth of feeling that couldn't be ignored.

Throughout her impassioned speech, Faye maintained an unwavering smile on her lips. Her eyes, locked onto Jack's, conveyed a mixture of resolve and intensity that captivated him. Her ability to maintain such a demeanor while addressing him left him momentarily taken aback. It was not the sweetness of her smile that struck Jack, but the steel-like resolve beneath it—a testament to her unyielding spirit. Faye's unwavering confidence seemed to declare, 'I will not be ignored, and I demand respect'. It was this aspect of her character that left an indelible impression on Jack, immediately igniting his admiration.

As he snapped back to the present, Jack couldn't help but appreciate how she had shifted his focus from her words to her unshakable presence. He acknowledged his initial underestimation of her, realizing that he had missed the intricacies of her message while being entranced by her ability to stand up to him.

"Wait a minute, I'm not some misogynistic ass. You don't even know me," Jack retorted, his words laced with a hint of defensiveness. He took a step back, allowing himself to lean against his desk, his arms crossed in an act of self-righteous indignation.

Faye, however, was ready with a retort that left Jack momentarily disarmed. "Don't I?" she began, her tone holding a touch of playful challenge. "Let's see. Born to William and Margaret Riddle. High school Valedictorian. Attended Saint Cornelia College on an academic, athletic, and ROTC scholarship. Oh, and let's not forget—you were on the college boxing team. Graduated Magna Cum Laude with a bachelor's in mathematics and physics. And, just a small detail—you snagged a silver medal in the Olympics for boxing in the heavyweight class."

Faye paused, a hint of satisfaction in her expression. "How am I doing so far?" she inquired, her tone almost teasing as she arched an eyebrow, awaiting Jack's response.

Jack's silent nod served as an unspoken agreement, granting Faye the permission to proceed with her revelations. She began to unravel more about Jack's past.

"Your next plan was to pursue a career as a professional heavyweight boxer, but your path took an unexpected turn when you were activated for active duty with your reserve unit. You were deployed to Iraq, where you served for a year. Upon your return, you were de-commissioned after earning a remarkable array of honors—a collection that includes the Army Achievement Medal, Army Commendation Medal, Meritorious Service Medal, the Bronze Star, a Silver Star, and a Purple Heart, all accomplished during a single tour." Faye's recitation held a certain weight, emphasizing Jack's impressive achievements.

Jack's scowl deepened, his expression reflecting his lack of enthusiasm for Faye's detailed knowledge of his history. He found her familiarity with his past accomplishments easy to dismiss, perceiving them as mere facts easily accessible to anyone with internet access. "Memorizing my résumé doesn't mean you know who I am," he retorted, a hint of irritation in his tone.

Faye mulled over Jack's response, silently acknowledging that he had a valid point. She rose from the couch with a deliberate grace, moving toward the small table to replenish her coffee cup. As she returned the carafe to its place, she remained standing, her gaze thoughtful as she pondered Jack's words. The chilly atmosphere of the building seemed to seep into the conversation, mirroring the slightly frosty exchange.

"You're right," Faye admitted, her tone thoughtful as she processed his perspective. "All those achievements, medals, and titles—while impressive—aren't the sum of who you are. They're the steps that shaped you, the milestones along the way." Her words held a warmth that contrasted with the cool surroundings, a contrast that seemed to bridge the gap between them.

A contemplative pause followed as Faye continued to reflect. Holding the coffee mug between her hands, she leaned into its comforting warmth. "Here's a thought," she began, her tone soft yet assertive. Intimate, in a manner that made it seem as if they were the only two individuals in all of the world.

"Your unit was engaged in a routine resupply mission. Departing from the supply base approximately forty-five minutes prior, you were en route back to your base camp. In an unusual twist, you as the platoon leader, took the driver's seat. Your platoon sergeant occupied the passenger seat—typically your spot," Faye recounted, her voice adopting a distant quality that suggested her mind was reaching back into history.

As she spoke, her tone grew softer, carrying an almost reverential quality. Her gaze seemed to drift into the past, lost in the scenes she painted. "An ambush of improvised explosive devices suddenly shattered the convoy's rhythm. The last vehicle in the five-vehicle convoy was immobilized, and the lead vehicle was overturned by the blast. That lead vehicle, tragically, was yours." Faye's words seemed to hold a weight beyond their literal meaning, conveying the gravity of the situation.

"You extricated yourself from the wreckage and swiftly rallied your platoon. Despite the chaos and confusion, you managed to organize a counterattack against the enemy, who held a strategically superior position and outnumbered your platoon." Faye's description painted a vivid picture of Jack's leadership in the midst of chaos, his determination and quick thinking steering his team in the right direction.

"Though your platoon was depleted, the result of both injuries and the efforts to tend to the wounded, you employed tactical brilliance to outmaneuver and encircle the enemy forces. Your skillful tactics forced their surrender to you and your determined platoon." Faye's words carried a sense of admiration, a recognition of Jack's ability to turn a dire situation to his advantage.

Her voice then took on a somber tone as she continued her narrative. "Yet, amid the triumph, tragedy struck once more. As your platoon was securing the surrendered enemy, a vehicle laden with explosives barreled towards the scene. The vehicle detonated near the overturned lead vehicle, the shockwaves claiming the life of your platoon sergeant, who remained trapped within." The weight of the loss was palpable in Faye's words, her recounting of the events honoring both triumph and sacrifice.

The room fell into a contemplative silence after Faye's words had settled, the weight of the story hanging in the air between them.

Jack averted his gaze from Faye, though she had never turned to meet his eyes as she spoke. The intensity of her words had stirred something within him, a feeling he struggled to confront. He couldn't bear to look at her, as if doing so might reveal the turmoil churning within him. Despite the years that had slipped by since that fateful incident, the wound it had left behind still seared and gnawed at him. The memories were an open wound, festering beneath his stoic exterior.

The weight of that day pressed upon him, threatening to shatter the walls he had meticulously built around his emotions. A tumultuous sea of feelings surged through his mind—anger, sorrow, loss, grief—all swirled together in a whirlwind of raw emotions that raced through his consciousness. "That doesn't tell you who I am either," he managed to say, his voice laced with a mixture of frustration and vulnerability.

In response to his admission, Faye turned on her heels, her movements fluid and deliberate. Jack felt a magnetic pull, urging him to face her. As she closed the distance between them, their proximity grew unnervingly intimate, a mere breath away from his hand encircling her waist. Her greenish gold eyes, soft and understanding, met his own expressive dark brown eyes. Jack found himself captivated by her unwavering presence, drawn to her in a way that unsettled him.

With the woman who had ignited a dormant pain standing before him, Jack was forced to confront his emotions head-on. Faye's words had struck a chord within him, revealing truths he had tried to bury. Her voice, steady and gentle, pierced through the maelstrom within him. "I know who you are, Jack, and I've only just met you," she said, her words carrying a quiet reassurance.

Faye's insight into his character was both disconcerting and strangely comforting. She saw through his defenses, recognizing the pattern he had woven around himself—a pattern of pushing people away to prevent them from getting too close. Yet, in the same breath, she acknowledged the innate goodness that resided within him—the willingness to put others before himself, to risk everything for those who needed him.

Her voice took on a softer, empathetic quality as she continued, unraveling the complex layers of his heart. "I believe you've closed yourself off from deep connections because you've convinced yourself that you don't deserve love, nor do you think you can give it in return." Faye's words were an affirmation of her understanding, an acknowledgment that transcended the superficiality of their first meeting.

Jack's towering figure cast a shadow over the petite woman before him. His emotions churned, a tempest of anger threatening to consume his thoughts. "You're treading on thin ice, Agent Atwood," Jack's words rumbled forth, laden with his smoldering ire.

Faye, undaunted by Jack's seething aggression, stood her ground without a hint of trepidation. She met his hostility head-on, unwavering and resolute. "Whether you're on board or not, Detective Riddle, we're in this together," she declared, her voice holding a calm but unyielding determination. "A judge is dead, and at the Federal level, people want answers. So, sooner you accept that fact, the sooner we can get to work. You'll have the answers to your 'whys,' for the other cases and I'll get a ticket out of your life."

Her coffee cup found its place on Jack's desk, the liquid still steaming within. Faye raised her gaze to meet Jack's, her eyes locking onto the depths of his brown irises. There was a well of pain within him, an abyss that beckoned her to explore. For an instant, she wondered if she could become lost in the sea of his emotions, her very identity swallowed by the intensity she glimpsed. But reality tethered her, reminding her of the duty she bore.

Faye understood that losing herself in someone else's world was a luxury she couldn't afford, not in the face of the case at hand. As much as Jack intrigued her, there was a line she couldn't cross, at least not yet. With a flicker of her lips, she offered a weak smile, a fleeting glimpse of the empathy she held. But beneath that fragility, determination thrived, strengthening her resolve.

Her fingers grazed his cheek in a gentle touch, an act loaded with empathy, before withdrawing. The momentary tenderness morphed into a light but impactful smack against his cheek. The sound resonated in the room, a physical punctuation mark to her declaration. It carried a message that transcended words—a fusion of seriousness and her unwavering intention.

Jack's head recoiled involuntarily, caught off guard by the unexpected smack. "What was that for?" His question hung in the air, a blend of surprise and curiosity as he sought to understand the reason behind the abrupt gesture.

A small smile played on Faye's lips as she responded, her tone light but pointed. "My new partner is a misogynistic ass."

The accusation stung, and Jack's retort was swift and sharp. "I am not misogynistic," he growled, the words lashing out in defense. Yet, his protest went unanswered as Faye moved past him, assembling her belongings with a purpose that left him slightly disoriented.

As Faye continued her preparations to leave his office, she glanced back at him with a playful gleam in her eyes. "So, you're okay with admitting you're an ass?"

Caught off guard once again, Jack found himself at a loss for words, his attempt to craft a suitable response falling flat.

"I got a copy of the files from the Desk Sergeant," Faye continued, her tone shifting to a more business-like cadence. "I'm heading back to my hotel to catch some sleep. Jet lag's a killer."

With those parting words, Faye exited Jack's office, leaving him alone with his swirling thoughts and unresolved feelings. The silence settled around him as he grappled with the realization that he might actually be able to work alongside Agent Atwood. Her defiance and self-assuredness had left an impression, compelling him to reconsider his initial reservations.

Faye's actions spoke volumes. She intended to be a partner, not just a subordinate. Her touch and her resolute demeanor conveyed a willingness to bridge the gap between them. Jack could sense the undercurrent of sincerity and purpose emanating from her, and he had no choice but to acknowledge it.

As Jack attempted to refocus on his work, a nagging thought wormed its way into his consciousness—a distant recollection of a faint sound when he had first entered his office to find Faye waiting. Almost as if on the edge of a dream, he wondered whether he had imagined the soft sound of purring, a detail he had dismissed until now.

The day had descended into a dreary rhythm, a cadence that Jack curiously found comfort in. The blend of an abrupt awakening and the ceaseless barrage of work's demands had drained him to his core. Weariness had taken hold, a well-worn companion he was intimately acquainted with. The longing for respite had settled deep within him—both his mind and body aching for the tranquility of slumber. As thoughts of escape and the allure of sleep dominated his thoughts, a sudden interruption shattered the impending stillness, jolting him from the edge of departure, his hand on the doorknob, ready to exit. The insistent ring of his phone cut through the air, like an unexpected gust that sweeps away the calm.

He glanced at the phone on his desk, a mix of annoyance and suspicion knitting his brow. It felt like a malevolent force, an entity hell-bent on derailing his fleeting peace. Oddly enough, it had remained silent for over ninety minutes, until the very moment he stood, hat in hand, poised to leave. The irony wasn't lost on him, and his instinctual response was to ignore it. He almost let it ring, a silent protest against the world's insistence on yanking him back. But he knew himself better than that; leaving things hanging wasn't his style.

His voice carried the weight of his waning patience. With a sigh laced with weary patience, he answered, "Detective Riddle speaking." The voice that came through the speaker held a familiar lilt, the same one he'd encountered earlier. "Heading out already?"

The question halted his exit in its tracks, a sudden pause in his determined stride. Weariness seeped into his response, coating his words. "Just about to step out. What's going on?"

"Are you headed home?" Faye's query held a delicate yet persistent note.

His reply carried a hint of surrender. "Home's the only destination on my radar." The honesty in his words rang clear. There were no grand plans for the evening, no elaborate agenda. The day had been a demanding marathon, kickstarted by Bob's call about an investigation that had rudely summoned him from his slumber at the ungodly hour of four in the morning.

"Come to my hotel," Faye's voice carried an unexpected invitation, breaking the mundane spell that had begun to wrap around Jack's thoughts.

His brows furrowed as he mulled over the proposition, uncertainty edging his words. "Why would I do that?"

"To share dinner. I'd rather not dine alone," Faye confessed, her voice echoing through the digital connection, her unseen smile somehow perceptible.

A suspended moment hung in the air, pregnant with Jack's unspoken response. It lingered, stretching the silence until Faye decided to pierce it with her words. "I gather you haven't had your dinner yet."

A touch of incredulity tinged his query. "How would you know that?"

A hint of sarcasm laced Faye's response. "Considering you're only just leaving the office, it's a safe assumption."

The conversation paused, punctuated by another stretch of silence. Faye took it upon herself to rekindle the discourse, her determination evident. "I'll be waiting. Shouldn't take you long to get here."

"I'll be there in about fifteen minutes," Jack's reply was brisk, a tacit agreement to her proposal. He didn't wait for her response, ending the call and setting his phone down. The wheels of action were set in motion.

True to his word, fifteen minutes later, Jack found himself navigating his way to Faye's location. The city lights painted streaks across the night sky, his mind filled with a blend of curiosity and uncertainty about the evening that lay ahead.

The neon lights that flashed from store fronts passed by in silence as he purposely kept the radio off. Reminded of the cacophony of noise he'd endured that morning on his way to that crime scene. He looked around to find a parking spot and having found one, decided to see about locating Faye.

The neon lights from storefronts painted fleeting streaks of color, as he passed by their silent dance. They were a marked contrast to the cacophony of noise that had invaded Jack's morning ride to the crime scene. He drove in contemplative silence, opting to keep the radio hushed. His focus shifted to the task at hand: locating Faye.

Parking his vehicle, he exited with a sense of purpose. The restaurant within the hotel complex was his destination, and he soon approached the table where Faye sat engrossed in her work. As he pulled out a chair and seated himself, their gazes met. Faye closed the folder she had been engrossed in, acknowledging his presence with a subtle nod.

His eyes trailed to the pizza box on the table, prompting a quizzical raise of his brow. "That's dinner?" he inquired, his voice tinged with mild surprise. A thought surfaced, reflective of the usual dietary concerns of those he'd encountered. Most women he knew would shy away from a meal like this on any kind of continuous basis, as if it were a dreaded specter. Yet, Faye's nonchalant contentment with the beer and pizza struck him as an intriguing departure from the norm. Jack did have to admit that he only knew a few women anyway so he couldn't be too sure about his assertions of women's choices in dining.

Faye's response was cheerful and unapologetic. "Yep." She reached for another slice, mirroring his casual approach to the meal.

Observing the hotel restaurant's surroundings, Jack's curiosity tugged at him. "How did you manage that?" he inquired, referencing her ability to have delivery pizza in a hotel dining establishment.

A sip of beer preceded Faye's explanation. "I had a hankering for beer and pizza. They had the beer, and I ordered the pizza. Showed my federal ID for the beer, and they didn't object to the pizza." A hearty bite of pizza accompanied her words, her appetite undeniably healthy.

Between bites, her question surfaced, words muffled by pizza. "How did you find me?"

A smirk touched Jack's lips as he offered his reply, tinged with a hint of humorous sarcasm. "I'm a detective—I detected."

Faye's retort was swift, her tone dry and unamused. "About as funny as a hole in the head."

Jack played along, gesturing melodramatically with a hand over his heart. "Like a joke with no punchline."

A wry grin curved Faye's lips, her retort sharp. "We're not talking about your life."

His expression shifted to one of feigned hurt, Jack's hands pressed to his chest in mock agony. "That's hurtful," he remarked with theatrical dismay.

Their banter took a more serious turn as Faye inquired about his method of locating her. Jack pointed towards the window. "Your contact info was in the briefing folder, and I caught sight of you through the window when I walked up."

The interplay between them carried an undercurrent of shared understanding, a dynamic that was a blend of teasing rapport and genuine curiosity. As they conversed over pizza, the barriers seemed to soften, hinting at the potential for camaraderie amid the complexities of their collaboration.

Faye's inquisitive gaze shifted over her shoulder, and then she refocused on Jack. A quirk of her head revealed her curiosity. "You parked on the street?" Her tone carried a playful note, a clear sign of her interest in his choice of parking.

Jack responded with candid honesty, a touch of amusement in his voice. "Yeah, I'm too cheap to pay for parking."

A mischievous glint danced in Faye's eyes as she pushed forward, her intention evident. "And here I was thinking you'd be buying the beer."

Jack's response was swift, his tone dry but not devoid of a hint of humor. "Why would I?" His question held a sense of genuine curiosity, more about her reasoning behind the suggestion than a refusal to go along with her playful banter.

With a subtle pointing gesture, Faye drew attention to the pizza box that held the remnants of a devoured slice. "I bought dinner," she declared, her words framed by the evidence of her actions.

Jack's raised eyebrow spoke of his surprise, his coat casually discarded onto an empty chair. He scanned the surroundings, seeking a waiter's attention. When he succeeded, the waiter started making his way towards their table. Jack gestured towards Faye's half-full beer and raised two fingers, a simple yet clear indication of his intention.

As the waiter turned to head to the bar, Jack's attention was momentarily diverted by the appreciative glance the man cast in Faye's direction. It prompted Jack to surreptitiously regard her himself, his initial assessment confirming her attractiveness.

Jack's senses were attuned to the subtle details of Faye's appearance, and his observant gaze took in the comfortable aura she exuded. "You look comfortable," he remarked, his tone casual yet laced with a hint of approval.

Faye was clad in an oversized, cerulean blue sweater that draped over her frame, paired with sleek black leggings. The sweater's off-the-shoulder slouch revealed a glimpse of a lace bra strap, adding a touch of casual charm to her ensemble.

"Thanks," Faye responded, a faint smile playing on her lips. Her gratitude was genuine, a subtle acknowledgment of his compliment. She shifted, considering her own words to return the favor, but finding none that fit the bill. The honesty she sought in her reply seemed momentarily elusive.

"You look..." Faye's pause was palpable, her search for the right words evident. Unfortunately, her quest led her to a linguistic dead-end, with nothing quite as positive to say as Jack's comment. He hadn't changed out of his work attire, after all.

"Like I just got off work," Jack supplied, the hint of a wry smile touching his lips. His self-awareness allowed him to acknowledge the truth in her unstated sentiment, a shared understanding between them.

Faye's lips curved into a companionable smile, a mutual understanding passing between them as they shared a lighthearted moment. Both their laughter resonated with a sense of camaraderie, bridging the gap between their appearances and paving the way for an easy rapport.

The waiter approached, bearing their requested beers. Faye's swift consumption of her first beer paved the way for a renewed conversation with Jack. He, in turn, acknowledged the waiter's subtle glances in Faye's direction but brushed them off with an air of nonchalance. There was no need for him to dwell on it; they had only become partners earlier that day, and their connection was solely professional at this point.

"I wanted to apologize about earlier," Faye began, her words holding a hint of earnestness.

Jack's brows knitted with a touch of confusion, his mind retracing their interactions to discern any situation that might warrant her apology. He couldn't quite pinpoint anything in particular that would prompt her to seek forgiveness from him. In fact, if anyone were to apologize based on their interactions, he assumed it should probably be him. Regardless, Jack harbored no inclination to deter Faye from her intention; if she felt the need to extend an apology, he had no qualms about receiving it.

Casually reclining in his chair, Jack regarded her with a mixture of curiosity and receptiveness. He voiced his inquiry, his tone laced with curiosity, "What are you talking about?"

Faye's gaze met his, her expression thoughtful as she seemed to grapple with the words she wanted to convey.

"Earlier I acted like I knew who you were. I said all those things..." she paused. Her hands lay folded on the table before her, her thoughts slowly coalescing as she pieced together the events that had transpired between them.

"You were right," Jack interjected, his voice soft but firm as he interrupted her introspection. "I do tend to push people away, and I wouldn't hesitate to put my life on the line for others, if it's the right thing to do." There was a straightforwardness to his admission, devoid of shame or pride. He acknowledged these aspects of himself with a sense of candid acceptance.

Faye regarded him with an odd expression, a mixture of amusement and surprise flickering in her eyes. "Well, you just stole my thunder," she quipped, her tone light. A smile tugged at the corners of his lips in response. The atmosphere felt notably more relaxed, as if the weight that had been present between them had lifted, leaving room for genuine conversation.

His lips curved into a gentle smile, and he offered an assuring response, "I didn't intend to." The air around them seemed to have cleared, allowing their dialogue to flow with a newfound ease.

A sense of openness lingered in the air, and Faye seized the opportunity to express herself more openly. "And I didn't mean to come across as a know-it-all. I hope we can work well together," she confessed, finally reaching the underlying reason behind her invitation to dinner.

Jack's smile widened, and Faye's reciprocated smile mirrored his. The exchange felt genuine and promising. "I'm sure we'll do fine together," Jack affirmed, his tone resonating with optimism.

Taking a leisurely sip of his beer, Jack set the glass back on the table, his gaze shifting towards her with a hint of playful curiosity. "So, is this your version of an apology?" he asked, his expression a mixture of jest and genuine interest, raising an eyebrow in question.

Faye, for all her assertions of being an adult, sat in the chair with a demeanor that contradicted such claims. Her feet were in the seat, arms wrapped around her knees, exuding a playful and carefree aura that defied the seriousness of their roles. She looked and acted like a playful kitten. If a ball of yarn were to appear, he wouldn't be surprised to see her chasing after it. With an air of jubilance, she leaned back, her greenish gold eyes dancing with mischief, and a broad grin gracing her features. "Nope, this is a bribe!" she declared, her tone filled with youthful exuberance.

Jack's laughter, genuine and hearty, resonated in the air as he shook his head in amusement. This unexpected interaction with Faye was proving to be a delightful departure from his usual routine, a spark of vitality that he didn't know he needed.

3

Donovan adjusted his glasses, nudging them higher on the bridge of his nose. Leaving his office behind, he moved through the facility, descending to a lower level before halting in front of a pair of unmarked doors. Throughout the entire complex, there was a conspicuous absence of labeled doors. Yet, anyone with legitimate business in the facility knew that these unmarked portals led to Dr. Brundle's lab—an unspoken understanding among those who frequented these corridors.

Stepping closer to the doors, Donovan engaged the security panel at the side, allowing it to confirm his identity and access privileges. The doors slid open smoothly, sinking into the recesses of the wall. As he entered, the doors sealed shut behind him. Donovan paused, patiently waiting until the figure of Dr. Brundle emerged within his line of sight.

Within the laboratory, Dr. Brundle moved with a measured deliberation around the perimeter of his domain. His thoughts consumed him, weaving an intricate web of contemplation that distanced him from the presence of another in the room. His laboratory was a manifestation of his intellect, a space where he could navigate the complexities of genetics and creation. Although deeply engrossed in his thoughts, Dr. Brundle's awareness was tethered enough to acknowledge the potential consequences of ignoring the man who had just entered his realm.

Dr. Brundle's credentials were those of a geneticist, and while his colleagues might bestow upon him the title of genius, he paid little heed to their opinions. Eccentricity was an indelible part of his character, a trait that colored his interactions and pursuits. Yet, the consensus among his colleagues was unanimous—his sanity was tenuous at best. The common metaphor painted him as a few cards short of a full deck, with the jokers being the only companions left in his hand.

Such perceptions held no sway over Donovan Pike. For Donovan, the genius aspect was the crux of their connection. Dr. Brundle's unconventional brilliance was an asset that Donovan coveted. He was willing to overlook the eccentricities, even the question of sanity. In Donovan's assessment, Dr. Brundle was a valuable investment—a repository of knowledge and capability that justified the attention and resources Donovan poured into him.

Donovan embodied patience—a trait his extended lifespan had provided him. He watched with practiced tolerance as the enigmatic doctor darted about in a seemingly haphazard dance within his own sphere of concentration. Instruments were scrutinized, and their data noted methodically. Figures were cross-referenced with readouts on an array of devices, gadgets, and intricate apparatuses. Donovan wouldn't have been surprised if the doctor's workspace concealed secrets as diverse as a cancer cure and the world's most formidable weapon, all confined within those four walls.

If left to his own devices, Donovan was fairly certain that the doctor would remain content, engrossed within his personal enclave like a tick nestled on a host. Amidst his test tubes, beakers, and computers, the doctor's unwavering commitment to his work was palpable.

A tube containing a viscous, oddly colored fluid caught Donovan's attention. He plucked it from a nearby tray, surrounded by other identical, unmarked tubes. Whether safety had ever been a concern for the doctor was unclear, given the lack of labels throughout the lab. Donovan's brows furrowed at the chaotic organization, yet he knew that the doctor's exclusive domain was designed only for his understanding.

Turning the tube, Donovan observed the fluid within. It defied the laws of physics, shifting within the glass in an inexplicable manner. Absorbed in his observation, Donovan was taken off guard by the doctor's sudden appearance at his side. With deft precision, the doctor retrieved the vial from Donovan's grasp, placing it back onto the tray he had taken it from. The doctor's actions were efficient, performed with a degree of expertise that spoke of his familiarity with his workspace.

Dr. Brundle's voice, an odd mixture of low tones and nondescript inflections, broke the silence. His words held a subtle warning as he addressed Donovan, drawing his attention to the peculiar vial and its unpredictable nature.

"Mr. Pike, while the contents of that particular vial are indeed interestingly colored and its properties cause it to move in unexpected ways, you would do well not to agitate the contents too much. I do not believe you would be interested in what occurs upon agitation of that particular substance," Dr. Brundle cautioned.

With deft movements, Dr. Brundle meticulously rearranged the other vials on the tray, all the while shifting his focus to the unwelcome visitor who had intruded upon his domain. He recognized that in order to continue his work uninterrupted, he would have to allocate some of his time and attention to Donovan.

"What can I do for you, Mr. Pike?" inquired Dr. Brundle, acknowledging Donovan's presence with a touch of reluctance.

"I came to check upon the status of subject Delta 67-3. How are things progressing, Doctor?" Donovan's inquiry was direct, his purpose clear.

Dr. Brundle's expression soured as he felt his work interrupted for what he deemed a trivial inquiry. He walked over to his computer station and began inputting the necessary commands to retrieve the requested information. The figures and data appeared on the screen, and he immersed himself in their analysis. Transforming the technical details into a simpler form for Donovan, he provided a concise overview of the situation.

"The telemetric data is continuously updated. Vital signs are stable, and brain activity is within normal parameters. At the current rate, we can work with the subject for about fourteen more days before synaptic breakdown leads to increased psychosis. At that point, we can either bring the subject back here for genetic material harvesting or retire it, depending on your decision."

Donovan's frustration was palpable as he interjected, "I asked about Delta 67-3's mission execution, not its physiological state."

Dr. Brundle's expression shifted to a more contemplative one as he processed Donovan's annoyance. "Ah, my apologies. As of the latest report, three out of the five mission objectives have been completed. One is currently in progress, and the last is in the initial planning phase."

Donovan took in the update, content with the progress thus far. The general outline of Delta 67-3's achievements sufficed for his overarching objectives. He entrusted the specifics to Dr. Brundle, believing that the initial instructions were comprehensive enough for the doctor to handle the finer details.

"And what of subject Alpha 06 that you redeployed?" Donovan inquired.

"Alpha 06 is on track. We can recall or leave the subject deployed as needed. Alpha 06's progress confirms that there's no threat to Delta 67-3's mission," assured the doctor.

"I'm sure you'll receive further performance data once Delta 67-3's mission is complete and you recycle the genetic material. Ensure the next target is dealt with," Donovan instructed.

As Donovan turned to exit the lab, he added, "Dr. Brundle, pass my instructions to agent Alpha 06. Make sure they understand their role and what's expected."

"Understood," Dr. Brundle affirmed, watching Donovan leave before focusing on his work once again. The lab's doors closed soundlessly as Donovan left to attend to his tasks.

Dr. Brundle waited for the anticipated call from Alpha 06, which came punctually.

"Alpha 06, are you there?" he inquired.

"Yes, sir," a clear voice responded, immediately recognizable to Dr. Brundle.

The absence of holographic communication didn't concern Dr. Brundle; the secure connection required mutual verification. His instructions were issued promptly and succinctly.

"You're to observe the subject, providing assistance if their task is compromised without hindering your own mission. Initiate the Zero-Sum protocol if Delta 67-3's safety is at risk, and report any changes. Maintain a low profile."

Dr. Brundle didn't seek confirmation; it was implicit that the instructions would be executed seamlessly. Similarly, he acted without hesitation when receiving directives from Donovan Pike. The understanding between them was founded on mutual expectation and unswerving compliance.

4

The early morning presented itself with a veneer of cheerfulness, yet Jack found himself far from prepared to embrace the new day's opportunities. Fatigue clung to him like a weight, and his mind felt as foggy as the mist outside. The alarm clock, ever insistent, had begun its blaring when he was least ready for its intrusion. Squinting at the flashing numbers through bleary eyes, he struggled to decipher the message it conveyed. After a few attempts, he managed to grasp its insistence that it was time to rise.

Casting a glance through his bedroom window, his gaze met a sky adorned with twinkling stars, a canvas still untouched by the sun's ascent. The angels, it seemed, had granted themselves an extension on their morning duties, hitting the cosmic snooze button. As the realization settled, Jack felt a pang of recognition—he was no longer the young and resilient man who had eagerly joined the police force. Inwardly, he chided himself for allowing the persuasion of a petite woman to sway him into a night of drinking.

"Why on earth did I let that little girl talk me into drinking last night?" he muttered, his frustration directed more at his own susceptibility to persuasion than anything else. The regret lingered, as potent as the remnants of a hangover.

The days of easily indulging in a few drinks and shouldering the following day with relative ease were now part of a bygone era. The battle against the morning after had intensified, and he now grappled with the repercussions of letting a seemingly harmless woman leave such a profound mark on him. The beer and pizza had flowed freely, a prelude to Faye's shift to tequila. At the time, thoughts of the impending early morning hadn't factored into the equation; the night was meant for enjoyment, a sentiment Jack had fully embraced. However, the intoxicating allure of tequila had led him astray, blurring his foresight. The impending responsibilities of dawn had faded into the background, overshadowed by the camaraderie and shared moments of the evening. Hindsight now weighed heavily on his shoulders as he regretted not urging the driver to make an earlier stop, opting for a swift exit instead of extending the night's festivities on the Tequila train.

The night prior had found Jack and Faye as the sole inhabitants of the bar until its closing hours. The clock's hands had extended towards two-thirty in the morning, marking the culmination of their shared revelries. Following the bar's closure, the path diverged for the two companions. Faye ascended the staircase, her presence fading into the sanctuary of her upstairs room, while Jack's journey led him to the welcoming embrace of an awaiting Uber, a vehicle that traversed the space between the night's merriments and the quietude of his own abode.

Despite the throes of a hangover that now clenched his head like an unforgiving vice, Jack couldn't deny the fun he'd experienced. Memories of laughter, shared stories, and the warmth of camaraderie held their own sway against the morning's repercussions. Regret didn't yet fully color his reflections; the night had been worth it, at least in some measure.

Jack, undeterred by the cost he was now paying, found himself navigating through his routine with a determination that belied the headache that throbbed within him. The police station's gym, a realm of dedication and discipline, beckoned to him. Resolute, he pushed aside the lingering discomfort, determined to navigate his customary ritual despite the cost. With each motion, he sought to erase the remnants of indulgence. Weights lifted and machines conquered, his body became a testament to his willpower, the pain of his muscles harmonizing with the discord of his hangover.

As the gym session unfolded, Jack's focus was unwavering. He began with a cardio regimen, commencing with speed rope drills that danced like a rhythmic pulse. Two miles on the treadmill followed, each step a testament to his commitment. Having primed his body, he took a moment to tape his hands with a methodical precision, the preparation for his next phase.

Gloves adorned and determination etched into his stance, Jack turned his attention to the gym's occupants: the speed bag and the heavy bag. Methodically, he switched between the two, the rhythmic symphony of his fists connecting with the bags harmonizing with the rhythmic cadence of his heart. The sweat that now gathered was evidence of his exertions, a testament to his devotion.

Amidst this physical ballet, Jack found himself invited into a sparring match, homage to his skill and reputation. Accepting the challenge, he peeled his shirt away, revealing the culmination of his dedication in the form of his physique. The ring awaited him, a stage where his abilities would be put to the test. As he stepped into the ring, the echoes of last night's revelries became but a distant murmur, eclipsed by the rhythmic dance of combat that now took center stage.

Faye's entrance into the police station gym had a purpose rooted in necessity. The hotel's gym had failed her, its incapacitated treadmill unable to satisfy her need for physical exertion. Unlike the remnants of fatigue that clung to Jack that morning, Faye was the epitome of vitality. Her ability to weather the effects of a night that had extended into the early hours was nothing short of super human. As dawn broke, her readiness to face the day remained resolute. In contrast to the turmoil of a hangover, the gym beckoned to Faye like a sanctuary of empowerment, a realm where she thrived.

Having completed her run, Faye found herself in the midst of a seamless transition as Jack assumed his position within the ring. The rhythmic cadence of her footfalls on the treadmill had provided the backdrop to his entrance into the arena of sparring. Exiting the room housing the treadmills, Faye's gaze gravitated towards Jack, his form a manifestation of power that was balanced by a sense of agility. It was a tribute to his dedication that his physique radiated strength without crossing the boundary into excessive bulk. For a man of his age, Jack's presence held an air of vitality that was undeniably appealing.

In her observation, Faye couldn't help but appreciate how Jack's movements seemed to embody a fluid harmony between strength and grace. As her eyes lingered on him, a realization crystallized: the man in the ring was far more than his age suggested. He was proof of the resilience and perseverance that came with experience, qualities that transcended mere youthful energy.

Sharing the ring with Jack was a younger counterpart, a testament to generational contrasts. Despite the difference in age, the younger opponent appeared to struggle under the weight of his own breath. His exertions left him winded, a telltale sign that his prowess might be eclipsed by his lack of endurance. The dynamics in the ring were palpable, the seasoned warrior and the youthful challenger engaging in a dance of skill and stamina.

As Faye watched, it became evident that the young contender was outmatched. His efforts culminated in a concession, a tap that signaled his recognition of Jack's superior prowess. With that, the stage transformed as yet another challenger stepped into the ring, a newcomer seeking to test his mettle against the seasoned veteran. The transitions within the gym mirrored the ebb and flow of life itself, a succession of challenges met and overcome, each sparring match a testament to the interplay between strength, experience, and the pursuit of excellence.

Twenty minutes had elapsed since Faye's entrancement began, and within that span, a question floated like a wisp in her thoughts: *Is he even human anymore?* The scene unfolding before her was no ordinary one; a captivated audience encircled the ring, bearing witness to a spectacle that had become synonymous with Jack's presence. His form, immersed in the ebb and flow of combat, was a portrait of otherworldly skill and endurance. It was as if the boundaries of human capabilities had been pushed to the brink and stretched beyond recognition.

Jack stood within the ring, a juggernaut that defied the concept of fatigue. Despite the passage of numerous opponents, his demeanor refused to yield to the telltale signs of exhaustion. The rhythm of his sparring sessions played out in a relentless cadence, a dance between warriors marked by rapid exchanges. Opponents came and went in five-minute intervals, yet Jack persisted, an embodiment of ceaseless determination.

Faye's gaze remained transfixed upon him as his body moved with a grace that belied the force he summoned. Each punch he unleashed set his chest muscles into a symphony of motion, a ripple of power that spoke volumes about his prowess. His feet, seemingly choreographed by an unseen hand, traversed the canvas of the ring with a fluidity akin to an ice skater navigating frozen terrain. Yet, amid this display of kinetic energy, his breath flowed steady and measured, a testament to his unshaken composure.

An astonished whisper escaped Faye's lips as the spectacle continued to unfold before her. "He looks like he could take on Atlas at this point. My god!" The very idea of facing Jack, as borne witness by his performance, was a formidable concept, one that only the mythic figure of Atlas might dare challenge. Faye's comment encapsulated the awe that this extraordinary display invoked.

As Faye's observation persisted, an unanticipated undercurrent began to weave its way through her consciousness. The image of Jack took on a new dimension, stealthily insinuating a desire to experience more than mere observation. Her thoughts wandered to the tactile realm, to the sensation of muscles flexing and relaxing beneath her fingertips. The contours of his thighs held an allure of strength, while the breadth of his chest conjured an image of rugged firmness.

Faye's own heartbeat seemed to synchronize with the rhythm of Jack's feet, racing in tandem with the intensity of the moment. Each breath she took appeared to echo his exertions, as if her very existence had become intertwined with his in this transcendent display of physicality.

Yet, as the spectacle neared its zenith, Faye's motivations evolved. No longer content with witnessing Jack's prowess, she found herself seeking the ethereal, the otherworldly element that set him apart. A singular purpose emerged, to savor this moment of marvel before the intensity of her own desires threatened to consume her.

A fleeting instant lingered before Faye chose to retreat, a conscious withdrawal from the precipice of burgeoning yearning. The gymnasium's threshold became her sanctuary, a refuge from the magnetic pull that Jack's enigmatic presence exerted over her senses.

Faye made her way to the women's locker room, seeking refuge within its confines. Alone before the mirror, she confronted her reflection, her gaze anchored on the enigma within her own eyes. Her fingers clung to the cool edge of the sink, a physical anchor in a moment of internal turbulence. Her heart galloped within her chest, its erratic rhythm mimicking her swirling thoughts. The reflection before her held a glint, a spark of something unfamiliar, an enigmatic allure that she grappled to comprehend.

Tension gripped her as she wrestled with the unfamiliar emotions surging through her veins. She yearned for an explanation, for something tangible to attribute her feelings to. A feverish blush, a wave of faintness—anything that could provide a rational justification for the overwhelming desire that had surged within her, unbidden, for a man she had scarcely met and, by technical accounts, hardly knew.

Faye's grip tightened on the sink's edge, her knuckles turning white as her thoughts tumbled like dice in her mind. She needed a lifeline, a rationalization that would sever the link between her and this magnetic pull she couldn't escape. The image that stared back at her from the mirror held a mysterious twinkle, a silent reminder of the uncharted territory within her heart.

Her thoughts formed a hesitant narrative, a web of rationalizations woven with threads of denial. She clung to the notion that it was mere fatigue, the aftermath of a vigorous run, coupled with the presence of an undeniably attractive man. Yet, her inner voice refused to be muffled by these flimsy excuses. Faye knew, deep down, that the intensity of her reaction defied such simplistic explanations. She attempted to diminish the overwhelming sensations by belittling them, casting them as fleeting figments of her imagination. "I'm imagining things," she whispered, the words a self-prescribed antidote to the potent brew of emotions that threatened to engulf her. The lie, so carefully crafted, was a soothing balm to her unsettled psyche.

Seeking a reprieve from her internal turmoil, Faye sought refuge in the solace of the shower. Water cascaded over her form, its touch a feeble attempt to quench the fire that had ignited within her. She was determined to wash away not just the physical exertion of her run, but the emotional intensity that had gripped her so unrelentingly.

With each droplet that caressed her skin, Faye sought to cleanse herself of the bewildering feelings that had taken hold. As steam filled the air, she closed her eyes, allowing the water to envelop her in a cocoon of sensory distraction. She lingered there, suspended between the mundanity of cleansing and the storm of emotions that had raged within her.

Emerging from the shower, a veil of calmness now draped over her, Faye's resolve solidified. She had succeeded in quelling the tempest of desire that had threatened to consume her. As she prepared to ascend the stairs and confront the day's tasks, she clung to the notion that her feelings were a fleeting aberration, a transient whisper amidst the cacophony of life's demands.

The euphoria of his workout enveloped Jack, leaving him invigorated and triumphant. He relished the opportunity to push his limits, to challenge himself beyond his familiar boundaries. It was a sensation he hadn't experienced in a while, a need to break through his own barriers. As he stepped out of the ring, a subtle wobble in his knees betrayed the intensity of his efforts. Friendly jabs and age-related jests from his colleagues followed him, a playful banter that he welcomed with a good-natured grin. The same colleagues who had swapped in and out of the ring after mere minutes, unable to withstand his unyielding stamina.

The residual shadow of the hangover had been banished to a distant memory, replaced by the vibrant pulse of his exertion. A contented sigh escaped him as he acknowledged, "that was just what I needed." The rush of endorphins had transformed his disposition, leaving him feeling equipped to face any challenge, no matter how daunting. His energy was renewed, his spirit indomitable.

Amidst his self-congratulation for defeating the lingering remnants of the hangover, fragments of the previous night's revelry tiptoed into his consciousness. A vivid image of Faye rose to the forefront of his thoughts, and a gentle smile graced his features. He wondered, with a mixture of intrigue and amusement, if he'd dare to engage in another round of drinking with that captivating little devil again.

Completing his morning ablutions, Jack felt a renewed sense of purpose coursing through him. He was poised to seize the day, determined to channel this triumphant energy into making progress on the intricate case of the three brutal killings. Hope simmered within him, a belief that perhaps Faye's presence could inject a fresh perspective into the investigation. An idea crystallized in his mind—a two-fold plan to tackle the investigation head-on. He envisioned immersing himself in the case files during the morning hours, followed by revisiting each crime scene in person. His intuition urged him to believe that these scenes held untapped insights, cryptic clues that could propel them toward solving the enigmatic puzzle.

As Jack set his intentions for the day, his excitement mingled with a touch of nervous anticipation. The combination of a revitalized spirit and the prospect of collaboration with Faye infused him with a renewed sense of purpose. He was determined to unveil the truths hidden within the shadows of the case, and if fate allowed, perhaps even those that danced behind Faye's enigmatic gaze.

Once again, Faye found herself waiting in Jack's office. She hadn't crossed paths with him at the gym earlier, but he was oblivious to the notion that he should have been searching for her in the first place. Seeing Faye in his office stirred memories of the previous morning when she had been curled up just as she was now. As he entered the room, a soft purring-like sound reached Jack's ears, which he attributed to the hum of the building's air conditioning. The aroma of freshly brewed coffee wafted from the office door, filling the air and triggering Jack's habitual longing for his morning cup. Coffee had become his one permissible indulgence, a small pleasure he allowed himself.

"Your cup is on the desk. I just poured it," Faye's voice broke the stillness. Her breathing remained steady, and she appeared to be in a tranquil slumber.

Jack glanced toward Faye, noting that she had spoken without opening her eyes to confirm his presence. He dismissed it, assuming she had noticed him approaching the office moments before reclining on the couch. Perhaps she had seized the opportunity to pour his coffee and then settled back down.

"Thanks," Jack expressed his gratitude. He felt a genuine sense of relief that he didn't have to wait for his coffee to brew, enabling him to relish his favorite drink right away. A contented expression transformed his features as he released a slow sigh, his shoulders relaxing.

Faye smiled, her eyes still closed and her posture unchanged. "Two creams and two sugars, right?"

"Yeah," Jack affirmed, giving her a side glance. He likened her to an 'aloof aristocrat', a moniker his niece had playfully bestowed upon her audacious cat. The image of Faye resembling his niece's feline companion brought a hearty smile to his lips, elevating his already buoyant mood.

Jack carefully hung up his coat, casting a brief glance at the corner where he noticed an additional gym bag. It was a logical deduction that the bag belonged to Faye; she was the only other person who might have reason to store one in his office.

Moving around his desk, Jack settled into his seat, cradling his cup of coffee. As he took a leisurely sip, his eyes wandered over to his new partner. Faye was draped in a snug, grey turtleneck sweater that accentuated her form, paired with a darker grey pencil skirt that elegantly stretched down to her ankles. Her unadorned feet rested delicately, one atop the other. The term 'slimming' only began to describe the skirt's effect; it clung fittingly to her curves, though his view was somewhat limited by her reclined position on the couch. A fleeting thought brushed his mind, envisioning Faye standing upright in that skirt, and he felt a sudden blush warm his cheeks.

Amidst his internal musings, Faye's voice interrupted, as soft as a whisper. "So you have a foot fetish now?" Her candidness never failed to catch him off guard.

Jack swiftly diverted his gaze, refocusing on the depths of her eyes. He reprimanded himself for his momentary lapse, resolving to avoid such unintentional intrusions in the future. Though Faye's gaze remained fixed, her head remained still, observing Jack without the need to turn her gaze toward him. He chose to brush aside the mystery of how she sensed his attention on her feet.

Unease gnawed at him, unsettled by her uncanny ability to discern his focus even with her eyes closed. His mind drifted to the day he had found himself fixating on her legs, just as he had a moment ago with her feet. Attempting to regain his composure, Jack cleared his throat and shifted his gaze elsewhere, sidestepping the need to respond to her playful query. A sense of mild embarrassment washed over him; being caught in such a reverie was not his intention.

While Jack was looking away, a noticeable silence fell over the room. It wasn't an uncomfortable one, nor uneasy. Jack's eyes darted back to Faye.

Faye concealed a smile behind her hand, a gesture that shielded her amusement from Jack's view but couldn't hide the twinkle of humor in her eyes. She savored the flattery of receiving a lingering gaze from a man she found quite handsome, in a refined, intriguing manner. Yet, she was determined not to let that acknowledgment slip through and took pains to ensure Jack remained oblivious to her inner thoughts.

"You looked like you were having fun in the gym this morning," Faye remarked, her words punctuated by an unintended mental image of Jack's muscles flexing during his boxing routine. Swiftly, she averted her gaze, dismissing the unbidden daydream.

For a fleeting moment, surprise flickered across Jack's expression, prompted not by her sudden movement but by her mention of his gym activities. The image of her gym bag from earlier resurfaced in his mind, leading him to glance toward the corner as though confirming its presence, a quirky detail that hadn't departed his thoughts.

"Yeah, I was actually enjoying myself. What led you to the gym this morning?" Jack inquired, genuinely curious.

"The treadmill at the hotel decided to be uncooperative. Speaking of uncooperative, after last night, I half-expected that from you this morning," she quipped, her tone a blend of teasing and casual observation.

"Credit where it's due, Faye. You gave it your all to drink me under the table. I was quite the disheveled mess this morning. But somehow, I've rallied," Jack replied with a grin, reliving the events of the previous night.

"You couldn't keep up, old man?" Faye retorted, easily slipping into their familiar banter, momentarily forgetting the fleeting image that had danced through her mind moments ago.

"Care to test that theory in the ring?" Jack countered, a mischievous grin curving his lips as he displayed an air of confidence.

"Alright then. Tomorrow morning?" Faye responded, her tone unexpectedly serious.

Jack's eyebrows raised with prominence, his smile widening. He hadn't anticipated this turn of events, but he found himself more than willing to embrace the challenge. A grin tugged at his lips, and he responded, "Consider me intrigued. Let's see if I can't make you yield after stepping into my world."

With a purposeful movement, Faye stood up, departing Jack's office and returning shortly with a vacant chair. She placed it next to him, positioned conveniently by his desk. Jack meticulously spread the case files across the surface, ensuring easy access for both of them. The morning was consumed as they delved into the contents, sifting through the information in search of that elusive lead that might finally crack the case wide open.

Around eleven o'clock, Jack suggested they take a breather and seek out some lunch. The files had been scoured repeatedly, every detail examined and scrutinized between the two of them. Crime scene photos were studied, hypotheses exchanged, and autopsy reports dissected. Their collaborative efforts left no stone unturned, yet they remained frustratingly short of any breakthroughs.

Yearning for a change of surroundings, Jack also desired to escape the confines of his office and visit the crime scenes before the day drew to a close. The locations spanned various parts of the city, making Jack suspect that they would spend more time traveling between sites than actually investigating them.

Leaving the office behind, Jack and Faye descended in the elevator to the garage. Jack briefly left Faye's side to secure a vehicle from the motor sergeant, an encounter that left him in high spirits. The sergeant's efficiency and professionalism contrasted starkly with the sometimes difficult colleagues Jack dealt with, putting him in an unusually jubilant mood when he returned to Faye in a spacious SUV.

"Why the cheerful demeanor?" Faye inquired, taken aback by his uncharacteristically jovial expression.

"Just appreciating a bit of positivity for a change. Some of the folks around here can be a handful. Come on, hop in, and let's hit the road," he replied with a smile.

Faye climbed into the vehicle, and they set off. Snow was falling outside, prompting Jack to opt for a four-wheel-drive SUV. Mindful of potential traffic, he had also equipped the vehicle with a light bar on top. Their initial destination wasn't far, allowing Jack to promptly guide them out of the subterranean garage and toward their first stop.

"Where are we headed first?" Faye inquired.

Jack glanced her way briefly before focusing on the road again. "Our first victim was Mr. Paul Weaton, a banker. His murder occurred at his residence, and it's not too far from here. That's where we're heading first."

A quarter-hour later, the big utility vehicle rolled to a halt in front of a warehouse, where Jack brought it to a stop.

"I thought we were heading to the banker's house first?" Faye inquired.

"We're already here," Jack replied, pointing toward the unassuming structure. He unfastened his seatbelt and exited the vehicle, and Faye mirrored his actions.

The locale, if one could even call it that, existed within an aging industrial park, its massive edifices largely decrepit and begging for demolition. The entire area seemed deserted, almost like a set for a movie portraying an apocalyptic world.

"So, these are like some sort of converted condos?" Faye asked, her curiosity tinged with caution.

Jack shook his head in response. "If only it were that simple. It'd certainly speed up our search. The guy owned the entire industrial park. This warehouse is his place," he explained, gesturing towards one of the sturdier brick buildings. "He turned it into his residence."

Jack located the entrance and ushered them in. Motion sensors activated automatic lights, casting an eerie phosphorescence into the space. The entire first floor was one vacant empty space.Looking from the door afforded a view of all four of the outer walls. Jack led them to a staircase. Ascending, they reached the second floor. Like the ground level, this story boasted an expansive open space. However, unlike the downstairs area, the second floor housed a living area. The lower floor remained completely barren.

The living quarters consisted of standalone walls strategically positioned to create two discrete bedrooms, each equipped with an attached restroom. Kitchen cabinets were affixed to the walls, effectively establishing the kitchen area. Beyond this, much like the ground floor, the rest of the space remained devoid of any contents.

"Making an entire warehouse into a living space? That's pretty wild," Faye commented, her voice tinged with amazement.

"All three of the victims had unconventional homes. The second one, the judge, had a three-floor mansion with hardly any furnishings, except for a fully stocked kitchen, a library crammed with books, and a bedroom with just a bed. The last guy inhabited a house that was practically fortified like a fortress," Jack shared.

Faye glanced at the time, her expression uncertain. "I'm not sure if we'll manage to review all this square footage before nightfall."

"The exterior footage isn't our immediate priority. I had half the detectives in the force meticulously combing through every inch of that area. My interest lies more in reevaluating this interior," Jack announced, striding towards the living area.

"It's hard to imagine ever being comfortable in a place like this. These rooms just sit right in the middle of the warehouse floor. It's like you're on display," Faye mused.

"Agreed. The whole setup gives me the creeps. Can you picture being here at night, only this small part illuminated while the rest fades into darkness? It sends shivers down my spine just thinking about it," Jack confessed, involuntarily shuddering."Having so much open space around me would make me uncomfortable." With that, they stepped into the living area.

The spacious warehouse was bathed in sunlight, pouring through the windows that adorned the north and south walls. This natural illumination offered ample visibility, although they supplemented it with strategically positioned lamps that vanquished any lurking shadows within the living space.

Directing their attention to the master bedroom, the site of the murder, Jack resolved to concentrate their efforts there while conducting a brief survey of the remainder of the living area. After an hour of methodical exploration, it became evident that no additional leads or evidence awaited discovery. With their search yielding no further results, they decided to conclude and retraced their steps toward the vehicle, preparing to depart.

"How did the killer gain entry?" Faye questioned.

"Our presumption is that the killer both entered and exited through the same means. The security company reported a break-in. When the uniformed officers reached the scene, they found the entrance wide open—or whatever passes for a front door here," Jack explained.

"So, the victim seemed to have been caught off guard. All indications point to that. The state of the food implies it was left uneaten, and he was found in pajama bottoms," Faye mused.

"The report indicates no signs of forced entry, and we haven't identified a feasible method for the door to be manipulated remotely," Faye added, summarizing their findings.

She paused, ruminating, hoping to conjure any potential insights that might lead them down a path of discovery. Anything that could offer a foothold in the investigation.

"So, the security company reported a sort of break-in?" she inquired.

"Exactly. It seems the killer set off the alarm by exiting through the front door. That's the current theory. The challenge now is figuring out how the killer got inside in the first place. There are no security anomalies anywhere else, and the video footage from the front door shows only the victim entering. Unfortunately, during the time the alarm was triggered, the video quality becomes distorted. You can perceive the door being opened, then a blur obscures the view, and the door is left wide open. About ten minutes later, the first uniformed officers arrive at the scene," Jack explained.

"Did they attempt any forensics on the video to enhance the blurry part?" Faye inquired.

"Indeed, that was attempted. The video recording unit is motion-sensitive, but its frame rate is suboptimal. The blurring results from the limitations in the frame rate. The killer moved too quickly for the camera to capture clearly, and so far, no amount of forensics analysis has managed to rectify that," Jack replied.

After a cursory examination of the exterior of the building, Jack and Faye found no new leads there either. Climbing back into the SUV, they turned their attention to the judge's residence. Their time there proved even more fruitless, with the house offering no breakthroughs. Disheartened by the lack of progress, they departed from the location.

Jack hesitated, his thoughts carefully considering the decision he was about to make. The journey to the last residence in the suburbs loomed ahead, but the weather had taken a turn for the worse. Snow and ice were beginning to fall, a treacherous mixture that could turn even the sturdiest SUV into a risky proposition on the road. Jack wasn't willing to take that chance; the potential rewards didn't outweigh the danger. He reasoned that waiting another day wouldn't likely make a significant difference in their investigation. After all, any additional clues or evidence would still need to be thoroughly processed.

Frustration gnawed at Jack's patience. "It's like we're just ticking boxes, not actually doing real police work," he muttered to himself, his inner monologue betraying his exasperation. He felt a growing need for a breakthrough, something substantial to propel their investigation forward.

Caught by surprise at Jack's muttered comment, Faye turned from her contemplative gaze out of the window. She lifted her head from where it had rested against the window pane, drawn from her thoughts by the sense that Jack might have said something significant. While the radio played softly in the background, her mind had been elsewhere, preventing her from truly focusing on his words.

Jack's casual response came with a hint of playfulness, "I didn't say anything important. Let's go grab a bite to eat. What're you in the mood for, Faye?"

Curiosity still present, Faye probed further, "What options are nearby?" The sensation of hunger had begun to assert itself.

"We can sit down or take it to go, so it's either: slow and easy, or fast and greasy," Jack replied, the rhyming pattern of his words punctuating his attempt at maintaining a serious tone despite the underlying humor.

With a grin that seemed to stretch from ear to ear, mirroring the Cheshire Cat's enigmatic smile, Faye responded, "Fast and greasy sounds good to me." Her expression was akin to that of a child who had just been told they were getting their favorite treats: fries, a burger, and a milkshake.

Jack observed her playful enthusiasm, recognizing the charm in her demeanor. He couldn't help but find her resemblance to an excited child endearing. Deciding to embrace the moment, he entertained the thought of indulging her 'little girl' side. He was determined to treat her to just what she wanted—a place where they could relish fries, a burger, and a delectable milkshake.

Jack had a destination in mind, a burger joint that wasn't too far from their current location. The place had an unassuming charm—affordable, abundant food in a setting that wasn't too shabby. The food's quality was impressive, the milkshakes crafted by hand, and the coffee, in particular, held Jack's fascination at the moment. His coffee cravings were hard to ignore. Even if Faye had opted for the slow and easy choice, Jack would have likely suggested the same place. The coffee and decent food were reason enough for his enthusiasm.

As they pulled up to the front of the establishment, an off-kilter neon sign dangled precariously, lending the storefront a somewhat disheveled appearance. The place seemed cramped, lacking any grandeur. The neighborhood wasn't exactly bad, yet it hardly boasted a reputation for excellence. Instead, it was the kind of hole-in-the-wall burger joint you'd encounter in the nooks and crannies of a bustling metropolis.

Jack parked the SUV, leaving the engine running without a second thought. Any concerns about taxpayer funds being wasted by burning gas or the sudden appearance of a rogue hopping into the driver's seat were swiftly dismissed from his mind. His sole motivation for leaving the engine running was uncomplicated—he simply didn't want to get back into a cold vehicle. It boiled down to that straightforward desire for warmth.

Faye, unfazed by the still-running vehicle, stepped out from her side. With a carefree demeanor, she approached the entrance, seemingly unaware of the SUV's engine humming behind her. Eagerly, she skipped toward the door, her enthusiasm palpable. Jack followed, his gaze alternating between her playful strides and the way her pencil skirt clung to her, accentuating her charm. The combination of her youthful behavior and sensual allure proved to be an intriguing dichotomy—one that both captivated and bewildered him.

As they neared the door, a somewhat startling thought flickered through Jack's mind, *Damn, I need a cold shower.* The skirt's effect on Faye's appearance had ignited an unexpected surge of desire, prompting a mental exclamation about needing to cool off. He couldn't help but acknowledge the puzzling contrast between her playful demeanor and the enticing sensuality she effortlessly exuded. This inner dialogue remained his personal revelation, wisely left unspoken.

"Those burgers smell incredible," Faye exclaimed as they stepped into the cozy warmth of the restaurant. Her grin was as infectious as ever, radiating her genuine excitement.

"And they taste even better," Jack replied with a knowing smile. Gesturing toward a small table nestled discreetly at the rear of the establishment, he suggested, "Let's take a seat over there."

Jack pulled out a chair, allowing Faye to settle in comfortably before gently guiding her forward. Though a flush of warmth crept to her cheeks, Faye resisted the urge to blush in response to his chivalrous gesture. She accepted it as a sign of his recognition of her as a woman beyond their roles as colleagues and partners. It was a refreshing shift, but she was cautious not to overanalyze it. After all, she had recently dealt with thoughts of Jack that had left her feeling off-kilter, and she wasn't keen on revisiting those emotions.

Seated across from her, Jack positioned himself with his back to the wall, his gaze fixed on her. Faye noticed the potential significance of this seating arrangement—the protective stance with his back to the wall and facing the entrance. She didn't voice her observations aloud, but she recalled that this behavior was often seen in individuals who felt uneasy with their backs exposed. Soldiers returning from war zones with PTSD often adopted this posture, as did those who remained vigilant against potential threats.

Faye contemplated these insights in silence, not wishing to pry into Jack's feelings or motivations. While she had an inkling of the reasoning behind his stance, she decided it was best not to bring it up, respecting the unspoken boundary he had set for himself.

Seated at the table, they mulled over the menu, considering the limited options that the humble eatery had to offer.

After a few minutes, Jack lifted his gaze to meet Faye's, his perceptive nature shining through. He couldn't help but notice the unspoken queries and contemplations flickering across her expression like subtitles. Choosing to provide her with an opportunity to voice her thoughts, he spoke gently, "Is something on your mind? If you've got questions, feel free to ask."

Faye, recognizing his willingness to engage, seized the opening he offered. She combined her thoughts into a statement and a question, asking, "PTSD?" Her eyes held an inquisitive glint as she observed his intense scrutiny of their surroundings.

"Huh?" Jack's response was a mix of surprise and confusion, as he attempted to follow the sudden direction of the conversation.

Undeterred, Faye repeated herself, simultaneously stating and inquiring, "Post-traumatic stress disorder?"

Jack's brow furrowed, his confusion deepening. "Why are you bringing that up?" he asked, genuinely perplexed by her line of questioning.

"You chose this spot, making sure your back is against the wall, giving you a view of both the front door and the people around us," Faye observed, gesturing discreetly to their surroundings before directing her gaze to the entrance they had just walked through. "Since we sat down, you've been keeping an eye on everyone and noting the exits."

Jack nodded, the truth of her words settling in. "Yeah, it's a habit I picked up during my time in Iraq. Not something I've been able to shake off, even after almost two decades."

"Hyper-vigilance—it's both a curse and a blessing in our line of work," Faye commented, acknowledging the complex nature of their profession.

"Tell me about it," Jack agreed, a touch of weariness in his voice. "This job molds you into someone different, keeps you on edge even when you wish you could relax."

Faye's demeanor shifted, a tinge of sadness reflecting in her eyes. "It's tougher for someone like me," she admitted, her gaze wandering into the distance, hinting at deeper concerns.

Jack picked up on her change in tone and demeanor, his concern rising. "In what way?" he inquired, leaning in attentively.

A dry laugh escaped Faye's lips, devoid of any amusement and laden with frustration. "When you're small like me, and you look like someone's teenage kid, gaining respect becomes a daily struggle. Add 'female' to that mix, and you get a parade of insufferable men who feel the need to play the role of my 'knight in shining armor'. They try to protect me while simultaneously attempting to do my job for me."

Jack's expression shifted to one of understanding and empathy, his features softening as he recognized the challenges she faced. The complexities of navigating a male-dominated field were not lost on him, and he respected Faye's tenacity in persevering.

"Is that why you're compensating with those cannons?" Jack inquired, indicating the pair of sidearms holstered at Faye's sides with a nod of his head.

Faye's head swayed gently from side to side. "Not really overcompensating," she replied, her tone resolute. "These 'cannons,' as you call them, are here because I'm not exactly towering over suspects. Being small means I'd rather not find myself in a physical confrontation. If it comes down to drawing and using my guns, I want the threat neutralized," she said with a touch of fierceness.

"Damn," Jack responded, a nervous chuckle escaping him. At that moment, he wasn't entirely sure if he should be slightly intimidated by her or not. "Rawrr. Easy, tiger!" he playfully chided, a quip that elicited laughter from both of them.

As Faye laughed, Jack grappled with mixed feelings. Her vulnerability had been on display, yet her choice of weaponry contradicted any notion of fragility. The guns she carried were not to be underestimated—the caliber alone indicated the sheer force they could unleash upon a target.

Watching her laugh, Jack's thoughts were a swirl of conflicting emotions. His protective instincts surged, driven by her revealed vulnerability, while his awareness of the destructive power of her firearms caused a shiver of unease he fought to suppress. He was torn, wanting to shield her from harm while acknowledging her capacity to wield lethal force.

Amidst their shared laughter, Faye interjected, her tone carrying a note of seriousness, "Just so you know, I'm dead serious about that, you ass."

Her intent was clear: she wanted to emphasize her reliance on her sidearms due to her physical limitations in direct combat. As if to emphasize her point, she swung her arm in a mock punch across the table towards Jack. He quickly sidestepped, narrowly avoiding her playful attack, causing her fist to sail harmlessly through the air. Her near miss almost collided with the waiter who had suddenly appeared at her side, yet even this misadventure was met with laughter all around. The waiter, unfazed, took their order and departed to relay it to the kitchen.

With the immediate amusement subsided, Faye seized the moment to revert to their earlier conversation. "As I was saying," she began once more, her tone now tinged with solemnity. "I could outperform most of the male cadets in endurance and various physical activities, but hand-to-hand combat training was my Achilles' heel. The instructor once told me, 'Girl, you're too light in the ass to be doing this without some kind of backup plan in place,'" she recalled, mimicking the instructor's words in a comical yet horrible southern drawl.

"Well that was an ignorant thing to say, as well as being overtly sexist to say the least. Did you report him to his superiors?" Jack's question was tinged with incredulity, clearly appalled by the instructor's words.

Faye chuckled before responding, a grin spreading across her face. "I didn't report 'her' to her superiors," she replied with a hint of amusement, savoring the twist in the tale and the moment's levity.

As they reminisced about that period in her life, Faye managed to infuse humor into the memories. "She was right, though. I am indeed 'light in the ass' when it comes to hand-to-hand combat. So, I specialized in weapons training instead—you know, to compensate for my flaw," she quipped, her tone playful yet revealing her practical approach to the situation.

Jack's response was one of authentic surprise mixed with mock shock. "You have a flaw?" His eyes widened, and he covered his mouth with a hand, an expression of awe concealed behind it.

The both of them shared a laugh, the moment serving as a testament to their developing camaraderie. Despite his comment, Faye didn't dwell on the topic, instead she let him steer the conversation in a different direction.

"Well, don't forget, we've got a date in the ring tomorrow morning. I don't want to hear crap about that hand to hand stuff as an excuse to get out of it because it ain't happening, Faye," Jack asserted, not giving her any leeway to back out.

"And I don't want you to have a heart attack in the ring when you're in there facing me. You better put your big boy panties on and suck it up. Deal with it like a man," Faye paused to give emphasis. "Wearing panties!"

Laughter echoed between them once more. In this exchange, Jack found himself appreciating Faye's company even more. She had a way of putting him at ease, making the interaction effortless and enjoyable. This connection felt refreshing, a genuine opportunity for them to understand each other better and share laughter in a relaxed, friendly atmosphere.

Their ordered food arrived shortly thereafter, and Jack watched in astonishment as Faye shifted from her playful demeanor to a focused one, attacking her meal with determination. She methodically devoured her burger and two baskets of the bottomless fries that accompanied their meals, all before announcing her contentment.

Her appetite didn't stop there, as she efficiently dispatched two large milkshakes as well. Jack couldn't help but wonder where she was stowing all that food, given she certainly wasn't hiding it in her pockets. Simultaneously, he pondered how she managed to maintain her physical fitness while consuming such quantities.

5

Jack entered the gym, his excitement palpable. Anticipation for his morning workout with Faye had him in high spirits. The session's plan was already laid out in his mind, and he had secured their time on the training ring. Setting up the various equipment and gear, he was pleasantly surprised by the efficient flow. He grinned as he surveyed the organized space; everything was primed for their training.

Faye walked into the gym with purpose, her determination matching Jack's enthusiasm. Shedding her coat and stashing her belongings in a locker, she was dressed for action in a sports bra and biking shorts. Her attire signaled her readiness to engage in a vigorous workout with Jack.

"Hey, Faye, ready for our workout?" Jack called out, a wide grin on his face.

Faye looked up from storing her belongings, a determined smile on her lips. "Absolutely, Jack. I've been looking forward to this."

He nodded, pleased with her enthusiasm. "I've got everything set up for us. We've got the ring blocked out and all the gear ready."

Faye's eyes scanned the well-organized space. "Impressive, Jack. You really came prepared."

He chuckled. "Well, I wanted to make sure we make the most of our time."

As they made their way toward the treadmill area, Faye spoke up. "You know, I'm excited about the cardio part. Let's kick things off with a solid two-mile run."

Jack matched her enthusiasm. "Sounds like a plan. It'll get our hearts pumping."

They hopped onto adjacent treadmills, Faye adjusting the settings on hers. "Ready to start?" she asked.

Jack grinned, his fingers poised over the controls. "Ready when you are."

With a shared nod, they simultaneously pressed the buttons, the treadmills coming to life beneath their feet. As they began their run, their synchrony echoed

After the invigorating cardio session, they transitioned to the boxing ring. Jack stripped off his shirt, revealing his well-defined muscles, and Faye found herself appreciating the sight. She couldn't deny her partiality for his impressive physique; it was something she couldn't help but notice. His easy confidence was matched by his physical presence, making it hard for her eyes to wander elsewhere.

As they got into position with gloves on and pads ready, Faye found herself studying Jack's form with more intent. It was almost expected of her, given the nature of their training. He guided her through the intricacies of stance and punch technique, demonstrating each move patiently. As he stepped into his role as her mentor, it was only natural that her focus remained on him.

"Alright, Faye, stance is crucial," Jack instructed, his voice steady and encouraging. "Spread your feet shoulder-width apart, balance your weight on the balls of your feet, and keep your guard up."

Faye mirrored his stance, absorbing his guidance. "Like this?"

"Perfect," he affirmed with a nod, admiring her perfect legs. "Now, let's work on the jab-cross combination. Left jab, then follow it up with a right cross."

She executed the combination, feeling the satisfying thud of her punches connecting with the pads. "Got it."

Faye followed his instructions, focusing on her footwork as she moved through the combination. Jack's attentive coaching made the process smooth, and she appreciated his patience.

As the session progressed, Jack introduced her to more advanced combinations and techniques. He showed her how to read punches and evade them, their dynamic evolving into a seamless exchange of movement and guidance.

Faye absorbed each lesson with keen interest, her determination evident in her every move. Her prior experience in various forms of hand-to-hand combat gave her a foundation, but boxing presented its own set of challenges and nuances.

By the time their training session was nearing its end, Faye wasn't sweating at all and her breathing was even, her energy was undiminished. She stepped back and met Jack's gaze. "Thanks for the lesson, Jack. I've got a lot to work on, but I can see the potential in this."

Jack's smile was genuine, reflecting his satisfaction with their progress. "You're a quick learner, Faye. Boxing takes time, but you're on the right track. We'll continue to refine your skills in our future sessions."

Jack effortlessly absorbed Faye's punches during their training session. She had intentionally held back her true strength, aware that her half-hearted punches were unlikely to pose a significant challenge for him. Her slender build meant she couldn't put much mass behind her strikes. Although her form wasn't perfect, Jack saw potential in her technique. And, he couldn't deny the aesthetic appeal of her physique.

As the training session came to an end, they both headed to the separate shower facilities the police station gym provided. After freshening up, they got dressed and convened in Jack's office, ready to dive into their work for the day.

About an hour later, Jack led Faye to the site of the first murder, their mission being to canvas the neighborhood for any potential leads. The area was predominantly filled with warehouses, offering little in the way of traditional neighbors. It made their task relatively straightforward, as there were no individuals who fit the standard description of residential neighbors.

The second crime scene, however, presented a different situation. This time, they had the opportunity to conduct a more traditional canvas of nearby residents. The outcome mirrored that of their previous efforts—no leads emerged. The neighbors had nothing significant to report, having seen nothing unusual or suspicious on the night of the murder. Their observations of the neighborhood since then had yielded nothing out of the ordinary, aside from an increase in police presence, which had not brought about any substantial changes.

As they wrapped up their canvas, Jack and Faye found themselves facing a frustrating lack of information. The investigation was proving to be a challenging

Back at the office, Jack and Faye settled in to undertake the less glamorous but crucial aspect of police work—calling known associates and colleagues of the victims. This was the grunt work, the backbone of investigations, the part that often led to tangible results. They knew that going out to canvas neighborhoods, making phone calls, and even relying on hotlines could yield the valuable leads they were hoping for. These techniques were the bread and butter of traditional police work, time-tested and proven.

As they dialed numbers and had conversations, the clock seemed to tick slowly. Their determination was unwavering, but each call that didn't bear fruit added to the growing sense of frustration. This was the nitty-gritty part of the process, and they were fully immersed in it. They methodically worked their way through contacts, hoping that someone would remember something, anything, that could be a clue.

Despite their efforts, the morning's work yielded no breakthroughs. The leads were sparse, and the pieces of the puzzle weren't coming together as they had hoped. Their collaboration was marked by a shared understanding that these moments of relentless grind were an integral part of the investigative process. There was no room for shortcuts or magical revelations; it was about putting in the effort, no matter how tedious.

With the morning's endeavors behind them, Jack and Faye found themselves back in the office, facing the mountain of files once more. They shared a moment of mutual frustration, a brief acknowledgment of the challenges they were up against. Then, without skipping a beat, they resumed their analysis from the beginning. This was the ebb and flow of investigative work, a dance between frustration and determination, with the ultimate goal of finding that elusive break that would unravel the cases they were tackling.

Around noon, a sudden rap at the door of Jack's office drew their attention. There, at the threshold, stood what would normally be considered an unfamiliar figure to a police station—a teen girl with vibrant red hair that cascaded around her ruddy, freckled cheeks. She lingered for a moment, her small hands planted firmly on her hips, an air of impatience about her. As a young adult that was small of stature, just a bit taller than Faye, she had grown accustomed to demanding attention, a necessity she knew well.

It was a skill she had mastered early on, one that proved remarkably effective in ensnaring a certain someone around her finger. A tactic wielded with devastating effects, much to the occasional chagrin of Jack. Unbeknownst to Jack and Faye, the girl stood waiting for acknowledgment, looking every bit of a lost, red-haired orphan if you didn't know who she was.

The occupants of the office were deeply engrossed in their discussion, their focus entirely on their work at hand. The teen cleared her throat in a deliberate, almost obnoxious manner, realizing that subtlety wouldn't serve her purpose in this instance. "Ahem..." the sound finally punctured the bubble of concentration that enveloped the room.

Jack's head snapped up at the sound, his eyes locking onto the unexpected visitor. His initial surprise gave way to recognition as he registered the red-haired girl standing there.

In the midst of this interruption, Brooke's voice broke the silence. "Hey, uncle Jackie," she said, taking a few steps further into his office. Faye, now aware of the newcomer, regarded the scene with curiosity. She observed the interaction between Jack and the young girl, her presence clearly holding significance for both of them. Brooke's entrance had effectively shattered the monotony of their investigative routine.

A broad smile spread across Jack's face as he quickly recognized the unexpected visitor who had inserted themselves into his office. This intrusion had caught him off guard, mainly because he wasn't meant to be in his office at that particular moment. Despite the surprise, Jack's grin conveyed his genuine delight at the sight before him.

"Hi, Brooke," he greeted warmly, his voice carrying a mixture of affection and mild apology. "Sorry, lost track of time," he added, his words hinting at the diversion from his usual schedule.

As Brooke's presence registered in his mind, Jack's gaze shifted to the wall clock while simultaneously closing the files scattered across his desk. He rose from his seat, his movement punctuating the fact that their work discussion had been temporarily halted. By the time he had fully stood, Brooke had advanced and was standing right before Jack's desk, her attention openly fixed on Faye. The subtle dynamics between the two adults hadn't escaped her observation as she entered the room.

Faye, sensitive to the unspoken exchange, directed her gaze toward Jack, her curiosity evident in her eyes. She was silently seeking an explanation for the presence of the teenager who now stood in front of his desk. She had already pieced together that Jack was her uncle.

That much was clear. Faye's question revolved around her desire to know more about the girl who had casually referred to Jack as 'Jackie'. Moreover, the striking similarities between Brooke and Jack had not gone unnoticed by Faye.

Recognizing Faye's inquiry, Jack turned his attention toward her, ready to offer the introduction that was due. Faye's curiosity was palpable, and Jack took a moment to address it. "Faye, this is my niece, Brooke," he introduced with a fond smile, shifting his focus to Brooke as he spoke. The connection between them was evident, a familial bond that explained Brooke's casual use of the name 'Jackie'. With a methodical sweep, Jack stacked the files into a neat pile on the corner of his desk. Jack made sure everything was orderly as he prepared to address the new development. Seeing Faye rise from her seat and approach Brooke, he turned to face them both, ready to facilitate the introduction.

"Brooke," Jack began, his tone warm as he turned to include them both in the conversation. "This is my partner, Faye."

Brooke's reaction was nothing short of astonishment. Her eyes widened in disbelief, a mixture of shock and joy dancing in her gaze. The impact of Jack's words seemed to hit her with a wave of emotions, and she looked as if she might burst into tears of happiness. Knowing her uncle's aversion to partnerships, Brooke's surprise at the revelation was palpable. That knowledge underscored the significance of the woman before her. But what was even more evident was the way she regarded Faye—as if she had just encountered a celestial being, an angelic presence, a true miracle.

Her incredulity shining through, Brooke managed to voice her amazement, still struggling to process the unexpected news. "You're uncle Jackie's partner?" Brooke queried, the suspicion ringing in her voice, a mixture of disbelief and elation painted across her expression.

Faye responded with a nod. Her eyes meeting Brooke's, Faye affirmed her query. The situation was peculiar, that much was certain.

The young girl's enthusiasm couldn't be contained. "But how did this happen?" she burst out, her grip on Faye's hands growing tighter, as if seeking assurance that this wasn't some fleeting dream. Her words spilled out, and she couldn't contain her frank assessment. "He's such an ass!" Brooke exclaimed, voicing a sentiment that appeared to be her uncle's reputation among those closest to him.

There was a momentary pause, and then, his hand met his forehead with an audible smack—the sound of realization and surprise meeting his palm.

Caught off guard by Brooke's candidness, Jack stood there, momentarily dumbfounded by the outburst from his niece. Jack's jaw practically hung open. He stared at the scene unfolding before him, a mix of shock and bemusement playing on his features. In his mind, he half-jokingly wondered if the scent of brimstone was in the air, as though the appearance of this young little devil girl defied all his expectations. A hearty groan escaped his lips, a sound that mirrored his internal confusion. *How exactly did I end up in this situation?* he questioned himself.

Faye's lips curved into a warm smile as her gaze settled on Brooke. "Oh, I think he's sweet," she playfully remarked, adding a touch of teasing humor to the moment.

In the shared exchange of glances between Faye and Brooke, a connection formed—a shared appreciation for the camaraderie they had stumbled upon. Suppressing their laughter was an exercise in futility, and the pretense of seriousness dissolved into a fit of shared laughter that echoed within the office walls.

Jack observed the scene with a mix of amusement and a touch of mock offense, fully embracing the humor at his own expense. His dignity, he figured, was a small price to pay for the genuine laughter and connection between the two women. As the laughter began to subside, a semblance of seriousness returned to Jack's expression—well, almost.

"That kind of talk isn't necessary, young lady," Jack chided, his words carrying a hint of mock indignation, the tone more playful than authoritative.

Brooke met her uncle's mock seriousness with a quirked eyebrow and a look that danced on the edge between incredulity and amusement. "You're right, uncle Jackie," she began, her tone just as playful, "but that kind of talk wouldn't be necessary if it wasn't true." The words were laced with humor and a dash of cheekiness.

Jack emitted a somewhat exaggerated huff, not particularly thrilled about engaging in this kind of conversation with his fifteen-year-old niece. The prospect of justifying his character and choices to a teenager was not something he had been looking forward to.

With his patience for the situation wearing thin, Jack decided to shift gears and opt for a different approach. He glanced at Brooke and then directed his question toward her, hoping to steer the conversation in a more manageable direction. "Are you ready to go?" he asked, his tone carrying a mix of resignation and readiness to move on.

The change in topic proved to be a wise maneuver. A noticeable shift came over Brooke as her previous exuberance returned, almost as if a cloud had lifted. Displaying her readiness by nudging the duffel bag at her feet, she replied with an eager grin, "I'm as ready as I'll ever be." Faye, curious and perhaps slightly amused by the interplay between uncle and niece, took the opportunity to ask, "Where are you guys going?"

It was as if a dam burst in Brooke's excitement, causing her words to tumble out in a rush. "Uncle Jackie and I are heading up to the family cabin in the mountains for a few days," she declared, her enthusiasm palpable. Her eyes practically sparkled with joy. "Took me only a few weeks to wear him down and get him to ditch work for some quality time with his favorite niece," she added, punctuating her statement with a victorious grin in Jack's direction.

"My only niece," Jack emphasized with a playful smirk, his response already hinting at their playful banter.

Brooke, seemingly unaffected, turned to Faye, seeking confirmation for her original wording. "That's what I said, right? I'm pretty sure I did."

Faye chimed in with an amused smile, "You did, Brooke. I heard it too."

Brooke's eyes lit up as she launched into an explanation of their plans. "Uncle Jackie and I are going to soak up some fresh mountain air and take a trek, if the trails are clear enough."

Faye raised an eyebrow, a hint of incredulity in her tone. "In the snow?"

The confident response came from Brooke, who seemed to have an answer ready. "We've got snowshoes, and it's a great workout. Plus, it's one of the few times I actually get to spend with my uncle Jackie." As if on cue, Jack joined in with a hearty bear hug for his niece, showcasing a side of him that was often hidden from the rest of the world.

Interrupting their interaction with a curious question, Brooke turned her attention to Faye. "What about you, Faye? Any plans for the weekend?"

Jack glanced at Faye, intrigued to hear her answer. His niece's unexpected question had him wondering how Faye might respond. He pondered her potential plans, recognizing that being new to the city might limit her familiarity with local activities. In fact, if Faye had approached him for suggestions, he would have likely been at a loss himself, despite being a city native.

"I was actually just going to stay in my room for the rest of the weekend," Faye replied casually.

Brooke gave Faye an exaggerated eye-roll. "There's no way we're going to let you do something so boring and pedestrian when you can just come with us," she declared, casting an affectionate glance at her uncle.

Jack sensed the impending request and knew he was unlikely to resist. However, before he could even respond, Brooke went ahead.

"Can she please come with us?" Brooke turned to Jack, her eyes pleading.

Jack chuckled, well-aware of his niece's persuasive skills. He was about to agree when Faye interjected playfully, "I was going to order in and watch television too. Can you top that?"

Brooke didn't miss a beat, her enthusiasm unwavering. "While watching television sounds like it would be fun, I think you should come with me and uncle Jackie. I'm sure he won't mind, and there's plenty of space up at the cabin for you to have your own room."

Faye hesitated, caught between not wanting to intrude on Jack's time with his niece and the prospect of a more engaging weekend. She glanced at Jack, seeking his input. Jack simply shrugged and said, "I don't mind, and I'm fine with it if you are."

Faye's face broke into a smile, her reservations melting away. She hadn't relished the idea of being cooped up in a hotel room all weekend, and this seemed like a great opportunity to experience a different side of Jack that the world didn't often get to see.

"Alright, if you're okay with me joining you guys for the weekend, then I'm going to need to stop by my room and get some clothes," Faye said with a nod.

Brooke clapped her hands excitedly. "Yay! This is going to be so much fun!"

Jack smirked at his niece's enthusiasm, his own reservations fading as he looked at Faye's genuine smile. This weekend might just turn out to be more interesting than he had initially expected.

Jack efficiently loaded his bag and Brooke's belongings into his SUV, and once they were all settled inside, he steered the vehicle onto the road. Their initial destination was Faye's hotel. Pulling up at the hotel entrance, Faye swiftly exited the vehicle and entered the lobby. She hurried to her room, where she efficiently packed a bag with items she anticipated needing for the weekend. Within twenty minutes, she was back downstairs, ready to embark on the trip.

With everyone on board, they set off on their journey towards the mountains. As they ascended, the atmosphere inside the vehicle was filled with laughter and light-hearted banter. This drive allowed Jack to witness a side of Faye he hadn't previously encountered during their work. While the relaxed pizza and beer encounter had offered a glimpse, this was a different kind of interaction.

Faye was engaged in genuine laughter, her demeanor illuminated by the shared fellowship. Jack couldn't help but feel a subtle sense of annoyance at a feeling of being left out somehow, his attention divided between Faye and the road ahead. He was jealous, he had to admit. He wanted to engage with Faye and see this side of her and felt an unreasonable desire to have it to himself. He observed her enjoying herself, a reminder of the multifaceted person she was beyond the professional sphere.

During the journey, Faye discovered a significant piece of family history—Brooke's father had been Jack's identical twin brother. Tragically, he had lost his life in a car accident shortly before Jack's return from one of his combat tours in Iraq. This event transpired just before Brooke's birth, which meant that her knowledge of her father was largely shaped by the stories and mannerisms of her uncle

Jack. Elizabeth, their mother, had attested to the remarkable similarity in mannerisms between Jack and his late twin brother.

As they chatted in the car, Faye turned to Brooke with curiosity. "So, Brooke, you mentioned earlier that your father was Jack's twin. That must have been quite a bond they shared."

Brooke nodded, her expression thoughtful. "Yeah, it was. My mom told me stories about how they used to do everything together when they were kids. I guess that's why my uncle Jack feels like a big part of my connection to my dad, even though I never got to meet him."

Faye's eyes held understanding as she listened to Brooke. "It must be comforting to have your uncle around, someone who carries a piece of your father's personality and memories."

Brooke smiled softly. "Definitely. Sometimes it's like I can catch a glimpse of my dad in the things my uncle says or does. It's a way for me to know him a little better, even though he's not here."

Faye's gaze shifted to Jack for a moment, a subtle understanding in her eyes. "I'm glad you have that connection, Brooke."

Their conversation shifted, but the bond between them grew stronger. Faye couldn't help but feel a sense of warmth in witnessing the special relationship between Brooke and Jack, one that bridged the gap between generations and brought comfort in shared memories.

Faye and Brooke hit it off famously, much to Jack's satisfaction. He couldn't have been more pleased with how well the two girls were getting along. However, to Jack's chagrin, he spent the entire drive up the mountain roads enduring what he dubbed 'girl talk'. He had to tolerate their secret giggles, firmly convinced that they were somehow at his expense. Despite their assurances, he couldn't be convinced otherwise. Still, he found himself enjoying the drive up the mountainside with their company.

The mountain air greeted them with its brisk, refreshing, and crisp embrace as they finally arrived. Faye had wisely taken the opportunity to change out of her pencil skirt and into a pair of jeans when they stopped at her hotel to pack for the weekend getaway. Brooke, on the other hand, had come prepared, dressed for the adventure she had in mind. As they stepped out of the car, ready to embark on their snowy trail experience, Jack found himself being the odd one out, the only one not dressed for the planned excursion.

Jack brought all of the bags into the house, taking a moment to change from his slacks into a more practical pair of blue jeans. Meanwhile, the girls had efficiently unloaded the groceries that Jack had purchased for their getaway. With a sense of careful preparation, he started a crockpot, allowing the aroma of the meal they'd enjoy later that evening to gradually fill the cabin. As the savory scent wafted through the air, the girls were already outside, embracing the refreshing atmosphere and taking in the scenic view.

Venturing towards a lean-to shed connected to the side of the cabin, Jack retrieved the snowshoes they would need for their hike and handed them out to Faye and Brooke. Once everyone had their snowshoes on, they stepped out onto the trail, ready to begin their mountain adventure. The path wound its way through the woods enveloping the cabin before ascending into the mountains, promising a journey filled with nature's wonders and breathtaking sights.

The trio continued to relish the early evening, spending it walking, conversing, and immersing themselves in the vast expanse of nature that surrounded them on the snowy mountain trails.

Upon their return to the cabin, Jack, displaying a considerate gesture, took the initiative to shower first. This not only allowed the girls more time, but it also gave him the chance to move to the kitchen and finalize dinner preparations. The enticing aroma of a well-prepared beef stew filled the air, indicating that their evening meal was nearly ready. With the main course almost complete, Jack turned his attention to the finishing touches, including preparing the accompanying dinner rolls and rice. As an additional treat, he set a pot of spiked, spiced apple cider on the stove to warm, envisioning a cozy post-dinner gathering around the fireplace, engaging in relaxed conversation.

Just before Jack delved into his culinary endeavors in the kitchen, Brooke made her way in to have a conversation with him. Although she hadn't yet taken a shower, she was en route, driven by the need to clarify the location of her bags and her uncle's belongings.

"My bag is in the second bedroom to the right. I put yours in the loft and Faye's bag is in the first bedroom," Jack informed her.

With gratitude, Brooke responded, "Thanks," as she planted a gentle kiss on her uncle's cheek and vanished from the scene, presumably to get ready for her shower.

Jack suspected that Brooke might opt for one of his sweatshirts for post-shower lounging. His intuition proved correct as Brooke, having emerged from the shower, donned his college sweatshirt. The garment tastefully adorned her petite frame, a sharp contrast to the pair of shorts that accompanied it. Jack couldn't help but silently hope that those particular shorts would remain confined to the cabin, given their skimpy nature.

However, what caught Jack off guard—and pleasantly so—was a sight that materialized just moments after his niece's appearance. Faye cautiously peeked around the kitchen corner, a hint of hesitance in her demeanor. Sporting one of Jack's button-down shirts, she'd rolled up the sleeves for practicality. A small but genuine smile illuminated her face as she made eye contact with Jack, infusing his night with an unexpected warmth and sense of connection just from wearing his shirt.

"I hope you don't mind. I borrowed one of your shirts to sleep in. I forgot to grab myself something to sleep in when I hurriedly packed my bag earlier," Faye explained, a touch of bashfulness coloring her words.

Chuckling softly, Jack replied, "Oh, I don't mind," though his inner thoughts were anything but casual. He struggled to maintain his composure, feeling a subtle warmth emanating from the situation, both from her choice of attire and their close proximity.

Truly, Jack's indifference was a façade. He actually reveled in the sight of Faye donning his shirt, which managed to enhance her attractiveness in his eyes. The shirt enveloped her, cascading down to her knees, giving her an endearing yet alluring appearance. Her jet black hair cascaded down her back, lending an additional touch of elegance to the scene. As much as he tried to play it cool, Jack's feelings were far from detached.

After enjoying their dinner around the kitchen table, they migrated to the hearth to bask in the cozy warmth of the fire. Carrying mugs of spiked, spiced apple cider, they settled into a circle and engaged in easy conversation. Jack couldn't help but notice how Brooke's chattiness seemed to blossom in the wake of her sips from the mug.

However, the cider's effects didn't spare Brooke from succumbing to drowsiness. She found herself unable to resist the siren call of early bedtime, yielding to her body's demands and nestling her head comfortably onto her uncle's lap. On the opposite end of the sofa, Faye took a seat, positioned at the foot of Brooke.

Recognizing that his niece was caught in the gentle embrace of sleepiness, Jack softly roused her. Waiting until she was coherent enough to heed his instructions, he then prompted her to head off to bed.

As Brooke gracefully rose from the couch, she leaned over to place a gentle kiss on her uncle's forehead, a gesture that spoke of their close bond. With a quiet smile, she left Jack and Faye to continue their conversation, making her way toward her resting place for the night. Despite having imbibed the spiked cider, Jack was reassured that the amount of alcohol he had added was modest; he trusted that Brooke would be just fine.

Faye observed Brooke's departure, her keen eyesight attuned to the dimly lit surroundings. The cabin's lights had been extinguished, casting the room into the warm embrace of the flickering firelight. In most circumstances, Brooke would have vanished into the darkness quickly, yet Faye's exceptional night vision allowed her to maintain a visual connection for a bit longer. She attuned her senses to the soft sounds that followed—Brooke's ascent up the ladder, the soft creak of a door opening and closing. Assured of her friend's safe arrival in her quarters, Faye turned her focus back to the lingering company around her.

Faye's fixed gaze remained on the crackling fire, the chaotic day spent with Jack and Brooke slowly receding into the background. The flames within the hearth flickered and danced, a ceaseless display mirroring the intricate whirl of thoughts that began to stir within her. As Brooke's presence faded from her mind, Faye confronted an emerging reality—a burgeoning attraction to Jack that she could neither disregard nor suppress. Despite her efforts to quell these feelings, she found herself unable to resist their pull any longer.

The acrid scent of the fire permeated the air, mingling with the comforting aroma of the mug cradled between her palms. Inhaling deeply, she absorbed the rich notes of nutmeg, cinnamon, and apples. As her focus shifted to the mug, she felt the warmth of the drink seeping through its sides, a fleeting comfort countering the chill of her contemplations.

From the fireplace, a hiss followed by a pop resonated, prompting the flames to intensify their dance. In this moment, Faye's mind wandered back to the day she had first met Jack, admitting to herself the undeniable initial attraction she had experienced. Sipping her drink, the infusion of apples and spices battled against the lingering smoke, their fragrant undertones vying for dominance.

In a hushed whisper, she confessed to herself, "I can't continue like this." Her words, soft and barely audible amidst the symphony of burning logs, were a testament to the overwhelming nature of her newfound feelings. The taste of cinnamon and nutmeg surged within her, as potent and encompassing as the emotions she grappled with.

The fire's relentless dance maintained its hold on her attention, casting its vivid movements onto the cabin walls. Amid her introspection, she found herself circling back to the same questions, the same uncertainties. She lowered the mug, entranced by the swirling liquid as if seeking answers within. The desire for clarity mingled with the undulating flames, yet the fire's mysteries remained intact, offering no solutions to her inner conflicts. Her grip on the mug tightened, warmth seeping into her skin, mirroring the way her emotions threatened to overwhelm her. "I'm in too deep," she confessed, her voice nearly lost amidst the crackling wood.

The fire crackled with a ceaseless restlessness, consuming the wood fed to it. Adjusting her position to a cross-legged stance, Faye's attention vacillated between the mug and the fire, both failing to provide the solace she sought. A fleeting glance at Jack reminded her of his proximity, a presence both near and distant. It felt as if an expansive chasm separated them, a visual metaphor for the internal chasm between her desires and responsibilities. The yearning for Jack's embrace stirred within her, a desire that seemed to engulf her entire being. She acknowledged her helplessness, acknowledging, "I'm only feeling this way because I can't act on it. Why can't I shape my own life? Why must my mission supersede my desires?"

Observing the fire's increased turbulence, she recognized the cacophony within her thoughts. The logs crackled, the flames shifting in color and intensity. A grimace accompanied a rising ache in her chest, though she resisted the impulse to clutch it—a gesture that might draw Jack's attention. He sat close, almost within reach, yet also frustratingly distant. A fire kindled within her chest, its intensity nearly driving her to a moan of agony. Slowly, her hand settled between her breasts, movements deliberately concealed from Jack. Gazing into the mug, she clutched it as images of Jack flooded her mind, accompanied by the echo of responsibilities that she couldn't evade.

Faye eventually realized—each breath that she took seemed to be his own breath, each beat of her heart seemed to be his heartbeat. She took a cleansing breath and released it slowly, realizing afterwards that the silence in the room was punctuated only by the fervent crackling. Faye slowed her breathing while the flames continued to wave back and forth in the hearth.

Gathering her resolve, she shifted her gaze to Jack, her curiosity piqued by the enigmatic expressions that flitted across his features. In an oddly contradictory twist, she found herself yearning to occupy the focal point of his contemplations.

A fleeting thought of how effortlessly Jack's affection flowed towards Brooke triggered a sharp pang of jealousy that briefly took root in Faye's mind, only to wither away in the next heartbeat.

Jack, meanwhile, was ensnared by his own inner musings. His contemplations remained benign, anchored in the interplay of firelight with the dark cascade of Faye's hair. More captivating still was the way those flames lent an iridescent gleam to her eyes, reminiscent of nocturnal creatures illuminated by sudden beams of light.

Although seated just a few feet away, Faye seemed to him somehow distant, not emotionally, but in the unspoken narratives she kept guarded. So deeply engrossed was Jack in his thoughts that he failed to recognize his gaze locked onto hers, the unspoken connection bridging the space between them. Unbeknownst to him, she posed a question, the words entering his ears as a distant murmur, necessitating repetition.

A sheepish smile curved Jack's lips as he admitted, "I'm sorry, what was that?"

With patience, she repeated her words of candid vulnerability. "I envy your relationship with Brooke. She really loves you." Her tone lowered, a softer murmur, not really intentionally inaudible, but heard by Jack anyway, followed, "You really love her."

A momentary unease fluttered in Jack's chest, hinting at unspoken layers beneath her words. What he'd actually heard in his subconscious was *Why don't you love me?* But he wasn't sure he should be interpreting the way that she looked at him when she said that as anything more than a direct meaning of her words. His throat tightened, an audible gulp punctuating the moment as he darted a furtive glance around, grappling with a surge of nervousness.

He faltered, "Well, I guess I am the only male presence in her life."

"I don't have that in my life," Faye confessed, her words heavy with regret, a palpable sentiment that Jack couldn't overlook. Avoiding his intense gaze, her eyes shifted away, and her pulse quickened briefly before settling into a calmer rhythm. Her attention returned to the fire, its flames dancing serenely in the hearth.

Jack's movements became restless, and he rose from his seat, making his way to the stack of firewood nestled by the hearth. With deliberate motions, he selected a log and added it to the fire. The resulting hiss and crack filled the cabin's small space, the renewed vitality of the fire accompanied by a symphony of sound. The added fuel fueled the flames, their intensity surging to new heights before settling into a smoldering glow, the additional energy required to kindle the blaze anew. Throughout his task, Jack kept up a conversation with Faye, striving to maintain a connection.

"A male role model, or just a male presence?" he inquired.

As he awaited her response, he turned back toward her, a momentary hesitation evident in his movements as he contemplated resuming his seat near her. His steps faltered briefly, but he eventually gathered the resolve to continue moving to settle back into his place.

Almost as soon as the question left Jack's lips, he felt a twinge of uncertainty about having posed it. Pausing in front of the couch, he waited, caught in a maelstrom of anticipation. He genuinely desired to know her answer, even if he was grappling with doubts about the timing and appropriateness of his inquiry. However, before Faye could reply, Jack extended his hand toward her mug, a gesture that served a dual purpose. On one hand, he was taking the initiative to help her, and on the other, he was inadvertently creating a distraction, perhaps hoping the question would recede from focus.

This seemingly casual action was a strategic maneuver on Jack's part—an attempt to sidestep any potential awkwardness that his question might have generated. He hoped that by taking charge of the situation, he could create an opening for them to move beyond the delicate topic.

"Would you like a refill for your mug?" Jack deflected, his intention clear in his tone, aiming to defuse the tension that had taken root between them.

With no better option at hand, Faye responded gracefully, her gratitude evident in her voice. "Yes, thank you." She handed her mug to Jack, the simple act carrying with it a tacit understanding that their conversation was shifting, if only momentarily,

Contemplation lingered within Faye's thoughts as she weighed the decision to respond to Jack's question. Uncertainty clouded her mind, battling against the notion that the information wasn't classified or detrimental if shared. Besides, she was in the process of sorting through her own feelings towards Jack. She considered that her answer might even provide her with a better understanding of her emotions.

In the midst of Faye's contemplation, Jack had ventured into the kitchen to refill their mugs. As he glanced back into the living room, he observed Faye rising gracefully from the sofa, her lithe movements resembling, once again, those of a lithe feline. However, a sudden awkwardness gripped him when his gaze inadvertently landed on the exposed waistband of her shirt, giving a revealing a glimpse of her panties. He found himself wrestling with confusion, his feelings for Faye a complex puzzle he hadn't yet unraveled.

After careful thought, Faye's voice carried across the room, breaking the silence. "The answer to both of those questions is a resounding—no." Her response held a certain conviction, leaving Jack uncertain about how to interpret the emotions swirling within him.

As Jack reentered the living room, two mugs of cider in hand, a mix of emotions danced in his gaze. He returned Faye's mug to her, finding her seated on the sofa, legs pulled up beneath her, arm resting on the armrest, and her focus fixed on the cup cradled in her hands. The quiet atmosphere enveloped them, and Jack resumed his place beside her.

In a voice tinged with a hint of remorse and a profound desire for affirmation, Faye ventured, "You seem to have quite an interest in my legs, don't you?"

Caught off guard, Jack began, "How did you—"

But Faye interjected before he could finish, her tone a mix of amusement and genuine understanding, "I can sense your gaze moving over me. Feel free to look. I don't mind. In fact, I'm flattered because it's you."

Silence descended once more, delicate as a slumbering newborn, draping over them like a veil. Jack felt his cheeks warm with a blush, a flush hidden beneath his deep complexion. Even if his blushing wasn't as evident due to his dark skin, the sensation was real, stirring a mix of emotions within him.

Faye drew a deep breath, steeling herself for the upcoming moment. With a sense of determination, she leaned forward and gently placed her apple cider mug on the coffee table before the sofa. Her voice, soft and gentle, broke the silence that had enveloped the room, "I hope you don't mind."

Her body shifted gracefully as she turned on the sofa, reorienting herself until her back faced Jack. A surprising yet not unwelcome move, he found himself somewhat taken aback but certainly not objecting. He was well aware that protesting a beautiful woman's desire to be close would be nothing short of foolish. As Faye leaned back, her head nestled into Jack's lap, he allowed her actions without resistance. When she pulled his right arm from its perch on the back of the sofa and draped it around her, he felt a pleasant tingle of connection. It was an intimacy they hadn't shared before, but one he was open to exploring.

With a gentle whisper, Faye spoke her intentions, her words carrying a mixture of vulnerability and gratitude, "I'm sorry. I know we've only known each other for a few days, but I just needed this, and right now felt like the perfect opportunity. I feel really safe having you close to me."

Jack's response was equally soft, a sincere "Thank you," escaping his lips. The situation might have caught him off guard, but he was willing to embrace it. After all, he liked Faye, and the chance to know more about her felt like an opportunity worth seizing.

Their eyes locked, his gaze meeting hers as he stared down at her while she gazed back at him. In that moment, he felt a certain unspoken understanding, a sense that their connection could grow even deeper without overstepping boundaries. He mustered the courage to lean in, his intention being a gentle kiss on her forehead—a gesture reminiscent of his interactions with Brooke. However, fate had other plans. Faye's head shifted upward at the last second, and their lips met in a soft and unexpected kiss. It lasted just a brief moment before Jack withdrew, his cheeks flushed with a mix of embarrassment and a feeling of crossing a line.

But Faye's devilish smile offered him a lifeline, a silent assurance that she was content with the kiss, and in fact, she had orchestrated it. She could see the fleeting shadow of shame pass over Jack's face, and she swiftly reassured him, "It's okay. I didn't mind that."

Jack, feeling relieved by her response, decided to let go of his embarrassment. He had momentarily overstepped, but it was clear that Faye had welcomed it. She had even played an active role in making it happen. As he looked into her eyes, he felt a renewed curiosity about her. He decided to revisit their earlier conversation, as it seemed a good starting point to delve deeper into her thoughts and feelings.

"Does your job make it hard for you to find a meaningful relationship?" Jack inquired, his words laden with genuine curiosity and concern.

With a newfound comfort in their closeness, Jack's right hand found a resting place beneath both of Faye's hands, positioned gently on her belly. Meanwhile, his left hand danced playfully through the strands of her silky, ebony hair, a seemingly idle yet intimate gesture that mirrored his growing ease with physical contact in this intimate setting.

Faye responded to his question with a slight intertwining of her fingers through Jack's, their hands forming a subtle yet tangible connection. "It's a lot more complicated than that," she revealed, her words hanging in the air, carrying a sense of mystery and reluctance to divulge further.

Jack, his half-serious inquiry lingering, pushed a bit deeper, "Could it be that you're dedicating too much time to the office?"

Faye's response was prompt but guarded, "It's not that, it's just... that I have obligations and commitments. My job requires all of my time."

The fire crackled and popped in the background, a soothing soundtrack to their conversation. As the flames danced, Faye's expression shifted, a hint of sadness softening her features. The firelight cast intricate shadows across her countenance, momentarily painting her in melancholy shades.

In this fleeting moment, Jack glimpsed a side of Faye rarely unveiled—an overwhelming weight of pressure that bore down on her. However, the moment was elusive, slipping away before he could fully grasp its significance. He sensed a door had been slightly ajar, granting him insight into her struggles, but it closed just as swiftly.

Jack grappled with the awareness that he might have missed an opportunity, a chance to offer comfort or understanding. Yet, he also recognized the delicate nature of the situation. Pressing further could potentially push her away when he desired nothing more than to draw her closer. As the present moment unfolded, he resolved not to force the issue, not now at least. It wasn't the right time, and he couldn't afford to let his curiosity jeopardize the connection they were building.

Amid their ongoing conversation, Faye's actions took an unexpectedly daring turn. With a mixture of intention and impulsiveness, she gently guided Jack's right hand beneath the hem of her shirt. As his fingers brushed against her skin, a dance ensued—a playful and nimble exchange that mirrored their developing connection. Each touch, each movement, sent ripples of sensation coursing through her, igniting trembles that seemed to shiver through her very core.

In that charged moment, Jack's touch confirmed a suspicion he had quietly held. His fingers traced patterns on the canvas of her smooth, alabaster skin, evoking responses that didn't go unnoticed. And within the midst of these physical exchanges, he confirmed the absence of a bra—his fingertips discerning the contours of her body with an acute awareness. Faye's form beneath the shirt was an alluring canvas, her silhouette subtly reshaping the fabric that draped over her, a sensual interplay of texture and flesh.

Jack consciously decided to navigate away from any physical exploration of her body, as it didn't align with his current intentions. The alluring image of her partially clothed form tugged at his senses, yet he chose to focus on the evolving conversation instead. He balanced on the precipice, reining in his own desires while allowing their genuine exchange to flourish. His hand ceased its ministrations of her body.

Faye felt a twinge of disappointment as Jack's hand abruptly ceased its movement, leaving the sensations to dissipate. Sensing the potential for awkwardness, she decided to fill the void that the ensuing silence had brought.

"Why aren't you in a relationship?" Her question hung in the air, a gentle prod that beckoned Jack to open up.

He took a beat before responding, allowing the tranquility of the moment to fill the space between them. As the silence enveloped them, he was keenly attuned to the rhythm of her heartbeat, a rhythm that seemed to dance between the chaos and calm, reflecting the intricate dance of their emotions.

"I don't know," Jack began, his voice carrying a note of contemplation. He paused, a momentary intermission to gather his thoughts and regain his composure. "Maybe I'm not ready to..." Jack trailed off.

Before he could elaborate further, Faye's soft interruption, like a whisper of destiny, shattered his words. In an instant, she bridged the space between them, her hands cupping his face, pulling him into a kiss that was both tender and intense. Their tongues danced, a delicate choreography of passion and hesitance, as if their desires were battling with their uncertainties.

Amid the exchange, Faye found strength, even as her resolve to take things slow wavered in the face of overwhelming emotion. For Jack, the kiss ignited a fire within, stoking the flames of his desires. Yet, Jack's conscious restraint tugged at him, telling him that if he let Faye continue, they would traverse a path unknown and potentially harmful.

Breaking free from the kiss, they settled into a serene quietude, their gazes locked in a gaze that held a thousand unspoken words. The swift, soft breaths they shared seemed to harmonize in the stillness, a symphony of their mingling feelings. As Faye felt her own emotions teetering on the edge of control, she shifted their focus, redirecting the conversation away from the precipice they had approached, aiming to restore a more comfortable equilibrium.

Faye found herself engulfed by a surge of conflicting feelings and emotions. Struggling to reconcile these internal tumults, they manifested in outward expressions—movements and a barrage of questions. The need to act became palpable as things started to shift in a different direction.

Jack, however, found himself acutely aware of Faye's every movement, attuned to the subtle shifts in her body's response to his touch. As the conversation continued, he couldn't shake the feeling of alarm that crept over him. Beneath her facade of a casual conversation, he sensed an undercurrent of desire that her body betrayed, despite her efforts to suppress it. Her languid movements, the exposure of her belly, the way she squirmed on his lap—all of it was a symphony of signals that he couldn't ignore.

Amid this charged atmosphere, Faye finally spoke, her voice breaking the tension. A mix of nervous energy. "I talked with your niece," she admitted, unaware of the storm her own body was brewing. "She told me that you spend just about all of your free time with her. Could it be that you're using her as a shield so that you can stay emotionally unavailable to any other woman?"

An honest answer would have been an acknowledgment of this truth, but Jack was unwilling to confront it, even within himself. He moved to change their positions on the sofa, a subtle retreat from the physical closeness they had been sharing.

"When was the last time you were in a relationship with a woman other than your sister and your niece? Any relationship?" Faye's follow-up question struck a nerve, prying into areas Jack had tried to keep locked away.

Jack's silence spoke volumes, his turmoil palpable. He gave a nonchalant shrug, hoping to deflect her probing, yet Faye was undeterred.

Her words carried the weight of honesty and vulnerability. "I'm actually willing to try because I like you, Jack. Even though it would be extremely complicated for me. So, does this have anything to do with your brother passing away while you were deployed? Do you feel like you have to be a surrogate father to Brooke because your brother died before she was born?"

Jack took a moment to process her words before responding, his voice measured and clear. "No, this has nothing to do with my brother James, my sister-in-law Elizabeth, or my niece Brooke."

Confusion mingled with his desires, as he wrestled with his own emotions and carnality. He yearned to embrace Faye, to explore their connection on a more intimate level, yet the conversation was pushing him to erect walls, to hold back.

"I think I should say goodnight," he finally admitted, the words heavy with unresolved tensions.

The room's atmosphere had shifted, leaving both of them on the precipice of uncertainty. Jack carefully repositioned Faye, lifting her from his lap while rising simultaneously. As she stood upright, he leaned in, granting her a passionate kiss before gently pulling away. Mumbling a quiet "goodnight," he left to retire to his room. Even Jack couldn't fathom why he had kissed her so passionately before bidding her goodnight. His intention had only been to give her a peck on the cheek or perhaps the forehead but her lips had been so inviting.

"What just happened?" Faye's voice hung in the air, directed more at herself than anyone else, a verbal attempt to untangle the bewildering events that had unfolded. She settled onto the couch, drawing her feet up and wrapping her arms around her knees, as if seeking refuge in this self-imposed embrace. A gentle shiver passed through her, mirroring the undulating play of firelight across the room.

Her thoughts were in turmoil. Reflecting on the recent sequence of events, she recognized that her own desires had spiraled out of control, leading her down a path that could have ended disastrously. A mix of relief and longing washed over her when Jack abruptly bid her goodnight, leaving her feeling both grateful for the distance and abandoned in its wake.

Unanticipated moisture traced her cheeks, her hands discovering the evidence of her emotional turbulence. With a deep, tremulous breath, she released the pent-up tension that had taken hold of her. It took a series of such breaths to finally reclaim her equilibrium. She couldn't fathom what had caused Jack's sudden retreat, but she realized that immediate answers were unlikely.

Faye's gaze fixated on the fireplace, where the fire emitted a final, vibrant burst before receding into quiet embers. Despite her desire to release the emotional turmoil that had engulfed her, she found herself returning to the maelstrom of questions once more before finally succumbing to sleep.

The first question emerged: *Does he like me?* Its origin was inexplicable, given Jack's hasty departure. Yet, it was tied to the second question that followed closely: *Why did he kiss me with such intensity when he left?* Absentmindedly, she touched her lips, reliving the memory of his passionate kiss.

The following day was marked by a palpable awkwardness between Faye and Jack, a tension that didn't escape her notice. Jack seemed to tread carefully, avoiding situations that would force them into isolation. The events of the previous night remained unspoken, hanging in the air like uncharted territory between them. He maintained physical contact when necessary, yet refrained from any extraneous touches.

The journey back to the city on Sunday carried the weight of uncertainty for both. Jack's mind was a battleground of conflicting emotions. He chastised himself for not seizing the chance to draw closer to Faye, yet the scars of his past held him back, locked within a mental compartment he was not ready to unlock. Faye's presence beside him intensified the internal struggle. She sat quietly, her gaze drifting over the passing landscape, while Jack wrestled with the demons of his past.

As they rode together, Jack couldn't help but acknowledge the missed opportunity that now seemed like a gulf between them. The yearning to know more about Faye clashed with his hesitation to expose his vulnerabilities. A conversation of such magnitude was unthinkable in Brooke's presence, yet Jack found himself unable to navigate the complexities of his emotions without addressing his past baggage.

Faye's gaze remained fixed outside the window as they traveled, lost in her thoughts as well. The tension was palpable in the confined space, a tension that she was certain Brooke, perceptive as she was, had noticed during their time at the cabin. As the miles passed, the silence only deepened, punctuated by Jack's intermittent glances in the rearview mirror, searching for clues in Brooke's demeanor.

Finally, they arrived at Faye's hotel. Farewells were exchanged with an air of formality, each word weighed down by unspoken emotions. Faye watched as Jack's car pulled away, a tangible sense of lingering between them. She could see Jack glancing at her in the rearview mirror, a moment of connection and uncertainty. He dropped Brooke off at his sister's house, the unspoken tension still hanging heavily in the air.

6

Jack's yearning for the forensic lab results from the crime scenes served as a shield against the emotional tempest churned up by his weekend with Faye. The aftermath of their time together had created a whirlwind he was trying to distance himself from. Recovering from the intensity of their encounter was proving to be a challenge. His relationship with Faye had spiraled into uncharted territory, pushing boundaries that nearly transcended their professional dynamic. Faye's poignant questions had dredged up emotional baggage he wasn't ready to unpack. The truth he had to admit to himself was that he couldn't handle both his internal turmoil and her presence simultaneously. The weight was too heavy, so he had retreated.

"I feel like a coward," he muttered to himself, his self-criticism gnawing at him. The mere thought of the potential hurt he might have caused Faye left a sour taste in his mouth. His attempts to distract himself at home had fizzled, prompting his visit to his sister-in-law's residence.

Elizabeth, the chief forensics examiner at the police station, offered a potential respite. Jack hoped to glean some insight into the cases by pestering her at her home. His focus remained tethered to work and what remained to be accomplished. This was only self deception to keep his mind off of what had happened with Faye over the weekend. However, several obstacles thwarted his intentions to distract himself. Firstly, it was Sunday, delaying the results of the autopsies until Monday. That was one nail in the coffin of distracting himself. Secondly, he found himself at Elizabeth's house. Elizabeth would read him like a book and know that something besides work was on his mind. Lastly, he had a prior commitment to care for his niece, a weekend excursion he was just returning from. A weekend that still wasn't over just because they were back from the cabin.

"Your mind's on work again, isn't it?" Elizabeth's perceptive inquiry pierced the air. It was a veiled deception. She wasn't going to bother Jack about revealing what was really bothering him just yet. She had a keen understanding of her brother's emotional landscape, far more attuned than he was himself.

Jack sat on a patio chair, staring into the distance. His gaze shifted upward to his sister in law, a figure he cherished deeply. Despite the loss of her husband, his brother, she had chosen to remain a part of their family. She took on the role of a real sister to her brother in law. Accepting the steaming cup of coffee she offered, he nodded his gratitude. Seated gracefully beside him, her red hair swayed gently in the winter breeze, creating an atmosphere of camaraderie.

The day held a chill, prompting Jack to lose himself in introspection akin to the snow drifts that the wind swept away. Despite the crisp air, the two of them found comfort in the subtle warmth that allowed them to savor the nascent days of fall.

Attempting to divert his focus from work since he couldn't get anything done in that regard, Jack aimed to immerse himself in the fleeting moments of the day. But an incessant pull tugged him back to his central preoccupation—the lab report. He yearned to confirm the identity of the individual responsible for the murders. He was also torn between his interaction with Faye, a subject he wanted to relegate to the back of his mind to pursue at a later time.

"Hello, Captain Jack, back to Earth," Elizabeth's voice broke through his reverie.

"Hmm, yeah, I'm here," Jack replied, his contemplation momentarily grounded.

Elizabeth's gentle smile held a hint of mischief. "Good, because I doubt you'll be great company for your niece if you're lost in space all day." Her words bore a hint of playfulness, yet her tone held an underlying truth. "Besides, we both know she's the only woman in your life right now."

Jack bristled at the implication. "That's not true," he grumbled. He looked over into the living room where Brooke was laying on the carpeted floor, her attention focused on whatever she was working on.

Observing his reaction, Elizabeth set her coffee down, her expression a tapestry of concern and understanding. Jack recognized the direction this conversation was veering toward, and he wasn't inclined to aid its progression. His reluctance was palpable. The emotional tumult between him and Faye over the weekend had already taken its toll.

With a determined demeanor, Jack picked up his coffee and retreated into the house. Settling on a bar stool by the counter, he found himself pursued by Elizabeth, a familiar presence following in his wake.

Elizabeth turned the corner, entering the kitchen to position herself on the opposite side of the counter, directly facing Jack. In the context of their now diminished family, she had adopted a maternal, older sister role, an anchor for him. This was despite the fact that they were basically only weeks apart in age.

She took on the responsibility of caring for him when he faltered in maintaining meaningful relationships with others. This facet of his well-being was her utmost concern, and her persistence in urging him toward a fulfilling partnership stemmed from that caring. However, he had chosen to disregard her counsel, a decision that had stung her.

Elizabeth's features bore a faint frown, her discomfort evident. Jack recognized the expression well; she was feeling put upon. He knew his swift retreat into the house had contributed to her unsettled demeanor.

Oh well, Jack mused to himself, his inner voice echoing his thoughts.

He justified his abrupt return, convincing himself that he had grown weary of the outdoors and the cold. A feeble excuse, he acknowledged, designed to shield him from the guilt of potentially upsetting his sister-in-law. But the shield proved porous, incapable of keeping the remorse at bay. Elizabeth had an uncanny ability to lead him down the path she deemed best, a trait that seemed to be shared by all the women in his life. He knew he would inevitably yield to her wishes, just as he always did.

His musings carried him further, his mind conjuring an image of Faye. "Oh god," he silently groaned, his thoughts straying into dangerous territory.

The mere thought of Faye orchestrating his movements made his palms moisten with sweat. He was all too aware of how she had turned his life on its head when they first crossed paths. That memory, laden with embarrassment, haunted him. He was forced to admit, however begrudgingly, that Faye had a way of keeping him on his toes. A fleeting smile crept onto his lips, an involuntary reaction to the thought of her.

Returning his focus to his sister, Jack foresaw her unrelenting determination. He knew she wouldn't relent until he acquiesced, leaving him metaphorically rolling onto his back, much like a compliant puppy. He understood that, in her eyes, this was a sister's prerogative—to subtly guilt her brother into complying with her requests.

"You can't keep running away from me, Jack," her voice carried a blend of sternness and gentle concern.

Shifting on the stool, Jack turned to cast a gaze into the living room. His niece, engrossed in a task on her computer, sat comfortably on the floor. The intricacies of whatever she was working on seemed light-years away from his grasp, complex concepts that he would only ever understand if she distilled them into simple explanations.

Elizabeth's words resonated with a truth he couldn't deny. Brooke was the sole woman in his life. He grudgingly admitted that, while it was a fact he often overlooked, Brooke's presence was something he treasured deeply. But then there was Faye—her presence refused to be relegated to the shadows of his thoughts.

His past relationships had clashed against the backdrop of his demanding career and unyielding sense of duty. When pressed to make a choice, he had opted for his responsibilities over his personal life. But with his niece, the equation was different. She would never demand he abandon his career or plead for more of his time. Her unconditional acceptance was a lifeline that fueled his determination to keep pushing forward.

Elizabeth, perceptive as ever, sensed his inner turmoil and knew what he longed for. "I'll get you the report as soon as I can. You understand the weekend staffing situation at the lab. We're juggling multiple cases, but yours will be prioritized," she assured him.

Turning his attention back to his sister, Jack managed a weak smile. Elizabeth, the stalwart leader of the Forensics Department at the police station, had held that position for as long as he had been in the force. The way she had navigated marriage, loss, and raising Brooke while advancing in her career left him in awe.

He couldn't help but marvel at her ability to maintain equilibrium amid life's turbulence. His respect for her was as steadfast as her commitment to her responsibilities.

"I guess I'll just have to be satisfied with that," Jack admitted, his coffee cup finding its place on the counter with a half-hearted clink. A troubled furrow etched his brow as he continued, "I guess what's really bothering me is the increasing aggressiveness of the perpetrator. What kind of person would do the things that he's done?"

Elizabeth mulled over Jack's words, her contemplation evident in her pause before responding. "You're onto something. The lab results might not be the linchpin in connecting these crimes. You don't really need the lab results to figure out it's the same person," she admitted, her tone a blend of analysis and concern. "The sheer strength required to dismantle a human body, to tear it apart limb by limb—it's beyond comprehension. The most recent victim was literally torn to pieces. It defies reason to believe this perpetrator is in any way sane," she mused, allowing herself a moment of thoughtful silence. Under her breath, almost as a continuation of her internal musings, she added, "Or perhaps beyond human," exploring the enigmatic possibilities the evidence might suggest.

Stepping away from the kitchen, Elizabeth took a seat beside Jack, the bond of their shared concern unspoken yet palpable. In the quietude of the moment, they both directed their gaze towards Brooke, who sat absorbed in the living room. Elizabeth's voice pierced the stillness once more. "I know this is bothering you. We'll catch this guy. You also have this thing with Faye that you've got to deal with."

Jack's response was a sigh—a mixture of appreciation for Elizabeth's understanding and trepidation for the conversation ahead. He leaned over, planting a gentle kiss on her cheek. He hadn't explicitly shared his feelings about Faye, underestimating Elizabeth's ability to perceive his emotions.

"I don't even want to know how you knew about my feelings about Faye," Jack chuckled softly. His eyes momentarily averted before locking onto Elizabeth's, a mix of vulnerability and connection in their gaze. "Things are..." he paused, having to resolve himself to the reality of the situation, "...complicated."

"You like her, don't you?" With a knowing expression, Elizabeth delved into her profound comprehension of her brother. Her words, an embodiment of sisterly insight, delved deeper.

"Yeah I guess I do. But it's not love. I can't do love, Lizzy." A sigh escaped Jack's lips, bearing a blend of introspection and revelation.

In Elizabeth's eyes, Jack's intricacies were a landscape she had traversed since she'd first met him. Brooke might know Jack's surface, but Elizabeth's understanding reached to the core of his being, fostering a connection that went beyond mere familiarity.

Allowing the emotionally charged conversation to fade into the background, Elizabeth deftly redirected their focus. A warm smile graced her lips as she transitioned, her tone shifting gears. "Well, I'll put my best people on your case for you on Monday. We'll get you an answer and more information by the afternoon on whether or not it's the same perpetrator, but I'm, pretty sure that it is. I've already seen the preliminary results."

Jack's features softened as a smile spread across his face, a rare glimmer of contentment breaking through his earlier unease. "Thank you," he voiced, his gratitude evident in both his words and demeanor, radiating a genuine sense of appreciation.

"Don't thank me," Elizabeth responded, a gentle smile gracing her features. "You've got to get your mind off that case and worry about this new girl in your life. Your niece was also grateful for the time that she spent together this weekend with her favorite uncle."

"I'm her only uncle, so of course I'm her favorite," Jack quipped, a chuckle escaping him.

Elizabeth's gaze flicked toward her daughter, engrossed in her laptop with a flurry of complex diagrams and images unfurling across the screen. Amid this technological symphony, she opted to let her daughter continue her work, but Elizabeth couldn't resist sharing Brooke's opinion on Jack's new connection. "Brooke loves Faye, by the way."

Jack's lips curved into a knowing smile. "The woman has that kind of affect on people," he acknowledged. He slid off the bar stool and headed to the living room, where his niece Brooke was absorbed in her activities.

His niece held a cherished place in his heart, a treasure beyond compare. His commitment to her spanned not just Friday and Saturday, but extended willingly into Sunday. As he strode across the room, a sudden sneeze caught him off guard, halting him in his tracks. It was an unusual occurrence for Jack, whose robust physical condition usually warded off such minor ailments.

Elizabeth rose from her seat and approached him, her concern evident in her gaze as she met his eyes. "Bless you," she uttered, her attention focused on his well-being. Her observant eyes stayed fixed on him, watchful for any hint of a follow-up sneeze. Finding none, she offered him a warm smile. "I was half-expecting you to notice. It took longer than I anticipated, though."

Jack's brow furrowed in confusion, his features a canvas of bewilderment as he scrunched up his face and narrowed his eyes at Elizabeth. "What are you talking about?" he inquired, seeking clarification.

With an air of mischief, Elizabeth replied, "The cat is in the living room." Her attention remained fixed on Jack, waiting for his reaction.

Though not strictly allergic to cats, Jack had a tendency to sneeze a few times upon their introduction, until his system acclimated. "Why is the 'cat from hell' out here?" he questioned, his gaze sweeping the living room to locate the elusive feline. He found it perched on the back of the couch, fixating on him with an almost unnerving intensity. The temptation to leap onto the nearest surface to evade the crafty creature was strong, but relief coursed through him as he realized the cat was safely across the room.

"He didn't want to go back to her room and he raised a fuss when she tried to take him back. I guess he knew that you were here," Elizabeth explained apologetically, her hands pressed together in a gesture of supplication.

"I'm allergic to cats," Jack protested, his tone holding a hint of defiance.

"You're not allergic," Elizabeth retorted with a mischievous grin, her words carrying a playful edge. "You just don't like him. I don't know why, but every time you're around him, you sneeze a few times, and then it's over."

Jack's gaze lingered on the cat for a moment, his thoughts gathering, before he noticed Brooke's smile directed at him. Encouraged, he crossed the room, intending to plant a kiss on the top of her head. But before he could take more than a couple of steps, the cat emitted a menacing growl, halting him in his tracks.

Elizabeth intercepted Jack before he could venture further into the room. Stepping in front of him, she fixed her gaze on the cat. "I don't know what it is between you two, but he's so damn protective of Brooke when you're around. The moment he sets his eyes on her, he's on a mission to shield her from every male presence."

In an attempt to ease Jack's discomfort in the feline's presence, Elizabeth continued, her tone reassuring. "Honestly, I can't fathom why he's so particular, but there are moments when he won't let anyone but Brooke come near him. If you want to get close to her, I suggest we call Brooke into the kitchen."

Jack found himself wholeheartedly concurring with Elizabeth's idea. The notion of moving Brooke out of the cat's protective sphere seemed like a wise move.

"You know," he said with a wry smile, "you really should've gone for a dog. This cat is basically Satan's personal valet. He absolutely despises me."

"Stop exaggerating," Elizabeth chided, waving off Jack's playful protest. She beckoned Brooke into the kitchen, excusing herself to attend to chores elsewhere in the house.

With warmth in his eyes, Jack gathered Brooke in his arms, embracing her tightly before he prepared to head home for the rest of the day. His mind was a whirlwind, preoccupied with both the ongoing case and the complex emotions surrounding Faye. "I had a great time with you this weekend," he told his niece sincerely.

Brooke's eyes widened in mock surprise, her tone teasing. "So, it was only me you had fun with?"

Jack caught her playful implication and couldn't help but chuckle. "I enjoyed spending time with Faye as well, but that's not something you need to worry about."

"Sure thing," Brooke laughed. "I'll give her a call and let her know, but I won't pry. Love you, uncle Jack. This weekend was amazing, and I do think you should consider Faye more seriously."

He wrinkled his nose at her persistence, her determination mirroring her mother's. "You and your mom are quite the team, huh? Always trying to meddle in my love life and convince me I'm lonely. I've got you, kiddo, and that's more than enough."

Brooke didn't relent, a mischievous glint in her eye. "Oh, come on. I saw the way you looked at Faye."

"Alright, alright," Jack surrendered, playfully ruffling her hair. Gathering himself, he was about to leave when he suddenly caught on to something she'd said earlier. "Wait a second, how do you have Faye's number?"

Before he could dig for more answers, Brooke hurried away to tend to her cat, leaving Jack amused and curious but ultimately in the dark. With a kiss to Elizabeth's forehead and a wave of goodbye, Jack took his leave from their company. As he walked out, Elizabeth assured him once more that she would delve into the case as soon as she got to the office on Monday.

As he entered his home, a smile still lingered on his lips. He went about his evening routine—eating, showering—and retired early, hoping for a restful night's sleep. The sanctity of his home gave him a chance to think things through. The weekend had granted Jack a respite, a welcome chance to spend time with his niece, Brooke.

Amidst her demanding college studies, these moments of connection had grown rare. The girl had easily graduated school early and was engaged in taking courses from the local college while she waited another year to attend at the age of sixteen.

Jack cherished these interactions, as they allowed him to momentarily escape the grip of work-related stress. Yet, his weekend had also intertwined with thoughts of Faye, an unexpected addition to his mental landscape.

That night hadn't been easy for him to deal with. He'd felt overwhelmed by how...fast paced, the events had unfolded. *Sure*, Jack thought to himself as he prepped for bed, *I'd love to get physical with a beautiful woman like Faye. Who wouldn't. But...* He left the thought hanging. There was too much to deal with. Too many bags that needed unpacking. He was willing to do the work but he was the first one to admit, *It's a helluva lotta baggage to unload.* He wasn't going to think about that now, however, his subconscious had other plans. He crawled into bed, intent to let his mind drift off into blissful oblivion so he could get some rest and challenge the day ahead but in the realm of dreams, his thoughts remained tethered to Faye, a constant companion even in slumber.

In his dream, he walked into his office, only to discover Faye lounging on the couch. A sudden sneeze heralded his arrival. Faye was curled up, her naked feet tucked under her. Her head rested on her arm, a tranquil scene that gave the illusion of deep sleep. Yet, beneath that façade, he sensed an awareness of his presence, an unspoken understanding.

"Are you going to come in and close the door or just stand there and stare at me?" Her soft voice broke through the silence. The lights seemed to be dimmer than they usually were in his office but he paid them no mind because his attention had been claimed already.

It took him a moment to register that Faye was awake and speaking. She rose lazily, stretching with a languid cat like grace. His shirt, which she wore, clung to her form as she reached upward, revealing hints of skin. A fleeting sense of discomfort and intrigue mixed within him as he watched her movements. The shirt rose up to reveal her flat belly and small waist. She was wearing only a pair of panties under the shirt.

Her gaze, fixed on him, conveyed an intense assessment. He felt as if she was sizing him up, contemplating her ability to overpower him if need be. The sensation was unsettling, but it dissipated when she inched closer, entering his personal space.

Without delay, Faye closed the gap between them, wrapping her arms around his neck. Her smile was magnetic, exuding a strength that thawed his defenses. Although his instinct was to retreat, her presence held him captive. He grappled with the mix of intimidation and attraction she stirred within him. Every aspect of her—her intellect, allure, and capability—fascinated him.

Her deliberate disregard of his hands on her waist made her intentions clear. She subtly leaned into him, their connection electric. Faye's actions conveyed her interest as effectively as words ever could. Jack tried to avert his gaze, his nerves betraying his inner thoughts. There was something captivating about her unpredictability, an enigma he was drawn to.

Before he could fully process the situation, Faye's voice, a blend of assertion and vulnerability, pierced the air. "Before we go any further, I just want to let you know that I can't stop thinking about you. This isn't open for debate."

Trepidation etched Jack's expression, the surprise softened by his grasp on his composure. Faye's admission took him off guard, yet he managed to retain his wits.

"You might believe that, but you don't really know me," he responded, his guardedness evident. The complexities of his past relationships loomed over his psyche, impacting his ability to fully engage.

Faye's proximity intensified as she whispered into his ear, her warmth a stark contrast to his internal uncertainty. His hands shifted along her body, guided by an unspoken attraction.

"Take all the time you need. I'll be patient," she murmured, her breath caressing his skin. As she leaned up to kiss him, the dream's intensity swelled, rousing Jack from his slumber. He was left panting, a powerful desire lingering even as he reentered reality. "Even in my dreams... I can't help but meet you," Jack said with a sigh, working desperately to get his heartbeat back under control.

Across town, in a hotel room, Faye awoke in a similar state, her own vivid dream having left her breathless and overwhelmed by the same inexplicable yearning.

7

Jack was a firm believer in certain unwritten rules that life seemed to follow, ones that should be adhered to. These guidelines were like the foundational steps of getting dressed: socks before shoes. Like topping off the gas tank before the needle reached empty. Just like stopping at a red light. Jack had his convictions, his compass of common sense. But he was no preacher of how others should navigate their own paths. No, he never claimed that these 'must-dos' were etched in stone for everyone.

Sure, he'd heard of yuppies defying convention, donning shoes without socks as a fashion statement. But Jack, well, he was no yuppie. As he embarked on what he was certain was one of his 'must-dos', he was fully aware that these principles he lived by weren't universal truths; they were more personal codes he abided by.

And today, as he walked with purpose, he carried a singular mission in his thoughts: he needed to dispel the lingering awkwardness with Faye. That undefined tension between them, like a crackle in the air, needed addressing. It had to be smoothed out, turned into something more manageable, less... well, awkward.

Lately, it seemed Jack was stuck navigating unwanted tasks on days that could only be described as downright crappy. There was that one dreadful day when he encountered a dismembered body—head and arm conspicuously absent—and now here he was, in the midst of yet another ordeal. At least this time, the weatherman's prediction had held true. The snowflakes were descending with a sense of purpose, almost mirroring Jack's turbulent state of mind.

He eased his vehicle to a stop in front of the large window adorned with a neon sign. This time, however, the neon's glow was conspicuously absent, casting an eerie shadow over the scene. Yet, Jack's focus remained unchanged. It wasn't the ambiance he was after, merely the coffee.

The early morning rendezvous had disrupted his usual routine, that much was clear. The usual ritual of sweating it out at the police station's basement gym had to be shelved for today. As much as he treasured those sweat-inducing sessions that fueled his day, Jack understood the pressing priorities that required his attention today. The gym's solace and routine would have to give way to more significant matters.

Among these pressing matters was a person who had recently become quite significant to him. A door had opened, revealing a new world, yet Jack had inexplicably swung it shut again. Today, he was determined to reopen it, to unravel the awkwardness that had enveloped their connection. The person on the other side of that door had become a vital presence, someone he needed to set things right with.

As he stepped out of the car, a gust of cold air reminded him of the snow's insistence. Adjusting his collar against the chill, he walked toward the entrance. There was a sense of purpose in his stride, a resoluteness that mirrored his commitment to addressing the uncertainties he'd allowed to take root. The door, once closed, was not locked—he was determined to find a way to open it again, to bridge the divide he himself had created.

Earlier during that morning, Jack made a conscious decision to deviate from his usual gym routine. He'd decided to make an apology, redirecting his steps toward a rendezvous with Faye at her hotel with coffee in hand.

Balancing on the edge of punctuality, he was well aware that Faye, too, had taken to the early morning regimen at the police station's basement gym. This shared ritual underscored their intertwined schedules. Yet, his aim for today was far different—he hoped to convince Faye to accompany him for breakfast, creating an opportunity to mend the strains that had crept into their dynamic.

Two cups of steaming coffee rested in his hands—one for him, the other for her. His own cup was customized with two creams and two sugars, a comfort concoction that fueled his mornings. Faye's, however, was starkly distinct—an unadulterated, 'straight black jet fuel', as she preferred it.

Navigating the intricacies of the hotel's elevator call button proved more perplexing than he'd anticipated. Jack couldn't help but chuckle at his own conundrum, an irony considering his position as the lead detective. *To be smart enough to become the lead detective, I sure feel dumb at the solution to this problem*, he mused, a wry smile playing on his lips. He momentarily placed his coffee cup on the floor to press the button, only to pick it up again as the elevator doors chimed open.

Once inside, he faced another challenge—deciphering the elevator's floor selection panel. His brow furrowed in concentration as he attempted to navigate the array of buttons, a skill that seemed oddly detached from his usual investigative prowess.

I suppose not every problem requires 'detecting skills', he chided himself internally, a groan escaping his lips as he realized he was even making puns about his own missteps.

Upon arriving at Faye's hotel room, Jack managed to bypass any awkward coffee-cup juggling and focused on the door before him. He lightly tapped his foot against it, a subtle signal that he'd arrived. From within the room, a series of sounds reached his ears—the unmistakable shuffling of movement. After a brief moment, a voice—distinctively Faye's—resonated through the door, assuring him she'd be there shortly. That sound was all it took to coax a genuine smile onto Jack's face, a response sparked by the mere thought of her.

With a delayed realization, he acknowledged the flutter in his chest and the barely perceptible moisture on his palms. The coffee in his hands seemed a convenient scapegoat for his slightly clammy grip, but he recognized the true source of his excitement. It was Faye. His heart raced at the prospect of seeing her again, a sensation reminiscent of a pimply high school teenager awaiting the answer to his first date invitation. As much as he might have wanted to attribute his unease to external factors, he couldn't deny the surge of emotions that Faye elicited within him.

After a brief wait, the door swung open, revealing Faye on the other side. Her reaction, however, was anything but expected. The surprise etched across her features mirrored the unexpectedness of Jack's visit. Stammering slightly, she managed to muster a hesitant greeting. "Ummm, hey," Faye's voice quivered, her astonishment palpable. Her expressive eyes, however, betrayed more than her words ever could, unveiling her genuine shock at Jack's early morning appearance.

Conversely, Jack was caught off guard in a different way. His gaze locked onto Faye, his jaw figuratively dropping as his surprise manifested in a moment of silent awe. His astonishment wasn't tied to any revealing attire; rather, it was the garment she wore that caught him off balance. The shirt she had borrowed at the cabin—he was certain she had returned it. Yet here it was, enveloping her form in a way that left him momentarily speechless. The thought to jokingly accuse her of being a 'shirt thief' flashed through his mind, but the sight of her in that shirt was somehow too charming for reprimand.

Faye's perceptive gaze caught the intensity of Jack's stare, prompting her own moment of confusion. She glanced down at herself, her quizzical expression shifting into amusement. "Do I have something on me?" she questioned with a hint of flatness in her tone, her eyes dancing with laughter.

"No, it's just... umm," Jack stumbled over his words, a familiar sensation overtaking him. He felt as if he were right back to their first meeting—a blabbering mess in her presence. An inward sigh echoed in his thoughts as he lamented, *How does she manage to do this to me?* Faye's exclamation indicated the source of Jack's mesmerized stare. "Oh," she chuckled softly, realization dawning. "Your shirt. I'm sorry. I kept it. I liked how comfortable it fit, and I forgot to give it back to you on Sunday morning." Her words carried a blend of apology and amusement

Faye harbored no intention of confessing to Jack that she had, in fact, purloined his shirt. Her reasons went beyond mere comfort or convenience; the lingering scent of him had etched itself into the fabric, evoking the sensation of Jack's arms around her. Wearing his shirt seemed to bridge the distance between them, comforting her in ways she struggled to put into words. She mused at how rapidly and intensely her feelings were developing for a man she had only known for a week. Despite the brevity of their acquaintance, there was an undeniable gravity to her emotions, an inexorable pull that defied logic.

Faye embodied independence—a trait that had defined her throughout her entire life. She had navigated the world relying solely on herself, forging her own path without leaning on others. This self-sufficiency was her hallmark, yet it had also rendered her devoid of any romantic entanglements. Jack, however, had upended this narrative. His presence ignited a flutter within her chest, a visceral response that was foreign yet exhilarating. The intensity of his gaze, especially when it lingered on her legs, sent delightful shivers coursing through her, a potent reminder of his magnetic effect on her. This fiercely independent woman was now inexplicably reliant on Jack to keep her heart racing.

Politely stepping aside, Faye extended an invitation for Jack to enter her suite. The hotel room exuded an air of sophistication, tastefully adorned with ample space. A cozy sitting area beckoned just beyond the vestibule, while a separate bedroom with an attached ensuite offered a sense of privacy. Adjacent to the suite's entrance was a convenient water closet, designed to cater to visitors.

With a welcoming gesture, Faye indicated one of the plush, overstuffed chairs in the sitting area, silently inviting Jack to take a seat. His gaze flitted from her to the chair, and a mischievous grin played at the corner of his lips. Faye caught his look and followed his gaze to the chair she had motioned towards, realizing the humorous aspect that had caught his attention.

"Oh, let me get that," Faye chimed in, a sheepish grin gracing her face. Her heart raced within her chest, but it wasn't solely due to the slightly embarrassing item she had hastily removed from the chair.

The chairs, once occupied by undergarments and a smattering of her clothes, now lay scattered with the articles Faye was picking up. As she moved about the room, her gaze flickered towards Jack in stolen glances, a quiet reassurance that he was indeed there, his presence no mere mirage. But her anticipation, her nerves, seemed to stoke a fiery flush within her, akin to standing before him entirely unclad, even though she wore his borrowed shirt.

With a nonchalant feigned grace, she strode to the open door of the bedroom and casually tossed the retrieved items inside. They landed haphazardly, scattered without concern. Tidiness was far from her mind, more focused on her own discomposure at having cleaned up earlier, only to leave behind this carelessly strewn array of clothes for Jack to see.

Upon her return to the sitting area, having quickly shut the bedroom door behind her, Faye accepted the coffee cup Jack offered. Settling into the chair opposite him, she felt her heart still thundering, the lingering traces of her hurried movements or the handsome man seated before her, she wasn't sure. Determining the cause seemed trivial, so she concentrated instead on steadying her nerves, calming the internal tempest that threatened to consume her.

Jack's perceptive nature picked up on the subtle signs of Faye's nervousness, the slight falter in her usual sharp demeanor. A gentle curve played on his lips as he discerned these cues, his own awareness sharpened by his understanding of her. The sight before him wasn't one to be ridiculed, but rather a moment that amused him in a different way—seeing her experience what he often did. It wasn't about exploiting her vulnerability; it was a genuine, refreshing shift in their dynamics.

The smile that graced his face held a touch of warmth, appreciating the role reversal in this fleeting moment. The universe had an odd way of weaving connections, and now it was his turn to find amusement in her unease, not as payback, but as a reminder of their shared humanity.

"Why are you here so early in the morning, Jack?" Faye's voice trembled as she spoke, her heartbeat echoing in her ears. It was as if the shirt she wore had transformed into a billboard for her racing pulse, a visible testament to her inner turmoil.

A flicker of apprehension crossed Jack's features, a testament to the realization that he needed to address his behavior, to navigate the complexities that had arisen between them. Taking responsibility was imperative, and he braced himself for the forthcoming conversation.

"Well..." His words hesitated momentarily, a pause punctuated by a clearing of his throat. With determination, he continued, "I wanted to apologize for how I acted on Saturday night and Sunday morning."

"Yeah, I couldn't understand what I said to upset you." Faye's response carried a hint of vulnerability, her admission shrouded in uncertainty.

In the wake of her words, her demeanor underwent a subtle transformation. Jack observed this shift, witnessing a facet of Faye that he hadn't encountered before. Her fragility surprised him, but what struck him even more was the way her vulnerability touched something deep within him. It wasn't a surge of protective instincts that welled up, but rather a sense of discomfort, an acute awareness of the impact he'd had on her emotions.

He sought refuge in the steady warmth of his coffee cup, cradling it between his palms as he leaned forward slightly, the chair's back no longer a resting place for him, an unconscious response to the gravity of the moment. Faye's words flowed on, each sentence unraveling another layer of her emotions. As she confessed her struggle, her admission seemed to hang in the air, vulnerable and unadorned. Jack felt a growing heaviness settle in his chest.

Her admission hung in the air, a confession that tugged at Jack's emotions. He processed her words, acknowledging the significance they held.

"I know I came across strong. I gotta confess, I'm having problems coming to grips with how much I like you," Faye's voice softened, revealing a layer of vulnerability he hadn't expected.

Jack's thoughts raced in tandem with his heartbeat, processing the weight of her words and contemplating his own response. *Wow,* he thought, caught in the swirl of emotions and revelations. He tilted his head to each side, eliciting a satisfying series of audible cracks from his neck, a physical manifestation of the tension he felt. His body settled back into the chair as he considered his next words, their significance and the reasoning behind them.

"That was just me, not you," he began, his voice a measured reflection of his thoughts. He paused, allowing the words to marinate in the space between them. "I wasn't ready to face certain things yet and didn't realize how deeply they still affected me."

"Yeah, I know what you mean about facing things," Faye confessed, her mind tracing back to the moments when she had grappled with her burgeoning desire and the rapidity with which it had taken root. She resisted the urge to shudder as the memories surged, instead focusing on a deep inhalation to rein in the emotions that threatened to consume her.

Her voice steadied as she continued, words carrying the weight of a truth she needed to share. "I need to tell you something, Jack."

Jack's nod, silent and understanding, encouraged her to proceed.

"This is the first time I've ever been in love," she confessed, the admission hanging in the air like a revelation waiting to be absorbed. Jack's world seemed to tilt on its axis, the significance of her words hitting him like a surprise bombardment. He grappled with the enormity of her confession, the realization that he was the one to inspire such a profound sentiment. He looked at her with renewed scrutiny, his gaze tracing the contours of her features as if discovering them anew: her raven-black hair, her delicate frame, her feline grace, her eyes reflecting a unique blend of green and gold. In that moment, he saw her more vividly than before, his understanding shifting into something deeper and more resonant.

Questions swirled in his mind, and he verbalized one of them, his brow slightly furrowed in curiosity. "How can I be your first love? Didn't you have any crushes while growing up? Maybe a boyfriend in high school?"

Faye's response was a solemn shake of her head, a gesture that conveyed a history of absence. "You're my first love, I'm sure of it. I've never had to navigate these emotions before, so they overwhelmed me. I didn't know how to handle the intensity of it all."

Jack's intuition whispered that something lingered beneath her words, a subtlety he caught in her fleeting pause. He dismissed the fleeting thought, recognizing that, in this moment, the focus was on guiding her through her feelings. "You loved your parents, right?" he inquired gently, as if extending a lifeline to an unraveling thread of emotions.

Faye's reaction was immediate, a momentary freeze that flickered across her expression. She averted her gaze from his, and the distance she created between them was palpable.

"I don't want to talk about that. It's not important," she deflected, her voice carrying a tone of dismissal that hinted at a layer of pain she wasn't ready to reveal.

Jack released a sigh, understanding the sensitivity of the subject and opting to respect her boundaries. He allowed the silence to stretch, a space for Faye to take the reins if she wished. Her pointed gaze prompted a question from her, laden with a blend of hesitancy and anticipation.

"So, are you ready now?" she ventured, her voice reflecting a mix of uncertainty and a glimmer of hope.

Jack, momentarily puzzled, signaled his confusion to her through his expression.

"Are you ready to confront those things you were talking about?" Faye clarified, her words cutting through the haze of ambiguity.

Understanding dawned on Jack, the clarity washing over him as he grasped her intent. "Oh, I'm getting there," he replied with a reassuring smile, seeking to ease the tension that had been building.

Faye's attention remained focused on the untouched coffee cup cradled between her hands. The conversation had drawn her in so deeply that she hadn't taken a single sip, her thoughts wrapped up in the emotional exchange taking place. Uncertainty gripped her, tugging at her like an anchor in the sea of her feelings.

"I didn't mean to upset you," she murmured, her words carrying a tentative edge.

Jack shook his head, offering swift reassurance. "No, no... it wasn't your fault. I just don't know how to respond to you because it's been so long I guess," he confessed, a hint of sorrow clouding his features. Internally, he grappled with his thoughts, marveling at the vulnerability she exhibited.

Goddamn, little girl, he silently mused, the phrase dripping with a mixture of endearment and exasperation. *You're killing me here.* His thoughts a silent testament to how her unveiled vulnerability was both endearing and overwhelming.

Her vulnerability clung to her like a cocoon of protection, a winter coat she wore to shield herself from the cold. Jack's yearning to enfold her in his arms was met with hesitance, as if she were a delicate prey ready to bolt at the slightest movement on his part. The predator and the prey, locked in an intricate dance of emotions and perceptions.

Within Jack, an ache resonated, reminiscent of a child who had lost a cherished pet, the pain of an irreparable void settling in. If he were younger, his lower lip might have quivered, a physical manifestation of the turmoil churning within him.

"A lot of things happened to me, back to back, during that time of my life, and I kinda shut down," Jack shared.

"It's okay. I can understand how all of that stuff can pile on and take a toll on you quickly." Faye's demeanor began to regain its steadiness, yet there was a lingering sense of emotional turbulence she still grappled with.

"You were right about me using Brooke as a shield. Spending time with her and my sister helps ease the loneliness." Jack's internal struggles mirrored his outward composure, as if he navigated an emotional sea with sturdy paddles.

"I don't know what to say to that," admitted Faye. Beneath her words lay a subtle twinge of jealousy, a yearning for a similar declaration from him without hesitation. She realized, though, that patience was key.

"You don't have to say anything. I heard what you said Friday night. You told me that you liked me." Jack's confession held a mix of sincerity and vulnerability.

"Yeah, well, I do... I do like you. I don't know why it happened so quickly," Faye reaffirmed, seeking assurance.

"I know what you mean. We've only just met a week ago." Jack shifted in his seat, a gesture that mirrored his internal reflections. His hand grazed his head, a subtle sign of his emotional unease.

"So what about you, Jack? Do you... like me?" Faye's question carried a hint of teenage vulnerability, reminiscent of a girl discovering a mutual crush. The poignancy struck Jack.

"I don't really know how to answer that yet. Your work record impressed the hell out of me. You get along famously with my niece, like you're two peas in a pod. I don't know anyone who handles firearms like you do, single or double wielding. Those are some pretty badass guns," Jack's voice softened, his admiration apparent. "And you are very intelligent and beautiful."

"I think that covers all the bases," Faye replied, her rueful smile acknowledging the completeness of his assessment. She playfully mimicked gun fingers, invoking a lighthearted air.

Faye's playful gesture signaled her return from the depths of emotional waters. Jack's laughter resonated, dissipating tension from his frame like melting ice giving way to water's flow. His shoulders eased, and he felt the familiar comfort he had before the weekend's disarray.

"I think you're very, very beautiful, Faye. Especially when I can see you in my shirt like that," Jack complimented, punctuating the moment.

Jack's gaze lingered on Faye's legs once more. A familiar hunger welled within him, a sensation dormant for a long time. It returned like a cherished friend, warm and gentle, snug like a well-worn sweater on cold winter nights. The feeling deepened as he absorbed the sight of her in his dress shirt and her panties. The thought triggered a memory of a whimsical fantasy book titled 'The Color of Her Panties', which brought a smile to his lips.

His smile spread lazily, a testament to the allure Faye's presence held for him. Evidently, the intensity of his gaze affected her too; she seemed to fidget slightly, struggling to maintain her composure.

Under Jack's unyielding scrutiny, Faye's discomfort grew palpable, sensing his mind might be wandering into more provocative realms. The notion sent a rush of heat through her veins, and she realized she needed something cooler. She took a sip of her coffee.

"I'm going to step into the bedroom for a quick shower. I'll be right back," Faye declared.

"Great. I was thinking of taking you out for breakfast before we head to the office," Jack proposed.

"Sounds wonderful," Faye agreed, her voice carrying a tinge of anticipation.

Rising from her seat, Faye maneuvered around Jack and the chair he occupied, her path leading to the bedroom. As she passed him, she planted a peck on his cheek—a simple gesture that set her heart aflutter, reminiscent of a schoolgirl stealing a kiss from her crush. She disappeared into the bedroom, gently shutting the door behind her.

Inside, Faye's heart raced. She embraced the sensation, allowing her thoughts to revisit their conversation, dissecting its words and the emotions beneath. As a newcomer to relationships, she grappled with uncertainty, feeling the urge to proceed cautiously. She yearned for their connection to evolve naturally, at its own pace.

During her shower, thoughts of Jack continued to swirl in Faye's mind, flustering her as she prepared for their outing. Clad in denim jeans and a snug red knit sweater, she stayed true to her word, ready within twenty minutes.

Jack expressed his intention to treat her to breakfast, and they set off, departing for a restaurant of his choice. As they left, Faye refrained from offering his shirt back, secretly hoping he had forgotten about it amidst their rush. Fortunately, his lapse of memory granted her a little more time to hold onto the shirt she would now wear to bed religiously.

Faye and Jack had just settled down at their table, barely having time to place their orders and make a dent in their meals, when Jack's phone rang. It was the desk sergeant from the police station, and without much thought, Jack answered the call, his initial annoyance at the interruption fading as he went into professional mode. The routine nature of his response stemmed from the acceptance that such interruptions were an inherent part of their job.

Faye watched with mild interest as Jack took the call. She understood the unpredictability that came with their line of work, and her fork hovered mid-air before she gently set it down on her plate. She caught fragments of Jack's side of the conversation, her curiosity piqued.

"Hey Mary," Jack greeted the desk sergeant, recognizing her voice even before she identified herself. The caller ID had given him a heads-up on who was on the other end.

"Jack, I'm sending you the address and preliminary information on another murder. Same M.O. as your current cases. The Chief wants you there pronto, and he said to take your new partner with you," Mary relayed succinctly.

Jack's gaze briefly met Faye's as he spoke on the phone, a silent assurance that he would fill her in once the call was done. "Alright, thanks Mary," Jack responded, trusting her to keep the information concise.

After ending the call, Jack relayed the limited information he had gathered to Faye. It wasn't much beyond what Mary had already shared over the phone. *We should try to gather more information from the computer while we're on our way,* he silently contemplated, aware of the need to be as informed as possible before they reached the scene.

Jack settled the breakfast bill before he and Faye swiftly made their way to his unmarked police cruiser. A fleeting regret crossed his mind for not leaving the engine running, not due to any expectation of an immediate call to action, but simply to avoid stepping into the frigid vehicle. Although a twinge of responsibility nagged him about the taxpayer dollars potentially wasted by an idling city vehicle, he braced himself for the cold bite of the early morning air. The chill pricked at his skin as they stepped outside, prompting him to instinctively hunch his shoulders. Cold weather was Jack's nemesis, a fact he often grumbled about, a fact not lost on Faye.

Once inside the car, he initiated the process of bringing his computer online, focusing on the task at hand. The text on the screen captured his attention as he delved into the preliminary information, leaving behind the discomfort of the cold weather and allowing his investigative instincts to take over.

"What's the situation? Another victim in this string of murders, I'm guessing?" Faye inquired as she settled into the passenger seat, loosening her jacket, a precaution she'd taken to ward off the cold's grasp. She had waited until after Jack had looked through the computer for additional information before she posed her question.

"The latest victim was something of a local celebrity, fairly well-off," Jack began, multitasking as he brought the computer online. "A confirmed bachelor, known around the city. His murder is already making waves in the local news, both print and TV," he concluded, a hint of distaste crossing his face. With the necessary data acquired, he punched in the address and set the vehicle in motion.

As they arrived at the scene, media personnel and their vehicles swarmed the front of the building. The noise was palpable. The chaos of the scene was amplified by a hovering news helicopter far overhead.

"This is turning into a goddamn circus," Jack remarked to Faye, his expression mirroring his sentiment.

Faye's thoughts reflected his own assessment of the situation. Uniformed officers and their cruisers joined the fray, helping to maintain order amidst the media frenzy. Curious onlookers added to the chaos, and the noise echoed through the narrow confines of the street. The situation was chaotic, and it was only destined to worsen as the day progressed. While the previous murders had garnered some initial attention, they had mostly faded from the breaking news cycle as they lacked substantial leads or suspects.

"Once the media starts connecting the dots on these murders," Jack ventured, fully aware that the situation would escalate beyond their control.

Jack and Faye maneuvered their way through the crowd of pedestrians, employing a mix of gentle nudges and friendly persuasion to carve a path. A blend of assertiveness and diplomacy. Their determined efforts continued until they reached the perimeter marked off by the police cordon. Jack's badge served as a key to access both the cordon and the building beyond. Instantly, they found solace from the clamor outside and the pressing proximity of the crowd. Respite from the bustling clamor outside and the crush of bodies. Their mission began in earnest as they stepped inside, greeted by the contrastingly hushed atmosphere of the lobby.

Within the lobby's confines, the abrupt shift from the chilly outdoor environment was immediately evident. A chaotic scene was contained just beyond the glass partition. Serenity pervaded the interior, standing in stark contrast to the bustling scene just beyond the expansive floor-to-ceiling windows. Soft, canned music drifted from concealed speakers, filling the air with a subdued ambiance. Standing adjacent to a reception desk, a uniformed officer stood in readiness. He offered Jack and Faye what insights he could, tasked with maintaining control over this crucial section of the crime scene. He provided them with specifics about the crime's location and outlined his role in managing the lobby's access, selectively permitting or denying entry to various individuals.

Jack acknowledged the officer's diligence with a friendly pat on the shoulder, coupled with a sincere smile and words of gratitude. "Keep your head up. You're doing fine."

Jack summoned the elevator with a simple press of the up button, the soft hum of machinery signaling its ascent. Side by side, Jack and Faye stepped into the cabin. The ascent to the penthouse suite on the fiftieth floor commenced in silence. Their shared journey was punctuated by an unspoken understanding of the somber task awaiting them—each engaged in their own private mental preparations, bracing themselves for the grim realities of a murder scene investigation, each engrossed in their own rituals of readiness.

At the pinnacle of the building, contrary to what one might assume, the penthouse suite was not confined to a solitary floor. Rather, it commanded the entire apex of the building, spanning two expansive levels. Dominating the building's uppermost floors, the penthouse suite spanned an impressive 3200 square feet of luxurious living space. Perched on the summit of the skyscraper, it boasted an awe-inspiring panoramic view of the city that sprawled below.

Its open-plan design created a sense of airiness, offering a harmonious blend of luxury and utility. The residence itself was a testament to opulence, characterized by the expansive open areas that seamlessly merged with the skyline. Adding to the allure was a rooftop garden and a key-operated private elevator that exclusively served this elite domain. Additional access to the floor included a stairwell. The stairwell, intended for exiting only, further bolstered the suite's security, prohibiting entry from the stair side. Surveillance was constant, as both the stairs and the elevator were under round-the-clock closed-circuit scrutiny.

Jack's thoughts weaved through the peculiarities. *Another odd home,* Jack mused inwardly, quelling the shake of his head to keep his contemplation contained. He contained the motion within his thoughts, preventing it from manifesting in his physical actions. *What's the deal with this eccentric setup? Could this quirk be the link connecting these cases?* His mind buzzed with questions, seeking to decipher the significance behind this peculiar living arrangement.

Undoubtedly, Jack stood as the designated lead investigator for this case. Not a single other detective was present at the scene. It wasn't lost on Jack that this situation was intentional. As this realization settled, it dawned on Jack that this orchestration was most likely the handiwork of Chief Eugene himself. It spoke volumes about two critical things: a potent display of trust in Jack's investigative prowess, and an implicit lack of confidence in others' abilities to measure up.

The subtle yet undeniable implication pushed Jack to comprehend the enormity of his role—not just a lead, but the solitary force driving the inquiry. Jack held the sole mantle of responsibility for solving this crime. The implied burden weighed heavily; success or failure rested solely on his shoulders. It was a strategic move. It was a way to offload accountability, to shift blame should the need arise. A way to divest accountability and culpability, a tactic that stirred a knot in Jack's gut and etched a grimace across his features.

As a sense of responsibility and pressure settled in, Jack's hands involuntarily clenched, a manifestation of his internal turmoil. His discomfort was vividly etched on his face. The weight of the task was clear: he alone held the power to shape the investigation's fate, for better or worse. The chief's strategic gambit to isolate Jack in this pursuit was a double-edged sword, granting him the autonomy he craved while simultaneously painting him into a corner.

Exiting the elevator, Jack and Faye had found themselves in a secluded lobby that functioned as a vestibule for the penthouse suite. Jack took note of the security layers in place. His keen observation didn't miss the nuances. Despite the possibility of an unauthorized ascent via either the elevator or the stairs, breaching the penthouse was another matter entirely.

The imposing door ahead emphasized this, its formidable presence a sentinel against unauthorized entry. It was a solid looking door set in a floor to ceiling bullet proof glass wall—an insurmountable barrier that safeguarded the interior from unwelcome intrusion. The layers of security were conspicuous. As his gaze settled on the formidable entrance, Jack recognized the layers of safeguards designed to maintain the sanctity of this space, a testament to the gravity of the crime scene they were about to explore.

Jack's gaze shifted to Faye, a silent attempt to decipher her thoughts. Her recent quiet introspection contrasted starkly with her usual animated personality. The absence of her usual questions and comments felt glaring to him, highlighting the incongruity with her typical bubbly demeanor. Despite her quietude, Faye's presence seemed amplified, her subdued actions and words somehow demanding his attention.

Upon closer observation, Jack discerned a woman engrossed in capturing even the minutest of details, her role as an investigator paramount in her mind. Her outward demeanor might suggest otherwise, but Jack recognized the subtle dance of her eyes as they absorbed the surroundings. He briefly entertained the notion that she might even be employing her sense of smell, an idea he dismissed as irrational. After all, there were no discernible pungent odors in the vicinity, and even if there were, he struggled to fathom their significance.

Faye caught Jack's watchful gaze and responded with a warm smile. Her transition from the initial seriousness to her familiar, easygoing self reassured Jack, alleviating any concerns he held for her well-being. Her nonchalant words carried an air of eagerness that matched the gravity of the situation without overwhelming it, and Jack felt encouraged to shift his focus to their impending task.

Jack had to acknowledge to himself that, despite the recent awkwardness in their personal lives and the vulnerabilities and uncertainties she had shown, Faye's professional demeanor hadn't faltered. She appeared to be fully engaged in her role.

"Let's get to work, shall we?" Faye's grin carried a determined enthusiasm, setting a proactive tone that resonated well with Jack.

The lobby presented two other doors, one presumably leading to the stairwell and the other likely granting access to the roof. Jack took the initiative to open the door leading into the penthouse, allowing both him and Faye to step through. Yet, their first encounter inside was jarring—a severed foot lay before them, demanding immediate attention.

"What the hell?" Jack's exclamation was a mix of disbelief and astonishment, his eyes fixed on the macabre sight.

Faye involuntarily took a step back, following Jack's line of sight to the unsettling discovery that had grabbed his attention. Their entrance had been marked by this grisly scene, casting an eerie pall over the investigation's beginning.

A uniformed officer approached Jack, his attention drawn by the detective's exclamation. He introduced himself as the first responder who had reported the murder. "Hey, Detective Riddle," he greeted.

Jack shifted his focus from the disconcerting foot to the officer before him. "Can you brief me on what you've gathered so far?" he inquired, his thoughts still grappling with the implications of the severed foot placed so conspicuously by the entrance. As the officer began recounting the details, Jack's gaze oscillated between the officer and the unsettling sight

"About an hour and a half to two hours ago, the maid arrives for work and finds our victim... um, well... all over the place," the officer explained, his hands gesturing vaguely in an encompassing sweep that spanned the penthouse suite's expanse.

Jack recognized the officer's literal accuracy in describing the state of the victim's remains. Having encountered the work of this particular killer before, he knew the gruesome nature of the scene they were about to navigate. His eyes darted around, scanning the immediate vicinity before inevitably settling back on the severed foot that marked their grim entry point.

"Please continue," Jack prompted the officer, his tone steady and focused.

"The maid understandably freaked out, rushed downstairs, and raised hell, as the concierge desk clerk recounted," the officer reported with a detached efficiency.

Jack appreciated the officer's professionalism, especially considering the disturbing circumstances that had initiated the investigation. The haunting specter of the murder scene cast a shadow over him, and he half-expected it to extend to the personnel on site. With his professional demeanor intact, the officer's response was commendable, maintaining an air of competence even in the face of a grisly tableau. Jack's thoughts briefly shifted to the media circus outside, a jarring reminder of the public's insatiable thirst for sensationalism.

"Why the media frenzy out there?" Jack inquired, his curiosity piqued by the pandemonium beyond the crime scene's confines.

"It seems likely that someone, maybe entering or leaving, caught wind of the commotion and dialed up the news. Could've been the doorman, desk clerk, security, or even the maid herself, for all I know," the officer explained, shedding light on the probable source of the media circus.

The officer shifted his weight, a subtle repositioning that managed to keep him upright. Jack's observant mind briefly wandered, imagining a healthier version of the officer shedding twenty-five pounds in just a few months' time. However, he promptly refocused his thoughts on the task at hand, steering away from fitness musings. The officer's physical condition wasn't a pertinent concern in the moment; Jack's interest was rooted in the man's capability to execute his role effectively. Jack's mental pivot away from the officer's weight demonstrated his concern for both his colleague's well-being and his job performance but not in a negative way.

"The desk clerk mentioned that he only saw regulars coming or going since his shift began this morning. He specifically noted that the maid was the sole person to use the private elevator to go up," the officer recounted, succinctly wrapping up his briefing.

"Have you reached out to security?" Faye chimed in from her position slightly to the side, her voice carrying an air of assurance that she was an active participant in the investigation process.

Her eyes had been intently roving over the interior, her scrutiny giving off an uncanny sense of perceptive acumen. There was a sharpness in her gaze that Jack's own awareness couldn't help but notice. Her eyes were scanning the interior as if they possessed an innate ability to uncover hidden truths, a heightened sense of observation emanated from her that Jack had to fully acknowledge. It demonstrated her attentiveness to detail.

"I've got that covered. A uniform is down there now, reviewing the feed," the officer responded, pivoting his attention to Faye and acknowledging her inquiry.

Jack's focus returned to the officer, shifting away from Faye's magnetic presence momentarily. "Alright, so show me...where...our victim is," Jack instructed, emphasizing the word 'where' to convey his expectation of investigating multiple areas.

Drawing from his experience with prior crime scenes involving this particular perpetrator, Jack was mentally prepared for the gruesome realities that awaited him. The distinctive modus operandi of the murderer had consistently revealed dismembered victims, their brutal deaths marked by a baffling absence of traditional weaponry or tools. Instead, evidence pointed to an extraordinary level of physical violence, a superhuman strength and an inexplicably violent act that defied conventional understanding.

Jack anticipated the officer leading him to a specific location, a central point where the bulk of the victim's remains were likely concentrated. Instead, Jack found himself surprised by the officer's static posture. The officer remained rooted in one spot, wearing a quizzical expression. This was an unexpected twist as he was ready to move further into the house and get started with his investigation.

"Are you inquiring about the biggest piece of the victim's body or should I focus on that?" the officer's finger pointed at the severed foot near the entrance. "Because if not... There's a piece here, then there's another in the bedroom, one on the balcony. Oh," he paused, a flicker of memory rekindling, "and one on the level beneath the bedroom..."

"Huh? Stop." Jack's response betrayed his momentary confusion, as if his mental gears had inexplicably shifted out of alignment just moments after posing his question.

The unexpectedness of the officer's answer had thrown him off balance, leading him to question his own understanding. Jack felt as if his intelligence had abruptly abandoned him, leaving him floundering in a moment of cognitive dissonance as his mind struggled to process the disturbing information.

"Yeah, Detective Riddle," the officer began, his tone carrying a sense of gravity. "The victim's all over the place, in big and small pieces.

There's even an ear over near the door, leading into the office over there," the officer detailed.

Jack's response was a mixture of disbelief and exasperation, a drawn-out sigh emphasizing his incredulity. "Just take me around and show me then," he requested, his tone a blend of resignation and determination, revealing his commitment to comprehending the unsettling scene before him.

With a casual shrug, the officer led Jack deeper into the penthouse suite, adopting a functional approach to their task. Faye trailed behind them, her quiet presence neatly fading into the background as the trio moved forward. Their footsteps resonated, the spaciousness of the penthouse amplifying the sound. The interior immediately unfolded into an expansive area extending the full height of both floors. Panoramic windows adorned three sides of the building, offering unobstructed vistas of the surrounding cityscape.

On the lower level, a series of rooms lay before them, each with its own purpose. There was an office, two guest rooms complete with en-suite bathrooms, a water closet, a wine cellar, a fully equipped kitchen, a formal dining room, and a living area that flowed seamlessly into a butler's pantry. A balcony overlooked this entire expanse, the glass railing providing an uninterrupted view. Glass steps led upward to a second level, which was divided into an open-concept master bedroom, complete with its own en-suite bathroom, and a library. An additional entrance in the kitchen offered access to the rooftop green space, providing a serene escape from the urban environment below.

The rooftop green space encompassed not only a garden but also featured a covered Olympic-sized pool, accompanied by a three-quarter bathroom and a sunroom. As the uniformed officer guided Jack through the various locations within the penthouse where body parts were discovered, Faye seized the chance to explore the rooftop area. While Jack couldn't quite fathom her motives for investigating the roof, he opted to let the matter be, refraining from voicing any questions.

Once the officer had provided Jack with a comprehensive tour of the gruesome scene, the forensics team conveyed their need for more time before offering their preliminary findings. With this avenue temporarily closed off, Jack shifted his focus toward locating Faye. It didn't take him long to spot her; her voice reached out from the kitchen, beckoning him. He swiftly moved towards her, his curiosity piqued by her summons.

Positioned near the opening leading to the roof access, Faye awaited Jack's arrival, her expression suggesting a mixture of discovery and intrigue.

"I believe our intruder gained access from the roof," Faye shared with Jack, her voice pitched low enough to avoid causing echoes in the penthouse's open design. She wanted to prevent any unnecessary reverberations, saving her voice from having to carry too far.

"Huh? How could the killer get in from the roof?" Jack's brows furrowed revealing incredulity. He concealed the hint of doubt though, not wishing to discourage Faye's willingness to express her ideas. He wanted her insights to the investigation.

"Follow me. I'll show you," Faye suggested, leading the way toward the staircase that ascended to the roof. Her movements were tinged with a restrained enthusiasm, embodying a genuine desire to contribute her unique perspective to the case.

Faye guided Jack to the rooftop, venturing beyond the confines of the pool enclosure. The winter cold was sharper. The higher altitude exposed them to a more biting winter cold, intensified by the relentless wind that transformed it into an almost cutting chill. Jack, though not thrilled about braving the outdoors again, appreciated Faye's commitment to the case.

The roof was a lush expanse of real grass devoid of a covering of snow, an unusual feature that lent an unexpected touch of nature to the urban setting. A waist-high glass railing encircled the roof, offering a sense of security while allowing for unobstructed views. Near the southern edge of the rooftop, about six feet from the railing, Faye came to a stop and directed Jack's attention to the ground.

"Take a look here. You can see the grass has been damaged from the landing," she pointed out.

"Are you suggesting the guy parachuted in?" Jack inquired, his gaze fixed on the marked patch of grass Faye had indicated.

He acknowledged the dent in the grass. Although he observed the evident depression in the grass, he still found himself somewhat skeptical of the notion that the killer had descended from the sky.

Faye gave a dismissing shake of her head. Without hesitation, she shot down Jack's parachute hypothesis.

"No," she responded with a firm seriousness that conveyed her certainty. Her expression unwavering. She glanced at Jack and stated, "He jumped."

Turning her attention to indicate a building situated to the south, Faye continued, "From over there," concluding her explanation.

Jack shifted his gaze toward the building Faye had indicated, his steps leading him to the railing where he peered down at the street far below, some fifty-odd stories down. His grip tightened on the rail. A surge of nausea swept over him as he grappled with the vertigo triggered by the view far below. He despised heights more than even the bitterest of cold days—a sentiment that spoke volumes given Jack's abhorrence of winter weather, which he deemed the work of the devil.

Turning back to Faye, he voiced his incredulity, "You're suggesting someone leaped from that building way over there?" Jack queried, his hooked thumb gesturing over his shoulder toward the building he'd just scrutinized. His features betrayed his skepticism.

Faye met his gaze squarely, addressing the logistical challenge. "Across roughly fifty to fifty-five feet, spanning nearly fifty-three stories in the air." Jacks finger traced the gap between the two buildings. "Only to then cover an additional six feet or so to reach this spot on the building here?" He indicated the location where Faye had identified the point of entry.

Faye's expression hadn't changed. Jack shook his head.

"That's impossible," he challenged.

Jack wanted to give her the benefit of doubt. He wanted to respect her input, but he struggled to accept the plausibility of the entry method she described and the implications it carried. Her explanation of the murderer's entry seemed far-fetched, considering the complexity and precision involved. That didn't even consider the ramifications of the physical abilities needed to accomplish such a feat.

Faye's response was direct, her tone firm. She was unwavering. "No, it's *improbable*, but not *impossible*," she retorted, her tone flat as she distinctly emphasized the two critical words, conveying their nuanced significance. Her use of the language showed that she understood the distinction between the terms and their implications.

"Nevertheless, however, I assure you that is exactly what happened," Faye stated with a note of finality.

Her unwavering gaze bore into Jack's, an intensity that caused a seed of doubt to take root in his own skepticism. It made him begin to seriously question his own disbelief in her theory.

The uniformed officer who had been the first to arrive on the scene joined Faye and Jack as they made their way outside and up onto the roof. Instructing him, Faye had the officer call two more uniforms from the cordon downstairs to head to the roof of the building on the southern side.

While it took some time for these officers to gain rooftop access, they eventually succeeded. Their inspection revealed a suspicious disruption of the tar and gravel covering on the opposite roof, hinting that something might have landed there. The maintenance team for that building corroborated that no scheduled work had required roof access, and they noted that the latch to the roof entry door had been intact about two days prior.

Jack, in response, dispatched a portion of the forensics team to gather potential evidence from the neighboring building's roof, hoping to shed light on this peculiar entry point.

Faye, however, had more to reveal to Jack. Leading him over to the door of the pool area, she opened it to reveal signs of damage that were clearer now. "The lock's been forced from the outside. It appears the intruder simply twisted the knob until the whole mechanism gave way."

Jack scrutinized the knob, conceding that it did indeed exhibit signs of torsion damage. No matter how he looked at it, the imagery was hard to explain logically.

"This whole case is nutty like a peanut candy bar," Jack admitted, his skepticism palpable. The peculiar patterns defied easy explanation. Doubt was clouding his judgment, and his thoughts were in disarray, his anxiety manifesting in sweat despite the cold. "This is crazy as hell and getting weirder by the moment. Each victim is brutally dismembered, and the perpetrator seems to perform incredible feats at each crime scene. He's kicked down reinforced doors with ease, twisted metal like paper maché, sprinting like an Olympic athlete on steroids, or vaulting over fifty feet of empty space like some sort of mythical creature or a person in possession of a magic carpet."

He shook his head, struggling to reconcile the strange occurrences with his understanding of reality. "I'm finding it hard to suspend my disbelief and fit this suspect into the my understanding of reality."

Jack turned his gaze to Faye, a glimmer of hope for grounding flickering in his eyes, only to find himself met with a somber expression that deepened his sense of disconnection. Her demeanor suggested a firm belief in the perpetrator's extraordinary abilities, leaving Jack with a lingering suspicion that she possessed insights beyond his grasp. His thoughts circled back to the enigma of why an agent of her stature had been thrust into this case. The incongruity of a judge among the victims refused to slot neatly into his understanding, casting doubt on the rationality of it all.

"I'm familiar with the saying, 'Once you have eliminated the impossible, whatever remains, however improbable, must be the truth,'" Jack mused aloud, pausing only briefly to scratch his head. He then continued, "And it's leading me to entertain the notion that we might be dealing with some sort of superhuman entity."

Faye's response seemed to hang in the air, her contemplative words carrying an air of casualness as if unintentionally uttered. "We could indeed be in pursuit of someone quite extraordinary," she added, almost as an afterthought.

In that moment, Jack's intuition crystallized. Faye's guarded demeanor and her calculated response left him with little doubt that she was holding back significant information. The unsettling feeling that she was privy to a more comprehensive picture gnawed at him, fueling his conviction that he wasn't being given the full story.

The dissonance stemming from Faye's potential professional secrecy gnawed at Jack's thoughts, particularly in light of their candid and honest personal interactions. The emotions they had untangled, raw and sharp, had undergone a shared negotiation—transitioning from an initial devastating impact to a more harmonious and mutual reconciliation.

The realization that Faye might be withholding information pertinent to the case weighed heavily on him. Jack acknowledged that if he wished to unearth these concealed details, he might have to confront Faye directly. Yet, such a confrontation was the last thing he desired. The burgeoning connection he felt towards her was undeniable, and the prospect of challenging her could inadvertently push her away. He recognized that he both yearned for her closeness and hesitated to jeopardize it through a forceful confrontation.

Despite his inner turmoil, Jack chose to keep his thoughts guarded. He held a deep desire to place his complete trust in Faye and was willing to extend her the benefit of the doubt. He hoped that time might allow her to share the information voluntarily, avoiding a potentially damaging confrontation. Jack understood the importance of her openness for the sake of their evolving relationship.

Meanwhile, he noticed that Faye appeared oblivious to his internal shift. Her focus seemed to be directed elsewhere, absorbed in details of the case—details that Jack was both conscious of and unaware of, creating an intriguing mystery.

Having completed their initial tasks, Jack and Faye made their way back to the building's lobby. Stepping out through the front doors, they were immediately met with the cacophony of the waiting crowd and a barrage of questions from reporters. As they approached the cordon, a cluster of reporters surged forward, bombarding Jack with inquiries. Among them were a few familiar faces that Jack recognized from his previous interactions with the media.

Faye, on the other hand, seemed to deliberately stay a step behind, avoiding the spotlight. Jack noticed her reluctance to engage with the reporters, attributing it to her desire to maintain a low profile. He assumed that her agency preferred to keep their involvement discreet, possibly to prevent the case from spiraling into unnecessary public attention.

"Detective Riddle," one of the reporters called out, trying to seize the initiative and Jack's attention. "Can you shed some light on what's happening?"

Jack felt a surge of caution, aware that every word he uttered could be dissected and analyzed by the media. He understood the potential consequences of sharing too much information prematurely, so he carefully selected his words to provide a semblance of transparency without compromising the investigation.

While the urge to be curt and dismissive tugged at him, Jack chose a middle ground. "At this stage, we're initiating an investigation into the death of Monroe Strickland. As we're still in the early phases, there are no concrete leads or suspects to report. The victim's maid discovered the body in his residence roughly two and a half hours ago. As we gather more information, we'll ensure that the media is kept informed."

By striking this fairness, Jack aimed to balance the public's right to know with the necessity of preserving the integrity of the investigation. He was keenly aware that his interactions with the media could impact not only the case itself but also public perception of law enforcement's capabilities.

Jack concluded his interaction with the reporters and turned his attention to Faye, intrigued by the intensity of her gaze directed somewhere within the crowd. Curiosity tugged at him, and he pondered what had captured her interest amidst the bustling chaos. He tried to follow her line of sight but found it difficult to discern the source of her focus.

Unbeknownst to Jack, Faye's acute senses had picked up on something that her conscious mind struggled to identify. A familiar scent wafted through the air, triggering a cascade of primal instincts within her. She scanned the crowd, her intuition on high alert, as her other senses chimed in with warnings of danger. The chill that gripped her went beyond the winter cold; it was a visceral response to an imminent threat.

In an instant, Faye's gaze locked onto a man in the crowd. His appearance was unremarkable, almost bland in its normalcy, yet Faye knew instinctively that he was no ordinary individual. When his eyes met hers and a smile spread across his face, she felt a rush of dread.

It was a chilling smile that revealed a set of razor-sharp teeth, an unsettling manifestation of his bloodlust.

Faye's hand instinctively moved towards her holstered weapons, her training and experience guiding her reflexes. Yet, she hesitated, acutely aware of the potential devastation that might follow if she engaged him here and now. The bystanders would be caught in the crossfire, innocent lives shattered by a confrontation that spiraled out of control.

As their eyes held, the man's smile faded, his lips covering his predatory teeth. He turned away, his hands disappearing into his jacket pockets as he melted into the crowd. Faye's senses remained on high alert, but the immediate threat had vanished, leaving her with a chilling awareness of the darkness lurking beneath seemingly ordinary exteriors.

"Faye... Faye... Agent Atwood?" Jack's voice sliced through the fog of Faye's thoughts, his concern evident as he attempted to snap her back to the present.

He couldn't help but worry at how deeply engrossed she seemed in whatever had captured her attention. Her gaze had been fixed with such intensity that Jack had to resort to near-shouting to break through her distraction.

Her response was somewhat distant, and Jack detected an unusual paleness in her complexion. "Yeah... Oh, yes," Faye replied, finally reorienting herself to their surroundings and his presence.

With a hint of apprehension in his voice, Jack asked, "Are you ready to go?" He could sense that something had unsettled her.

Faye nodded in response, her mind racing. She cast a look at Jack, the man whose handsome features and magnetic presence had captured her heart. But now, her worry tinged her expression, and a shadow of concern danced in her eyes. Her heart began to quicken its pace, and her breath caught just a little, as her thoughts swirled.

I've got to get this mission completed before any outsiders get hurt, she silently affirmed, a mantra to keep her focused. She followed Jack's lead, allowing him to guide them back to their waiting vehicle, all the while feeling the weight of her responsibilities pressing upon her.

As they began to move, Jack's curiosity got the better of him, and he surreptitiously glanced over his shoulder toward the direction that had held Faye's focus. There, he spotted a man in a nondescript beige jacket, ambling away from the scene.

Casually, Jack inquired, "Who was that?" He didn't want to make Faye even more uneasy, but his curiosity begged an answer.

Meeting his gaze, Faye's eyes held a hint of something he didn't quite like. *Is that fear?* Jack's thoughts raced as he analyzed the subtle shift in her expression.

"I don't know," Faye replied, a lie that masked her deeper awareness of the mysterious man. Gathering herself, she turned toward the patrol car that had brought them, a whirlwind of thoughts consuming her.

Meanwhile, Jack observed her retreating form, his own steps resuming after his momentary pause. The image of that fleeting, raw fear in Faye's eyes gnawed at him, leaving him with unanswered questions and a sense that there was much more to this situation than met the eye.

8

As Jack and Faye returned to the vehicle, Jack exhibited a gentlemanly demeanor by holding the door open for her. This wasn't about Jack displaying any sexist tendencies; rather, he genuinely wanted to assist Faye. His actions were spurred by his observation of her unease after she had noticed the peculiar man in the crowd.

The unforeseen situation at hand had disrupted their initially promising morning. His plan for a leisurely and unhurried breakfast as a part of their reconciliation had been abruptly derailed by the emergence of a new murder case. This grim development had intensified Jack's workload, a weight he was eager to alleviate. The recurring instances of murder within the city had exhausted his patience. While these cases had led to his acquaintance with Faye, he couldn't escape the moral conflict of deriving positivity from circumstances that were born out of someone else's tragic demise.

Life's lack of fairness was a bitter pill to swallow. Regardless, the harsh reality of life's unfairness was a truth Jack had come to terms with over time. The challenges it presented, epitomized by the series of troublesome cases he was grappling with, had become a persistent thorn in his side. Concurrently, the introduction of Faye into his life stirred up an array of conflicting emotions—a mixture of exasperation and an intriguing allure. Amidst all this, his feelings toward her had taken on a romantic turn, a realization he couldn't ignore.

Well, considering everything, my life's a real masterpiece, he mused laced heavily with a hint of sarcasm.

Given this complex backdrop, Jack was now compelled to prod Faye about the events that transpired at the crime scene. Her distraction had been palpable, and the fear he glimpsed in her eyes had left him unsettled. There was also the thought to contend with that beneath the surface, he sensed that she was withholding something. As they wrapped up their investigation, he had a growing awareness that she possessed information he wasn't privy to—information that seemed increasingly critical.

Settling into the driver's seat, Jack closed the car door and prompted the engine to a roar of life. Seeking solace from the pervasive chill and combatting the cold with vehemence, he cranked up the heat to a level that could only be described as 'two degrees hotter than hell'. Amidst this, the thought of coffee beckoned, but he pushed it aside, acknowledging it as a luxury that could wait. Presently, his focus was squarely on Faye, thoughts of her demanding his immediate attention.

"What was that back there?" Jack's inquiry bore a mix of concern and a touch of frustration, spurred by the fear he had detected in Faye's eyes concerning the mysterious man.

Unbeknownst to Jack, his tone was tinged with a hint of anger as his thoughts were colored by his awareness of Faye withholding information about the case. A protective instinct was surfacing within him, though he grappled with the realization that Faye was more than capable of handling herself without his intervention. He recognized her strength and knew that if she did seek safety, she could ask for it independently.

Faye, still not entirely present in the moment, responded with a slightly perplexed tone, "What do you mean?" Her thoughts remained entwined with the enigmatic man, diverting her from sensing Jack's emotional undercurrent.

Adjusting in his seat to face her, Jack's gaze bore intensity. "The man in the jacket. You were locked onto him. Did you recognize him?" His anger seeped into his tone, harder to conceal this time.

The temptation to avert her gaze from Jack's penetrating stare and focus on the passing scenery crossed Faye's mind. She resisted the urge, allowing her shoulders to release the tension she hadn't even realized had built up from the encounter. She sought a way to diffuse the situation and ease Jack's rising frustration, all while safeguarding her secrets.

I guess it's better to share a diluted truth than to drown in an outright lie, she fooled herself into thinking.

Deciding on a course, she replied, "He just seemed out of place and odd. I didn't think it was worth bothering you with." Her words were carefully chosen, a partial truth but a lie all the same.

Jack understood the deception. It might not have been a bold lie, but it was a lie nonetheless. He recognized it, and he sensed that she was offering it to shield him from worry.

"Alright," he conceded, opting not to confront her about her deception. "I was just worried because you were really focused on that guy. I guess I was going at it full tilt.". He refrained from mentioning the fear he'd glimpsed in her eyes, choosing to keep that revelation to himself.

Jack's gaze lingered on Faye, a touch of scrutiny etched in his features before he acknowledged that she had divulged as much as she was willing to share. The intensity of his stare softened. His hand moved slightly toward her, hinting at reassurance, yet he withdrew it, conscious of their professional roles. He understood the need to maintain a distinction between their personal lives and their duty. He recognized that he would have to release the matter and hope for a more open conversation in the future, though her guarded demeanor made him skeptical.

Faye, perceiving Jack's withdrawal from the topic, visibly relaxed. Although she yearned to share the truth, she understood that the timing wasn't right. Her mission and assisting Jack with the case had to remain separate endeavors. She also realized the necessity of delineating her emotions for him. Offering a faint smile, she hoped it would ease his unease.

Jack responded with a gentle shake of his head and a subdued smile, though he wasn't entirely content with the answers he had received. Shifting his gaze away, he initiated the vehicle, transitioning into drive mode and maneuvering through the congested traffic. It took time to distance themselves from the chaotic scene and set a course back to the office.

Returning to the police station, Jack and Faye barely had a moment to breathe before the chief of police summoned them to his office in a storm of frustration. While Faye wasn't under his direct jurisdiction, the chief made sure to channel his discontent through Jack. The chief's theatrical display of anger, a performance designed for the benefit of the officers stationed nearby, was well-known to both Jack and Eugene.

Amid the uproar, Eugene, his voice a mixture of irritation and pressure, let his grievances loose. "The mayor is breathing down my neck and now I've got the media crawling up my ass. Get your shit together, Riddle, and get me some goddamn results," Eugene scolded, his voice laden with annoyance. His hands hadn't stopped moving during the entirety of his tirade.

"I'm doing the best I can, chief," Jack responded, a touch of petulance in his tone. His demeanor was aloof, almost as if he couldn't be bothered by the chief's attempts to pile on the pressure for quicker results.

Observing Jack's apparent indifference, Eugene scowled and when he deemed the scowl inadequate, he intensified his glare. He didn't mince words in his response. "Get the hell out of my office, Riddle, and shut the door behind you," roared Eugene. The two shared an unspoken understanding of the charade they were playing. If not for the unseen audience lingering outside the office, they might have chuckled together at the unspoken irony of it all.

Eugene's roar dwindled into a mutter, punctuated by sarcasm. "'Doing the best I can, chief', my fucking ass."

Following Jack, Faye entered his office and took the initiative to set the coffee brewing for him. With a graceful ease, she settled onto the couch, making herself comfortable in her preferred spot. Jack, meanwhile, leaned against the front of his desk, positioning himself to face Faye.

Alright, so the chief wants some 'detecting' done, and I suppose that's the gig they're paying me for, Jack mused, his words more rhetorical than seeking active participation. It was a glimpse into his thought process, a methodical way he often worked through cases. Faye, however, wasn't privy to this facet of him yet. Their acquaintance was too fresh.

Slipping off her pumps, Faye crossed her legs momentarily before readjusting herself comfortably on the couch. She watched Jack intently as he embarked on his audible deliberation, unraveling the case step by step. Her admiration for his method was apparent, though hidden beneath her observant gaze was a playful twinkle, alluding to her mischievous thoughts.

Unaware of Faye's internal musings, Jack continued his verbal dissection of the case. "We've got a timeline here. The banker's decapitation about two months ago kicked off this series. A month later, the judge met the same fate," Jack paused, gathering his thoughts.

As he paused, Faye picked up where he left off, her mind attuned to his process. "The consistent patterns in the injuries and body damage led your department to suspect the same killer for both instances. The attorney's murder, two weeks after the judge's, solidified the conclusion due to matching modus operandi," Faye continued, following the thread of investigation.

In a subtle shift, Faye's movement managed to catch Jack's attention. His focus wavered as he watched her sweater glide over her figure, a momentary distraction he swiftly recognized. Shaking his head, he closed his eyes momentarily, attempting to regain his concentration from the pleasant yet diverting image in his mind.

Undeterred by Jack's momentary lapse, Faye carried on, seemingly unperturbed. "Today's crime scene, which we investigated, unfolded a week after the attorney's murder. It appears the time span between each incident is halving, suggesting the next victim might surface in a matter of two or three days," Faye astutely deduced, maintaining her composure even as she playfully acknowledged Jack's distraction.

As the coffee pot gurgled, signaling the imminent completion of its brewing cycle, Faye detected a subtle shift in Jack's demeanor. She could sense his attention briefly diverted by the thought of fresh coffee intertwining with the backdrop of their conversation. Nevertheless, he maintained his outward engagement.

"Faye, there's still no tangible link connecting these victims. Aside from their wealth and solitary status, the common thread eludes us. It all feels oddly haphazard. A banker, a judge, a corporate tax attorney, and a playboy billionaire—where do they intersect?" Jack pondered aloud.

"I agree. It's not that straightforward. We're overlooking something," Faye concurred, rising from the couch and making her way to the coffee pot.

She sensed Jack's gaze tracing her movements, aware that his eyes lingered lower, focused on the jeans she wore. Though unspoken, the dynamic between them was palpable, a current that flowed beneath the surface.

Faye gracefully moved to pour both of them a cup of coffee. She handed Jack his cup, prepared just the way he liked it, in their customary routine. Settling back onto the couch, Faye remained keenly attuned to Jack's reactions to her every move, a dynamic that added a layer of unspoken tension to the conversation.

"My team's been on this from the start," Jack shared after Faye resettled. He exhaled a breath he hadn't realized he was holding, a release that coincided with her returning to her spot. "They can't find a connection either. Even though I sometimes think that they all share a single braincell between the lot of them, there is no way that they could not have stumbled on a connection by now."

"Speaking of logic, what can we ascertain about the perpetrator?" Faye inquired, her hands cradling her cup for warmth as they continued to dissect the intricacies of the case.

"The blurry video clip, if it's our guy, indicates he's between five foot ten and six foot one, with an average build," Jack sighed, a tinge of frustration in his voice. He rubbed his head as if massaging answers out of his thoughts.

"We managed to secure DNA samples, as he took bites out of each victim. Originally, we were banking on those bites to link the cases. However, the DNA results have been a mess. The lab suspects contamination, but even that explanation doesn't hold up, because the samples are consistently showing the same anomalies," Jack continued, his voice carrying a sense of bewilderment.

Faye, on the brink of taking a sip from her cup, halted mid-motion. Jack's revelation struck a chord, inviting her curiosity.

"What's causing the lab technicians to be so sure about contamination?" she inquired, her interest piqued.

"According to what I've been told, the results are all over the map. The DNA doesn't match regular human markers, and there's a discord between the samples that's hard to explain," Jack disclosed, the mystery deepening. "I managed to glance at the results on my phone while we were at the last scene. While you were on the roof."

Acknowledging the complexity, Faye contemplated the situation. "So, if we disregard the DNA angle and focus solely on the physical evidence, we're looking at someone incredibly strong, fast, smart, patient, and utterly ruthless," she summarized.

"Yeah, it's almost like we're dealing with a superhuman, a blended version of the Batman, Hulk and The Flash," Jack chuckled, a hint of disbelief still lingering in his words. The notion of their killer surpassing the realm of human capability and venturing into the territory of a superhero was challenging for him to fully embrace.

"Be serious, Jack," Faye chided, her tone turning reproachful as she groaned at his humor attempt, her hands reaching to rub her forehead as if to erase the ill-timed jest.

"I am being serious," Jack retorted, a touch of exasperation in his voice. He placed his coffee cup on his desk, his arms folding across his chest. "We got nothing we can use to pinpoint this prick down."

Faye leaned forward, her voice carrying the weight of a revelation. "He eats a piece of each victim. This is a detail we've kept under wraps, something the public doesn't know."

Jack's brows furrowed as he considered her words, his arms falling to his sides. "Yeah, but the bite marks look like a bite from a shark with the mouth of a human. How do you even begin to explain the cause of that? How do we begin to make sense of clues and evidence like that?" Jack's hands gestured upward, his frustration evident as he grappled with the enigma they faced.

"We approach it seriously and take it step by step," Faye responded, her voice grounding their conversation even as her thoughts seemed momentarily distant.

Jack raised his hands in mock surrender, his earlier humor now conceding to their weighty situation. "Okay then, let me grab the files," he declared, rounding the corner of his desk and collapsing into his chair.

With anticipation, Jack pulled open the drawer meant to contain the essential case files. His gaze shifted to Faye, a puzzled look etched across his features. "Did you by any chance move those case files?" he inquired, a genuine note of confusion in his voice.

In response, Faye mustered her best 'confused-but-game' expression, a playful retaliation. "Nope, they were definitely placed in that drawer before we left on Friday," she assured.

"They're not here," Jack stated, frustration causing his words to come out sharper than he intended.

He moved on to check the other drawers, searching for the elusive files. The rest of his desk remained undisturbed, offering no hints. Deciding on a course of action, he dialed the Desk Sergeant's number.

"Detective Riddle," came Sergeant Pembroke's voice through the phone.

Jack's tone was terse, reflecting his consternation. "Sergeant Pembroke. Can you come to my office, please?"

The line clicked as it disconnected, and moments later, Mary appeared in the doorway, her presence swift and efficient.

"Mary," Jack began, his tone carrying a hint of concern, "have you come across the case files for these ongoing murder investigations? Or have you seen anyone other than Special Agent Atwood and myself in my office?"

Sergeant Pembroke contemplated for a brief moment before answering, "No, I haven't observed anyone entering or exiting your office while I've been at the desk."

Jack's murmur of dissatisfaction was barely audible, an expression of his growing unease. "Alright, I guess I'll just have to reprint them then. Thanks, Mary," he concluded, his gratitude sincere.

"No problem," Mary responded crisply, pivoting on her heels and disappearing from the doorway,

Jack powered up his computer, determined to retrieve the essential information from the police database. Though he was certain he had accessed the right database, Jack found himself unable to locate any file names that matched the information he sought. After navigating out of the system and then logging back in, Jack eventually managed to locate the digital files he needed. However, upon opening them, a disconcerting emptiness greeted him—none of the fields contained any data, and the images were absent. Each image file displayed nothing but a blank expanse of white.

Jack leaned forward from behind his computer screen, his voice carrying through his office door. "Bob, bring me your hard copies for the psycho murder cases," he called out, urgency tainting his tone.

Bob's affirmative response provided a glimmer of hope, yet Jack's patience dwindled as he awaited the delivery of the requested duplicate hard files. Frustration simmered within him, his expectations bordering on impatience. He couldn't help but wonder why Bob was taking longer than he deemed necessary to retrieve the folders, especially considering Bob's familiarity with his workspace. The air soon filled with the sound of Bob's curses and the violent slam of drawers.

An ominous sensation tightened around Jack's heart, a lump of discomfort lodged in his throat. That familiar sinking feeling took root in the pit of his stomach, a sensation he recognized well—when things went from bad to worse. Reacting swiftly, he left his office, striding to Bob's side and his desk. The leaden weight of unease settled within him as he confronted the reality of missing files.

"I can't find them, Jack. They were in my drawer, but now they're gone," Bob's bewildered voice held a note of defeat.

With Bob left dumbfounded in his wake, Jack quickened his pace to seek out Sergeant Pembroke. Meanwhile, Faye, having donned her shoes, trailed after Jack toward the Desk Sergeant's domain.

"Jack," Faye called out, her voice an attempt to draw his attention.

Jack acknowledged her with a glance, his focus torn between her and the pressing situation at hand.

Faye presented her rental car keys, outlining her plan. "I'll head back to my hotel room to retrieve my copies of the files," she offered as a solution.

"Alright," Jack replied, his attention briefly captured by her before she changed course, striding towards the motor pool exit. The urgency in her movements mirrored the gravity of the circumstances, leaving Jack to ponder the intensifying enigma surrounding their investigation.

Jack located Mary at her desk and appealed to her for help in gaining access to the digital records. Unfortunately, Mary encountered the same issue that Jack had faced. Together, they attempted access from several other computers within the police station that were linked to the database, only to encounter the same results.

Jack took responsibility for the situation and made his way to inform the police chief about the distressing turn of events—a loss of physical records and the corruption of digital files. He found himself hoping that Faye would swiftly return with her own copies of the files, stored in her hotel room. As her copies weren't in the police station, he wished that she wouldn't encounter the same challenges in locating them that he was experiencing.

While Jack diligently scoured the police station's resources, Faye had departed to retrieve her files from her hotel room. By the time Jack had completed his investigation and reported the situation to the chief, Faye had already returned to the station. Spotting Jack, she hurried over with a disappointed expression etched upon her face. Jack shared Faye's bafflement and concern.

"No joy. Nothing else was missing except the files. Someone broke into my hotel room and took them," she recounted, her voice tinged with despondency. The intrusion into her personal space seemed to weigh heavily on her mind.

Perplexed and frustrated by the escalating situation, Jack exclaimed, "What the hell is going on here? They broke into your hotel room and took the files?"

Faye's expression remained troubled as she replied, "There were no signs of forced entry. However they did it, it wasn't by physically breaking down the door. That only leaves hotel staff or the possibility of an electronic hack of the digital lock on the door."

Jack positioned himself in a way that unintentionally made him a pretty effective barrier, causing officers to adjust their paths around other desks. Deep in thought, he scratched his chin, his expression contemplative as he pondered their current predicament. Eventually, an idea emerged, and Jack suggested they visit the forensics lab to determine whether a digital or physical copy of the files existed there. The forensics lab operated on a separate server from the police database, raising Jack's hopes for more success in that avenue.

Setting off for the forensics lab, Jack and Faye had covered about half the distance when Jack's phone suddenly began to ring. With a quick glance, he noted his sister's caller identification on the screen, prompting him to answer on the third ring.

"Hey. I was just coming to see you," Jack greeted, his voice carrying his surprise at the unexpected call.

Elizabeth's voice came through the receiver, her response revealing a twist in their conversation. "If you're heading to the forensics lab to see me, you'd be wasting your time. I'm not there right now, I'm at home."

Curiosity piqued, Jack inquired, "Why are you at home?" His confusion etched into his furrowed brows.

Elizabeth's response held a note of secrecy. Unwilling to delve into the details over the phone, Elizabeth's voice took on a conspiratorial tone. "Don't ask. I don't want to talk about it over the phone. How soon could you get here?"

The question prompted Jack to instinctively glance at his wrist as if to check the time, though he realized he wasn't wearing a watch. Suspicion gnawed at him, driven by the secretive undertones of Elizabeth's request.

"It would take me about fifteen minutes to half an hour, depending on how bad the traffic is between here and there. It's about lunchtime now, so the roads are likely to be packed," Jack estimated.

"Okay, then. I'll see you in about half an hour," said Elizabeth. However, she hadn't completed her thought and interjected, "Oh, Jack... I need you to bring along Special Agent Atwood with you as well."

Concerned, Jack responded, "We've got an issue here, and I don't know if I can solve it and be there in half an hour."

Elizabeth's response was firm and resolute. "Jack, get in your damn vehicle and get your ass here. It's important, and you'll thank me for it later."

Jack, despite his frustration, couldn't help but shake his head, though Elizabeth was unaware of the gesture over the phone call. He sighed, acknowledging the loss of a perfectly good gesture. It was an act he had displayed solely to Faye, yet now it was inadvertently wasted.

"I just wasted a good gesture on you," Jack admitted with a hint of resignation.

"You can shake your head at me when you get here," Elizabeth responded, perceptive enough to discern what he had done. "Now, hurry up and get here."

"Alright, I'll see you soon," Jack replied. Before ending the call, he added, "With Agent Atwood."

Jack and Faye swiftly departed from the police station, their destination set for Jack's sister's house. However, a gnawing sense of incompleteness lingered within Jack. There were tasks left unresolved, and he keenly felt their weight. He needed to unearth the fate of the vanished physical files, unravel the mystery behind the blank digital records, and identify the culprit who had infiltrated Faye's hotel room to seize her copies of the case files. Of all these tasks, the last one gnawed at him the most. The realization that someone was privy to the existence of those files in Faye's room was deeply disconcerting to Jack.

Compounding his concerns was the unsettling reality that someone had infiltrated Faye's personal space without her awareness. Just that very morning, they had stood within those four walls, and now, in their absence, the files had vanished. The mere thought of an intruder in her room sent a chill down Jack's spine. The breach of her privacy ignited his worry for Faye's safety in this unsettling situation.

Jack did not manage to navigate through the afternoon traffic in less than thirty minutes, a feat he hadn't expected. He had initially thought the journey to his sister's house would be a quick one, but reality proved otherwise. The drive ended up taking nearly forty five to fifty minutes due to an unexpected surge in holiday shopping traffic, something he had failed to anticipate. His frustration grew as he realized his oversight; he mentally chided himself for not accounting for the seasonal congestion. However, he was well aware of the rules and refrained from considering the illegal option of using his emergency lights and siren to bypass the traffic.

The subdued mood that had settled over Jack at the police station still lingered as he finally pulled up to his sister's residence. The extended time on the road had only added to his irritability, but he was determined not to let it affect his interaction with his sister. He recognized that it wouldn't be fair to take out his frustrations on her; after all, he cared deeply about her well-being. Suppressing his annoyance, he resolved to keep a composed demeanor.

Upon arrival, his sister warmly greeted them at the door, her presence a welcome contrast to the day's exasperating events. Aware of Jack's unease, she led them inside

Seated comfortably on barstools in Elizabeth Riddle's kitchen, Jack and Faye engaged in a quiet coffee break. The clinks of ceramic mugs meeting the wooden countertop created a soothing rhythm in the air. Both cups held steaming coffee—one as bold and dark as jet-black diesel fuel, the other a concoction of sweetened, creamy indulgence. This kitchen was a place of solace for Jack, his second-favorite spot for coffee after the donut shop that held the top spot in his preferences.

As he sipped his coffee, Jack puzzled over an enigma that had been gnawing at him. Despite using the same brewing techniques and creamer at home, Elizabeth's coffee always seemed to possess an ineffable quality that made it taste better. He had come to a conclusion: it wasn't just about the coffee itself but the company he shared it with that elevated the experience.

Interrupting his musings, Jack inquired, "What's the reason behind summoning us here, Izzy? There was a minor crisis back at the police station that demanded my attention."

With a tinge of weariness coloring her words, Elizabeth leaned against the counter, her expression marked by a sigh of exasperation. She brushed a hand through her hair before responding, "I'm sure you've noticed it by now, Jack. All the information pertaining to your ongoing murder cases has mysteriously vanished from the servers." Her frustration was evident.

Jack leaned back on his stool, a mixture of concern and confusion on his face. "Yeah, I noticed that," Jack affirmed with a furrowed brow, a hint of frustration tugging at his tone. "The data is still there, but it's like the heart of the files has been hollowed out. The information is missing. What I can't wrap my head around is how this is even possible." Leaning forward, he rested his elbows on the countertop, his coffee momentarily forgotten as he delved into the perplexing situation.

His brow furrowing deeper, Jack continued, "And it's not just the digital information. Someone actually breached our physical security as well. They entered my office and made off with the hard copies, including Detective Skipple's. It's like they had inside knowledge of our every move." The unease in his voice was palpable as he reflected on the audacity of the breach.

Faye, her expression mirroring the shared concern, interjected, "It's even more unsettling, Elizabeth. Whoever is behind this knew about the files I had in my hotel room too. They managed to infiltrate my space and snatch those hard copies as well." She shook her head in disbelief, her eyes reflecting a mix of astonishment and indignation.

Elizabeth's expression froze, a mixture of shock and concern evident in her widened eyes. Her attempt to compose herself resulted in a hesitant response, her voice a blend of uncertainty and empathy. "I'm afraid I can't provide a solution for the missing hardcopies or shed light on how that happened," she admitted, her sympathy for their predicament palpable. "However, when it comes to the digital files, I do have some insight to offer."

Jack leaned in, his curiosity undiminished by the unfolding complexities. "Alright," he responded, his tone a blend of anticipation and readiness. "Tell us what you've discovered."

Running her fingers through her hair in a gesture of thoughtfulness, Elizabeth began to unravel the digital mystery. "It appears that someone infiltrated the server and introduced a malicious program known as the 'Zero Sum' virus," she explained. A touch of pride tinged her voice as she continued, "Oddly enough, I stumbled upon it almost by accident. Data was disappearing without explanation, and I repeatedly re-uploaded it, only to watch it vanish once again. It was my daughter, Brooke, who helped uncover the virus. Having a computer-savvy daughter turned out to be a blessing in disguise."

A look of bewilderment enveloped Jack's features, his confusion palpable. His jaw hung slack, giving him an air of comical incredulity as if he were wearing a metaphorical sign that read, 'Hello, my name is stupid.'

He voiced his perplexity, seeking clarity, "So, what exactly is a 'Zero Sum' virus, and how does it relate to the disappearance of the digital case files?"

The question hung in the air, underscoring the gravity of their predicament and the urgency of finding answers. Elizabeth's explanation carried a sense of helplessness, her words hinting at the complexity beyond her reach.

"I'm afraid I can't provide a clear explanation. Brooke would be the one to untangle it for you," she conceded, her voice tinged with resignation.

She took a moment to gather herself. Drawing a deep breath, she paused briefly and then called out to her daughter, invoking a familiar ritual. The sudden volume of the call caught Faye slightly off guard, though Jack's familiar reaction showed that he was accustomed to these impromptu summonings.

From the back of the house, Brooke breezed into the kitchen with an air of vibrant enthusiasm. Her arrival was marked by an audible bounce in her step, her spirited demeanor impossible to miss. The interplay between Jack and the female agent accompanying him had not escaped Brooke's observant eyes. She relished their dance—it was a spectacle she couldn't resist watching from her metaphorical front-row seat. She noted with amusement that her mother was equally tuned in to the unspoken exchange.

"Mum, you called?" Brooke chimed in with a cheerful lilt to her voice. She effortlessly settled beside her mother, a casual arm looping around Elizabeth's shoulders in a display of camaraderie. Her gaze then shifted to Faye, a friendly smile brightening her features before extending the same warmth to her uncle Jack.

Elizabeth seemed to absorb a portion of her daughter's boundless energy, allowing it to spill over onto her own demeanor. Her face lit up with a radiant smile directed at Brooke, a clear testament to the love shared between a mother and her child. The bond between them was tangible, a connection forged through countless moments like these. Jack recognized the affectionate exchange, knowing firsthand the feeling of being uplifted by the presence of family. It was a shared dynamic, an unspoken familiarity that existed in their midst.

Turning her attention to Brooke, Elizabeth requested an explanation, seeking her daughter's technical insight. "Why don't you explain to your uncle what that Zero virus sum thingy is that you found"

Brooke's response was immediate, her explanation delivered in a breezy, confident manner. "Sure thing, Mom. It's essentially a root command that embeds itself deep within your drive's software. This command is programmed to identify specific keywords, phrases, and numerical sequences within designated file string identifiers. Once detected, it triggers a rewrite of the file, resulting in a 'zero sum' balance of data. And just for the record, Mom, it's called a 'Zero Sum' virus, not the 'thingy' you called it," Brooke corrected with a playful twinkle in her eyes. Her technobabble was a jumble of terms that sailed over the heads of everyone in the room, including the seasoned law enforcement agents. Yet, her confidence made even the most intricate of explanations seem like it should have been easy to understand.

Jack regarded Brooke with a perplexed expression, his eyes locked onto her as if she were reciting a cryptic incantation. To him, her words formed a conundrum in an unfamiliar language. The English words were recognizable, yet the arrangement defied his brain's attempts to unravel their meaning. The result was a verbal jumble that remained stubbornly resistant to comprehension. Brooke's linguistic proficiency was like a foreign tongue, and as long as those words remained strung together in that specific order, Jack's understanding seemed an unattainable goal.

Faye's gaze remained fixed on Brooke, her stare an amalgamation of disbelief and confusion. To her, it was as if Brooke had sprouted an improbable arm from the center of her forehead—an occurrence that would have, somehow, made more sense than the explanation she had just received. The technical intricacies had woven a thick blanket of bewilderment in Faye's mind, necessitating a comprehensive unpacking of the explanation itself.

Amid this exchange, Elizabeth's smile was one of affectionate understanding. Her role as a mediator between tech-savvy Brooke and the rest of the room was a familiar one. She addressed her daughter with a touch of gentle guidance, aware of the need to simplify.

"Sweetheart, remember to use small words for us non-geeks," she advised with a playful glint in her eyes.

Jack's astonishment shifted from Brooke to his sister, his eyebrows rising in disbelief. He voiced the question that mirrored his thoughts, incredulous that anyone had grasped the intricacies Brooke had detailed.

"You understood that?" he asked, his tone a mix of surprise and admiration.

Brooke glanced at her mother, a perplexed expression creasing her brow. She had done her best to simplify her explanation, believing she had chosen the most straightforward terms available to describe the situation with the digital files. As she shifted her gaze toward Jack and Faye, the looks on their faces mirrored her confusion. It became evident to her in that moment that her explanation had soared well above their comprehension, leaving them adrift in a sea of technical jargon that made no sense to them whatsoever.

Clearing her throat, Brooke made another attempt to convey the essence of her earlier explanation. "Essentially, it's like a piece of the computer's brain, and the person who made this 'Zero Sum' thing can program it to find specific stuff and make it disappear," she simplified, hopeful that her new explanation would bridge the gap.

Jack responded with a genuine smile, the kind that came from both affection and relief. "Thanks for being kind enough to break it down into plain English. But here's the thing—can't you just put the data back on the system?"

Elizabeth chimed in, her tone carrying a note of resignation. "I actually tried that already, Jack," she confessed, her words a testament to her efforts and the complexity of the issue they were facing.

Brooke responded to her uncle's query with a subtle shake of her head, a gesture laced with a hint of incredulity. It was as if she were silently conveying, 'this is something so simple that even a child would understand and you cannot get it; are you a neanderthal?' Her exasperation, though unspoken, underscored her attempt to bring clarity.

"Uncle Jackie, it's not as simple as that," Brooke retorted, her tone carrying a touch of patient explanation. Her words flowed with the confidence of someone well-versed in the intricacies of technology. "Once these triggers are activated, they remain in effect for the altered data. Changing filenames won't help because the value of the data remains constant. This mechanism keeps running until the person who initiated it decides to deactivate it. And it's persistent—whether you rename the file or not. Not only that, if the system gets networked, then the command jumps to another system. It will go from computer to computer, continuing its data erasure spree."

Jack's frustration reached its zenith. In a gesture of exasperation, he threw his hands into the air, his voice laced with irritation. "Seriously, is there even a way to put a stop to this?"

Brooke's response was swift, carrying an air of nonchalance that bordered on a revelation. "Ah, now this is where it gets simpler," she chimed, her tone carrying the weight of an 'ah-ha' moment. "To tackle it, you've got to go back in time a bit—revert to an analog approach. Hard copies!" A triumphant grin tugged at the corners of her lips, an infectious self-satisfaction gleaming in her eyes.

Jack's frustration simmered beneath his voice as he began to speak, his patience wearing thin due to the ongoing predicament. "So, what's our plan now?" he inquired, his tone tinged with irritation. "All the hard copies at the police station have been taken. Where does that leave us?" His question was a plea for direction, a way to navigate the quagmire of challenges they were facing.

"Fortunately, for us, my computer is set up to automatically back up to a server Brooke established for her school work," Elizabeth began, her eyes briefly meeting Jack's as she explained the arrangement. She gave a small nod of gratitude in Brooke's direction before continuing. "She generously allows me to utilize some of that space, so I make regular data backups every few days."

Jack leaned back on the stool, his expression contemplative of the possibilities he was seeing.

"Once Brooke identified the issue," Elizabeth continued, "she took her server offline as a precaution. The data remains secure on her server, provided it remains disconnected from the network."

Faye chimed in with an affirming smile, her support for Elizabeth's daughter evident in her eyes. "It's clever, really. A sort of digital quarantine."

Elizabeth's response carried a note of agreement as she appreciated Faye's assessment. "Exactly. And she's also ensuring data transfers occur using an isolated, offline computer."

Jack's eyebrows lifted in acknowledgment. He admired the foresight and caution they were exercising. "So, Brooke had an old computer just sitting around?"

Elizabeth chuckled softly, a fond look exchanged with Faye. "She's always had a knack for saving things. Turns out, her old computer's newfound purpose is quite the lifesaver. It hadn't been online for a significant period, so it's devoid of the virus. Making it the ideal tool for printing multiple copies."

"Great, thanks, Izzy. That solves one problem, but it still leaves us with two other problems. Who could steal all of the hard copies from the police station and also break into Faye's hotel room and steal the hard copies from there as well?" Jack pondered aloud, his hand now rubbing his chin as his mind worked through the puzzle.

Faye, ever attentive and precise, leaned in and tapped Jack gently on the shoulder to interject. "I hate to correct you, Jack. We actually have three problems that need solving."

Jack turned slightly, raising an eyebrow at her. "What did I miss?"

A knowing smile graced Faye's lips as she clarified, "You forgot about the virus. The one responsible for deleting all of the information from the system. I think all of these events might be interconnected, possibly linked to our killer."

"That's just great," Jack retorted, frustration evident as he threw his hands up in the air. "We have a computer geek, sociopathic, homicidal, cannibal on the loose."

Faye leaned back slightly, her response tinged with a touch of humor. "That's a lot of adjectives, Jack."

A smirk tugged at Jack's lips. "I'd like to throw some adjectives and adverbs together with a few choice nouns to talk about how I'm feeling right now about everything that's been happening."

Faye's eyes danced with suppressed laughter, her voice holding a lightness as she redirected the conversation. "At least we got the files again," she said, managing to contain her amusement.

"Okay," Jack responded simply, his mood lightening a bit as he acknowledged Faye's point.

He waited until Elizabeth returned with a refilled coffee cup, using the moment to ensure her attention. Once she had placed the cup before him, Jack resumed speaking.

"So, I can understand us being able to use the photographs and notes, but what about the lab results that came back from the DNA and the bite marks? The DNA showed all kinds of stuff, and the lab tech said the sample had to be contaminated."

"That's just it, Jack," Elizabeth's voice broke the silence, her words carrying a sense of intrigue that instantly piqued Jack's curiosity. As the head of the laboratory, her insight held potential knowledge he might not possess. "The samples weren't compromised in any way. I meticulously reviewed the results from various samples," Elizabeth continued, delving into the heart of the matter. "Each victim's DNA sequences were uniform with a particular marker. Oddly enough, all the murdered individuals shared the same peculiar DNA." Elizabeth's hand brushed through her hair slowly. "And whatever caused those bites left behind DNA that's a mix of canine, reptilian, and human. There's no room for doubt. Even that DNA has the same marker as the victims."

Jack's response was emphatic, laced with disbelief. The direction the conversation was taking seemed to traverse into the realm of science fiction, leading him to question the plausibility of such a scenario.

In the midst of this exchange, Faye's presence served as a subtle reminder. Her words carried a gentle assurance, her smile radiating a sense of understanding. "Improbable, as I mentioned, not impossible," Faye's response delicately underscored the scientific possibilities being discussed.

Jack's gaze drifted over to where Faye's hand lay, her touch light against his own. A flicker of contemplation crossed his mind, wondering if there might be more significance to this seemingly trivial connection. Could her touch be imbued with meaning beyond mere attention-seeking? The uncertainty of his interpretation left him torn between a somber undertone and a more neutral assessment. Regardless of the depth he attributed to the touch, he found solace in it, relishing the simple comfort it brought.

Gradually, Jack refocused his attention on his sister, a thoughtful glint in his eyes. "So, I'm meant to be on the lookout for a scaly green guy with dog ears and a tail who's in dire need of a dental surgeon?" he quipped, his tone carrying a note of wry humor.

Elizabeth's response was swift, her voice holding both authority and knowledge. "No, Jack. This individual won't stand out visually. His distinctiveness lies beneath the surface, on a genetic level. He'll blend in seamlessly, his appearance ordinary. However, his genetic makeup will set him apart. Enhanced healing, heightened senses—smell, hearing, vision—and a muscle density that grants him five to ten times the strength of an average man. His uniqueness is his secret; unless he speaks, you could be right next to him without knowing," Elizabeth explained, her words revealing her expertise in the subject matter.

Jack's mind flickered with a memory, the fragments of Elizabeth's recent conversations converging in his thoughts. He recollected observing a man clad in a beige jacket walking away from him and Faye, fading into the crowd. Just as he was on the verge of voicing his recollection, an unexpected interruption jolted his focus. Something—a presence he wasn't anticipating—brushed against his shin, accompanied by a soft meow that reverberated through the air. The burgeoning memory dissipated as Jack's muscles tensed involuntarily. He remained immobile, aware that any sudden movement might provoke the feline's defensive instincts, leading to an unwanted swipe of its razor-sharp claws.

"What in the hell is that demon cat doing here?" Jack exclaimed, his voice a mixture of surprise and incredulity.

Faye's attention was captured by the sound of a soft purring. Swiftly turning on her stool, her eyes fell upon the entrance of the cat in question. Its imposing size didn't deter her; she was already on her feet, cradling the large feline in her arms with unexpected speed. The suddenness of her action left no room for anyone to caution her about potential danger. The cat, notorious for its challenging disposition, was an exception when it came to Brooke's company. Others, including Jack and Elizabeth, had learned to approach with caution.

Amid the collective amazement, all three pairs of eyes—Jack's, Elizabeth's, and Brooke's—were fixed upon the scene unfolding before them. The cat, playfully dubbed the 'cat from hell', comically flopped over backward in its attempt to revel in Faye's petting. The scene was a testament to the peculiar bond that Brooke shared with the feline, one that no one else dared to test by attempting to rub the cat's belly. After a moment of mutual admiration, Faye gently placed the cat on the floor, an invitation for it to continue basking in the attention.

As the enigmatic scene played out, Jack's voice broke the stunned silence, his words reflecting his bewilderment. "What in the —"

"Hell..." Elizabeth finished for him, her voice trailing off in amazement.

Brooke, with a soft chuckle, joined the exchange. "Aww. He's just showing his love for you," she commented, her affection for both Faye and the quirky cat evident in her words.

However, Brooke's attempt to recreate the same interaction met with a swift escape as the cat sprang to its feet and darted away. The feline raced toward the back of the house, its final destination clear to Brooke. She was certain that it was headed for her room, likely to curl up on her bed and snooze the day away.

Observing Faye's slightly puzzled expression, the dynamic between the group shifted.

Faye looked between Jack and Elizabeth, fueled by perplexion at their reactions.

"Did I miss something?" Faye's query hinted at the amusing contrast between her lack of awareness and the cat's mysterious antics.

Elizabeth shook her head in response, her expression holding a touch of amusement as she exchanged a knowing glance with her daughter. "No, dear, you didn't miss anything," she assured Faye, the corner of her lips quirking into a faint smile.

Jack climbed down off the barstool. He walked off into the living room. His exit from the kitchen seemed to signal the end of the curious feline episode.

Unbeknownst to Faye, Jack's muttering carried through the space, a mix of exasperation and jest escaping his lips as he walked away.

"Of course, you didn't miss anything," he said, his voice laced with both fondness and light frustration. The muttered words gave way to more diatribe. "Damn evil cat would fall in love with her too."

9

Donovan Pike found himself once again in the presence of Dr. Brundle. However, this encounter differed from their previous ones solely in terms of location. This time, Dr. Brundle rendezvoused with Donovan in the expansive board room of the installation. Casually sipping on a fruity alcoholic beverage, Dr. Brundle launched into an explanation about the sex determination of hens and the fate of male chicks.

"...so, you insert a probe into the chick's orifice. If it doesn't reach the designated marker on the probe, it's a male chicken. You then toss the male chick into the auger on the side of the table. In under thirty seconds, that baby chick turns into a paste that's sold to dog food companies," Dr. Brundle explained, engrossed in his macabre topic.

Donovan, however, had little interest in this particular discourse on hen sex determination. Despite his disinterest, he refrained from interrupting the doctor. Donovan believed it was wiser to allow the mad doctor to share his thoughts freely. Much of what Dr. Brundle discussed outside his lab was either irrelevant to the current circumstances, like the hen lecture, or simply irrational rambling. Yet, Donovan recognized that amidst the erratic speech, there occasionally emerged a valuable insight, a nugget of wisdom.

It was precisely such a conversation, five years earlier, that had set them on their current path. Donovan vividly remembered the pivotal moment that initiated it all. With crystal clarity, he recalled Dr. Brundle's comments.

"Viruses, that's a good topic. Viruses aren't cells," Dr. Brundle began, his tone contemplative. "They lack the capacity for self-replication and aren't categorized as 'alive' are they? Well in the technical definition they aren't. Viruses lack the ability to independently replicate their genetic material or synthesize their proteins. They rely on other life forms' cells to perform these functions. They are indeed efficient in eliminating this need in order to survive. Saves energy, saves space. What's truly captivating is that viruses are essentially tiny clusters of nucleic acids and proteins, devoid of cellular structure, yet they possess the potential for immense devastation. They're like Machines. Simple machines. Machines can be programmed. I have the power to manipulate them at my will. I can program viruses. I can create designer viruses," he had concluded with an air of confidence.

In response, Donovan had posed a seemingly innocuous question, nothing so much to do with the topic that Dr. Brundle was discussing. "Can we create designer soldiers?"

At the time, Donovan hadn't anticipated any substantial outcome from that question. He had regarded the conversation as one of Dr. Brundle's nonsensical ramblings. However, after a brief pause, Dr. Brundle had surprised him.

"Certainly. I can craft a series of genetically engineered soldiers for you in no time, from a genetic standpoint," said Dr. Brundle.

Now, five years later, Donovan Pike stood on the threshold of his ambition—an army of genetically manufactured soldiers. The means used to achieve this end were ethically and morally questionable, but they were undeniably accomplished.

Returning from his contemplation of the past, Donovan redirected his attention to the present and the scientist in the room.

"Dr. Brundle," he began, adjusting his glasses onto the bridge of his nose, "I want to extend my congratulations and gratitude for your exceptional work on that computer virus. It performed admirably."

"Thank you, Mr. Pike. It was a matter of simplicity, really. Identifying the correct insertion point in the root destination command of the operating system proved to be crucial," Dr. Brundle began to explain.

"Dr. Brundle," Donovan interjected, his tone firm but polite, "while I have no doubt that your explanation of the virus's construction would be both educational and intriguing, it would also be somewhat redundant at this juncture. Besides, we don't want to risk being late for our imminent meeting with the others."

The doctor's lips parted momentarily, but they soon sealed shut in a reflexive, mechanical manner. He had been on the brink of objection, yet his own internal assessment left him lacking any significant retort. Opting for silence seemed a wiser choice in Dr. Brundle's estimation, and this very decision appeared satisfactory to Donovan.

Before the forthcoming meeting, Donovan had an obligation to fulfill—a call to provide an update on the progress thus far. Lifting the phone receiver, Donovan dialed the necessary numbers with precision. The click of connection resonated in his ear, although he had no need to confirm the presence of anyone on the line. The call's successful connection was itself an assurance that the right person had responded.

"Sir, I'm on the verge of commencing the meeting. Additionally, the final detail has been addressed, and it concluded this morning at his residence. Following the meeting, I will reach out to you with the outcomes," Donovan relayed purposefully into the phone.

The line on the other end of the call faded into silence, signifying a disconnection. Donovan carefully returned the phone receiver to its cradle. A soft beep from the desk diverted his attention towards the virtual computer terminal. Donovan's fingers danced over select keys on the floating digital interface before him, prompting a holographic display to materialize in his immediate view.

The message relayed that the scheduled meeting with the organization's members was set to commence in approximately ten minutes. Donovan settled into his seat, a portrait of patience, his thoughts dwelling on the ramifications of this upcoming assembly and how its outcomes would inevitably impact his strategic plans for the future.

"Doctor," Donovan's voice carried a hint of command, his intention to draw the mad doctor's focus.

Dr. Brundle was caught in his own mutterings, a manifestation of his maniacal disposition.

"Did you manage to dispatch the packages I requested for the Conferences?" Donovan's query shifted the doctor's demeanor into a more pragmatic mode. The madness that typically dominated Dr. Brundle's eyes was somewhat subdued.

"I've successfully sent four units of the old Delta 66 series. They were the last ones of that model. I had saved them for this specific purpose. All four units have arrived at their designated locations and are prepared for deployment," Dr. Brundle reported methodically.

"Thank you, Dr. Brundle. I'll notify you when it's time to activate each of them. Please ensure they're on standby," Donovan's tone remained casual, his authority implicit.

The doctor acknowledged with a nod as Donovan pressed a key on the hovering control console before him. The far wall of the boardroom, shared by Donovan and Dr. Brundle, illuminated with a holographic display portraying four identical boardrooms, mirroring their design and layout.

After a brief pause, the meeting commenced, and Donovan's attention was drawn to the holographic images before him. His gaze swept methodically across the screen, starting at the upper right quadrant and tracing a clockwise path. The initial grouping identified itself as the Eurasia Conference, followed by the African Conference, Pacific Conference, and lastly, the South American Conference. With the representation of all five Conferences, a global presence was established.

Each of the Conference's had five to six personnel present for the meeting. These individuals were the board members for their

Conference. The global Conference's were responsible for the part of the world in which they were established.

"Welcome, esteemed Shepherds. Shall we inaugurate this assembly?" Donovan's tone adopted a formal cadence.

A chorus of murmurs resonated from the various holographic feeds, infusing the room with an undercurrent of sound. Yet, before any further words could be exchanged, the meeting's rhythm was disrupted.

"Point of order, Mr. Pike," interjected a man with a dark complexion on the screen displaying the African Conference. He was the Prime Speaker for his conference. "Where are the rest of your Conference members? Where is your Prime Speaker?"

This interruption ignited a pause, the air momentarily charged with anticipation as the question hung in the room, urging Donovan to respond.

Donovan's gaze swept around the conference room, a feigned expression of astonishment gracing his features, as if he had only just realized the conspicuous absence of his Conference members. The carefully contrived concern was evident in his demeanor. A brief furrow creased his brow before he shifted his attention back to the holo projections before him.

He responded, his voice carrying a measured tone, "Their absence today is not without reason. I'll provide a thorough explanation of this matter at an appropriate juncture. Rest assured, I will ensure that the discussions we engage in during this meeting find their way to the individuals who require this information."

"This is undoubtedly an unusual circumstance, Mr. Pike, yet hardly one that necessitates further postponement of our proceedings. I implore you to proceed. After all, it was you who convened this meeting," the dark-skinned man articulated with a tone that carried a hint of sternness.

Donovan cleared his throat, his action a prelude to addressing the assembled members. Amidst his words, some participants in the virtual gathering visibly adjusted themselves in their seats, seeking a more comfortable position. Donovan's voice assumed a rhythmic quality, ebbing and flowing with a deliberate cadence and the precise tempo of his discourse. "We Shepherds have guided the fate of the world and these humans for several thousands of years."

In the midst of the audience, a sneer rippled through as the word 'human' was spoken, as if the term were an unsavory morsel hastily expelled in speech—an expression that had to be endured but was far from welcome. It carried a resemblance to acknowledging a bodily function while shying away from discussing it openly in genteel conversation. The collective disdain held for humanity was palpable and didn't go unnoticed. Everyone in the room shared the sentiment. This awareness wasn't lost on Donovan either, and he found himself disheartened by the fact.

The shared sentiment, the unanimous undercurrent of contempt, served as a stark reminder of their alignment, and Donovan would have preferred not to be so keenly reminded of the common sentiment that bound them together.

"With our extended lifespans and heightened intelligence," Donovan's voice remained steady, "we've operated from the shadows, molding the world into its present form. Our approximately 200-year lifespan grants us insight into trends and patterns that elude humans. Manipulating these dynamics to our advantage is well within our grasp.

"We've orchestrated wars to redraw global boundaries, deposed governments when expedient, and forged fresh regimes from the remnants to sway nascent societies. We've woven religions to wield control through faith, and deployed diseases to manage populations and impede their expansion. Our influence extends to technological advancements, driving growth as we deem fit," Donovan concluded succinctly.

A member of the Pacific Conference interjected, seizing the floor from Donovan, her voice firm, "Mr. Pike, what significance do these deeds hold? They've been our practices since our earliest generations, etched into our collective memory."

Echoes of agreement resonated through the assembly, confirming her sentiments. She paused, allowing the quiet murmurs to subside before resuming, "You're not unveiling new revelations. Spare us the preamble and address the true point you're driving at. Don't insult our intelligence by assuming we've forgotten our history and essence." Her tone carried a hint of irritation, supported by voices chiming in to affirm her sentiments.

A hint of mild annoyance traversed Donovan's porcelain countenance. Dealing with these individuals, who, in his estimation, appeared ignorant of the what was coming in the future, was a source of frustration. In his audacity, he was determined to set his own plans into motion, determined to reshape the impending future irrespective of the sentiments of his fellow Shepherds. His conviction set him apart; he alone possessed the insight required for effective action. He was resolved to persist, regardless of the toll it might exact. Donovan resumed speaking, his voice purposeful.

"The crux of the matter is that, regardless of our actions, humans appear undeterred in their trajectory toward self-destruction. Intentionally or inadvertently, they're marching toward an outcome that spells not only their own demise, but also jeopardizes our existence. Personally, I refuse to stand by and witness a bleak conclusion."

The woman from the Pacific Conference, who had previously voiced her opinions, emerged once again as the collective voice of the attendees. "We've been following the same path for generations. What alternative approach are you proposing?"

Donovan didn't hesitate in his response. "I believe it's time to shed our secrecy. We should reveal ourselves to the world, stepping out from the shadows to assume leadership positions. This way, we can instigate change while we still possess the means." His suggestion carried a note of boldness, a divergence from the clandestine strategies they had long adhered to.

Another member of the conference found their voice, this time hailing from the South American Conference. "Mr. Pike, this is nothing short of absurdity. Our species numbers less than twenty thousand across the globe. It's a meager presence scattered sparsely. How then, with so few of us, do you expect us to exert control? Our approach has always been to operate from the shadows."

The question posed was precisely what Donovan had been anticipating. It was the inquiry that unlocked the gate for his departure from the starting point.

"I do have a solution for achieving that," he responded, his tone measured. "I've taken the liberty of dispatching a representative to each of your conferences. If you'd be so kind, I request that you now invite this representative into your conference rooms."

In response to Donovan's reference, each group commenced actions to bring the designated agent into their respective conference room. These agents bore perfect resemblance in every aspect—from their uniforms to their equipment and even their composed demeanor. They stood before the Shepherds, a collective embodiment of cold dispassion. It was a unified tableau stretched across vast distances, settling within diverse environments yet unified by a peculiar similarity.

The dark-skinned representative, serving as the Prime Speaker for the African Conference, voiced his thoughts once more. "They are indistinguishable, to the smallest detail," he noted, his gesture encompassing all four agents regardless of their distinct locations. "This certainly captivates our attention, but how does it align with your audacious scheme? Relying solely on clones won't suffice; you'd never amass enough of them simultaneously to create a substantial impact."

His question revealed a probing skepticism, the sentiment shared among those present. It underscored the challenge of relying solely on cloned soldiers to bring about substantial change.

"That might indeed hold for clones resembling either us or humans, but these soldiers possess strength and swiftness magnified by a factor of ten. The paramount quality is their unwavering loyalty, ensuring they execute orders without hesitation," Sai Donovan explained.

Raising his right hand, Donovan conjured a holographic file suspended above his open palm. A subtle flick of his wrist directed the file toward the wall of monitors. The gesture prompted a command that transmitted the contents of the file to the other Conference rooms. Donovan maintained his composure as he awaited acknowledgments from the members, confirming they had received the file.

"What precisely is the content of the file you've distributed to us?" queried the Prime Speaker of the African Conference, his complexion displaying an array of emotions.

The recipients, including the Prime Speaker, had already accessed the file Donovan had transmitted. Each individual was examining the digital contents at their own pace. The file unveiled information about the clones, coupled with imagery harvested from police records of the recent macabre dismemberment homicides.

"These are our own colleagues... fellow Conference members... What transpired here?" demanded the Prime Speaker, his voice carrying a blend of concern and frustration.

"I had initially contemplated showcasing the unarmed capabilities of these soldiers. However, upon reflection, I'm inclined to believe a live demonstration would be even more enlightening," Donovan addressed the assembly. His gaze shifted to Dr. Brundle, who had been quietly attentive throughout.

"Dr. Brundle," Donovan called, "Select a soldier and instruct them to eliminate all members in the boardroom they occupy. Following that, order the soldier's self-retirement."

As Donovan surveyed the startled faces on the projected screens, he continued, "This demonstration aims to underscore the instantaneous efficacy of orders being transmitted and executed." His words carried an air of calculated intent, designed to illustrate a profound point.

The room erupted into a cacophony of voices, each person clamoring to be heard above the others. Amidst the chaos, Dr. Brundle's actions only fueled the pandemonium, a chaotic symphony orchestrated by Donovan Pike's instructions. Fingers danced across the keyboard, issuing rapid-fire commands that were executed with practiced precision. The orders were sent before the board members could even fully process the situation, their protests drowned out by the whirlwind of events unfolding.

The live feed from the Pacific Conference flickered to life on the screen. In an instant, the scene unfolded in a surreal and almost incomprehensible manner. It was a swift, almost imperceptible sequence of events that played out, as if the fabric of reality had been torn asunder. The brutality of the scene defied any reasonable expectation.

Within seconds, the agent stationed at the Pacific Conference drew his sidearm, and with lethal precision, dispatched the two guards present. Swift and deadly, he closed the distance to the first Shepherd at the conference table, snapping the man's neck with a fluid motion that prevented any defense.

Screams were silenced abruptly, stifled in the throes of terror as lives were extinguished. Crimson blossoms erupted from foreheads, chests, and backs of heads, transforming bodies into gruesome canvases of violence. The act of entering life became an act of departing it, an expulsion of existence.

In the span of a heartbeat, it was over. Lives were extinguished in rapid succession, leaving only the lone agent standing amidst the aftermath. He was a solitary figure amidst the sea of destruction, a testament to unwavering obedience. His mission had been to end lives, and he executed it without hesitation or query. Surveying the grim tableau before him, he turned his gaze to the screen, his weapon drawn once more.

The agent's movements had been a blur, too swift for any to recall the holstering of his weapon or its subsequent withdrawal. His actions were a display of lethal efficiency. Yet again, his weapon found its mark, this time aimed at his own temple. A gunshot echoed, and his head exploded in a horrifying display of violence.

All of this transpired within the span of three to five minutes, a fleeting window that could scarcely accommodate half a dozen breaths. Lives were extinguished with wanton disregard, an indiscriminate slaughter that left behind a senseless void. The bloodshed had been swift, the loss immeasurable, and the purpose behind it all remained obscured in the wake of unnecessary devastation.

A collective sigh of relief swept through the survivors of the demonstration as they finally exhaled the breath they had been holding in uncertainty. Mixed emotions of relief and understanding dawned upon them, realizing they could now draw subsequent breaths without hesitation. It was as if a weight had been lifted, allowing them to respire freely, at their own pace.

Silence enveloped the scene. Immobility reigned. Each person was cautious, guided by an unspoken force that inhibited any impulsive action. They found themselves suspended in a moment of uncertainty, uncertain about how to navigate the aftermath of the event they had just experienced. The unfamiliarity of this situation paralyzed them, leaving them unsure of even the simplest steps to take.

In this atmosphere of confusion, Dr. Brundle's claps echoed in the background, accompanied by his lighthearted muttering. Rather than offering reassurance, his actions only deepened the unsettling nature of the situation.

"That went well. It went rather well," Dr. Brundle began his rant, his thoughts flowing unchecked. "I didn't like that bit at the end with looking about. He should be certain of every kill. That can be fixed in the next batch. Eye and hand coordination and dexterity improvement. I did like the execution of the retirement command though."

Amidst his monologue, Dr. Brundle's words were abruptly interrupted by Donovan. "Doctor," Donovan called out quietly, his voice cutting through the doctor's ramblings.

Donovan's intention was to redirect the doctor's attention, putting an end to his purposeless and unnecessary tangent. The doctor blinked, his focus shifting to Donovan. Once Donovan was confident, beyond any doubt, that the doctor was back in the present moment—as sane as could be reasonably expected of him—he shifted his gaze back to the remaining members of the Conference.

Donovan's dedication to his cause did not resonate deeply among his fellow Shepherds, or at least, that was his assumption. He was determined to ensure that they comprehended the gravity of the situation at hand. From Donovan's perspective, it was crucial for the Shepherds to assume a supporting role in relation to humanity.

The Shepherds constituted a rare and limited presence in the world. Their species didn't reproduce in great numbers; gestation took two to three years for their kind and necessitated the attention of their specialized medical staff. Moreover, interbreeding with humans was a complex endeavor that had so far failed in every attempt. The human population had surged far ahead of the Shepherds', growing exponentially.

Given these circumstances, Donovan believed the Shepherds had limited options. Their influence over the population paled in comparison to that of humans. Short of devising a pathogen to induce partial human sterility, there seemed little else the Shepherds could do to address this discrepancy.

Donovan's motivations extended beyond a simple desire for Shepherds to rule and control the world. He held a firm conviction that the Shepherds needed to take decisive action to disrupt the existing order; otherwise, the human race faced the bleak prospect of extinction. Unfortunately, many Shepherds either displayed indifference to this impending threat or were driven by a hunger for power. Donovan was resolute in his determination to ensure that his fellow Shepherds understood the urgency of his cause. To underscore his commitment, he contemplated orchestrating another demonstration, hoping that this time they would grasp the gravity of the situation.

His resolve was unwavering. While Donovan was prepared to take extreme measures, even eliminating all members of the other Conferences if required, he preferred to avoid such a drastic course—at least for the time being. He remained optimistic that such extreme actions wouldn't be necessary. He recognized that those who displayed a willingness to contribute still held value, and he intended to make use of their potential.

"As you've all just witnessed and been privy to, these soldiers exhibit remarkable efficiency in close quarters," Donovan's tone was devoid of excitement, akin to discussing the gas mileage of a new car. "They are essentially living weapons, independent of whether they're armed or directly involved in hand-to-hand combat. What's even more noteworthy is their ability to function as weapons without any physical movement whatsoever."

Donovan's gaze once again shifted toward the doctor. The prospect of losing his audience didn't overly concern him—he had their undivided attention, and it had been that way for quite some time. His listeners were captive, their focus entirely fixated, a direct result of the agent's presence within the room. The Shepherds' extended lifespans, a perk of their heritage, held no sway against a bullet's lethal potential. That tiny piece of copper-plated lead could terminate them as effectively as it could anything else.

"Doctor, kindly activate the self-destruct mode for one of the remaining three agents," Donovan's request was calm and deliberate. He believed in ensuring that he effectively conveyed his point. With this additional action, he thought he could persuade the remaining conferences to relinquish control of their territories without additional bloodshed or confusion. It was also because it was part of the plan that two of the remaining Conferences be taken down to alleviate issues of rebellion. Deviation from the plan would not be allowed.

The eccentric doctor appeared positively elated to have been entrusted with carrying out this particular command. His excitement was rooted in his confidence in the technology's functionality. After all, he was the mastermind behind its conception, design, and construction. The prospect of finally conducting a real-world test of the capability exhilarated him. Dr. Brundle pivoted back to his keyboard and swiftly initiated the command. Simultaneously, the dark-skinned Prime Speaker from the South African Conference erupted into a piercing scream.

"That—" the Prime Speaker's words were abruptly cut off.

A momentary flash played across the screen displaying the Eurasia Conference before the feed was abruptly severed at its source. The Prime Speaker managed to finish his sentence slowly, accompanied by a discernible sigh of relief, "...won't be... necessary."

The relief was palpable in his demeanor, clearly visible in the sigh he released—his Conference had evidently been spared. His dread was reserved for the tall, bespectacled figure with an angular countenance. It was evident that the remaining Shepherds within the Conferences shared this fear.

"Have I finally captured your undivided attention, ladies and gentlemen?" Donovan inquired somberly.

Silence ensued, not a single voice daring to break it.

"I appreciate your presence today. Rest assured that when I require your assistance, I will be in touch," Donovan's words concluded the meeting with a sense of finality.

Donovan's left hand executed the requisite gesture, terminating the video conference communication. One by one, the holographic images dissolved, leaving Donovan alone in the conference room. His gaze remained fixed on the wall, lost in thought. Stretching his arm, he picked up the telephone handset and deftly pressed the necessary keys to establish a call with the individual he needed to converse with.

"Sir, were you able to observe the conference?" Donovan inquired, his voice carrying a note of anticipation as he waited for a response at the other end of the line. "Sir, I believe that we have demonstrated our resolve already," said Donovan before he paused and waited for the party on the other end of the phone."Yes, sir. I'll make that happen," Donovan responded, acknowledging the reply. A decision had been made and it was up to him to see through its execution.

After a brief pause, Donovan gently returned the handset to its cradle. "Doctor," Donovan addressed with another momentary pause, his voice devoid of fervor. "Proceed to activate the self-destruct sequence for the remaining agents," he instructed. Donovan's tone remained resolute as he walked away from the room. *I tried,* he thought to himself.

10

Faye could have easily returned to her hotel room, but an opportunity had presented itself—a pretext to both extend her time with Jack and deepen their connection. She confided in Jack, revealing her reluctance to go back to her room due to the recent break-in. The incident had led to the disappearance of her hard copies of their investigations. There was also the loss from several other locations, leaving them both perplexed and suspicious.

United by a growing conviction, both Jack and Faye sensed that the string of murders they were investigating held an air of extraordinary mystery. With new hard copies in their possession, they recognized the chance to dive into the files once more, dissecting every detail. This time, however, the setting was different—they decided to convene at Jack's place instead of the confines of the office.

As the conversation unfolded, Jack proposed the idea of swinging by the hotel room to conduct a thorough search for any potential clues. Faye, however, managed to sway his enthusiasm, expressing her belief that it might ultimately lead to a dead end. She assured him that her initial inspection hadn't yielded anything substantial—the confined space of the room hardly provided any opportunity for significant oversights during her quest for evidence.

Gradually, Jack came around to her perspective, though it wasn't purely due to the logic of her argument. There was an unspoken underlying desire—a pull to spend more time with Faye beyond the confines of their investigation. With an unspoken understanding, they reached a consensus. Their plan shifted as they left Jack's sister's house—they decided that heading over to Jack's place would be the course of action to follow.

On their way back to Jack's house, they made a brief stop to grab some food. Faye insisted on fast and easy, which translated well as unhealthy and greasy. Jack couldn't help but marvel at how someone of her stature managed to maintain her figure despite her culinary inclinations. He realized he might need to step up his game during his next gym session, considering how Faye's eating habits contrasted with his own.

Swiftly, they arrived at Jack's place after collecting their food. Once there, they settled into the cozy living room of his modest two-bedroom house.

Years back, Jack had made the purchase as an investment, a gesture toward a future that remained a hazy and elusive concept. The house itself didn't align with his vision of a future home, but he grappled with a pervasive uncertainty about what lay ahead. Driven by the hope of eventually making sense of it all, he navigated his journey without a definitive roadmap.

His niece's resolute urging had played a pivotal role in the house acquisition. Nestled within the city limits, the small ranch-style residence occupied an unheard-of two-acre plot in its neighborhood. Its unique features included a capacious, open-concept basement that he and Brooke had transformed into a lively game room. The backyard boasted a petite swimming pool, a seasonal oasis primarily designated for Brooke's occupancy during the summer break. Currently, the pool lay dormant beneath its cover, partially drained and winterized for the colder months.

The food that they had picked up for dinner had been decided by Faye. She had enlisted Jack to fetch a spread of pizza, meaning a one less than half a dozen small pies, and hot wings. Jack, in his culinary contribution, unearthed a stash of imported German beer from his pantry.

This touch of warmth to their menu was a nod to his penchant for international flavors. As Faye ventured into the realm of sipping room-temperature beer, she was pleasantly surprised by how harmoniously it paired with the meal. Jack, ever the connoisseur, felt compelled to offer her a caveat—not all beers were suited for, nor should be, consumed at room temperature. He pointed out that Bitburger beer, in particular, excelled in its warm rendition.

Amid this culinary adventure, Faye's enjoyment of the meal was evident. She deftly wiped her fingers of their savory residue, ensuring that the files they pored over wouldn't bear the marks of their dinner. "Pass me a napkin," Faye called out, her voice a mix of necessity and amusement.

In response, Jack embarked on a semi-blind mission, his dexterity challenged as he navigated a file in one hand and sought out a napkin with the other. The slice of pizza, precariously wedged between his teeth, seemed to teeter on the brink of abandoning its place. Toppings threatened a gravity-defying escape onto his lap. Despite the complexity of the situation, Jack's determination remained strong, driven by a desire not to become a canvas for pizza artistry.

After a series of careful maneuvers, Jack successfully delivered the napkin to Faye. The triumph was accompanied by a sigh of relief—his pants remained unadorned by pizza toppings, as did the file he held.

"Here you go," Jack stated with a chuckle, extending the napkin to her. The gesture was met with a reciprocal amusement.

Faye reclined on the shared sofa, finding a moment of respite amid the dual activities of delving into the files and partaking in dinner. Close to twenty minutes had elapsed since they had begun this combined endeavor. With each of them having consumed a duo of beers along with a generous portion of the accompanying wings.

While the pizza had been a shared indulgence, it was evident that Faye had managed to claim the lion's share of the substantial pie. Among the six slices that comprised it, Jack had succeeded in persuading only two into his stomach. An empty pizza box stood testament to their collective appetite, and an unvoiced suspicion brewed in Jack's mind—had Faye clandestinely concealed a stash of pizza slices in a pocket he remained oblivious to?

Amid the gentle buzz of satiety and the tenacious pursuit of leads within the case files, Faye emitted a hearty groan. This dual-toned sound emanated from both a belly comfortably full and a mind mildly vexed by the seemingly stalled progress of their investigative efforts. With a flourish that echoed her exasperation, she deposited the folder she held onto the table. A seemingly precarious landing proved more steadfast than expected, as the folder defied the laws of physics by remaining in place rather than skidding off the table's edge.

"Which file are you looking at?" Faye inquired, a calculated question aimed at understanding which avenues of investigation remained unexplored from her side.

"The third one, the lawyer," Jack replied, his tone carrying a mixture of contemplation and frustration. The vivid memory of the lawyer's house, a fortress-like sanctuary, seemed to underscore the challenge they were facing.

Faye's expression mirrored her sense of letdown, a tangible disappointment stemming from the scarcity of progress made thus far. As the documents and clues accumulated, so did the complexity of the puzzle.

"So, at this point, we've established a narrowing timeline. Additionally, all the victims were single and inhabited these peculiar houses," Jack summarized, his voice carrying the burden of their collective puzzlement. His words carried an undertone of contemplation, as if he was turning over each piece of information in search of a hidden pattern.

Faye's gaze remained locked on the documents, her mind navigating the labyrinth of information. Jack's observation echoed her sentiments, their shared thoughts merging in the acknowledgment that, despite their incremental progress, the larger picture continued to elude them.

"Yeah, we've got the 'when' locked in, but the 'who' and 'why' are still elusive," Jack concurred, his tone reflecting a blend of understanding and exasperation. The knowledge of the imminent danger's timing was only significant if the rest of the pattern held steady. Yet, as Jack pondered aloud, the reliability of that assumption hinged on the consistency of the killer's behavior—a variable they had yet to decipher.

Faye's agitation was palpable as she shifted restlessly on the couch. The uncertainty of their investigation gnawed at her, manifesting in her restless movements. Eventually, she settled into a more composed posture, her resolve taking over.

"We can't possibly safeguard the entire city," Faye lamented, her voice tinged with frustration. The limitations of their resources were evident; they lacked the manpower to provide personal protection to every individual. Even if such a feat were achievable, Faye recognized the fundamental truth that their primary objective was apprehending the murderer responsible for the terror that had gripped the city.

She lowered her head, her gaze fixed on the hands clutching her beer, an intimate moment of contemplation. Jack's hand extended, delicately tucking a stray strand of hair behind her ear. The gesture made her look up, and as her eyes met his, a genuine smile graced her lips.

In a tone laced with gentle concern, Jack broached the topic, "Did you want to go back to your room tonight? I could accompany you and help check it out, just to make sure there are no surprises." His words seemed sincere.

Faye's smile, while still present, seemed to carry a tinge of melancholy. Uncertainty clouded her thoughts as she parsed through the possibilities. Was Jack subtly suggesting she leave, forgetting her earlier declaration, or perhaps ensuring she was still comfortable with the idea of staying the night?

Observing the shift in her expression, Jack was puzzled by the undercurrents of disappointment he sensed. He felt a pang of concern, a feeling that he might have unintentionally done or said something that had upset her.

Seeking clarity, he asked the question that had been forming in his mind, "Are you upset with me? Did I do something to bother you?"

"I'm not upset," she responded, her head swaying gently in denial. "I was just kind of hoping you'd ask me to spend the night."

Jack's grin seemed to expand spontaneously, an outward manifestation of his heart's rapid rhythm.

"Would you like to stay here tonight?" he inquired, the words carrying both sincerity and a hint of vulnerability.

The erratic beats of his heart had subsided, replaced by a steadiness that reflected his effort to reconnect with Faye. Although he could have offered the option of the spare bedroom, a sense of intuition told Jack that it wasn't what Faye wanted. In this pivotal moment, as they sat side by side on the sofa, his emotions clarified. The realization that he, too, had no desire for that arrangement resonated within him, a newfound sense of closeness with the woman he had encountered merely a week prior.

Responding to the atmosphere that had shifted, Faye gracefully rose from her seat, her movements embodying a feline fluidity. With an air of ease, she inquired if she could utilize Jack's shower—a proposition he readily agreed to. As she leaned in, seemingly poised to plant a gentle kiss on Jack's forehead, the intention was disrupted abruptly. The distance between her lips and his slightly furrowed brow hung suspended in a fleeting moment.

Jack, his curiosity piqued, met Faye's gaze in an attempt to fathom the unexpected halt. The intensity in her expression was unmissable as her focus remained locked onto the open folder before her.

Seeking to comprehend what had captivated her attention so fervently, Jack followed her line of sight, his own gaze sweeping over the contents of the photograph that held her attention. Despite his scrutiny, he couldn't discern the elusive element that was pulling at her, prompting this profound concentration. A sense of mystery hung in the air—what was it that had ensnared her so?

Her eyes were transfixed, drawn to something subtle yet compelling within the image before her. The file's photographs, a collection she had been poring over for a week, seemed to have unveiled a previously concealed detail that now demanded her full attention.

Concern laced his words, Jack probed gently, "What's on your mind, Faye? Is there something you've noticed?"

With a sudden jolt, Faye returned to the present, internally reproaching herself for the fleeting lapse that had allowed her gaze to linger too long on the photograph. Recognizing the need to smooth over the unintended pause, she embarked on a swift course correction. Redoubling her effort, she leaned in, aiming to carry out the interrupted kiss on Jack's forehead. However, the original spontaneity had been marred by the momentary distraction, and the resulting kiss felt slightly strained, devoid of its initial grace.

Faye was determined to recover from the minor disruption, preserving her lighthearted demeanor as best she could. Her eyes shimmered with a playful glint, and her lips curved into a smile as she withdrew from the scene, making her way toward the back of the house. Humming a light tune, she left the room, the musical notes accompanying her exit.

"It was nothing, really," she confided, her words carrying an air of reassurance.

A sense of unease crept over Jack. His intuition sensed the falseness in her words, as if she were trying to pull the wool over his eyes. The untruth was palpable in her voice, evident in the subtle shift of her gaze, and even apparent in the touch of her lips. A lie held between them, unspoken yet present. Though his instincts urged him to confront her, Jack remained silent, allowing her to retreat. A pang of self-reproach gnawed at him for not challenging her, as he watched her leave, wrestling with his own sense of vulnerability.

The sound of running water from the back of the house caught Jack's attention, marking her path to his ensuite. An awareness dawned—she had ventured into his personal space, his bedroom. The thought provoked a mix of emotions, a blend of curiosity and unease.

Left with the photograph that had held Faye's unwavering focus, Jack felt compelled to retrace her steps. Removing the photo from the file, he studied it intently, a hope kindling within him that he might grasp the insight she had gleaned. Yet, his efforts yielded no revelations. He could feel the absence of something, a puzzle piece eluding him. An unspoken understanding solidified—Faye was harboring an awareness that she wasn't sharing. Jack's certainty on this point was as strong as a dog's instinct to lick its own balls. The realization added another layer to their dynamic—he was keenly aware of the mystery but unable to decipher it.

Setting the photograph aside, Jack chose not to gnaw at the issue like a toothless old dog. He recognized that Faye's withholding of information was a choice he had to respect. There existed no obligation for her to divulge her thoughts or knowledge, regardless of whether she held them or not. Despite this acceptance, a sense of disappointment crept over Jack, casting a shadow on his mood. It seemed that Faye's reticence implied a lack of trust in him, an inability to confide in him.

Jack's assumptions about the state of their relationship were rattled. He had presumed they were beyond this point, a belief founded on the mutual enjoyment of each other's company. A growing connection had been unmistakable, an intangible thread that seemed to weave itself between them. Jack had wanted to cultivate this budding sentiment, to nourish it into something more profound. Yet, confronted by this barrier of trust, his optimism dimmed. The question of whether their connection could mature into full-blown love now loomed large, as they were faced with a hurdle that demanded careful consideration.

The impart of their evolving dynamics was further compounded by the demands of the case they were entangled in. Jack's concerns extended beyond their interpersonal issues, spanning into the labyrinth of the investigation.

With the master bedroom shower occupied by Faye, Jack calculated that his best option was to retrieve his belongings from his own room and make use of the guest bathroom down the hallway. Over the sound of the running water, he caught fragments of Faye's melodious singing—a stark contrast to the tension that had hung in the air earlier. Gathering what he required, Jack left the room, his footsteps carrying him to the nearby bathroom.

Amidst tendrils of steam wafting out of the bathroom, Jack emerged, a damp towel nonchalantly draped over his shoulders. As he turned the hallway corner, he found himself mere inches away from Faye, the unexpected proximity nearly resulting in a collision. In that instant, it became evident that Faye hadn't been idle during his absence; her actions spoke louder than words.

A swift glance revealed her secret—she had explored the contents of his closet. The evidence was unmistakable as she stood before him in yet another of his dress shirts, its sleeves casually rolled up, a sign of functionality over fashion. The shirt hung on her frame, a borrowed intimacy that whispered of defenselessness.

"Hi," Faye uttered shyly, her words emerging once she had regained her composure, having narrowly avoided a collision with Jack's chest. As she stood there, a silent thought echoed in Faye's mind—'Jack is a cheat.' And her reasoning? Well, there he was before her, shirtless. The sight of his expansive chest, resembling the sculpted contours of a Grecian deity hewn from marble, left her momentarily speechless.

Summoning the courage to speak, she continued, "I hope you don't mind. I ventured into your closet and appropriated a shirt. It's just that I hadn't anticipated staying over, and I didn't have anything suitable to wear to bed."

Jack welcomed it with open arms, his heart racing in sync with Faye's presence. Before him stood Faye, a vision with damp hair cascading over her back. Her eyes, like twin beacons of light, held him captive—just as they had when their paths first crossed. The tug of conflicting desires gnawed at him, each vying for his next move. And yet, it was as if some unspoken force guided his hand.

His fingers extended of their own accord, tenderly grazing her cheek before finding refuge in the tangle of her damp locks. He let his touch linger, smoothing her hair along the graceful curve of her spine. The gentle caress seemed to evoke an unexpected response—a soft, almost imperceptible purring, as if her very being responded to his touch.

As if magnetized, Faye's hand found Jack's, coaxing his arm around her waist in a gesture that seemed to bridge the chasm between them. Proximity heightened their connection, Faye's face nestled close to his chest. She drank in the clean scent of him, a fragrance that stirred an intoxicating thrill within her. Encircling him in a warm embrace, her fingers wove behind his neck, a gesture that spoke of both familiarity and a burgeoning yearning.

With a decisive impulse, Faye elevated herself on tiptoe, sealing the distance between them with a lingering kiss. The shirt that draped her frame lifted as her arms rose, revealing a tantalizing expanse of skin. Jack's hands, large and unyielding, traversed her exposed backside, the sensation sparking a dance of sensations that pulsed through her.

Faye's body responded with an involuntary quiver, subtle tremors rippling through her like the aftershocks of a powerful jolt. Each touch from him ignited a current of exhilaration, racing up and down her spine, an electrifying sensation that sparked and arched in an exquisite dance of intimacy. The science of electromagnetism paled in comparison to the sheer physicality of their connection.

While Jack was conscious of not rushing ahead too hastily, he could no longer deny the truth that surged within him. Faye had stealthily captured his heart, a revelation that both thrilled and unsettled him. The implications of this newfound emotion were a territory he hesitated to navigate. Yet, a fierce determination stirred within him, a desire to stake a claim on her heart, to be the one who shielded it from potential heartbreak.

In Jack's world, Faye held two names—she transcended the mere label of Faye to embody beauty and love. A yearning pulsed within him, an urgency to convey that within him resided all she sought to feel needed and cherished, that her every desire for love and reassurance had a haven within his embrace. Amid a world teetering on the precipice of chaos, Faye stood as his anchor, her presence a soothing balm that tamed the tumult within him.

The torrent of emotions swirling within Jack threatened to render his words incoherent. The intensity of his feelings was such that any attempt to articulate them would result in a cascade of disconnected thoughts. Instead, he allowed the charged silence to linger, an unspoken promise of devotion that flowed between them.

Jack's body craved her with a fierce intensity, the primal desire pulsating through his veins. Yet, his heart remained entangled in a web of hurt, tracing back to the sting of her distrust evident in her hesitance to confide in him about the photograph. The internal struggle was palpable, a conflict between the raw yearning and the emotional wounds he couldn't ignore.

Amidst this emotional maelstrom, he arrived at a resolute decision. He recognized the need for a foundation built on mutual trust, an assurance that was non-negotiable before he could navigate their relationship into deeper waters. Though the allure of what lay ahead beckoned like uncharted oceans, he realized that his footing on this shore of longing was already precarious. Jumping into the waters without addressing the underlying issues would only serve to complicate matters, something he was resolute on avoiding.

For Faye, the situation had her adrift in unfamiliar territory. She was swept up in a tempest of emotions, buffeted by the waves of heat and passion that radiated from Jack. The intensity of their connection elevated her to uncharted heights, igniting sensations she had never fathomed before. She imagined herself riding those peaks, the pinnacle of ecstasy within reach.

But like the undulating waves, the valleys followed, a contrast that made the peaks even more exhilarating. In those depths, she was vulnerable to losing herself, submerged in the intoxicating present. Faye acknowledged that if she surrendered to those depths, the world would narrow down to the next heartbeat, the next breath, a relentless cycle of yearning and fulfillment.

After a fleeting moment, Faye detected the gradual cooling of Jack's ardor, the fervor that had surged in him now receding, leaving behind a fading ember. The intensity had diminished, almost extinguished—yet not entirely. Faye's acute awareness picked up on this subtle change, a shift in his demeanor that she couldn't fully fathom. While the reason eluded her, the mere presence of this retreat offered her a foothold, a chance to regain her inner balance.

In response, Faye yielded the lead to Jack, a decision rooted in the understanding that he was the one who had undergone the cooling transition. It was a silent exchange of roles, a recognition of the ebb and flow between them.

Although Faye had anticipated the gradual descent from passion, the reality left her with a twinge of disappointment. The contrast between the intensity they had shared and the current state of affairs was stark, leaving her feeling adrift in unfamiliar waters. It was as though the oars of her metaphorical rowboat had slipped overboard, and she found herself caught in the pull of a relentless tide that kept her stranded far from the comfort of the shore.

As she followed in Jack's wake, a sense of vulnerability gnawed at her, yet her footsteps remained meekly aligned with his. Her fingers were entwined with his, a connection that spoke of intimacy and an unspoken bond. With one hand grasping hers, the other notched around his neck, Jack led the way, the physical touch between them offering a reassuring tether in the midst of emotional uncertainty.

Guiding Faye into his bedroom, Jack led her toward the inviting expanse of the bed. Faye observed as he deftly drew back the covers, creating a cocoon of comfort and warmth. With an unspoken invitation, he nestled into the bed's embrace and extended his hand to her. Faye, drawn by his magnetic presence, allowed herself to be drawn in, settling beside him. There, she lay on her side, her back fitting snugly against his broad, bare chest. A sense of intimacy, unspoken yet deeply felt, enveloped them.

Jack, clad in nothing but pajama bottoms following his shower, exuded a casual vulnerability that resonated with Faye. While she sensed that their connection might remain within the bounds of this gentle embrace for the night, the sheer comfort of his scent enveloping her and his arms enfolding her felt like an unspoken promise. His solid arm, muscles beneath the surface, wrapped around her form like a protective shield, creating a sense of grounded security.

As Jack drew the duvet over them, safeguarding against the encroaching chill of the night, Faye nestled her head against his other arm. She inched close, seeking solace in the proximity of the man she had come to see as a tender giant—a paradox of strength and gentleness.

The metamorphosis Faye had undergone was undeniable; her life had irrevocably shifted from its prior course. As the days had unfurled, so too had her heart, yielding to the compelling pull of Jack's presence. The brevity of time paled in comparison to the depth of their connection, a connection she could no longer deny. The realization dawned upon her that Jack had managed to stealthily pilfer her heart, leaving her forever changed.

Faye confronted a series of decisions demanding her attention. She recognized that hoping for a different tomorrow would remain a futile endeavor if she allowed the shadows of yesterday to continue dictating her present. While the prospect of surrendering to what lay ahead incited a palpable nervousness, the promise of countless tomorrows blooming before her made the uncertainty worthwhile. The decision ahead wasn't a challenge, not if she attuned herself to the symphony resonating within her chest—an internal timpani that harmonized with her heartbeat, a rhythm that spoke of love.

As the clock struck eleven in the evening, Faye and Jack retired for the night. Three hours later, Faye's eyes fluttered open, the hushed stillness of the house enveloping her senses. With the room cloaked in darkness, she lay there, her stillness mirrored by the world around her. Immersed in silence, she remained perfectly motionless, attuning herself to the subtle symphony of the night.

In the tranquil embrace of the darkness, Faye's senses came alive, her surroundings gradually unfurling before her as her vision adjusted. With each heartbeat, her awareness deepened, and the obscurity seemed to dissolve, revealing a world alive with muted details. The transition from drowsy slumber to keen alertness transpired in mere moments.

The room lay before Faye as if illuminated by sunlight, every detail etched in her vision despite the encompassing darkness. This remarkable sight was owed to the unique constitution of her eyes, allowing her to navigate even the pitch-black expanse with clarity. The rhythmic cadence of Jack's breathing provided a soothing backdrop, confirming that he was still ensconced in slumber. Gathering her resolve, she slipped out from under the blankets and silently slid off the bed. Her jeans were swiftly donned, followed by her socks and shoes.

Faye moved with an otherworldly grace, her steps reminiscent of a wraith, a spectral presence gliding effortlessly through the room. Every movement was devoid of sound, an ethereal dance that extended beyond the bedroom, down the hallway, and to the front of the house. A ghostly figure, she skillfully navigated around every creaky floorboard, rendering them as nonexistent. Standing at the door, she deftly utilized a phone app to secure a ride. Before leaving, she fitted herself with the harness of her dual holsters, a preparation for the unknown that lay ahead. Slipping on her jacket, she emerged from the house and stepped outside, the cool night air embracing her.

With her rental car still parked at the hotel, Faye's chosen transportation arrived without a hitch. The journey unfolded seamlessly, propelling her toward the hotel.

As the front door clicked shut, Jack's eyes opened, drawn from slumber by the telltale sound. Alertness had seized him when Faye had subtly slipped away from his embrace. He chose to remain motionless, a silent spectator to her movements, curious about her nocturnal agenda. Before succumbing to sleep, a vague premonition had settled within Jack—a sense that Faye might depart in the night.

Mixed emotions swirled within him; a fusion of validation for his intuition, yet an uncertainty about her departure unshared.

With a sense of urgency, Jack swiftly donned a pair of jeans and a lightweight sweater, the latter to be layered beneath a jacket. A tactical mindset informed his choice of attire as he equipped himself with practicality. His feet slipped into tactical boots, remnants from his military days, providing both stability and warmth amid the snow and ice. He secured his ballistic glasses in anticipation of the unforeseen challenges that might lie ahead. An air of uncertainty clung to his preparations, a result of Faye's withholding of specifics about the circumstances he might encounter.

A final check of his sidearm ensued, the ritual of ensuring readiness for the unknown. The weapon found its place in his shoulder harness, the snug rigging reinforcing his commitment to preparedness. Jack's actions were imbued with determination.

Slipping into his jacket, Jack swiftly emerged through the front door mere minutes after the echo of Faye's departing ride had faded. With an unwavering certainty in her initial destination, he set his sights on the hotel where he surmised she would seek refuge. His old truck, nestled within the confines of the garage, awaited his command. The engine roared to life as he embarked on his pursuit.

Entering her suite, Faye made a beeline for the bedroom. The bed hosted an array of files, and she meticulously sorted through them until the sought-after one was in her hands. Extracting a photograph from the file, she fixed her gaze upon it. The image was an exact replica of the one she had examined in Jack's house—a sweeping view of the entryway into the attorney's residence, marred by the splintered remnants of a kicked-in door. But what held particular significance for Faye was an additional detail.

In that frame, adjacent to the battered door, a framed newspaper clipping caught her attention. The clipping featured the attorney, standing beside an individual Faye believed she recognized. Yet, obscured by a glare on the glass, a third and fourth man in the photograph eluded her identification.

The urgency of confirming her suspicion compelled Faye. The need to ascertain the identity of these men took precedence before she could approach Jack and unveil the truth. She was steadfast in her belief that Jack deserved to be presented with a clear narrative. And to achieve that, she needed a closer look at that newspaper article, for only then could she corroborate her beliefs.

Retrieving the keys to her rental car from the nightstand, Faye moved with purpose. Her cell phone, temporarily replaced by another, was tucked away in the drawer to prevent any digital trace. The decision to employ a burner phone underscored her intent to avoid any surveillance while engaging in her upcoming mission. This strategic maneuver was crucial; anonymity was her ally in this venture.

Ensuring the readiness of her firearms, Faye methodically checked both their magazines and the weapons themselves. Each action resonated with a sense of precision and control. Content that her tools were primed, she descended the stairs and approached her waiting vehicle. A mental note to discreetly return the files to the police station underscored her commitment to tidying up her tracks. Navigating the route she had etched in her mind, Faye arrived at her destination with swift efficiency. It was the residence of the lawyer. Cutting the engine and extinguishing the lights, she allowed a few minutes to pass before emerging from the car. Stepping onto the front porch, she suddenly registered the telltale signs—the door had been boarded up. With a seasoned instinct for subtlety, she pivoted her approach, discreetly retreating to the back of the house via the side yard. The objective was clear: discreetly infiltrate the house from its rear.

Navigating to the rear of the house, an unsettling intuition permeated Faye's awareness. Instead of relying solely on her instincts, she exercised caution, pausing to confirm with her own eyes the nagging sense of something amiss. It didn't take long for her to corroborate her suspicions. The backdoor, usually a barrier, was agape, its handle a disfigured testament to some intense force. Its appearance spoke of an intrusion, a disturbance in the equilibrium she had anticipated.

With measured decisiveness, Faye gripped one of her guns, cradling it in her right hand. The other hand emerged from her pocket, brandishing a flashlight. The two instruments were poised in a tactical stance as she advanced, a blend of stealth and readiness defining her movements.

The flashlight's focused beam augmented her vision, the pale illumination revealing only what was essential. Her proficiency rendered it an option rather than a necessity, yet she welcomed it for its tactical utility. Its purpose wasn't mere illumination; it was a means to blind any potential threat, a calculated disruption of their night vision should they cross her path.

As Faye's footsteps carried her deeper into the house, each movement underscored the intensity of the situation. Her approach was a balance of caution and precision, reflective of her seasoned expertise. No lurking figures sprang forth from the depths of closed doors, nor did any unexpected echoes pierce the silence. The house stood vacant of life beyond Faye's presence. In her solitary passage, a resolute determination propelled her forward, a mission underscored by the resolve to bring an end to the sinister trail of murders. With every step, her focus was unwavering—each stride carried a weight, an impetus to reach Jack and share the vital information that could quell this cycle of violence.

As the dark expanse enveloped her, Faye was driven to finalize her mission, to relinquish the weight of secrets that lay between her and the man she had grown fond of. The dichotomy within her—partially a young woman immersed in the burgeoning depths of love for Jack, and partially an agent bound by duty and an unrelenting mission—had begun to blur. The intricacies of reconciling these two facets of her existence weighed heavily upon her, a challenge she grappled with as she navigated the house.

Her search led her to the anticipated picture frame, but the expected newspaper clipping was absent. In its place, a knife protruded from the wall, impaling a fragment of a street map. This makeshift arrangement marked a circled location, etched with a sense of urgency. As Faye studied the map and the imposing hunting knife that had been employed to anchor it, the intent behind the message became clear. While the blatant communication beckoned her attention, she remained resolute, memorizing the address before moving forward, determined to unveil the truth concealed within the cryptic symbol.

Left deliberately by the killer, the knife stood as a chilling testament to its intended recipient—Faye herself. Its significance was further underscored by the absence of the expected framed clipping. The missing photograph served as a clear message: the killer was well aware of Faye's connection to the individuals within the image. This insight fueled her conviction that the confrontation she had anticipated was now imminent. With the framed newspaper clipping inexplicably gone, the address that remained served as an undeniable beckon from the killer—a directive guiding her towards an impending face-off.

Acknowledging the purpose behind the killer's manipulative move, Faye pivoted to exit the house. Yet, her steps faltered just before crossing the threshold. Stretched out on the walkway, a paradox emerged—a picture frame holding the very newspaper clipping she had sought. Its presence baffled her; its emergence, timed to her departure, defied logic.

The frame hadn't adorned the space when she had initially entered; her heightened senses confirmed that much. No footsteps marked the passage of a retreating presence, dispelling any possibility of someone sneaking in and planting it during her tenure inside. This observation unveiled two unsettling truths—first, that the killer was well-versed in her identity and purpose, and second, that he had an uncanny ability to elude her perception.

A shiver traced the length of her spine, a stark reminder of the peril she faced. She recognized that relying solely on her heightened senses would not suffice against an adversary who wielded such control. The disconcerting incident outside the building, when she had unknowingly reacted to the killer's presence during Jack's media engagement, echoed in her thoughts. Resolute, she made the decision to augment her instincts with caution, acknowledging that her formidable opponent could manipulate his presence at will.

Deciding that waiting around to see if the killer lingered would prove futile, Faye concluded that if the killer had intended to confront her, he wouldn't have left behind the telltale clue to his whereabouts. With resolute determination, Faye pressed forward, her footsteps purposeful. She reached out and took hold of the framed newspaper article clipping, the artifact that had guided her to this point. She deftly turned it, angling it to capture the moonlight just right, revealing the faces of the three individuals depicted.

On the left, she identified the slain attorney, a haunting reminder of one of the crimes that had set this chain of events in motion. To the far right stood the current governor of their state, a juxtaposition that underscored the gravity of the situation. Yet, it was the pair of faces in the center that held her gaze with an almost surreal intensity—faces she could scarcely believe she was encountering beyond the narrow confines of her expectations.

In the heart of that visual polyptych, the countenance of Mr. Donovan Pike stared out at her, a frozen moment of time forever encapsulated in the newspaper's ink. And at his side, Dr. Brundle's visage stood in eerie juxtaposition. The arrangement of these figures in the framed article revealed an unexpected connection.

The memories rushed back to her with an unexpected intensity, like a floodgate suddenly swung open. The images and sensations hit her all at once—the sterile corridors, their antiseptic scent permeating the air. She could almost feel the cool touch of the hospital gown against her skin, a reminder of vulnerability. The soft hiss of recycled air whispered through the ventilation shafts, a constant reminder of the clinical environment she had been trapped in.

These memories pressed upon her psyche, their weight suffocating her as if they were squeezing the air from her lungs. She found herself instinctively hunching over, her head bowed, trying to suppress the rising tide of nausea that threatened to overcome her.

The recollections of electrodes and jolting shocks surged to the forefront of her mind. She vividly recalled the parade of needles, each one a pinprick of agony on her tender flesh. The humiliating exposure of her body during those invasive physical examinations was etched into her memory, a deep source of shame and violation. And through it all, there he was—his face, his unsettling smile, a constant presence that made her skin crawl. The man named Dr. Brundle, with an oily demeanor that sent shivers down her spine.

One particularly haunting memory lingered—being half-dragged out of a testing room by two stern-faced orderlies. Her nakedness felt like a flagrant symbol of her vulnerability, suspended between the two figures while Dr. Brundle looked on with his unsettling gaze, as though finding amusement in her plight.

Faye's thoughts then returned to those agonizing days spent within the walls of the Shepherds facility. Each passing moment etched a deeper line of despair into her psyche, leaving scars that went beyond the physical.

11

Faye settled back into the driver's seat of her rental car, her breath forming small clouds in the chilly night air. With a turn of the key, the engine roared to life. She cranked up the heat to dispel the biting cold that had seeped into the vehicle's interior. Warm air gushed from the vents, and she instinctively shifted the airflow away from her face, finding instant comfort in the change.

The heater core still retained a modicum of warmth, preventing the air from turning icy, but it was evident that the laws of thermodynamics were at play, as the heat was yet to reach its maximum potential. Though she had a pressing task ahead, Faye knew she needed a moment to steady her nerves before making a call she'd been dreading. The photograph frame she'd retrieved provided a tangible connection to her objective, a small victory amid mounting tension.

However, Faye couldn't remain idly parked in the car, avoiding the impending conversation with Dr. Brundle. An unexplainable restlessness urged her to act. As she reached for her cell phone, her fingers felt slightly clammy—she attributed it to the warmth pouring into the car. With a deep breath, she initiated the call, connecting with her true superiors, a departure from the federal agency she impersonated.

Dialing the numbers prompted a series of prompts, familiar codes, and a mechanical female voice. Faye's voice was curt, spoken in a succinct code, leading to successful connection.

Dr. Brundle's voice, despite its artificial undertones, carried authority as he inquired, "What do you have to report, Alpha 06?"

Gathering her thoughts, Faye relayed her updates efficiently. "I've secured hard copies of the files from the police station. Digital copies are irrecoverable. The investigation's progression has been hampered. I'm closely monitoring Detective Riddle to prevent connections between victims or exposing Delta 67-3. I've removed a photo from a victim's home to eliminate potential leads. No further developments to report."

Dr. Brundle's reply was concise, "That's good."

Faye's stomach churned at the prospect of enduring Dr. Brundle's presence any longer. Steeling herself, she pressed on, "Do you have any instructions for me, sir?"

"Nothing new. Continue derailing the police investigation. Observe Delta 67-3 until his mission concludes," Dr. Brundle instructed.

Faye ended the call, her decision crystallizing. The conflict between her allegiance to the Shepherd Institute and her growing feelings for Jack had reached its zenith. She could no longer straddle both sides. Resolute, she knew what she had to do. She'd confess everything to Jack, including her true identity, and aid him in capturing the killer. She was done playing both sides. Her newfound determination to embrace the life she desired surged within her.

The omission of the remaining case files was intentional. Faye feared jeopardizing Elizabeth and Brooke's safety. She couldn't predict the orders she'd receive, and her conditioning to obey her superiors, even if it meant carrying out reprehensible acts, weighed heavily on her. It wasn't the memories of what had happened to her at the Shepherd Institute that drove her decision, it was the new found feelings she had for Jack.

As Faye's thoughts swirled, her curiosity lingered on Delta 67-3's unexpected encounter yesterday. Why had he shown up outside the scene? Their objectives were clear, with no need for personal interaction. She contemplated this enigma, wondering if a significant reason lay behind his request to meet.

Refocusing her thoughts, Faye buckled up and adjusted her seat. With the car in drive and headlights illuminating the path, she set off toward the warehouse sector of the industrial park, south of the city. The journey was relatively smooth in the early morning hours, and within fifteen minutes, she'd arrive at her destination.

Donovan found himself within the confines of Dr. Brundle's laboratory when the call from Agent 06 came through. The ringing of the communication device echoed within the sterile environment, and the words spoken to Dr. Brundle reverberated through the space. Engaged in his work, Dr. Brundle was deeply absorbed, his attention riveted to notes and data that eluded immediate comprehension. Despite having lingered there for around thirty minutes, Donovan remained unnoticed, a silent observer waiting for acknowledgment.

The doctor's erratic conduct, fueled by the maelstrom of his thoughts, intrigued Donovan. He had witnessed this scene many times before, yet it never failed to captivate him. The distinct and disjointed chatter that emanated from Dr. Brundle's lips was a testament to his unique state of mind—a blend of genius and madness that permeated his existence.

"Hormone levels are hyper-optimal. Pheromone response is hyper-optimal. I have to adjust uptake parameters and the typical response to pheromone stimuli will have to be minimized as much as possible. Testosterone response causes an increase in dopamine production and uptake. Mating hormone response increase..." Dr. Brundle muttered, his words a glimpse into the intricate web of his thoughts.

Casually slipping his hands into his pockets, Donovan's subtle movement seemed to coax the doctor into shifting his focus, diverting from his previous contemplation.

"She is lying," Dr. Brundle's words were directed at Donovan, but they bore an air of detachment, as if they stemmed from a mind momentarily unburdened by its typical chaotic musings.

This unexpected pronouncement jolted Donovan. He sought clarity, urgently inquiring, "What doctor? What did you just say?"

The doctor's statement held implications that resonated deeply within Donovan. Agent 06 held a significant place in his world, and her actions impacted his plans more than he'd care to admit.

"Well, she's not technically lying but it's possible that she knows something that she is not sharing," Dr. Brundle stated with an odd blend of conviction and uncertainty. His coherence seemed fleeting as his thoughts veered into their customary irrational patterns. "Alpha 06 may not have told me everything that she knows about what we were talking about for the points that we were discussing and the things that she said," he rambled, blurring the lines between lucidity and madness.

Observing this exchange, Donovan marveled at the doctor's ability to shift from moments of seeming clarity to episodes of frenetic disarray. He couldn't fathom how Dr. Brundle maintained a grip on his thoughts well enough to produce the remarkable results his work demonstrated.

"I was taking notes," the doctor interjected, steering their conversation in another direction, albeit briefly grounded. He gestured toward figures displayed in the holographic image before him, attempting to decipher the cryptic patterns before them.

"I was taking live readings and observations when she called me. It is at this point in the conversation where she was under intense stress. The neural pathways shift slightly, followed by changes here and here," Dr. Brundle indicated two distinct readouts.

While the readouts remained unintelligible to Donovan, his faith in the doctor's expertise remained unwavering. Despite his lack of understanding, he trusted that Dr. Brundle possessed the insight to glean meaningful information from the data and provide an accurate interpretation.

Donovan's response was pragmatic, dismissive of the complexities that had just been unearthed. "It doesn't matter. Her only function was to slow down the investigation by the police. She has done quite well in that," he concluded, aware of the doctor's past inclinations to modify 'genetic material' that yielded unforeseen actions he wasn't happy with. He was wary of exposing Agent 06 to similar risks.

The doctor's silence spoke volumes, his attention once again wandering into the labyrinthine corridors of his mind. Donovan recognized that he had lost the doctor's engagement, his thoughts wandering along paths that were exclusively his to traverse. Accepting the inevitable, Donovan decided to leave, understanding that the subject would resurface when Dr. Brundle was ready to delve into it again. As he exited the laboratory, Donovan left behind the enigma that was Dr. Brundle's mind, a realm where genius and madness intertwined inextricably.

Jack observed Faye emerging from the rear of the house, her purposeful strides leading her to her waiting car. With a deft turn of her key, the engine in her car rumbled to life, breaking the stillness of the dark morning. He watched intently as she initiated a phone call, deducing that she must have found what she was searching for in the house. The time she had spent inside indicated success; had the house remained impenetrable, she would have returned sooner.

Faye was completely oblivious to the existence of his personal vehicle. Drawing from his own experience as a trained policeman, he employed his skills in covert surveillance, ensuring he trailed her discreetly. As the chilly night air seeped into his truck, he couldn't help but shiver, the cold permeating his surroundings while he awaited Faye's return to her own car. Yet, the cold's numbing grasp extended beyond the physical, a sensation he prayed wouldn't infect his burgeoning feelings for her.

As the moments dragged on, Jack's thoughts grew as somber as the night that enveloped him. *What is she keeping from me?* he pondered, his mind clouded with doubt. Memories of Faye's hesitant statements from their past interactions resurfaced in his mind. He also recalled the faint whispers she had uttered under her breath, unaware that he had overheard. It was the unspoken words, the gaps in her communication, that set off the loudest alarms within him. Those silences, pregnant with meaning, stirred the greatest concerns in his heart.

Aware of the need to remain inconspicuous, Jack resisted the urge to trail Faye as she departed into the pre-dawn obscurity. It was crucial that he didn't arouse her suspicions. In anticipation, He had devised a 'poor man's' tracking device in order to keep tabs on her location. It was a rudimentary tracking solution—a makeshift method of monitoring her movements.

During Faye's presence in the house, he had surreptitiously enabled location sharing on his personal phone. He discreetly nestled it within a crevice in her rental car's bumper. Simultaneously, he activated the location service on his police-issued cell phone, which facilitated the reciprocal sharing of their positions.

Before pursuing Faye, Jack conducted a thorough sweep of the house. Regrettably, his search yielded no valuable clues, serving only to heighten his frustration. Unbeknownst to him, the torn map fragment and the newspaper-clipping-adorned photo frame that

Faye had sought were absent by the time he entered the house. Their significance would remain veiled until a later revelation.

Strangely, an eerie sensation of being watched settled upon Jack during his time within the house. He attributed this unease to his own apprehension, a natural response stemming from his covert activities. Dismissing it, he attributed his heightened nerves to the tension of tailing Faye.

Resuming his pursuit, Jack settled into his truck and steered it toward the shared location indicated by his cell phone. Grateful that Faye remained oblivious to his truck's existence, he recognized the advantage it afforded him in avoiding the need for excessive vehicle concealment. Her background as a trained operative meant she would likely possess the instincts to detect anyone tailing her, thus necessitating Jack's cautious maneuvering.

The world around him felt desolate and cold, its darkness and silence amplified by the absence of sunlight at this early hour. Despite his vigil, he found himself alone, devoid of any other soul in his surroundings. He found himself following after a woman he was growing fond of and now was very suspicious of.

12

Faye guided her rental car into a parking spot and silenced the engine. She had reached the destination indicated by the map she'd found. The industrial park sprawled across a vast expanse, with the warehouse sector constituting around half of its total area. Stretching out wider than three football fields and nearly two-thirds as long, this section hosted dozens of warehouses arranged in orderly rows. Although varying in size, most of the buildings shared a uniformity in their dimensions.

Amid the many warehouses, numerous structures lay vacant, their emptiness suggesting a daunting challenge for Faye to locate the right one. In contrast, the warehouses still in operation bustled with nocturnal activity. Night crews tirelessly moved goods from one static location to another, guided by the luminance of their forklifts' work lights. These beams cut through the night, revealing only what was immediately ahead, while the encompassing darkness and the cold of winter remained steadfast.

Remaining in her car for a brief moment, Faye's attention fixated on a single building as a solitary light flickered to life within. The feeble glow barely illuminated a semi-abandoned dock strewn with discarded and fractured pallets. This light appeared unfit for a nighttime working environment, offering only a limited radius of visibility around the door. The expansive bay doors of the warehouse slid open, and an unremarkable man in a beige sports jacket emerged. Positioned beneath the muted radiance of a sodium gas lamp, he assumed an unassuming stance.

In the presence of the dim illumination, the man stood by the bay door for a fleeting succession of breaths. His gaze pierced the darkness that stubbornly resisted dispelling, its expanse lying beyond the lamp's limited reach. The nondescript figure retraced his steps, disappearing into the warehouse through the entrance's threshold.

Stepping out of the rental car, Faye approached the waiting entrance with a purposeful stride. Her training as an agent kicked in, and she became hyper-aware of her surroundings, meticulously absorbing even the slightest details.

Her self-awareness was profound. She acknowledged both her strengths and her vulnerabilities, humbly admitting to the latter. Despite her extensive capabilities, an insidious feeling crept over her—a sensation akin to a mouse walking deliberately into a trap. Yet, she dismissed this emotion, refusing to succumb to it. With a resolute determination, she withdrew both of her guns from their holsters, clasping one in each hand.

"No," she silently affirmed to herself. "I am the hunter, and he is my prey," she repeated like a mantra, a prayer to quell her nervousness.

This unease was a familiar companion, one that invariably accompanied her tactical actions. Oddly, it was a sentiment she welcomed, a constant reminder of the gravity of her tasks.

With graceful movements and almost soundless steps, Faye glided into the warehouse, her presence transforming the space into an arena fraught with potential danger; a potential killing arena that she would dominate.

Faye had ventured about thirty feet into the depths of the warehouse when the massive dock door clanged shut, swallowing her surroundings in darkness as the lights abruptly extinguished. Yet, the abyss held no fear for her. Her night vision outmatched that of an ordinary person by fourfold. Beyond sight, her heightened hearing, scent, and strength surpassed human norms, though she acknowledged her physical inferiority to the man she pursued. However, agility and reflexes were her true weapons—her swiftness a potential edge in a confrontation that might lie ahead.

"Delta 67-3," she called out confidently into the obscurity, her earlier apprehension vanished, "I came because you sent word to meet. My orders were to hinder the police investigation; I wasn't informed that we would be meeting face-to-face." She felt the accomplishment of what she'd set out to do in this meeting pulsating through her veins, overshadowing her unease.

The voice that emerged from the darkness had a haunting quality, punctuated by an unsettling lisp in some words. Faye strained to locate its source within the cavernous space. Her extraordinary hearing struggled to pinpoint the origin of the voice—a voice she had never heard before.

"Your name is Faye. I don't have a name, just a designation. Do you know why they did that?" The voice lingered with a certain eerie resonance.

Faye's grip on her guns tightened in response to the voice's words. Her determination surged, dispelling any remnants of anxiety. Her fingers caressed the weapons' handles as she steadied her breathing. She recognized the importance of maintaining control—of not allowing this unseen figure to dictate the terms.

"Me and my brothers are expendable so we are given no real name, unlike our sisters. Unlike you," said Delta 67-3.

"I am not your sister," Faye retorted vehemently, her words seeping with defiance.

The solid weight of her guns offered a sense of security, contrasting the shifting shadows that concealed her opponent. Faye yearned to reveal his position, to disrupt his current advantage. The impetus to seize control from the elusive figure propelled her.

"Oh, but you are. All of us brothers and sisters share the same source for genetic material. The free sisters and the many brothers," Delta 67-3 responded, a mix of calmness and eeriness embedded in his words.

Faye thought there might be a meaning behind the specific words that he used but the meaning eluded her.

"What do you want?" Faye's patience wore thin. The ongoing hide-and-seek was tiresome; she longed to strip away the facade and confront him. *Where is he?* she pondered, determined not to remain in the reactive role.

"I wanted to see you again. I wanted to meet you. We brothers never get the opportunity to meet one of our sisters," the voice continued to insinuate itself into Faye's consciousness, an unsettling charm woven through his words.

"Well, we've met and I am leaving. Do not contact me again or I'll kill you," Faye's declaration carried weight, masking her intention to maintain her vigilance

She had no qualms at all in carrying out the threat she had issued. She also intended to maintain the initiative, to force him out of the shadows, to level the playing field.

"I got no strings to hold me down," Delta 67-3 sang, invoking a line from an animated movie.

As the overhead lights surged back to life, Faye shielded her eyes with her forearm, adapting to the sudden brilliance. Amid the flood of light, an object hurtled toward her.

Faye pivoted, ready to fire. Yet, a realization stayed her fingers—the object posed no immediate threat. She traced its trajectory until it skidded to a halt at her feet. A faint glow emanated from the object, casting an eerie aura.

Emerging from behind a stack of crates, Delta 67-3 stepped into view. His form materialized in the renewed illumination, a tangible presence after a shadowy dance of words and intentions.

"Oops. Maybe I should have exercised more caution with that," he admitted sheepishly, referring to the luminous object he had flung her way.

Faye's gaze lingered on the object, her curiosity piqued as she nudged it with her foot. Its oval shape emitted an otherworldly glow, but that wasn't the sole enigma. It seemed to oscillate in her vision, as though it existed slightly out of focus, regardless of how she inspected it.

"You might want to handle that with care," Delta 67-3 interjected, imbuing his words with a tone of caution.

"What is it?" Faye inquired, her morbid curiosity overcoming her initial reluctance. She begrudgingly admitted he had succeeded in diverting her focus toward the object.

"Are you truly unfamiliar with it, sister?" Delta 67-3 feigned shock, his hand raising theatrically to his mouth.

"It's obvious if I'm asking you," she snapped back, her irritation palpable.

Delta 67-3 brushed off her question and resumed singing the remaining lines of the animated song he had started earlier. "I got no strings to hold me down. I got no strings on me." His feet tapped out a simple dance, arms hanging at his sides, resembling a marionette that had been set free from its controlling strings.

He motioned toward the back of his skull, his gestures enigmatic and unhelpful. Just as she thought she had him cornered for a potential exchange of gunfire, he slipped into a row of crates, vanishing in the blink of an eye. Faye rushed to the row, her eyes scanning for any trace of him. He had evaporated with disconcerting ease. Frustration welled within her; she had allowed him to toy with her mind and slip through her fingers without resistance.

Returning to the object, Faye grasped it in her hand, intent on examining it closely. Yet, its nature eluded her. She sensed its weight, felt its solidity, yet her vision could not fully reconcile with what she held.

"That's what they used to know what we think and what we feel. That's what they use to control all of us," Delta 67-3 confessed, his voice emerging from an elusive point once again, leaving her with more questions than answers.

"I thought they controlled us through the conditioning they put us through," she inquired, her confusion evident.

"That. Is. A. Lie," Delta 67-3 retorted, enunciating each word deliberately. "We can resist that conditioning if we focus hard enough. That multi-dimensional phase device amplifies the conditioning and compels us to obey."

Faye's eyes scanned her surroundings, hoping to catch a glimpse of Delta 67-3 and maintain visual contact.

"We're conditioned from birth to obey our superiors, and now you're suggesting that we can break free from it by removing this thing?" Her curiosity ignited, she wanted to learn more. The control exerted over them had always been a concern, but she had never known how to challenge it.

"You now understand perfectly well," Delta 67-3 replied with a hint of sarcasm.

Faye contemplated the implications of the device in her hands. *If it controlled them, and he had removed it...* Her mind raced, the implications of her thoughts hitting her with a jolt. She breathed in sharply, panic edging into her demeanor. She glanced around, her voice a hushed desperation.

"So you're going around killing Shepherds now because you're free from this thing?" Accusation colored her words, delivered in a half-whisper.

"No. Half right, half wrong," he replied with honesty. "I'm going around killing Shepherds because I was *ordered* to *and* because I want to."

Faye could almost envision the eerie smile that might have accompanied his words. A shiver ran down her spine, her skin tingling. "How can you harm them when they could simply command you to stop, and you'd be forced to obey? How did you break free from that control? Don't tell me it's just because you removed the device. I know you've done it recently—I can still smell the blood on it. It's overpowering."

"Oh, I told you. You're both right and wrong at the same time."

Without warning, Delta 67-3 materialized to Faye's left, emerging from between rows of crates. Rather than puzzling over how he had managed to maneuver around her, Faye focused on his words and focused her guns on him. He leisurely approached her, stopping about ten feet away.

"That device I handed over to you tracks us and transmits biofeedback data to Dr. Brumble at the Shepherd Institute. It forces obedience, contains a serum to kill us, and, most importantly..." he paused, letting the suspense build.

Faye's patience waned as Delta 67-3 reveled in his dramatics.

He read her impatience, and it fueled his penchant for playing games. His eyes shone with glee. With a flourish of his arms, he teased, "Wait for it. Wait for it."

"What the hell!" Faye's frustration broke through in a loud exclamation.

Delta 67-3's restraint crumbled. Words poured out in a rush. "The fun part is that its also a bomb that is capable and powerful enough to take out about one third of this industrial park. But the doctor can remotely control the overall yield. It's a method to get rid of us when they want or to use us as a weapon as well since the yield can be controlled at will."

Calm descended over Delta 67-3's features. He slipped his hands casually into his pockets, adopting a relaxed and nonchalant demeanor. His smile carried a razor-sharp edge, feigning boredom. Faye's desire to wipe that arrogant smile off his face surged—an urge to put another hole in his head with a bullet from her gun.

"How did you break free from your leash, you rabid dog? How can you kill Shepherds? What sets you apart?" Faye hissed, her patience stretched to its limits.

The urge to unleash a barrage of heavy metal objects at high speed toward his face gnawed at her. Delta 67-3's mission worried her. She became aware of the Shepherds being killed when she began her mission and wondered how Delta 67-3 could execute such an order when they were conditioned to obey Shepherds. Those Shepherds he had killed should have been able to make him stand down. This small detail was why Faye was curious. She didn't understand how Delta 67-3 was capable of killing Shepherds.

Delta 67-3's laughter rang out. "You were correct, we're conditioned from birth to obey Shepherds. There's no difference between the programming I received and what you received."

"Then how did you defy the programming and kill four of them?"

"The English language is fascinating in its nuances. By adding one word or altering word placement in a sentence, we can subtly change circumstances, and most would never notice. I expected you to catch that difference." Delta 67-3 said calmly. "Control is needed. That's why the device was created."

"What are you blathering about?" Faye's confusion grew, teetering on the edge of exasperation as she struggled to make sense of his words.

"We're conditioned from birth to obey *a* Shepherd," Delta 67-3 repeated slowly.

It hit Faye like a revelation. The distinction became clear. Delta 67-3 hadn't disobeyed a Shepherd; he hadn't broken free like a rogue dog. She remembered the constant mantra drilled into them: 'You must obey a Shepherd's orders.' He hadn't betrayed the Shepherds by killing those four. He wasn't an escaped renegade, but an obedient agent, sent on a deliberate mission to execute those specific Shepherds. He was carrying out a Shepherd's command.

"Donovan Pike," Faye spat with venom.

A chilling and malevolent smile twisted across Delta 67-3's face.

"That's correct, Alpha 06. Donovan Pike. It's on his orders, the orders of *a* Shepherd, that I'm doing this and killed those four Shepherds. I'll tell you the truth, if I could have I would have done this without his orders. Murder is... well," he paused, relishing the word, "*delicious*." He hugged himself, shivering visibly. Delta 67-3's twisted smile was unrecognizable, radiating his unsettling pleasure in taking lives.

Faye turned away, spitting at the ground near his feet. "Dogs like you should be put down."

"Oh, there's no doubt about that at all. You are definitely right but they won't be putting me down with that thing at least," Delta 67-3 retorted, pointing at the device in Faye's hand.

Faye's eyes involuntarily flicked down as he pointed, cursing herself for the lapse. By the time she looked up, Delta 67-3 had vanished again.

Faye's brows furrowed in frustration. "What's Donovan Pike's scheme? Why is he having Shepherds killed?"

Delta 67-3 responded petulantly, "I don't think I want to tell you." He crossed his arms and pouted, a grotesque expression.

"Why? You're foaming at the mouth to tell me, you animal." Faye's nausea grew, her tolerance for Delta 67-3's presence wearing thin.

"No, no, no, sister. You need to watch your mouth. By the way, dear sister, you still have one of those things in your head. They know everything you feel." Delta 67-3 reappeared and then vanished into the shadows, leaving Faye shaken by his revelations. "They know when you're happy or sad. They can sense when you lie. I got no strings to hold me down... I got no strings on me," his ominous voice lingered.

"Where are you, you bastard? Did you call me out here to kill me or to brag?" Faye's scream reverberated through the rows as she searched.

"I just wanted to meet you, nothing more. I've never met a sister so I was curious after seeing you on the street that day. But you should respect your elders and not talk to your big brother that way. I'll have to punish you for that," Delta 67-3 hissed, his lisp more pronounced. The realization dawned on Faye gradually. Despite never receiving an order to meet up with Delta 67-3, and the likelihood that it wasn't in his orders either, that didn't prevent him from taking the initiative to arrange this meeting on his own.

Gears whirred overhead, catching Faye's attention just before she leapt aside. A crate crashed down, splintering as it hit the ground. The cacophony echoed outside the warehouse, triggering a response neither Faye nor Delta 67-3 anticipated.

Not far from where Faye had taken refuge after evading the falling crate, the side door of the warehouse burst open with a resounding crash. Jack had forcefully barged in, the door nearly torn from its hinges by his impact. For a brief moment, he was framed in the doorway's opening, rushing in right behind the shattered wood.

"Faye! Faye! Are you okay?" Jack's voice echoed with genuine concern as his features displayed his worry.

Although Jack wasn't entirely sure if he had entered the correct warehouse, it was the closest one to where Faye had parked the rental car, and the illuminated interior coupled with crashing sounds had led him to take this risk. He had smashed through the door to get inside.

A glint of light caught Jack's eye from his right, drawing his attention. Swinging his revolver in the direction of the glimmer, he noticed a shadow of movement on his left, compelling him to shift his focus. The shadow danced across the tops of nearby stacked crates, hurtling toward him at an astonishing speed.

Jack struggled to track the shadow's trajectory with his eyes, but he managed something else. He deduced enough about its path to realize it was about to collide with him. Whatever was rapidly approaching was going to strike him head-on, and there was little Jack could do to alter or prevent this impending collision.

Jack had instinctively reacted to the glint of light, directing his attention to the closer target. His hand clenched the trigger of the weapon he held, and the gun's discharge echoed like the growl following a thunderclap. The recoil sent a jolt through Jack's grip, and the world seemed to shift into a slowed state, moving at a pace that defied normality.

Following the gunshot, a scream pierced the air. Then, impact struck Jack, and he was knocked off his feet as if by a high-speed tackle. This was succeeded by another scream, close in the heels of the previous ones. The surreal, drawn-out experience gave way to reality's regular rhythm. The time dilation, which had distorted Jack's perception, snapped back to its normal flow.

Untangling himself from the limbs that had entwined with his own, Jack remained vigilant, ready to fend off any potential attacks—blows, kicks, or the glint of a knife. However, no further assaults came. Gradually maneuvering himself to a position that allowed him to identify his assailant, Jack was astonished and disheartened to discover that it was none other than Faye tangled up with him on the floor.

As he took in the situation, he couldn't help but notice the apologetic expression that initially graced Faye's face. Yet, that look swiftly morphed into one of pain and discomfort. Her condition was alarming to Jack, evident in the lines etched across her face. The agony she radiated was palpable, and he knew she was in a bad way.

"Are you alright, Faye?" Jack's voice was soft, laced with genuine concern. He reached towards her face, sweeping aside the strands of hair that obscured her eyes.

"Yeah... hi, Jack," Faye managed, mustering a faint smile that thinly veiled the pain she was enduring. "I hate to tell you this, but I think I might have ruined your shirt. I hope you're not mad."

Her attempt at humor amazed Jack, reminding him of her resilience even in dire situations. It was then that Jack realized Faye was still wearing the shirt of his that she had borrowed earlier. But more importantly, he noticed a length of pipe extending about a foot from her lower back on the right side. Its other end protruded from her abdomen, poking him in the belly. The realization hit him like a shock: if Faye hadn't knocked him down by landing on him, that pipe might have impaled his chest, a life-threatening injury.

"Hold on, Faye," Jack began, a sense of urgency propelling him into action. He found his footing and rose to his feet, lifting Faye with him. Cradling her carefully, he decided to rush her to the hospital.

"I'll get you to a hospital," he declared urgently.

Faye, however, was resolute in her refusal, shaking her head with desperation. "No. Don't," she implored, her urgency causing Jack to pause and freeze in his tracks. "Please. No hospital, there will be too many questions to answer. There's gotta be... another... way," she begged, her voice fading as she slipped into unconsciousness.

With few alternatives and fueled by a lack of better options, Jack placed her in his truck and reached out to his sister, Elizabeth. Explaining the situation, he conveyed Faye's resistance to going to a hospital. He knew that his sister, a medical professional, could help guide him.

"Take her to the morgue at Saint Elwood Hospital," Elizabeth suggested, acknowledging the peculiarity of the situation. "I have a colleague there. He'll understand. I'll be there by the time you arrive."

Jack followed her advice, driving to the hospital and parking by the entrance to the morgue. He cradled Faye in his arms, his touch gentle and cautious, as he carried her inside. The package he held was precious, a life to be protected. Elizabeth and her friend, Jason Conwell, were waiting, assisting him in transferring Faye onto a gurney. Together, they wheeled her into the sanctuary of the morgue, locking the doors behind them to ensure privacy and security.

Dr. Brundle burst into Donovan's office, his agitation immediately shattering the peaceful tranquility of the sparsely furnished and decorated space. Emotions radiated from the agitated scientist, disrupting the room's serene atmosphere.

"There's no more data. It's stopped," Dr. Brundle stammered, his hands waving frantically in the air as if grasping at elusive threads. "I need that data for my research. I can't make corrections without it."

Donovan glanced up from his work, his expression quizzical. "What's the commotion about now, Brundle? You're in quite a state," he remarked calmly, a touch of disinterest in his tone.

Taking a deep breath, Dr. Brundle paused, his gaze fixed on Donovan as if seeing him for the first time that day. His eyes held a distant, glazed look.

"What's the matter, doctor?" Donovan inquired with a more composed demeanor, once the scientist's frenetic movements had subsided. "Please, explain."

"The data stream has ceased. I can no longer retrieve information from Delta 67-3 or Alpha 06," Dr. Brundle replied, his agitation now contained within his speech. He shifted restlessly from foot to foot, as if caught in a complex dance.

"Are they inoperative, then? Could they have malfunctioned?" Donovan stepped closer, maintaining a cautious distance, unsure if the scientist's agitated state might turn volatile.

Dr. Brundle seemed momentarily puzzled, as though the notion of their devices being inoperative had not crossed his mind. "No, not inoperative. The data should indicate any malfunction. It's just... stopped."

"Do you think there's a technical issue? A malfunction in the devices themselves?" Donovan's voice held a hint of optimism, his probing questions intended to guide the scientist toward a solution. As long as the agents were still functional, Donovan was content. He required their performance, nothing more.

Dr. Brundle wore the same perplexed expression once more. "Unlikely. The probability of simultaneous, consecutive malfunctions is astronomically low. The devices were functioning properly. The data flow simply ceased."

With a meaningful look, Dr. Brundle gazed at Donovan, conveying unspoken implications. Instead of elaborating, he abruptly turned and left Donovan's office, departing as abruptly as he had entered.

A hush settled over the office, enveloping Donovan in a cocoon of tranquility. Resuming his task, Donovan attempted to dismiss the incident. Yet, the encounter tested even his considerable patience. He relied on Dr. Brundle to fulfill their shared objectives, and he couldn't afford to strain their relationship. Such strain would hinder progress, a situation Donovan couldn't permit. He resolved to check on the doctor later, hoping to restore the equilibrium they desperately needed.

13

In the grand scheme of things, about an hour and a half elapsed before Elizabeth finally came to fetch Jack from his anxious wait. Throughout that span, Jack wrestled with his impatience, suppressing the urge to interrupt their efforts on behalf of Faye. The quiet desperation in his heart had transitioned from frenzied pacing to a somewhat calmer state, though his nervous energy now manifested in nail biting. Repeating the mantra aloud, "I can't lose her, I can't lose her," he battled his fears, closely followed by the thought, *I've only just welcomed her into my life.*

Whether the passage of time was actually longer or perhaps surprisingly shorter, Jack couldn't accurately gauge. Such trivial matters were eclipsed by the weight of his concern for Faye. From the moment he had brought her in until now, he could hardly entertain any other thoughts. The world had narrowed down to the critical space between those two points. Elizabeth's demeanor, as she emerged to retrieve him, didn't signal any dire developments, and that was a small relief to Jack.

However, Elizabeth didn't lead him immediately to Faye's recovery room. A shadow of apprehension darkened her expression, prompting her to guide Jack into one of the small offices scattered across the floor. The intensity of Elizabeth's concern mirrored itself on Jack's face as he absorbed her mood. Her expression seemed as if she had patented it—etched with an air of gravity. The decision to confer in the office conveyed a desire for a semblance of privacy. Oddly, this puzzled Jack; they were in a relatively isolated part of the hospital, occupied by only himself, Jason, Elizabeth, and Faye.

Needless to say, the prospect of speaking with Elizabeth before seeing Faye left Jack increasingly anxious. Tears seemed to lurk beneath the surface, ready to pounce like predators—much akin to how Elizabeth herself stood, a sentinel blocking the door and hemming him into the office. It wasn't a situation he relished; nonetheless, he confronted the inevitability of the impending conversation, fervently hoping for a positive outcome.

"What's happening, Lizzy? Is Faye awake? Can I see her?" Jack beseeched, his desperation evident.

He'd gladly have discard his pride and kneel if it meant gaining his sister's consent to be by Faye's side; his dignity seemed a small price for his beloved's well-being.

"She's on the path to recovery, Jackie," Elizabeth offered, aiming to quell Jack's anxieties, yet her own unease lingered beneath her words. Despite her attempt at reassurance, something else weighed on Elizabeth's mind, casting a shadow across her features. Jack discerned it in her eyes, the way she evaded his gaze.

Elizabeth allowed a pause, meticulously arranging her thoughts like puzzle pieces, each word a crucial part of a delicate reveal. She wasn't about to dive headfirst into the conversation; her aim was precision, ensuring both the content and delivery resonated with Jack. Additionally, the brief respite served another purpose: allowing Jack to regain composure and clear his head, making room for rational thought. An audible whoosh marked Jack's release of the breath he'd inadvertently held since entering the office. Elizabeth caught this sign of emotional unburdening, a cue to proceed.

With a determined steadiness, Elizabeth resumed, her tone deliberate and measured, "Jack, there's something else I need to share."

Her eyes locked onto Jack's, willing him to grasp the gravity of what was to come. She gave him the space he needed to absorb her words, to reflect and respond.

Elizabeth turned away, a fleeting moment of contemplation preceding her pivot back toward her brother. "You need to tell me what's going on right now Jackie."

Jack's head tilted, a physical manifestation of his uncertainty regarding the specific clarification she sought.

"What do you mean? I told you already what occurred in the warehouse when I got there. I don't know what else you could be talking about," he responded with a determined clarity, hopeful that his statement might dissolve any lingering confusion. Regrettably, it did not.

Elizabeth's frustration found involuntary expression in the motion of her hands, a gesture born from her struggle to convey her point.

Exhaling an exasperated sigh, she continued, "I am not talking about what happened at the warehouse."

"Then what are you talking about, Lizzy?" Jack's voice betrayed escalating frustration. The conversation's baffling turns grated on him, exacerbating his already taut nerves. "Can you please just tell me, Lizzy? What the hell is going on?"

"I'd like to know my damn self, Jackie. That's why I'm in here with you asking. There's more to her than meets the eye you know."

"In what way?" Jack's question bore the weight of his bewilderment.

"First off, we attempted to match her blood type, in case a transfusion became necessary after removing that steel pipe from her side. But, as it turns out, a blood transfusion wasn't a concern," Elizabeth explained, accompanied by a relieved exhalation. She unconsciously began to wring her hands, a telltale sign that the information she was about to reveal carried significant weight.

"So what's the problem then if she didn't need to get a blood transfusion? Isn't that a good thing?" The force of Jack's emotions infused his question. Struggling with his longing to see Faye and his need for understanding, he grappled to reconcile these conflicting sentiments.

Elizabeth's response carried the heaviness of revelation. "Jason and I got the pipe removed and when we got ready to do an assessment of the damage we would have to repair, we were shocked when we saw the tissue repairing itself," she conveyed. Her face revealed astonishment and wonder, mirroring the disbelief she felt when witnessing the phenomenon firsthand.

This concept stretched the boundaries of Jack's immediate comprehension. His mind drifted to their prior speculations about the superhuman nature of the elusive killer they were pursuing. The implications of Elizabeth's account and his own thoughts toyed with his sanity. Internally, he reasoned, There's no way what Lizzy is saying is true but she wouldn't lie to me about something like this.

The soft buzz of a fluorescent light overhead seemed to match the buzz of thoughts in Jack's mind. The room felt sterile, almost too clean, in stark contrast to the complexity of the situation they were grappling with.

Suppressing his internal musings, he inquired, "What do you mean?"

Elizabeth's tone blended incredulity and sincerity. "I mean we were ready to go into that hole in her to repair or remove her kidney, which got perforated by the entry of the pipe into her body. The tissue was regenerating and growing back together right as we watched." Her voice betrayed her own disbelief. "It was surreal, Jack. It was the freakiest thing I'd ever seen in my life."

"Wait, are you serious?" Jack's disbelief was palpable.

Elizabeth's response held a touch of exasperation. "Of course I'm serious. Tissue regrowth and repair that should take months, even post-surgery, occurred within minutes. At this rate, she'll likely be fully recovered in a day."

Utterly stunned, Jack grappled with the enormity of the revelation. He turned away, his hand passing over his head. His shoulders rose and fell with each heavy breath he took, his entire being grappling with the staggering implications.

"What the hell, Lizzy? What the hell is that about?"

"As if that wasn't peculiar enough, we discovered something even more unusual," Elizabeth began, her words charged with an air of disbelief. "Faye regained consciousness while we were extracting the pipe. She didn't utter a single word—just let us carry on as she observed. We were oblivious to her being awake until I glanced at her. Those eyes of hers were fixed on me."

Elizabeth's voice trembled slightly, a shiver traversing her spine as she recollected Faye's gaze. It was a detached look, as though someone were extracting a mere foreign object from her body, devoid of any response to pain. Anesthesia hadn't been administered; concerns over her unconscious state and potential blood loss took precedence.

"It was eerie, to say the least, working on a critical injury while your patient silently watched. Her expression could've been the same she'd wear during a pedicure," Elizabeth added, her words tinged with an unsettling reminiscence. She retrieved an object from her pocket, its faint glow casting an ethereal luminescence.

"Jack, there's something else," she continued, presenting the faintly glowing object—an oval-shaped device, about the size of a quarter. Flipping it towards him, it bounced against his chest before he grasped it with both hands.

Jack scrutinized the mysterious object, his brows furrowed in bewilderment. An aura of confusion surrounded it, amplified by his inability to focus his gaze. It was as if the device defied his attempt to fully comprehend it, shifting between states of reality and illusion.

"What is this?" Jack inquired, frustration evident in his tone.

His quick examination revealed that unraveling its nature was beyond his individual capacity. The device seemed to toy with his perception, residing in a liminal space between existence and imagination.

"Drawing from Jason's and my extensive knowledge in science and the medical field, along with our best assessment..." Elizabeth paused, punctuating her words with a hint of irony, "...hell if we know!"

Elizabeth swiveled around, seeking solace in a nearby seat. The fabric of her lab coat whispered as it brushed against the upholstery, a small echo in the aftermath of her revelation. The night's revelations had taken a toll on her psyche, and she was on the brink of conceding defeat.

"It's unlike any technology either of us has encountered before," Elizabeth admitted.

Its faint glow cast an ethereal luminescence across the room, painting shadows that seemed to dance in rhythm with her words. The object pulsed gently, its light creating a subtle halo.

Jack was turning the device over in his palm and still trying to get his eyes to focus on it. *Where did this thing come from?* Jack's inquisitive and analytical nature kicked into gear, his mind honing in on the investigative angle.

"Faye had me take it from the base of her skull. It had these tiny tendrils—microfilaments, infiltrating the spinal cord," Elizabeth explained, punctuating her words with demonstrative wiggles of her fingers. "If she had not assured me that she would heal, I would have left it there. I caught hell just in my attempt to maintain the incision opening for my work, given how rapidly she was healing."

"Wait, was she was conscious when you removed it?" Jack's incredulous inquiry widened his eyes.

Elizabeth's head shook in resigned acknowledgment, a heavy sigh escaping her lips. "She insisted on it. Nothing I could do about it. Initially, when I refused, she got a scalpel and was about to cut it out her damn self. Jason and I struggled to get the scalpel from her grip, and even combined, we could barely keep her arm from moving anymore. The girl is stronger than you know. Far greater than her petite frame suggests. I only got the blade from her after agreeing to take that device out."

"That's insane, Lizzy," Jack murmured under his breath, his voice hushed by the weight of the staggering revelations. Weary and overwhelmed, he sought a chair, his shoulders sagging under the invisible burden that now felt all too real—a burden he no longer had the strength to resist.

"I couldn't agree more," Elizabeth responded, her hands finding their way to her forehead, supporting her as she leaned forward. "I witnessed it firsthand, and still, it feels utterly unbelievable. After I removed it, she fell asleep. The healing process seems to have taken a toll on her."

Jack observed his sister, a keen recognition that there was more to this strange tale lurking beneath the surface. Elizabeth appeared poised to share, yet an unspoken hesitation held her back, as though she wasn't quite ready to divulge the entire narrative.

Seizing the moment, Jack prodded, hoping his prompting would coax the rest of the story from her. "What else is there, Lizzy? It's almost as if you're holding something back right now."

Jack's insight was on target. Elizabeth was indeed withholding, understanding her brother far more deeply than he realized. She'd witnessed his pain over the years, grateful that he hadn't turned to self-destructive vices like drugs or alcohol to cope. His workaholic tendencies, while not ideal, were manageable, a struggle she could support him through. Even his use of his niece Brooke as a shield against meaningful relationships, Elizabeth had managed to endure. But those coping mechanisms were no longer viable.

The mere presence of Faye had upended everything. She had instigated a transformation in Jack, a shift that had prompted him to reopen emotional avenues he had long shut down. Now, Elizabeth grappled with the uncertainty of what lay ahead for her brother, now armed with this newfound knowledge about the woman he had fallen deeply in love with.

Jack's inquiry pierced the air, his voice tinged with concern and curiosity. The words floated between them, carrying a weight of anticipation like a heavy breath suspended in the air. "What's going on, Lizzy? What are you not telling me?"

The soft creak of the chair beneath Elizabeth's slight movement created a subtle undercurrent, like a melody echoing in the background. Meeting Jack's gaze, Elizabeth took in the intricate mosaic of emotions painted across his countenance, her insight guiding her timing in revealing the information. His eyes radiated an unquenchable curiosity, urging her to proceed.

"The autopsies for the victims of the serial killer you're pursuing... Jason performed them," she disclosed, her words hanging in the air like a fragile thread.

A hesitant pause followed, a breath held in anticipation of the revelations that were yet to come. The room seemed to hold its breath, a quiet reverence settling over them as the weight of the unspoken truth lingered, suspended between them. In that momentary silence, Jack seized the opportunity to pose his question. "And what does that have to do with Faye?" he inquired, though his thoughts gravitated more toward grappling with the realization of Faye's extraordinary nature. An internal dialogue of uncertainty unfolded, *Can I even manage more revelations about Faye? How much more can I bear?*

"Just hold that thought for a second, because I'm about to get to that," Elizabeth prefaced, her words brimming with anticipation. She urged Jack to pause momentarily, letting the suspense linger in the air.

Elizabeth continued, her voice steady and measured, "Did you know that there were absolutely no dental or medical records for any of the victims? Not a single trace of them ever having seen a doctor or a dentist, as far as our investigations could determine."

Jack responded with a sense of nonchalance, his curiosity not fully ignited yet. "Doesn't strike me as odd, honestly. People can avoid medical care for various reasons."

Elizabeth, however, was intent on unveiling the unusual pattern she had discerned. Her voice took on a contemplative tone as she guided Jack's understanding. "Think about it, Jackie. All four of them, according to DMV records, were in their forties or older. Yet, not a single cavity, sprain, molar extraction, broken bone—none of the common ailments you'd expect with age. No prostate exams, nothing. These men could've theoretically lived well into their hundreds with the sheer level of health they exhibited."

The weight of the extraordinary reality was tangible in her words, conveying both her astonishment and resignation in accepting the inexplicable.

Jack's response was swift, revealing his familiarity with the challenges posed by the case they were pursuing. "And you're telling me that this pattern held true for all of them?"

"But perhaps the most intriguing piece of all is their blood type," Elizabeth continued, her voice carrying a weight of anticipation. "As part of the autopsy, Jason conducted blood tests. The results came back with a blood type that's virtually unheard of. In all of history, there's been only one documented case of this blood type. Jason stumbled upon it buried in some obscure medical journal during grad school, while he was researching rare blood disorders. It was a mere footnote, hardly explored further."

Her words came forth cautiously, laced with a sense of concern for what lay ahead. Elizabeth pondered the impact of her forthcoming revelations, wondering if they might be the last straw to burden Jack's already heavy load. She dreaded the thought of him breaking under the weight of it all.

"Until now?" Jack's response held a mix of inquiry and affirmation, a fusion of both question and statement.

Elizabeth nodded, her expression serious. With a small gesture of reassurance, she reached across the divide between them, placing her hand on his knee as a show of support. "Yes, until now."

Taking a deep breath, Jack sought clarity, his voice steady despite the mounting astonishment. "So, what does all of this imply?"

"Jackie, the blood type we found is incredibly rare—so rare that it's only been documented once in the entire history of medicine," Elizabeth unveiled, each word carrying the weight of the revelation. "And in the span of just two months, we've encountered not one, but four individuals with this same rare blood type. That's the link."

In the midst of the emotional rollercoaster that had recently gripped Jack's life, this revelation brought a glimmer of happiness. "Incredible, truly incredible. But in the grand scheme, it's just a piece of the puzzle. We still have no idea who else shares this blood type, how the killer identifies them, or even how to track them down," Jack mused, his voice a blend of awe and frustration. The magnitude of unanswered questions loomed large.

Elizabeth's response held a subtle challenge, a suggestion that Jack investigate closer to home for answers. "Perhaps you should consider probing those questions within your own circle."

Perplexed, Jack leaned in, his voice carrying a cautious curiosity. "What are you getting at?"

Elizabeth paused for effect, her tone laden with significance. "Jason conducted the blood tests, and the results came in moments ago. But here's the kicker... Faye," she hesitated briefly, the weight of her revelation palpable, "...Faye also has this same rare blood type."

Jack's initial reaction was speechless surprise. His mouth opened, but no words emerged. The realization left him stunned, a whirlwind of thoughts racing through his mind. His desire to speak with Faye surged within him, a longing to untangle the complexities of this situation and make sense of a world that had become increasingly bewildering.

For any of those desired outcomes to become reality, Jack realized the essential first step was to have a conversation with Faye. In the midst of this bewildering and chaotic situation, Faye was the one individual who potentially held the answers to the countless questions haunting him. Yet, she was also the person who had intentionally kept him in the shadows, withholding crucial information and leaving him adrift in uncertainty.

A surge of emotions swept through Jack—beyond frustration, teetering on the edge of fury, and comfortably nestled in a cocoon of seething resentment. He was practically simmering with anger, his emotional temperature rising steadily. He felt like he was standing on the precipice of full-blown ire, ready to unleash the storm of his emotions upon Faye.

To say he was irate seemed almost an understatement—it was more like an inferno of indignation brewing within him, heating up every fiber of his being. He yearned to vent his frustration at Faye, convinced that her deliberate omission of truth amounted to a betrayal of trust, a sentiment he could not easily dismiss.

Guided by Elizabeth, Jack left the office and entered the room where Faye was recuperating. The sight of her small, delicate figure extinguished the flames of his anger, replaced by a different kind of fire. The intensity of his emotions surged anew, reigniting an internal struggle he had been wrestling with ever since he encountered the fragile woman who now lay before him, vulnerable in a hospital bed. He reached a breaking point, the weight of unspoken emotions becoming too heavy to bear. With an exhale, the tension that had slowly coiled within him began to dissipate. All of his anger at Faye had not dissipated yet though. The act of admitting his feelings provided an unexpected sanctuary, a moment of solace he hadn't anticipated.

"I love this little girl even though she turned my whole world upside down," the words finally found their way out, whispered to himself as he drew closer to her bedside.

Jack's emotions churned within him like a tempest, a storm of anger and love intertwined. He recognized the need to cleanse himself of this roiling fury, fearing its potential to damage the tender bloom of his affection for Faye. As he gazed upon her, lying in that hospital bed, he couldn't help but feel a fierce urge to shield her from the harshness of the world. She appeared fragile, a porcelain figurine amidst the sterile surroundings, and he longed to envelop her in his arms, a bulwark against the tides of adversity.

The pallor of her complexion was disconcerting, a subtle ashen hue that spoke of the ordeal her body had endured. Dark crescents clung to the delicate skin under her eyes, a testament to the physical toll she had paid. The medical professionals, Jason and Elizabeth, had carefully stripped away her clothes, an act driven by necessity in their pursuit of healing. Now, she lay beneath the thin veil of a hospital gown, her vulnerability heightened by the exposure.

A folded blanket rested at the foot of her bed, a modest sanctuary against the room's coolness. Jack's hands tenderly embraced its edges, shaking it out before draping it lovingly over Faye's diminutive form. His actions were a silent vow, an unspoken promise to shield her not only from the chill but from the adversities that life might throw her way.

Faye's voice, though weakened by exhaustion, carried a hint of playful warmth. "So you don't want to stare at my legs anymore?"

A soft smile tugged at the corners of her lips, revealing a gentle spirit undaunted by her recent trials. The healing process, extensive and miraculous, had sapped her energy, yet her resolve remained unshaken. She understood the source of her weariness, a consequence of her body's remarkable recuperation, and the passage of time would surely mend her completely.

Faye's eyes remained shut, a shroud of mystery concealing her thoughts. Jack's curiosity, persistent as ever, prodded him to seek answers from the enigmatic source itself.

His voice held a gentle intrigue as he queried, "How do you know when I'm looking at your legs?" He was determined to unravel the nuances of her extraordinary abilities while the subject was fresh in his mind.

A hesitant pause yielded to Faye's revelation, her words resonating with both reluctance and candidness. "Your pheromones spike. I can smell them. They drive me to distraction."

Unveiling this aspect of her heightened senses, she involuntarily echoed her own inner reaction, realizing the extent to which Jack's emotions had a hold over her. The notion of her awareness was almost overwhelming in its intensity, particularly now, as Jack's emotions seemed to swirl around him like an intoxicating mist.

As Jack grappled with this newfound insight, his amazement painted a vibrant smile across his face. The revelation of Faye's olfactory prowess filled him with a mix of fascination and pride.

"How in the hell do you smell my pheromones?" His intrigue bordered on disbelief, his curiosity spurring him to further understanding.

With an effortless laugh, Faye responded, her playfulness surfacing once more, a sign of her gradually returning ease.

"I just do. I can't explain how it smells, but if I had to describe it, it's kinda like a sweet musky smell." Her playful tone sought to lift the veil of tension that had lingered over their interactions, shrouding the weight of secrets they now shared.

Jack's curiosity wasn't quenched, his desire to delve into the intricacies of her senses pressing on. "Is that a good thing or a bad thing?" His inquiry, laced with genuine interest, illuminated his determination to comprehend her experiences.

A soft laugh escaped Faye, a mixture of amusement and mild frustration. "Kind of both," she admitted, her tone tinged with a blend of honesty and vulnerability. "I like it, but it makes it so that all I can think about is you. I can also hear your heart speed up." The words carried a confession that echoed the intensity of their connection.

The moment shifted, Faye's eyes fluttering open to meet Jack's gaze. This was the first time he had the chance to peer into her unguarded eyes, and it felt like a revelation in itself. Adjusting her position in the bed, she oriented herself to face him fully, seeking to engage in this moment of mutual discovery.

Jack's voice was imbued with both wonder and a touch of realization as he observed her eyes. "Your eyes... they really are like a cat's eyes." The recognition of this unique characteristic deepened their connection, as if each revelation drew them closer, transcending the barriers between them.

Faye paused, deliberating the path of her words. She had kept much hidden, a choice born from a desire to unveil her truth on her own terms. Yet, circumstances had unraveled her secrets sooner than she had intended. "Yeah, I usually wear contacts to make them look more..." She hesitated, caught between honesty and the remnants of her previous secrecy. Her words danced on the precipice of truth, revealing a secret she had long held close.

"Human," Jack interjected, offering the word that matched her unspoken thoughts.

"I was going to say 'natural', but I guess you could use that term too," Faye replied, a touch of equivocation shading her words. The weight of Jack's newfound knowledge rested heavily between them, a secret shared that had shifted their dynamic.

The ensuing silence carried an unspoken tension, the space between them filled with the echoes of revelations and concealed emotions. Jack, unyielding in his pursuit of truth, broke through the quiet with a single query that encapsulated the essence of their enigma-laden connection. "So... what are you? Are you human?" His words lingered in the air, a question that held the promise of unraveling the mysteries that had bound them together.

"I am and I'm a little bit more, I guess," Faye began, her voice carrying both the weight of her confession and a touch of vulnerability. The truth she was unveiling held the potential to reshape their understanding of her identity.

"I am a genetically engineered being. I was designed to fill a specific purpose, just like the guy we are chasing." With these words, she sought to offer Jack the clarity he had long yearned for, a stepping stone toward unraveling the enigma they were entwined in.

The revelation sparked a cascade of thoughts in Jack's mind, his thoughts naturally gravitating toward the killer they were tirelessly pursuing. The fog of uncertainty that had shrouded the investigation seemed to be lifting, replaced by the glimmers of understanding.

"So... what are you designed for? And him?" Jack's question, though simple in form, carried the weight of an insatiable curiosity and a thirst for comprehending the intricate tapestry woven around them. As Faye began to unravel her truth, he felt the tendrils of revelation tugging at his grasp, pulling him further into the heart of the mystery.

Faye's voice bore a mixture of emotion as she responded, a blend of anger, sadness, and a hint of resignation. "He's a killer. He's a common soldier," her words were tinged with a palpable disdain, the emotions she had repressed now finding a voice. Jack could sense the depths of her hatred and frustration, her connection to the killer a complex web of intertwined pasts.

Her tone shifted as she continued, revealing the stark contrast between their roles. "Me, I am different. I'm analogous to a spy and assassin, I guess."

The vulnerability of her confession was evident, her voice tinged with a touch of self-consciousness. The burden of revealing so much about herself weighed heavily on her shoulders, a burden she had never faced before. Jack's presence seemed to create a space for her to share her truths, a rarity in her life until now.

The dynamic between Jack and Faye had evolved significantly over the course of their conversation. What began as a guarded exchange gradually transformed into a deeper connection, laden with revelations and shared vulnerabilities. Faye's admission allowed Jack to glimpse the complexity of her existence, the fusion of science and humanity that defined her identity.

Jack's attention shifted to Faye as he noticed her attempting to sit up in the hospital bed. The subtle protest of the bed's creaking accompanied her movement, a small detail that underscored the significance of her actions. Without hesitation, Jack rose from his seat, his purpose clear as he adjusted the bed to accommodate her, ensuring she could rest in a more comfortable position. The act was both gentle and considerate, a silent gesture of his care for her well-being.

Returning to his seat, Jack's focus remained on Faye as she began to speak again, her words laced with a mix of hesitation and an underlying sense of urgency. The space between them seemed charged, both with the weight of the revelations she was about to share and the unspoken connection that seemed to grow stronger with each passing moment.

"I can try to tell you more," Faye's offer held the promise of deeper understanding, despite the difficulties that might arise from disbelief.

Her admission about her ability to reveal more created a bridge of trust between them, a willingness to navigate the uncertain territory of truth together. As Jack settled back into his seat, their proximity rekindled the unspoken exchange of pheromones that seemed to heighten their awareness of each other.

The narrative shifted as Faye began to unravel her past, each word a thread woven into the intricate tapestry of her existence. Her admission about her origins and purpose was a revelation that could easily fracture the delicate understanding Jack had crafted about the world around him.

"I was created by the same people that created him," Faye's voice carried a mixture of resignation and self-awareness.

The complexities of her identity, tied to the same source as the killer they pursued, created a web of intrigue that Jack couldn't ignore. The dichotomy of her cover in law enforcement and her covert assignment further highlighted the interplay between her humanity and her engineered nature.

As the conversation delved deeper into the nature of the soldier and the entity pulling the strings, Jack's detective instincts kicked in. His question about catching the soldier illustrated his determination to bring justice to the situation. The layers of intrigue were piling up, and Jack's desire to unravel the mystery was palpable.

But then, the narrative took an unexpected turn as Faye mentioned the Shepherds. The weight of her revelation hung heavy in the room, a silence settling like a shroud as Jack processed the implications of what he was hearing. Faye's words painted a picture of a clandestine force that operated behind the scenes, orchestrating events with a sense of superiority that transcended human understanding.

"The Shepherds don't exactly identify themselves as human, and in that regard, they might be accurate. They're undeniably a breed apart, true homo-superior in every aspect. They possess heightened intelligence, physical prowess, and a lifespan that extends anywhere from two hundred to potentially even two hundred and fifty years. Existing for centuries, they've remained concealed in the backdrop of human history, subtly steering its course to suit their own aims," Faye explained, succinctly capturing the essence of the Shepherds' unique status and influence.

Faye's eloquent description of the Shepherds, their intelligence, longevity, and hidden influence, expanded the scope of the narrative dramatically. The concept of a hidden race shaping history from the shadows was a concept that challenged everything Jack thought he knew.

"The individuals Delta 67-3 killed are Shepherds," Faye disclosed, observing the visible unease that washed over Jack in response to her revelation.

Despite his attempts to maintain composure, Faye was attuned to the subtle twitches at the corner of his lips and the slight raise of his eyebrow before his self-control masked his involuntary reactions.

"I don't know why Delta 67-3 would target his own," Faye continued, her voice tinged with a mix of curiosity and concern. "My orders didn't encompass that bit of information. What I do know, though, is that the Shepherds place little value on life in general, especially when it comes to humans. They regard humans as mere sheep, which explains their chosen moniker. To them, we're meant to be guided, controlled, exploited, and disposed of when expedient. Eliminating their own wouldn't likely trouble them if it served their goals," she explained, her words heavy with the truth of what she had revealed.

Faye felt stripped of defenses, laid bare by the truths she'd told. This was further amplified by her personal connection to the very beings she discussed. The fact that she was genetically engineered made her practically one of them, a reality that left her feeling exposed and vulnerable.

"So, essentially, we're nothing more than commodities to them, manipulated as part of their grand scheme?" Jack inquired, seeking to grasp the gravity of the revelation. Faye confirmed his understanding with a solemn nod.

In the quiet that ensued, Jack allowed his thoughts to settle, the puzzle pieces of information interlocking within his mind. He wove together what he already knew with the fresh insights, molding his next line of inquiry. As he pondered, he decided to change course, opting for a lighter approach—uncovering the mundane curiosities about Faye, rather than delving into weighty matters.

His question broke the silence, carrying a lighthearted tone, "So, how old are you actually, given that you were genetically engineered?"

Faye's response was a surprised burst of almost-laughter, her hand rising to her mouth to stifle it. Jack's unexpected inquiry had an unintended effect, lightening the atmosphere and brightening her mood. Amidst a brief shuffle on the bed that produced accompanying squeaks, she managed to gather herself and speak, "Biologically, I'm in my late twenties to early thirties. But chronologically, I'm only about ten years old. I understand how strange that must sound," she added, chuckling softly to herself as she considered the disparity.

Amidst the levity, Faye's thoughts couldn't help but amuse themselves. "After all I've shared, that's what he chooses to ask?" she mused inwardly, a hint of playful exasperation coloring her inner dialogue.

"With everything laid out, where does that leave us now?" Jack inquired, shifting the conversation in a new direction.

Faye's response followed, revealing her determination, "I don't know about you but I want to find out what's being planned that requires the execution of Shepherds. I'm driven to uncover the truth." The gravity of her words underscored her commitment.

Jack's curiosity persisted as he asked, "Were you even aware that the victims were Shepherds?"

Faye shook her head, her gesture mirroring her spoken words. "No, I had no way of knowing initially. I only got the assignment to come and slow down your investigation and look after Delta 67-3. But somehow, that soldier knew his prey. In the evidence photos, there was a picture frame on the wall. One of the faces seemed familiar to me, prompting me to investigate further. When I arrived at the scene, Delta 67-3..." Her voice trailed off, her fists clenching as she held back the rest, her thoughts drawn inward as she processed the memories and actions that followed.

"Delta 67-3. He left behind a clue, a breadcrumb for me to follow," Faye explained, her voice resolute. "He anticipated that I'd eventually discover that photograph, and he orchestrated the situation at the lawyer's house, counting on me to come. It felt like it was a trap, and I walked right into it but I'm not sure. My secondary objective is to neutralize him if I receive the order. Somehow, that deranged psycho prick must have deduced that and decided to strike first but again, that's just me guessing. It didn't seem like he wanted to kill me at first. At the end though, it seemed like if you hadn't arrived when you did, he would have ground me down, unrelenting, until he ended my life. I know that those bastards possess an uncanny endurance, even greater than mine."

"Well, I think I scared him off somehow. When you tackled me, absorbing the impact of that pipe, he didn't bother with us while I took you out of there," Jack recounted, his tone tinged with a mix of relief and grim realization.

"That's because you shot him. I saw that much before I got hit," Faye explained, her voice carrying a mixture of observation and analysis. "I don't believe you managed to kill him, though. I wouldn't be too concerned about him anymore for now. He's slipped his leash and I'm pretty sure that they know it by now. They're probably gonna order him to retire." A touch of resignation laced her words, revealing a longing for Jack's attempt on the man's life to have been successful.

What Faye refrained from telling him was that she had a strong suspicion they were aware she was no longer entirely under their control. She was confident they could no longer monitor her as they once had, thanks to the removal of that device. Reflecting on it, her belief that Delta 67-3 had slipped his leash rested on this very fact.

Jack's brows furrowed, perplexed by the use of the word 'retire'.

"The Shepherd Institute is gonna have him kill himself," Faye clarified, her words cutting through the uncertainty. Jack absorbed this with a solemn nod of comprehension.

"Prior to embarking on this mission, when I was still with the Shepherd Institute, I stumbled upon an enormous chamber housing tens of thousands of clone generation pods," Faye revealed, concern etching lines on her face, evident to Jack and anyone observing. "The only thing I can think of as a reason for having that many clones is for an army."

Jack's reaction was immediate, his skepticism laid bare with an incredulous snort. His hand instinctively rose to cover a hint of amusement. "Seriously, Faye? This isn't a Star Wars movie," he retorted, his tone flat and dismissive.

"I'm deadly serious; this is no joke. Returning to my birthplace is my way of putting an end to this," Faye asserted firmly, her resolve unwavering.

Jack's response was immediate, his tone charged with a mixture of frustration and concern. "Why are you so willing to risk everything by yourself?" he questioned vehemently, a complex blend of emotions evident in his voice.

The fact that Faye would entertain such a notion infuriated him, but what irked him even more was the idea of her jeopardizing her life for this cause. Both sources of his frustration collided, leaving him feeling excluded and left in the dark.

"You won't be going in there alone. I'll be going with you," he declared resolutely, the determination in his voice unwavering

The thought of Faye being harmed again was unacceptable to him. Recognizing that he couldn't dissuade her once she'd set her mind, he chose to stand beside her instead.

"I can't ask that of you," Faye responded, her awareness of the inherent perils in such an undertaking apparent in her voice.

"You're not asking. I'm stepping up and volunteering," Jack retorted, his chest pulsing as he firmly thumped it with his clenched fist.

A grin of determination, a blend of strength and pride, spread across his face. The echo of his military days resonated within him as he made this proclamation, the memories of camaraderie and shared purpose returning vividly.

Faye closed her eyes, a conflicted expression forming as she shook her head. The unexpected offer of help from Jack had set her heart racing, but uncertainty gnawed at her.

"I have something I want to protect the future for. I don't want you to get hurt for that," she admitted, her voice tinged with a mix of gratitude and concern.

Her gaze dropped, her posture slumping as if under the load of her worries. Jack's response was unwavering, his words carrying a seriousness that matched his resolve.

"You don't have to worry about me getting hurt. I closed my heart off after Iraq," he disclosed, the pride and camaraderie of earlier moments fading as he recalled the profound losses he'd endured during his years of military service.

Faye sensed a misalignment in their conversation, a divide between the types of hurt she was concerned about.

"I mean physical pain, the risk of losing your life or being injured," she clarified, her voice a mix of caution and concern.

Jack's acknowledgment was swift, his response carrying a weight of understanding.

"I knew what you meant. You were right about me with the things you said when we were at the cabin. Do you want to know why it's like that?" he ventured, using her concern as a gateway to unburden himself, a doorway to reveal the painful events that had shaped his past.

Faye extended her hand, her fingers finding Jack's in a firm grasp. The significance of Jack's forthcoming disclosure wasn't lost on her. She recognized that this exchange could set into motion a profound shift in their lives, an alignment of their paths that would weave them together, inextricably intertwined.

This realization had been growing within her, a desire for a connection that went beyond the surface, something she both wanted and needed in her life. She saw the potential for that connection with Jack Riddle, a potential she believed could be nurtured if he was open to it.

Jack bared his heart, unveiling not just his history but also his pain—the most tragic chapter of his life. The passage of time hadn't dulled the ache; instead, it lingered, ever-fresh and tender, a wound still pulsating with agony at the slightest touch. This pain had taken on a life of its own, an entity suffused with palpable energy. At last, Jack stood prepared to confront this beast, to quell its power and find closure.

"I was on the brink of marriage, but we decided to postpone it until after my deployment. Seemed like the wiser choice," he recounted, his voice tinged with vulnerability.

"Did she call it off while you were in Iraq?" Faye inquired gently, her concern tangible.

Jack's response was heavy with emotion, "No, she... she passed away." His emotions lay bare, a raw and unfiltered display of his inner turmoil, an open window for Faye to perceive.

"I'm sorry to hear that. How did it happen?" Faye inquired.

Jack's silence stretched for a moment, a poignant pause that held more weight than words ever could. His hands enfolded Faye's smaller ones, a physical connection that seemed to mirror the emotional bond they were forging. His gaze remained fixed on their interlocked hands, as if seeking solace and grounding in their touch. The rhythm of Faye's heartbeat flowed through their joined hands, an unspoken synchronicity that resonated deep within Jack's chest. With a gradual shift, he lifted his eyes to meet Faye's, revealing a wellspring of tears that spoke to the fresh pain stirred by the memory he was about to share.

His voice, soft and laden with emotion, finally broke the stillness. "You already know how she died."

The weight of those words hung heavy in the air, a palpable echo of the grief that Jack had carried for so long. Faye's response wavered, caught in a moment of uncertainty and realization.

"I don't know what you're talking about..." Her voice faltered, then softened to a near whisper. "No... wait. The platoon sergeant in the Humvee was your fiancé?"

Jack's affirmative nod held both a confirmation and a doorway into the depths of his pain. The confession flowed, a torrent of remorse, guilt, and sorrow that had remained locked away. "Yes. I was able to save everyone but her. She was trapped there. I know she was scared and she was alone and I couldn't save her. She died alone, probably thinking that I had abandoned her. Everything was happening so fast and I couldn't keep up with all of it. I thought that she had gotten out. My carelessness got her killed."

Faye's empathy was palpable, her voice gentle yet firm as she sought to ease the heavy burden Jack carried. "You didn't get her killed. You can't take that on yourself. You can't blame yourself for something that was beyond your control."

But Jack's self-reproach was deep-seated, his guilt an insidious force that clouded his perception. "She was my soldier. I was the platoon leader and she was sitting in my spot in that vehicle. I should have been the one to die there that day."

Faye's words were a beacon of reason, a counterpoint to the darkness that had consumed Jack's thoughts. "Hey, you don't know that and you can't say that for certain. If you had died, then what's to say your whole platoon wouldn't have died too? You rallied them and led them when they needed it most, and because of that, you saved their lives."

Jack's pain was tangled with regret, his belief that he should have been the one to pay the ultimate price gnawing at him. "But I couldn't save her life. I... I should have died instead of her."

Faye's response carried an unwavering strength, a refusal to let Jack's guilt rewrite the narrative of his fiancé's sacrifice. "It obviously wasn't meant for you to die there that day. Every time you say something like that, you lessen her life and you cheapen the sacrifice that she made. She was a soldier too. She knew the risks just as much as you did. She knew what it could cost her by choosing to serve, and she did it anyway. Don't take that away from her because you feel guilty that you're alive and she isn't. That's just selfish."

The exchange laid bare the complexities of grief, guilt, and survival. The depths of Jack's pain were matched by Faye's insight and unwavering support, a testament to their evolving connection. The final moment of vulnerability, as Jack looked into Faye's eyes with his heart still haunted by the past, was a powerful reminder of the journey they were on.

"Faye, from the first moment I met you, I wanted you in my life."

Faye's heart leapt at those words, the warmth of Jack's voice penetrating the layers of sorrow. Her own joy and longing mirrored his sentiment.

"I could tell you felt something. Your pheromones made it pretty damn obvious that you had more than a passing interest in me. To be honest, I felt the same way. In fact, it's more so now. I've never needed anyone as much as you in my whole life—all ten years," Faye interjected with a shared chuckle, infusing the heavy conversation with a touch of lightness. "When I met you, Jack, I knew that I needed you. I wanted to have your arms around me."

A brief, contemplative pause hung in the air, a moment of shared introspection that seemed to call for further honesty and understanding. Faye, feeling the weight of a withheld truth, took a deep breath, breaking the silence with a confession that she felt compelled to share. Her words held a vulnerability that resonated deeply, bridging the gap between them.

"Jack, the reason I acted like that in the cabin is because of my age," Faye's voice carried a mixture of hesitance and sincerity. Her revelation echoed with a sense of raw authenticity. "I had never felt love before. The emotion was so intense and I wasn't ready for it. I didn't know how to deal with it because I didn't have the experience learned from growing up."

Jack's response was a gentle shake of his head, a silent assurance that he didn't want Faye to carry any unnecessary burden. However, the conflict within him was palpable, his own emotions a swirling storm of confusion.

"Somehow I feel like I'm betraying her memory," he confessed, the weight of his past relationship still heavy on his heart.

"Who, your fiancé? How so?" Faye's skillful redirection shifted the focus, allowing them to explore Jack's feelings without dwelling on her own confession.

Her ability to navigate sensitive topics showcased her emotional intelligence and growing connection with Jack.

"I have just felt I've never deserved to be happy again because she made me happy and I lost her," Jack's admission was laden with a mix of sorrow and guilt.

The memory of his late fiancé, Lauren, was a shadow that he struggled to escape. Faye's curiosity extended beyond mere conversation; she wanted to grasp the essence of the woman who had held Jack's heart.

"What was your fiancé's name?" Her inquiry held a tenderness, a desire to understand the woman whose memory still held sway over Jack.

"Lauren Beck," Jack's voice wavered slightly as he spoke the name that carried a world of emotions.

With sincerity and conviction, Faye countered Jack's self-doubt. "Well, I'm sure Lauren would approve of us," she declared, her words a beacon of reassurance in a sea of uncertainty.

Jack's skepticism crept in, a self-imposed barrier to happiness. "How do you know that? I mean, isn't saying something like that self-serving for what you want?"

His grin carried a hint of self-deprecation. Faye, though, wouldn't allow Jack to undermine himself. She was resolute in her belief that he deserved happiness.

"If she truly loved you, she would want you to be happy. Even without her. Didn't she love you?" Faye's question cut through the fog of Jack's doubts, laying bare the essence of love's selflessness.

"Yeah, I know she did," Jack admitted, his tears wiped away, replaced by a genuine smile fueled by Faye's unwavering support.

As the conversation lightened, Faye playfully led Jack through a series of questions, her intent clear: to free him from his own emotional restraints. The banter revealed the lighter side of their connection, the shared humor that could mend the cracks in their hearts.

"Million-dollar question coming up. Did she want you to be happy or sad?" Faye's playful tone was a balm, soothing the wounds that had been exposed.

A hearty chuckle escaped Jack's lips, an infectious laughter that seemed to release the tension he had been carrying. "That's an easy question to answer. She wanted me to stop being an ass since I wasn't misogynistic."

Faye's surprise was written all over her face, her playful expression shifting to disbelief. The unexpected twist caught her off guard, and she playfully punched Jack's shoulder, a gesture that blended affection and mock indignation. Jack, in response, leaned in and planted a gentle, playful kiss on Faye's lips, the gesture a continuation of their shared intimacy and the journey they were navigating together.

14

As the morning light spilled lazily through the window, Faye stirred from slumber to the inviting aroma of breakfast wafting through the air. Inhaling deeply, she savored the scent before exhaling in contentment. It was as though a weight had been lifted, a newfound ease settling over her. With her secrets unburdened and her heart's affections laid bare, including her deep love for Jack, Faye felt the tendrils of tranquility embracing her. Her desire was clear: to revolve her world around Jack, her love and devotion finding their focal point.

Yet, a solitary task remained, a promise she intended to fulfill. Whether time would present the opportunity or whether she'd need to seize it, she was determined to complete this last piece of their intricate puzzle.

Shifting onto her side, Faye's gaze fell upon the pillow where Jack had rested his head earlier that morning. She reached for it, cradling it against her chest with a gentle embrace. Nuzzling into the fabric, a joyous whoop bubbled from her lips as her legs kicked playfully upon the bed. The swell of love she felt was nothing short of intoxicating, a completeness that transcended the physical. Astonishingly, their relationship had yet to venture into the realm of the physical, and yet Faye sensed an undeniable connection to Jack, a sensation that lingered even when she adorned herself in his shirts.

Faye and Jack had returned to his place after leaving the morgue at the hospital. The ordeal had left Faye exhausted, a fact she had shared with Jack. She explained her unique healing process, which depended on injury severity and energy consumption for tissue regeneration

The rapid healing she had triggered earlier had drained her energy, necessitating hours of unconsciousness. Jack now understood why she had such a substantial appetite—her heightened senses and strength demanded an extraordinary caloric intake. The contrast in their dietary needs was stark: Faye, at five foot two and one hundred pounds, required almost twice the calories as Jack, a six-foot, two-hundred-and-fifty-pound man.

Entering the kitchen, Faye discovered Jack engrossed in whisking eggs behind the counter. The cozy space boasted a minimalistic aesthetic, a testament to Jack's functional decorating taste. The arrangement reflected his attention to practicality, with cool tones on the walls, light-colored cabinets, and well-organized counters.

As Jack tended to the stove, his attention seamlessly shifted to preparing the eggs. Faye, still recovering from her recent ordeal, settled onto a stool. Her presence exuded a sense of relief, a testament to their shared connection.

With exchanged smiles, Faye's playfulness shone as she teased Jack. "You know you're stuck with me now."

Chuckling, Jack responded in jest, "That's okay. I like stray cats."

Faye's response was a playful display of her own as she stuck her tongue out and blew raspberries, evoking a light-hearted atmosphere.

The mood shifted as Jack's straightforward declaration resonated, "I'm glad I found you, Faye." His sincerity held a sense of grounding, an acknowledgment of their intertwined journey.

Faye's blush spoke volumes, her vulnerability evident as she confessed, "That's not fair. I've never been in love, so I'm still learning how to deal with how I feel, and you're embarrassing me."

A wide grin adorned Jack's face as he deftly began crafting omelettes in a skillet, the sizzle of cooking eggs filling the air. Once cooked to perfection, he plated a generous breakfast for himself and an even heartier one for Faye. Complemented by a tall glass of juice and a serving of diced melon, the meal was a testament to Jack's thoughtful nature.

As the plates found their place on the table, Jack's actions were not the only thing to change the atmosphere. He approached Faye from behind the counter, a decision that spoke of his unspoken intentions. Wrapping his arms around her, he enveloped her in a warm embrace, their physical closeness echoing the emotional bonds they were forming. Faye responded, her hands finding their place on his forearms as she leaned her head back onto his chest.

"Did you know that you'd be surrounded by my love when we first met?" Jack's curiosity drove him to probe deeper, seeking insight into Faye's innermost thoughts, a desire to forge a connection that went beyond the surface

His words were laced with a hint of vulnerability, an unspoken invitation for her to share her feelings more intimately.

"I didn't know on the first day, but I definitely felt that it was something I wanted by the end of the week," Faye admitted with a hint of sheepishness.

Sharing her feelings in such a direct manner was still a bit embarrassing for her, a revelation of vulnerability that made her heart race. Jack's admission followed suit, a declaration of his protective instincts.

"I want to keep you safe," he said sincerely, his words echoing the depth of his emotions.

Faye's response was marked by a proud stance, her hands confidently on her hips, and her shoulders squared.

"I'm stronger than you," she declared, the sentiment reflecting her newfound self-assurance.

Amidst their exchange, Faye's posture had an unintended effect. As her chest swelled with pride, the fabric of her shirt accentuated her figure. Jack's gaze flickered briefly, his thoughts venturing into territory he quickly tried to steer away from. He turned away, a flush of embarrassment tingeing his cheeks. Her display of strength had inadvertently provided him with an unintended glimpse of her panties, momentarily clouding his mind.

Faye, seemingly unaware of the effect her stance had on Jack, playfully flounced back onto the stool, causing it to skitter across the hardwood floor. Jack's attempt to diffuse the situation with humor was evident in his light-hearted response.

"Tomato, tomato," he said, pronouncing the word exactly the same both times, a whimsical attempt to bring levity to the moment.

"I can't imagine my life without you in it anymore, Jack," Faye admitted, her words carrying a weight of emotion.

"You won't have to. I'm not going anywhere," Jack reassured her, sealing his words with a gentle kiss on her cheek before taking his seat and preparing to enjoy their meal. "After about a week, you'll probably tell me to go to work and detect something."

Faye playfully shook her head from side to side, clearly amused by Jack's playful banter.

"What?" Jack exclaimed in mock offense, a mischievous grin on his face. "I'm funny."

"Like a hole in the head," Faye responded with a theatrical flair, punctuating her statement by pointing a finger to her temple.

"Joke with no punchline," Jack retorted, his tone deadpan, echoing a playful exchange from their first shared meal together.

Faye's incredulous expression morphed into one of surprise as she processed Jack's response. Their eyes locked, and the tension broke as they both burst into infectious laughter, sharing a moment of unfiltered joy.

Eventually, Faye managed to regain her composure, shifting from their light-hearted banter to the task at hand: a hearty meal. With a newfound sense of seriousness, she dug into her food with gusto. Jack watched her with a sense of fulfillment, pleased that he could provide for her and contribute to her well-being in such a meaningful way.

"You know I don't have any clothes here to wear. How am I supposed to go out in just your shirt? I'm not doing the hospital gown again like this morning," Faye quipped with a playful tone, highlighting her concern about her attire.

Jack, quick on his feet, had an immediate solution at the ready. His swift response indicated to Faye that he had already considered this issue, effectively dismissing her worries.

"Brooke seems like she wears the same size clothes as you. She has clothes in the other bedroom you can borrow until we can get you to the hotel later this morning."

"Thanks, we'll do that," Faye agreed, her focus already back on her breakfast. "Breakfast smells great," she complimented.

Observing her plate, Jack teasingly pointed out, "You're a little late saying that now," causing Faye to break into a foolish grin. Eagerly, she picked up her fork, ready to tackle the remaining half of her meal. Meanwhile, Jack eyed a delectable piece of bacon on her plate and concocted a cunning plan.

"Pass me the ketchup, please," Jack requested, gesturing towards the ketchup bottle placed on the opposite side of Faye. It was a sly attempt to divert her attention and execute his bacon-heist scheme.

Faye turned and reached for the ketchup bottle, intending to hand it to Jack. However, Jack's maneuver to snatch the bacon was thwarted by the swift descent of Faye's fork, which came down between his hand and her plate, its tines clinking against the counter.

"You can try, but you'll come back with a nub," Faye warned with a playful glint in her eye, her tone a mix of humor and affection.

"I thought you loved me," Jack playfully whined, adding a touch of petulance to his voice.

"I do, that's why you'll come back with a nub and your life," Faye retorted, laughter dancing in her eyes, underscoring the lighthearted and affectionate dynamic between them.

Jack playfully lunged at Faye, sweeping her up into his arms with a joyful laugh. Despite his playfulness, he remained mindful of her healing process, relying on his instincts and her cues. He guided her effortlessly, the chemistry between them evident in their movements. With Faye cradled in his arms, he eased back onto the couch, their laughter filling the air.

In the midst of their play, their lips met in a kiss that felt like an unspoken affirmation. Faye allowed her body to relax against Jack's, a sense of contentment settling between them. She shifted her head, nestling it against his chest to feel the comforting rhythm of his heartbeat. As her gaze wandered, she noticed something on the television screen, capturing her attention. Jack had the news on, but the volume was muted.

"Turn that up," Faye requested, her posture becoming more upright as she gently moved off of Jack. Her focus shifted entirely to the news broadcast, her curiosity piqued by what was being shown on the screen.

"In international news, the multi trillion-dollar technology giant, Shepherd Institute, fell victim to a series of terrorist bombing attacks. Offices spanning Europe, Africa, South America, and the Pacific were simultaneously targeted in this coordinated assault. No group has claimed responsibility for these attacks, but it's believed to be the work of an extremist faction protesting the company's recent shift towards manufacturing weapons components. The attacks resulted in the deaths of several key leaders. The remaining corporate headquarters, located locally in the city, did not respond to inquiries," the news anchor reported.

Jack muted the television again, his expression pensive as he exchanged a glance with Faye. The weight of the information settled in their thoughts as they considered the implications of the news they had just heard.

Faye broke the silence, her voice laced with a mix of concern and suspicion. "I can't help but think that labeling this as a terrorist attack is a flimsy cover-up. If I were to venture a guess, the person who's been giving me orders might have a hand in this. It feels like he's eliminating competition, consolidating power."

Jack nodded in agreement, his mind working to connect the dots. "It's not unheard of. Sometimes these kinds of attacks are strategic moves to centralize control. This might mean that our killer's mission isn't over yet."

Faye's eyes held determination as she voiced her insight. "I believe the next target might be the governor. My reasoning is based on the photograph with the newspaper clipping I told you about. It featured the governor, the lawyer, and Donovan Pike."

Jack's interest was piqued, and he leaned in. "So you think the governor might be a Shepherd?"

Faye nodded firmly. "Yes, and that makes him a likely target."

As they discussed their theories, a sense of urgency settled over them. The pieces of the puzzle were falling into place, leading them closer to the heart of the conspiracy they were unraveling.

Donovan's gesture of neglecting to offer a seat went unnoticed by Delta 67-3, and he saw no reason to raise the issue. Their rapport was rooted in a profound understanding, a silent accord that negated the need for formalities. In their dynamic, misunderstandings were nonexistent. Their communication was a subtle dance: one held the reins of command, the other executed without question or hesitation.

Delta 67-3 approached his meeting with Donovan Pike devoid of nervousness. The notion of such an emotion was a foreign concept to him, as distant and inscrutable as the intricacies of circumnavigating a black hole's event horizon. Abstract sentiments like love, hate, and fear held no sway over his synthetic being. He was impervious to them all. With an emotional spectrum as unyielding as his programming, he stood before Donovan Pike, poised and unaffected, much like he would before a prospective target.

Donovan, however, existed in stark contrast. While Delta 67-3 could establish fleeting empathic connections with others, especially his victims, Donovan remained an enigma. The man's detachment from humanity was so profound that he appeared to hover on the periphery of human existence.

Seated behind an opulent, antique desk that occupied a commanding presence in the room, Donovan exuded an air of calculated detachment. The desk, a relic of time, was perhaps the only item in the world he deemed worthy of consideration. Yet even this attachment held a fragile quality. Donovan would consign the desk to ashes without hesitation should necessity dictate. This inanimate object occupied space within his private sanctum, a space that Donovan granted with fleeting significance, acknowledging the transience of possessions in his world.

To Donovan, Delta 67-3 mirrored that very desk—a mere object devoid of personal connection. In his estimation, Delta 67-3 held less value than a worn pair of socks, a disposability exemplified by Donovan's habit of never wearing the garments twice. The same disposability applied to other clothing items, with these items serving as a metaphor for the fleeting nature of their worth.

In public, Donovan might acknowledge Delta 67-3's existence as casually as he would mention something else having a utilitarian function, devoid of any emotional weight. But as with items that had outlived their utility, Delta 67-3's worth hinged solely on his capacity to execute tasks. Should that capacity falter, his destiny would align with that of worn-out socks—discarded, replaced without sentiment.

Donovan's focus transcended the ephemeral realm. The fleeting existence of items like his opulent desk paled in significance compared to the forces that commanded his attention. His sphere of consideration encompassed matters of such profound importance that it extended beyond the boundaries of the human experience, even though he himself lived outside it. While he projected an image of extreme detachment, this veneer concealed a profound connection to humanity that defied verbal expression.

Setting his longevity aside, Donovan acknowledged the inevitability of change. Actions taken in the distant past had a ripple effect on the present. He harbored concerns about an ancient action, buried deep within the annals of human history, long faded from collective memory. And yet, he possessed an unshakable awareness. It became imperative for him to devise strategies to alter the enduring consequences of these long-forgotten events on the world. With this objective in mind, he adopted a perspective that extended beyond the temporal confines most mortals could perceive, and he crafted his plans accordingly.

It was solely for these reasons that Donovan found himself relying on individuals like Dr. Brundle, Delta 67-3, and Alpha 06. These individuals became the instrumental agents he required to enact transformation. His strategies for change were nothing short of radical, a fact evident when measured against conventional norms.

Given the profound implications of the alterations he aimed to bring about, along with the dire consequences if those changes were to falter, he operated on a grand scale that surpassed the grasp of ordinary perception. His overarching perspective compelled him to sidestep conventional moral frameworks when rationalizing his actions, for he recognized that in a future beyond his influence, notions of right and wrong would lose their significance.

Donovan observed Delta 67-3 as the man came to a halt before the desk. A new addition caught his attention—the bandage covering Delta 67-3's eye, an alteration that hadn't been present before.

"What happened to your eye?" Donovan's inquiry held a note of curiosity.

Delta 67-3's hand instinctively went to the eye patch, his suppressed anger emanating palpably.

"I was shot in the eye by the detective. Detective Riddle," he hissed, the intensity of his emotions making his sibilant words stand out sharply.

Donovan, never one to waste effort on insignificant details, skipped any further queries about the incident. Instead, he redirected the conversation.

"What happened to your tracker?" he inquired, choosing to focus on more relevant matters.

Donovan was only aware of the loss of Delta 67-3's ability to be tracked because of the fuss Dr. Brundle had made upon discovering it.

Delta 67-3 didn't evade or equivocate. He provided a straightforward response, "I cut it out of my neck."

"Why?" Donovan's tone remained flat, reflecting his indifference towards the answer.

Despite his apparent lack of interest, the mere act of posing the question conveyed its importance. Whether or not the answer satisfied him held minimal significance; he operated on a principle of calculated efficiency, where every word and action served a purpose.

"I'd rather face the person who's going to kill me than be blown up without even realizing I'm about to die. There's something impersonal about that kind of death, even for me," Delta 67-3 admitted without a hint of remorse.

Donovan acknowledged the response, recognizing the genuineness in Delta 67-3's words. Such honesty was expected from a man of his demeanor.

"I'll need you to wait outside below the balcony," Donovan issued his directive.

Delta 67-3 nodded in clear understanding of his orders. Donovan adjusted his tie and pushed his glasses back onto the bridge of his nose. Exiting his office, he was followed by Delta 67-3. With a composed demeanor, Donovan proceeded down the wide corridor of the grand mansion, his footsteps muffled by the opulent carpeting beneath. Rich hues of red and gold adorned the flooring, and matching subdued colors adorned the walls, lending an air of regal refinement to the surroundings.

Oil paintings depicting dogs leading mounted men in a fox chase added an attempt at character. Donovan, however, remained oblivious to these decorative touches, dismissing them with disinterest. Having spent enough time in the mansion, every detail was etched into his memory.

He paused before an elegant desk, where a young woman greeted him with a warm smile before rising from her seat. Her attention then shifted to a pair of double doors, which she lightly knocked on before gently opening. Engaging in a hushed conversation with the room's occupant, her words mirrored the succinct nature of the individual she conversed with. Soon, her focus returned to Donovan.

"Lieutenant Governor Pike, the Governor will see you now," her voice carried a sweet inflection. Retaking her seat behind the desk, Donovan made his way into the office.

"Ah, Donovan," greeted the Governor. He was a tall figure, his dark hair and bushy eyebrows imparting a grand and almost paternal air to his countenance. Nonchalantly, he discarded the morning paper onto an adjacent table, its headline detailing the recent series of incidents at various Shepherd Institutes.

"Our plans seem to be proceeding quite satisfactorily," he spoke with a sense of satisfaction, a touch of joviality gracing his tone. "With those other bothersome Conferences out of the way, we should soon be in a better position to exert our influence on the world."

Donovan settled into one of the well-appointed chairs that adorned the governor's office. Each pair of chairs had been thoughtfully placed to create an ambiance of intimacy, transforming the room from a mere locus of minor power into a more engaging space within the broader tapestry of authority.

The governor, much like Donovan, was a Shepherd, bound by the common threads of longevity and a willingness to embrace ruthlessness when circumstances demanded. However, the similarities ended there. The governor possessed an insatiable greed, harboring aspirations of expanding his dominion towards the precipice of world control.

The Shepherds' technology afforded him the means to fulfill this ambition, but his focus was less on overt domination and more on orchestrating control from the shadows. The trappings of political power and the intricate maneuvers it entailed had served their purpose during his tenure as the state's governor. Now, he aimed to master the art of control without actively engaging in the rigors of governance.

Driven by this overarching objective, the governor had successfully enlisted Donovan as a partner in his scheme, seeking an advantageous edge over their fellow Shepherds. While Donovan harbored a desire to stand by the governor's side, their paths diverged significantly beyond that common goal. World domination and similar pursuits held no appeal for Donovan; his motivations were of a different nature.

Preservation, Donovan's inner thoughts resonated resolutely. *If we fail to adapt, we're doomed.* His contemplations delved into intricacies that transcended immediacy, extending to his overarching aim of safeguarding the very existence of the human race as a species. A complex web of motives propelled him forward, reaching depths that stretched past moral considerations. He was resolute—whatever it took, he would bend the arc of fate towards humanity's survival.

"We've encountered no hindrances thus far. Your swift and decisive action in dismantling the remaining Conferences effectively quashed any prospects of an organized Shepherd opposition," Donovan recounted, his focus transitioning to the subject at hand—their shared strategy.

"Indeed, for the present. But we mustn't harbor illusions that this state of affairs will endure indefinitely. As we advance our plan, the remaining Shepherds will undoubtedly become adversarial. Our sudden rise to a position of absolute power in this world will stir discontent," Governor Morgan Dupont foresaw, his gaze penetrating the horizon of possibilities. "It's imperative that we bring our intentions to light, step out of the shadows a bit to excerpt a little power while using the remaining position in the shadows to control it all. I'm thinking presidency might work."

"You're right, Governor Dupont. Progress has been promising, and the next phase of our operation can soon be initiated. We must adhere to our meticulously crafted timeline. The recent Shepherd Institute attacks could be leveraged to advance our agenda. The timing is conveniently opportune, and public support for uncovering the culprits can facilitate the implementation and acceptance of the changes we seek. Our strategic influence within Congress ensures the passage of our bills without undue resistance," Donovan communicated, his neutral expression a veil concealing his profound inner calculus.

"Does this indicate that the deployment of our new troops is imminent?" inquired Governor Dupont. His inquiry pertained to the clones currently being produced by Dr. Brundle.

"Yes, preparations are underway, and we've positioned a portion of them, primed to be allocated in alignment with our objectives," Donovan replied, a calculated untruth weaving through his words.

The truth remained that clones were indeed in production, albeit not to the scale the governor assumed. Their numbers served Donovan's ends, no more, no less.

"These genetically engineered soldiers are proving remarkably effective. Their operational records showcase their efficacy. It's unfortunate that our fellow Conference members within our facility couldn't grasp the transformative path we're embarking upon. Their participation would have bolstered the realization of our new vision," remarked Governor Dupont.

"You're absolutely correct. That's precisely why I took the initiative to eliminate them. Additionally, we have an operative within the police department, assuring the obstruction of the murder investigation," Donovan revealed, alluding to Alpha 06's role. "Our clone operative adeptly accomplished the task of removing the other Conference leaders. Speaking of which, you've yet to meet one of these soldiers. I can arrange an introduction to the one who's been pivotal in orchestrating our endeavors within our territory."

"I must admit, I've yet to witness one outside of Dr. Brundle's labs," Governor Dupont confessed. He found himself oddly intrigued by the callous and calculated demeanor exhibited by the clones, albeit in a rather macabre way.

"If you'd care to join me on the balcony, we can rectify that," Donovan suggested.

Governor Dupont agreed, and they proceeded to the balcony adjacent to his office. The governor poured himself a potent drink before stepping outside, locking his liquor cabinet behind him. The morning air retained a touch of chill as the sun was still climbing in the sky. Down on the veranda stood Delta 67-3, attired in a somber dark suit, unfazed by the cold despite the absence of a coat.

"Ah," the governor exclaimed, his breath visible in the chilly air. "There's the soldier below." He turned back to Donovan, a sense of pride evident, as if it was his initiative that had brought about the creation of Delta 67-3 and his counterparts. His attention then returned to Delta 67-3, his curiosity piqued. "I wonder, why the eyepatch?" he inquired, a note of genuine interest tinging his question as he observed Delta 67-3 once more.

"A local police officer shot him in the eye, sir," Donovan stated matter-of-factly. "Interestingly, the same officer is heading the investigation to find him."

"Is he alright," the Governor asked. Concern filled the governor's voice as he pointed his glass-laden hand downward, inadvertently causing the liquid within to swirl dangerously close to the rim.

Donovan was momentarily taken aback by the question. "Does it matter, sir? His ability to fulfill his assignment remains unaffected."

Governor Dupont shrugged dismissively. The well-being of Delta 67-3's eye was inconsequential. The wound seemed to have been excruciating at some point, but Governor Dupont suspected that an ordinary person would have succumbed to it. Donovan signaled to Delta 67-3, who acknowledged with a nod, advanced two steps, and then effortlessly leapt from the ground to the balcony—a feat far beyond human capability. He positioned himself before Donovan, remaining utterly still.

"They are undeniably robust and unwaveringly loyal," Governor Dupont commented as he circled around Delta 67-3, his eyes appraising the soldier. Upon completing his circuit, he halted and turned his gaze to Donovan, his curiosity apparent.

If Donovan were inclined to display emotions, a smile might have graced his features. "And they follow orders unwaveringly," he added. Turning away from the governor, Donovan began retracing his steps back into the mansion. His tone remained dispassionate as he threw a final instruction over his shoulder. "Make it appear as an accident."

"What?" The Governor's response trembled with confusion. His eyes darted back and forth between Donovan and Delta 67-3. Before he could process the situation fully, Delta 67-3's iron grip closed around him in a single-handed vice.

Delta 67-3 effortlessly hoisted the governor off the balcony and flung him into the air. The governor's face contorted in shock as he soared through the sky, the descent to the ground below too swift for any sound to escape his lips. He collided with the marble veranda, his neck snapping upon impact.

As Donovan moved through the office, the resounding thud of the governor's collision reached his ears, echoing the abrupt end of a life. He neared the doors to the governor's office, opening and then closing them behind him as he exited. His gaze met that of the secretary—another Shepherd, loyal to Donovan.

"It appears that the Governor requires medical attention. He slipped on some ice on the balcony and fell off," Donovan announced to her calmly. "Would you be so kind as to call for help?" With those words, he continued on his way toward his own office, leaving the secretary to make the call with practiced efficiency, her loyalty unwavering.

Faye and Jack's quiet day took an unexpected turn when they received a call to visit the governor's mansion. Their lack of surprise was a testament to their readiness, having already devised a plausible reason for their visit. However, their preconceived plans now felt futile in the face of the abrupt change in circumstances. Faye, draped in borrowed clothes from Brooke's closet, finished her preparations and was ready to face the situation at hand.

The news of the governor's death hit both Jack and Faye with a sense of disbelief. Regardless of the official narrative surrounding his passing, they shared an unspoken certainty that foul play was at work here. Their intuition defied the initial appearance of an accident, dismissing explanations like 'act of fate' or 'will of God'. This was a meticulously executed plot, and both Jack and Faye were resolute in their commitment to uncover the truth behind this staged accident.

As they approached the governor's mansion, the scene was chaotic, with news vans lining the road and concerned citizens mingling with the media, all eager to glean any information about the unfolding situation. Jack smoothly navigated the checkpoint with his badge, allowing him and Faye access to the mansion's grounds. Jack chose a discreet spot to park the car, ensuring it didn't obstruct any potential emergency vehicles.

Exiting the car, Jack's protective instincts kicked in, prompting him to instruct Faye to stay close to him. The memory of her wielding a steel pipe during a previous encounter lingered in his mind, a haunting reminder of the danger she could face. The thought of losing her was unbearable, and he was determined to keep her safe at all costs.

Faye, however, detected a nuance in Jack's demeanor, uncertain if she appreciated being told to stay by his side. She wondered if there was an implicit message that he doubted her ability to handle herself independently. Jack, attuned to her thoughts, sought to clarify his intentions. He acknowledged the limitations of their investigation here due to jurisdiction constraints and the forthcoming involvement of her agency's own agent. Jack emphasized that their presence was largely a formality, with the bulk of the investigation falling under state jurisdiction. His unspoken fear of her being harmed remained hidden beneath his composed exterior, a sentiment he wasn't ready to vocalize.

Faye's frown mirrored her contemplation of Jack's words, yet his explanation helped ease her concerns. His genuine fear for her safety touched her, even as she grappled with her own sense of self-reliance.

Despite her prowess, Jack's protective instinct resonated with her, fostering a shared understanding between them.

Faye's agreement to Jack's request was wordless, a nod that communicated her understanding of the situation. The urgency to leave the scene was mutual, driven by a shared determination to resume their pursuit of the elusive killer. Her mind churned with the need to uncover leads, even though she hesitated to mention a specific thought to Jack just yet. For now, her focus was trained on the present moment, hoping that a clue might manifest itself amidst the chaos.

Jack, adopting a methodical approach, opted to observe and absorb the environment before proactively seeking information. Both he and Faye were essentially placeholders, representing the local law enforcement in this scenario. Faye, remaining close behind Jack, followed him as he led the way, ultimately reaching the balcony where the incident had unfolded.

Their timely arrival seemed advantageous, as most of the forensic procedures had concluded, leaving the balcony unoccupied. The lack of significant findings left them to investigate the patio where the governor had tragically landed. Jack's interaction with the staff was methodical, a series of questions and notes that added to their understanding of the situation. The secretary's account of the events matched what had been told to state investigators—the governor's solitude in his office, the scream that had echoed through the corridors, and the missed appointment with the Lieutenant Governor.

While Faye adhered to Jack's directive to remain by his side, she couldn't shake a growing suspicion about the secretary's behavior. There was something peculiar about her demeanor, an emotional detachment that struck Faye as odd given the circumstances. However, she didn't voice her observations to Jack, as they weren't substantial enough to warrant further investigation at that moment.

As Jack concluded his inquiries, Faye stood beside him, her attention drifting momentarily while her gaze surveyed the people bustling in the hallway. Amidst the activity, a door farther down the corridor creaked open, and a man dressed in a dark suit emerged. An uncanny feeling washed over her, a sense of familiarity tinged with uncertainty. Her spine tingled as her eyes locked onto him. It was when he turned, flashing a grin that unveiled his razor-sharp teeth, that her recognition crystallized. The eyepatch that covered his eye, a reminder of the injury inflicted by Jack's gunshot, cemented her realization. Faye knew who he was.

The encounter sent a chill down her spine, the pieces falling into place with chilling clarity. Faye was face to face with the man they had been chasing, the man behind the governor's death. The tendrils of his dark influence had crept into their lives once again, leaving Faye grappling with a mixture of trepidation and determination. The urgency of her pursuit took over Faye's mind, overriding any considerations of sticking close to Jack as he had suggested.

Her singular focus shifted entirely to the pursuit and apprehension of the man before her. This new mission consumed her thoughts, prompting her to recalibrate her approach to neutralize the immediate threat he posed. While her instincts screamed for her to draw her weapons and engage, Faye exercised restraint. The risk of collateral damage held her back—the potential chaos of a firefight endangering innocent lives outweighed her desire to eliminate the target in one swift motion.

She couldn't reconcile being the catalyst for a disaster that claimed additional lives while attempting to subdue Delta 67-3. Her determination to prevent him from taking any more lives clashed with her commitment to preserving the safety of bystanders. The ethical dilemma gnawed at her, but she resolved to find a way to capture or stop him without jeopardizing others in the process.

Pushing her way through the crowd in the hallway, Faye's focus intensified. She navigated the faces that turned towards her in surprise, leaving astonished voices in her wake. Her relentless drive to apprehend her target caused her to lose sight of him, her headlong rush only providing a momentary advantage to his escape. The towering figures that obstructed her view acted as an unwitting shield, allowing him to slip from her grasp.

As the minutes ticked by and her search yielded no results, Faye came to a pivotal decision. Recognizing the necessity of involving Jack in the hunt for Delta 67-3, she retraced her steps back to where she had left him. Despite having initially disregarded his instructions to stay close, Faye's actions were motivated by a shared understanding of the severity of the situation. She found Jack where she had abandoned him and without hesitation, she grasped his hand, her fingers closing around his.

Before he could even inquire about the urgency in her expression, Faye took the lead, her grip on his hand propelling them both down the hallway.

"We need to go now!" Faye's urgency was palpable in her words.

Jack's brows furrowed as he registered her fervent statement. "What's going on?" His confusion was evident.

"He was here," Faye declared with a resolute tone, leaving no room for doubt.

Moving with purpose, Faye strode down the hallway, her focus unwavering as she made a deliberate turn towards the stairs. Her intention was clear: she aimed to reach the front of the mansion and potentially spot Delta 67-3 outside.

Jack, struggling to keep up both physically and mentally, sought clarification. "Who was here?"

Faye, conscious of the need for discretion, scanned their surroundings before leaning in closer to Jack. She didn't want anyone else overhearing their conversation. The last thing they needed was unnecessary attention or the need to answer probing questions that might derail their pursuit. She understood the stakes—losing the trail of the killer at this critical juncture was a risk they couldn't afford to take.

Her words were measured and hushed, designed to convey the gravity of the situation without drawing attention. "The soldier, Delta 67-3, my 'brother'. He was here."

Jack's eyes widened almost comically as he blurted out, "Are you serious?"

Faye's response was swift and no-nonsense, her impatience palpable. "Would I *joke* about something like that? Let's go!"

Releasing Jack's hand, Faye dashed down the stairs with a reckless abandon. Her rapid descent involved taking two or three steps at a time, her movements so intense that it appeared she might lose her balance at any moment. However, her feline reflexes and inherent agility enabled her to maintain her trajectory, deftly navigating the stairs without faltering.

Jack, although keeping pace, exercised more caution. He followed closely behind Faye, navigating the stairs with deliberate steps. Unlike her, he lacked the same level of natural grace and athleticism. The last thing he wanted was to injure himself with a clumsy fall down the mansion's staircase, especially considering the series of intense events he'd been caught up in over the past week.

As they burst out of the mansion's front door, Faye skidded to a controlled halt on the gravel driveway, closely trailed by Jack. Their eyes were fixed on a seemingly inconspicuous four-door sedan that was steadily pulling away, its tires crunching over the gravel. The ordinary appearance of the car was in stark contrast to the danger it represented.

Their breaths were slightly labored from the haste of their pursuit as they watched the sedan blend seamlessly into the flow of city traffic beyond the mansion's grounds. The elusive Delta 67-3 had slipped through their fingers once again.

"Damn, now what?" Jack's irritation was palpable in his tone.

His frustration manifested physically as he vented by kicking at the gravel underfoot, sending several pieces scattering against the sides of nearby parked vehicles.

"We won't be able to catch up to him now, and we daren't call in an All-Points-Bulletin for a traffic stop," Jack continued, his concern evident in his words.

However, Faye was already on the move. She headed briskly toward the car they had arrived in, her determination apparent in her stride. It was as if she hadn't even registered Jack's comment.

"Hey," Jack called out to get her attention.

Faye halted and turned to face Jack, her expression focused. She met his gaze and stated firmly, "I think I know where he might be going. Let's go."

Curiosity mingled with Jack's frustration as he asked, "So where exactly are we headed?"

Faye's response was direct and carried a weight of significance. "I've been considering this earlier. We're going to the place where I was born. Coincidentally, that particular Shepherd facility is right here in this city."

Jack's eyebrows lifted in a mixture of surprise and intrigue. Faye's past and the Shepherd facility held a connection that had piqued his interest before. Now, it seemed, they had a destination—a place that might hold answers to the puzzle they were trying to solve.

With a renewed sense of purpose, Jack and Faye began to move, their path leading them not only towards the potential location of Delta 67-3 but also deeper into the heart of the mysteries that had entangled their lives.

15

Entering Dr. Brundle's lab had become a scripted ritual for Donovan, a choreography etched across time, unfolding once more. As he traversed the threshold, he allowed his senses to embrace the technological symphony unfurling before him. Dr. Brundle's form, a shadowy figure ensnared by the allure of the screen, emerged like a sentinel amidst the digitized torrent. A holographic device projected intricate data streams and luminous figures, an otherworldly ballet of information that danced at the precipice of comprehension. The hum of machinery assumed an almost rhythmic cadence, a pulsating heartbeat that underscored the room's immersion in innovation.

The doctor's posture, a perpetual hunch over his workstation, was a testament to his distraction and immersion. Every stroke of his fingers upon the holographic interface was an intricate step in a complex choreography of creation. Data materialized and dissolved in ephemeral wisps, his focus like a gravitational force tethered to the luminous spectacle. Donovan's presence was an understated intrusion into this symphony of technology, a disruption woven with patience and intent.

A quiet throat-clearing emerged from Donovan, a note slicing through the resonant hum. It was a signal, a subtle assertion of his presence that sliced through the digital hum, akin to a melody piercing through silence. Each attempt to redirect Dr. Brundle's attention became a crescendo of patience, a measured rhythm that sought to break through the walls of the doctor's concentration.

Finally, Dr. Brundle yielded, his gaze momentarily relinquishing its hold on the holographic marvel. This concession, begrudging though it may have been, was a nod to the tacit hierarchy governing their interactions. Donovan's role as overseer was a thread woven deep into the fabric of their collaboration, a truth that lingered beneath the surface of their exchanges.

"What can I do for you, Mr. Pike?" Dr. Brundle's voice carried a veneer of formality, underscored by the recognition that true authority flowed from realms beyond his technological dominion.

"We're finished with the first phase of the plan, doctor. How goes the preparations for activation of our additional soldiers?" Donovan's words echoed with gravity, an embodiment of the weight that their shared pursuits bore.

"Every piece is moving in alignment with the prescribed cadence. To refine the accelerated growth formula for the subsequent soldier model, I shall need to dissect Delta 67-3. Extracting the requisite data, while navigating the labyrinth of deviations, is an unavoidable prerequisite for our march towards optimized growth," Dr. Brundle's explanation was a scientific sonnet, delivered with an unwavering dedication that mirrored his commitment.

Deciphering the intricate technobabble that Dr. Brundle often favored proved to be a challenge for Donovan. Impatience simmered beneath his composed exterior, urging the doctor to arrive at the heart of the matter. However, Donovan's calm demeanor remained steadfast, a facet intrinsic to his character. The ebb and flow of time was a resource he possessed in abundance. If a task demanded a specific span to be completed, then so be it. Time's passage held no urgency.

Efficiency was Donovan's paramount concern. At present, this aspect seemed lacking in Dr. Brundle's discourse, an observation rooted in Donovan's perspective.

Remaining patient, Donovan kept his attention fixed on Dr. Brundle, even though he harbored reservations about the doctor's ability to deliver relevant information in a timely manner. The desire for clarity warred with his growing impatience, a subtle clash beneath the surface of his composed exterior.

"Doctor, this Delta 67-3 seems to have a mind set that is a bit unsettled. The Alpha series needs to be adjusted so that independent actions are less likely. Increase the programming for both so that they are more obedient. Strengthen the programming of both series to fortify obedience," Donovan's directive was cast in iron, a command underscored by the unyielding need for allegiance.

Donovan couldn't deny that despite meticulous planning, errors were an inevitable part of the equation. The recent behavior of operative Delta 67-3 had been far from ideal, a consequence most likely rooted in the series' programmed mental state. While this mindset rendered them efficient for executing termination missions without hesitation or empathy, it also posed a challenge when it came to steering and restraining their actions during moments of heightened intensity. This predicament was far from tolerable in Donovan's perspective.

"I pledge, Mr. Pike, to program the upcoming iterations with an emphasis on amplified triumph. Progression and advancement are the cornerstone of our future trajectory," Dr. Brundle's response bore a tone woven from confidence and unwavering determination, a testament to his resolve to elevate their creations beyond current constraints.

"Good," Donovan's resolve to exit was evident in his stance, his form poised for departure. Yet, a fleeting thought clutched him, a revelation demanding immediate sharing. He pivoted on the brink of leaving. Prior to departing, he informed Dr. Brundle of his some future plans.

"I've ordered Delta 67-3 to report to you. He should be here within the hour. I must take myself to a press conference where I'll be assuming the role of the governor of this state. We are almost at our goal so keep up the good work doctor. I will not be returning back here today so make sure your tasks are accomplished for the day. I'm depending on you, doctor."

Faye offered Jack precise directions, guiding him towards the facility where her existence had been shaped, honed, and eventually unleashed upon the world for her assigned missions. The familiarity of this place was etched into her memory, a homecoming that stirred both nostalgic sentiments and the resonance of her origin. As Jack maneuvered his large truck, it came to a halt in front of a parking garage nestled on the fringes of the downtown area. He killed the engine quickly. With a quizzical look, he turned towards Faye, seeking confirmation.

His query hung in the air, a testament to his uncertainty. "Are you sure this is the right place that we're supposed to be at?" he inquired, his hand gesturing toward the parking garage situated on his left side, its form outlined against the urban backdrop beyond the window.

Faye met his gaze with a certainty that bespoke her connection to this place. "Why would you doubt me? You don't think I know where I spent the first six months of my life?"

Jack's skepticism lingered, his doubt evident in his raised eyebrow. "Then why didn't you mention this place yet?"

A rueful smile tugged at Faye's lips, a gentle playfulness coloring her expression. "It was on my mind this morning to talk to you about it but we got distracted while eating breakfast," she recounted, the memory the feeling of his arms as he had scooped her up and tickled her earlier, dancing around in the room. "We saw that news report and then got called out to the governor's mansion. There just wasn't any time to talk to you about it."

Jack's response came in the form of a nonchalant shrug, a tacit acknowledgment of the situation at hand. The ignition brought the truck's engine to life, propelling them forward as they meticulously adhered to Faye's guiding instructions. With every turn of the wheels, they descended deeper into the heart of the garage, until they came to a halt before a substantial garage door, a formidable portal guarding their entry.

Suspended overhead, a sign asserted the realm beyond as a maintenance shop area, an inscription that did little to quell the air of intrigue shrouding their destination. Positioned adjacent to the expanse of the garage door, an unassuming office played host to a solitary security guard, a peculiar juxtaposition that didn't escape Jack's scrutiny.

As his gaze shifted from the security guard to the layout before them, a perplexed expression knit Jack's brow, his contemplation evident. His voice carried the weight of curiosity as he gestured towards the enigmatic area unfolding in front of them. "How big does a maintenance area for a parking garage need to be and why would it need a security guard?"

Faye's voice carried the resonance of revelation as she unraveled the mysteries veiled beneath the surface. "The zone you're observing houses the cargo elevator," she explained, her words exuding a sense of unveiling secrets long guarded. "A conduit for supplies, it serves as a lifeline to transport essentials down to the concealed facility below. In essence, the facility itself resides underground, nestled directly beneath the very expanse of this parking garage."

The security guard sauntered out of the office, an aura of disinterest wafting around him like a cloud. His uniform bore the telltale signs of neglect, a disarray that seemed to echo his general demeanor. Unkempt and worn, his appearance hardly held any menace, but Jack knew better than to be deceived. A quick once-over, an assessment that came naturally to someone like him, categorized the guard as a potential threat. The exterior façade of indifference did little to obscure Jack's keen perception of the man's every move, each step taken with a measured precision that spoke volumes about tactical training.

Jack remained unperturbed. The guard's façade of indifference was a smokescreen. The telltale markers of a trained operative were too evident to escape Jack's discerning eye. The shabby uniform was a ruse, as the gear he sported bore an entirely different story. From the military-grade baton to the pristine pistol belt and the handgun that exuded an air of familiarity, it was clear that this was no ordinary security guard. The way he carried himself and the meticulousness of his steps hinted at a background steeped in professional military training.

As the guard drew closer to Jack's truck, the disparity between his appearance and his armament became more conspicuous. The holster on his thigh cradled a 9mm automatic handgun, while a stun gun rested on his opposite hip. A subcompact assault rifle, and a tactical shotgun was strategically mounted inside the security office door and Jack was barely able to make them out from where he sat in his truck. Each piece of weaponry carried an air of authority, a stark contrast to the banal role the guard was supposed to play.

The driver-side window lowered at Jack's prompt, providing a medium for conversation between the two.

"Do you need some help, sir?"

Despite the nonchalant query that greeted him, Jack heard a subtext that lay beneath the seemingly casual words. It whispered a challenge: 'You're out of your depth here; turn back and retreat.' But Jack was far from one to be easily intimidated.

"Yeah, we..." Jack's sentence was interrupted by a swift realization. His gaze darted to the passenger seat, only to find it conspicuously vacant. Surprise mingled with urgency, compelling him to refocus on the unfolding situation outside.

In the split second that followed, a gunshot-like crack rent the air, and the guard's body convulsed as a stun gun discharged its incapacitating charge. A muffled grunt mingled with the sound before the guard slumped, collapsing onto the ground beside the truck, his facade of indifference shattered. The unexpected turn of events had unfolded in mere moments, leaving Jack reeling and the situation drastically altered.

"What the hell, Faye?" Jack's voice crackled with incredulous shock. His thoughts spiraled, a tempest of possibilities dancing through his mind. The mere thought of the jeopardy Faye had placed herself in sent shivers down his spine, intertwining with the urge to reprimand her for the recklessness that could have gone awry in countless ways. The conflicting emotions swirled within him, a chaotic blend of concern and a desire to protect, even if it meant channeling it through an exasperated anger.

Faye's response, a casual shrug paired with a wild grin, did little to alleviate Jack's turmoil. The display of audacious amusement clashed with the gravity of the situation. She wielded the discharged stun gun with an air of playful victory, an incongruous image against the backdrop of their mission's stakes. The striking juxtaposition left Jack momentarily floundering, caught between his urge to chastise her and a bemused amazement at her audacity.

"He wasn't going to let us in," Faye's words held an irreverent tone, as if the act of incapacitating the guard was nothing more than a whimsical diversion.

Her nonchalance rubbed against Jack's lingering anxiety, a friction between their differing perspectives on the situation. With a calculated ease, Faye dragged the unconscious guard into the confines of the security station. The metallic clink of handcuffs resonated as she secured him to a desk within. The removal of his equipment and weaponry followed, the systematic precision a testament to Faye's methodical efficiency. The door shut, leaving the guard confined within his self-imposed prison.

"That should keep him out of our way," Faye's tone bore a matter-of-fact assurance, as if she had merely dispatched a minor obstacle, her nonchalant attitude both unnerving and oddly captivating to Jack.

Steering the truck to a discreet corner, Jack parked it with the intention of deflecting attention. Every nuance of his actions was orchestrated with precision, a dance of calculated movements intended to cloak their presence in the mundane. Positioned next to a smaller door adjacent to the larger rolling garage entrance, Jack assumed his place, his senses sharpened for the next step of their covert mission.

"How are we getting past that?" Jack's finger indicated the security keypad embedded in the wall beside the door, his voice laced with both curiosity and concern.

Faye's response was a confident smile, her fingers dancing across the keypad as a series of numbers were entered. "There. My codes still work. Then again, I don't see why they wouldn't," she stated, a fusion of pride and amusement tinting her words. Her perspective seemed to wrap the world in its own brand of logic, a skewed lens through which she viewed the reality around her.

Jack regarded Faye with a mix of incredulity and bewilderment. He couldn't understand how this seemingly carefree individual embodied the essence of an agent within anybody's organization? Her nonchalant attitude, despite the gravity of their mission, was nothing short of perplexing. He still harbored a miffed undertone, his emotions a tangle of lingering annoyance for her earlier impulsive actions and a deeper concern for her well-being. The contrast between her carefree demeanor and the imminent danger at hand left him torn between exasperation and a heightened desire to ensure her safety.

Jack wondered to himself about the complex tapestry of emotions within him. Concern for her safety intertwined with the desire to choke her, just for good measure, until she got the idea to keep herself out of harms way when it wasn't necessary to be there.

"If your codes still work, then why the hell did you stun the guard?" Jack's words held a miffed tone, an edge sharpened by the lingering irritation.

He struggled to reconcile the incongruity of her actions and her explanations, grappling with the apparent contradictions that characterized her approach. Faye's response came with an air of self-assuredness, her words carrying an unspoken assumption that her perspective was self-evident.

"He would have let me in, but he wasn't going to let you in." Her tone hinted that this was an immutable truth, an obvious reality that required no further elaboration.

Her gaze held his, as if daring him to dispute this singular, albeit unusual, logic. "If he had seen me with you, he wouldn't have let me in at all and would likely have called for backup," she concluded, the statement offered with a matter-of-fact certainty.

As her words settled, Jack found himself reluctantly considering the validity of her argument. The truth in her assessment gradually began to dawn on him, forcing him to grapple with a realization that defied conventional wisdom.

"So there are more guards?"

His words carried a shift in tone, a transition from mild annoyance to a tactical mindset. He was delving into the heart of the matter, his thirst for information now guiding his actions. The battlefield before them was gradually coming into focus, every detail a crucial piece in their intricate puzzle.

"Yeah. The control room knows I'm here because I used my access codes, but the rest of the guards won't know that we're here," Faye's voice took on a more serious tone as she shared crucial information with Jack. The transition from their earlier banter to the gravity of the mission was palpable.

"Faye, how can you be so certain that they haven't detected us beyond your key code usage?" Jack's inquiry was laced with a mix of caution and curiosity. He needed a complete understanding of their situation to make well-informed decisions about their safety throughout this operation.

Faye's response came in the form of a pointed finger, directed at a hidden camera nestled inconspicuously between a nearby wall and a supporting pylon. Its strategic positioning ensured that its presence remained hidden until a vehicle approached a specific point, eliminating any chance for occupants to react in time. The camera's field of view, once revealed, extended into the control room below them, situated deep underground.

Her explanation continued as she revealed her swift actions. "I disabled the camera as soon as I got out of the truck. Fortunately, you stopped before the camera's line of sight, so I didn't need to mention it. If the control room guards had observed what we did to the other guard, they would have initiated a lockdown and summoned reinforcements. With the camera presumably disabled, they'll likely attempt to verify its status through the guard in the shack. We should seize this moment to move while we still can," she concluded, her words driven by a combination of urgency and strategic insight.

"Do you have an idea of how many guards are here?" Jack inquired, his concern evident in his voice.

"I'm not certain. Probably around a dozen or so. The facility's layout doesn't have that many floors, usually two guards per floor, and a minimum of two in the control room. As for the exact count, I can't be sure," Faye replied, her tone carrying a hint of uncertainty mingled with her experience. She was providing Jack with the information she had, despite the limitations of her knowledge.

"Don't hesitate to use deadly force if necessary. They won't hold back either. It's a shoot-to-kill situation," she advised with a pragmatic edge.

"Just great," Jack responded, his sarcasm underscoring the gravity of the situation.

With a determined resolve, he drew his weapon from its holster, methodically checking the magazine and chambering a round. The distinct metallic sound echoed in the tension-laden air. Switching from his customary revolver to an automatic, he made a calculated choice for quicker reloading if the need arose.

Faye carefully unholstered her weapons one by one, mirroring Jack's preparation. Their synchronized actions demonstrated their shared readiness to proceed. Unspoken agreement propelled Faye into the lead position, a decision that made perfect sense given her familiarity with the facility's layout. The situation dictated that her knowledge and expertise be harnessed for their advantage.

With a swift and silent grace, Faye guided them down the stairs, each step taken with precision. The staircase led them to the first level of the underground complex, a detail she communicated to Jack. They stood at the threshold of a five-floor labyrinth, concealed beneath the surface. Passing through the security door marked a crucial transition, granting them access to the heart of the facility. Here, the choice between the elevators and the distant stairwells was pivotal.

Faye explained the implications of each option to Jack. The elevators provided swift transportation but came with the risk of alerting others to their presence, a danger they weren't prepared to face just yet. Worse, the control room held the power to halt their movement, potentially entrapping them and manipulating their exit point for an ambush. This outcome was unacceptable to both Jack and Faye. They settled on the stairwells as the wiser route.

Their descent into the stairwell shrouded their footsteps in muted echoes. The well-engineered design of the stairwell, with double sets of doors on each level, acted as an acoustic buffer, preventing their sounds from escaping into the hallway. Faye and Jack were relieved to know that their movements remained concealed as they advanced downward. The sound-locking setup, ensuring their covert progress wouldn't betray them to any lurking threats beyond the stairwell's confines.

As they entered the door leading from their current stairwell, a security checkpoint came into view, occupied by a lone guard. Faye took the lead, instructing Jack to follow her after a brief delay. Their plan unfolded: Faye would maneuver past the guard first, and when Jack approached, the guard would inquire about his identity, providing Faye the opportunity to incapacitate him from behind. Executed seamlessly, the plan enabled Faye to swiftly neutralize the second guard they encountered in the facility.

With Faye at the forefront and Jack covering their rear, they advanced towards the first distant stairwell, moving with utmost stealth and precision. Faye signaled Jack as they approached a door on the left side of the hallway, indicating their initial objective. Faye halted by the door, motioning to the control panel nearby. She activated a buzzer, drawing the guard's attention momentarily. Her gaze shifted upward to the single camera positioned within the facility, mounted above the door.

As the numerical keypad beside the door illuminated, Faye deftly entered a series of digits, a combination that would grant her unimpeded passage. This intricate dance of codes and tactics showcased her expertise, as she deftly navigated the facility's security measures.

As events unfolded seamlessly, Jack couldn't shake the growing sense that things were progressing too smoothly. Having military experience under his belt, he understood that the notion of an operation proceeding without a single hiccup was simply unrealistic. He found himself grappling with the paradox of wanting their plan to go off without a hitch while simultaneously being wary of unexpected complications.

Beneath this veneer of cautious optimism, his primary concern was Faye's safety. The possibility of her getting hurt weighed heavily on his mind. He wanted to shield her from harm, but he also recognized the futility of dissuading her from taking part. These conflicting feelings swirled within him, but he knew he needed to push them aside for the task at hand. Faye was a capable agent, more than capable, and her determination was unshakable. He found solace in the fact that they were in this together, despite the risks.

Jack's thoughts were brought back to the present by an audible click. They stood before the unlocked door. Jack's musings were momentarily set aside. Faye's actions spoke to her strategic thinking; she holstered her sidearms before using the intercom, not wanting to arouse suspicion from whoever was beyond the door. Once the click of the lock sounded, Faye resumed her stance, guns ready. Jack, having positioned himself out of the camera's view, rejoined the formation, allowing Faye to lead them into the heart of the installation's control room.

The corridor lay cloaked in dim lighting, with the distant hum of cooling fans providing a constant backdrop. The fans whirred diligently, dissipating the heat generated by the servers housed within the short corridor. Their noise, initially the only auditory presence, yielded to the rising chatter of the two individuals stationed nearby. Faye and Jack pressed onward, the increasing volume of the voices serving as a marker of their approach.

Amidst the ambient sounds, one of the figures within the control room called out, projecting their voice down the corridor. "Hey, if you're reporting in, Alpha 06, the doctor is on his way to the lab. You can meet him there."

"Alright, I'll move there now," said Faye.

Her response was seamless, fitting the narrative she had crafted, one that concealed their true intentions. The information she provided was a calculated fabrication, a thread woven into their fabricated reality. Jack observed the scene, recognizing the fluidity with which Faye navigated the deception, reinforcing his faith in her ability to manage even the most intricate details of their mission.

A voice emanated from the control room, its tone projecting through the corridor once more. "We lost the camera up on top, and Parker isn't responding over the radio. I think he's headed to check on that camera by his station, but we're not entirely sure. I'll head up to the surface to find him."

As the voice drew nearer, its speaker unconsciously approached Faye's position. Their proximity reached a critical point when the speaker inadvertently collided with Faye, their proximity emphasizing the barrel of her weapon pressing up against the side of his rib cage. Acting deftly, Faye contorted her lips into a subtle gesture, conveying the message that silence was paramount.

With a slight push, she guided the guard toward the narrow wall, positioning him within Jack's reach. Faye's intention was clear: Jack was to incapacitate the guard while she seized the opportunity to slip by, advancing unhindered towards the confined control room just ahead, her movements executed with the precision of a seasoned operative.

Jack silently celebrated. This successful entry into the control room had prevented any chance of the facility's defenders coordinating a lethal response against them. As Jack systematically disconnected cables from the control board, plunging the room into darkness, a sense of accomplishment washed over him, despite his unconventional method of disabling the system.

After securing and incapacitating the guards, Jack and Faye moved onward through the facility. The current floor held little of interest aside from vacant offices, an unoccupied barracks, and a deserted dining hall. The elevators were deliberately bypassed in favor of the stairwell at the opposite end of the facility, which led them downwards to the next levels.

Approaching the entrance to the subsequent floor, Faye positioned herself to cover Jack as he prepared to open the door. With a silent countdown, Faye signaled their approach, and the door swung open. Faye rushed forward, prepared to engage any potential threats. However, her momentum came to an abrupt halt as she encountered not just guards, but a more formidable assemblage. In their midst stood Dr. Brundle and the killer they had been searching for, making for a startling and unexpected confrontation. The realization struck Jack as he rounded the corner of the door, his heart sinking at the unexpected sight before him.

"Oh, shit," Jack exclaimed, voicing the shared sentiment that hung heavily in the air.

Tense moments unfurled, stretching in the silence that bound them. Each face wore the same mask of astonishment, caught off guard by the unexpected tableau that now confronted them. Dr. Brundle and his retinue had not been seeking out Faye and Jack. This encounter was the result of fortuitous circumstances.

The world seemed suspended, ensnared in the grip of those fleeting seconds—time dilated, akin to a house of mirrors where the passage of each tick was elongated, drawn out to match the gravity of the situation. In this temporal suspension, every detail etched itself into consciousness: each movement, each bead of sweat, every breath of air.

Faye, her senses attuned to the subtle dance of the room, mapped the spatial dynamics like a painter mapping hues on canvas. She sensed the guards' positions, their unease palpable. The glistening bead of sweat poised on a guard's lip, a testament to his apprehension. Even amidst the silence, Delta 67-3's breathing scraped like sandpaper, a raspy counterpoint to the tableau.

Her eyes traced the deliberate arc of another guard's hand, inching towards his weapon with a deliberate slowness. In tandem, she moved her head with painful precision, a languid sweep from left to right and back—an unspoken signal that words needn't be spoken; that the weapon should stay where it was. She knew the guard wouldn't listen but was hoping to defuse the situation somewhat before it descended into the chaos that it was headed in. The doctor, caught in this web of confrontation, chose retreat, edging back slowly, step by step, as if distance could shield him from the inexorable.

For Jack, the eruption of events was a cacophony that burst forth as though orchestrated by the gods of chaos. The narrow corridor became a crucible of sound, movement, and danger. The confined space morphed into a battlefield, and as if scripted by fate, all hell shattered loose. Delta 67-3 loomed, a hulking presence on Jack's left, a harbinger of turmoil.

Time fractured as Jack's finger found the trigger, the resonance of gunfire rending the air. The gun in his hand became an instrument of staccato, a quicksilver blur of motion that expelled its payload with intent. Rounds were unleashed, each bullet seeking its mark with precision honed through practice. The aim was focused, the impact intentional—center mass, a vital point. The gun's recoil surged, a tactile reminder of power, and with each recoil, the muzzle rose, but Jack compensated, keeping his target locked.

The symphony of shots was punctuated by the thunderous applause of recoil and the staccato rhythm of trigger pulls. The air danced with lead, and most, if not all, of Jack's rounds found their destination. Delta 67-3's form absorbed the impact, center mass struck with a clinical efficacy that only Jack's experience could yield.

In that moment, the corridor was a crucible of hell, a convergence of fate and action. The exchange of gunfire was an incantation, an unspoken dialogue between life and death. And as the last echoes of shots reverberated, the aftermath hung like suspended reality, a tableau of violence etched in time.

Jack's intended target crumbled, a marionette cut from its strings, under the combined impact of the unleashed hollow point rounds. The force of the bullets wasn't just absorbed—it was channeled, creating an explosive ripple that hurled Delta 67-3 back, a staggering eight feet. The corridor itself seemed to shudder in response, bearing witness to the raw force unleashed in that fleeting moment.

In the wake of the precision chaos, Jack found himself gifted with stolen seconds, a pocket of time to survey the battlefield that had been thrust upon them. His eyes flickered with the practiced rhythm of an observer, absorbing every detail with the keen perception of a strategist. The tableau unfurled before him, each player a cog in the complex machinery of the confrontation.

Faye, embodying a blend of finesse and power, moved with the grace of a feline predator and the precision of a sniper. The twin handguns she wielded were an extension of her will, their barrels fixed on targets with an uncanny determination. Two well-aimed three round bursts erupted from her, each bullet a whispered promise of impact. The three-round symphony was orchestrated with eerie synchrony, a testament to her uncanny strength taming the formidable recoil that erupted with each shot.

The guards on their right side found themselves caught in the lethal crosshairs of Faye's focus. Two lives extinguished by her lethal precision. Her shots were a ballet of accuracy, honed by more than just skill—an inhuman reflex, a remnant of the manipulation etched into her very genes. Her eyes tracked their fall, a symphony of death met with the quiet orchestra of her unwavering purpose.

In the chaos of her balletic violence, Faye was an observer as well as a participant. The second set of guards, the surviving half of the quartet, scrambled in desperation. Their fumbling hands sought weapons, their instincts screaming for cover. Doorways became sanctuaries as they sought refuge down the corridor, further away from the epicenter of the storm. Amidst this, a missing piece emerged—the doctor, vanished into the shadows, swallowed by the chaos.

Jack's attention was diverted, his gaze slipping from his own target's descent. Faye's focused mind, however, seized every detail. Her perception noted the doctor's departure, a trail of absence that he left behind. It was as if she had mapped the doctor's escape in the blink of an eye—a cartographer of chaos. The maze of passageways, intricate in their architecture, became her canvas, and she sketched his route with a mental precision that only heightened her deadly intent.

In a symphony of violence, their individual contributions harmonized. Jack's bullets found home, Delta 67-3 toppled, and Faye's bullets sang the dirge of two guards. Amidst the storm, the doctor's retreat, a fleeting enigma, and Faye's dual focus, a testament to her hyper-reflexes, painted a picture of a battlefield that was equal parts theater and reckoning.

A forceful oath erupted from Jack's lips, punctuating the acrid air already laden with the tang of gun smoke. The staccato echoes of the fired rounds still rebounded off the corridor's walls and in the stairwell, a relentless reminder of the violent symphony that had just played out. It was a scene both fraught and reckless, as if reason had taken a backseat to dire necessity. The straight expanse of the hallway offered no respite, no refuge from the storm of bullets and chaos. Jack's thoughts cut through the turmoil, a wry observation crystallizing in his mind—staging a gunfight in this corridor, devoid of cover, bordered on the brink of lunacy.

In the forge of this moment, the reality was unyielding. The options were stripped down to raw survival, and the luxury of a tactically sound battlefield was an indulgence they couldn't afford. It was an unspoken acceptance, a pact forged in the face of unrelenting odds. The hallway, once a mundane conduit, now bore witness to the intersection of fate and desperation.

Jack's practiced movements unfolded with the grace of a choreographed dance, a well-honed routine born from countless repetitions. The expended magazine was expelled with a quick flick, landing in a subdued clatter on the ground. His hand moved with purpose, deftly plucking a fresh magazine from its resting place on his harness. The mechanical snap of the new magazine engaging was followed by the authoritative thud as he slammed it home. Swiftly, the slide release was pressed, orchestrating the familiar ballet that ushered a round into the chamber, completing the transformation from reloader to the ready.

In those precious moments of reloading, the battlefield had shifted. Faye, a symphony of violence and precision, continued her lethal dance. Another guard fell under the caress of her bullets, and her unrelenting focus shifted to the last remaining sentinel of chaos. Her poise was an embodiment of vigilance, a testament to her unbroken awareness even in the midst of the chaotic symphony of gunfire. She was a conductor of precision, her gaze untamed by the storm that raged around her.

Yet, even amidst her fluid motions, Faye's perception reached beyond the immediate. Without the need to physically turn and look, she sensed it—a danger lurking in the shadows.

Her voice, as sharp as a blade, cut through the turmoil, calling out to Jack with a command that was both urgent and precise, "Jack, watch your back!"

The words echoed in the air, a bullet aimed at his consciousness. Jack's instincts, honed through survival and necessity, shifted him on a dime. His body twisted, a rapid pirouette to face the source of the threat that had eluded his attention. In the unfolding instant, time seemed to elongate, his reflexes racing against the inexorable march of seconds.

The gun he had so deftly reloaded swung up, but not quickly enough for a proper aim. The opponent, an agent of controlled force, surged forward with premeditated violence. The blow's trajectory was calculated, a swing aimed not at his head but his shoulder. In a rush of instinct, Jack's shoulder dipped and his head retracted, a macabre dance of evasion.

The impact landed with a jarring force, a symphony of flesh meeting force that resonated through his nerves. The world swayed in that instant, his arm suddenly deadweight, his fingers disconnecting from his weapon. In the aftermath, a numbness extended down his arm like a hate-filled embrace. As his gun tumbled from his grip, he found grim solace in the fact that the blow had struck his shoulder, sparing his jaw the devastating impact Delta 67-3 had initially intended. The dance of fate had veered, and in the twisted choreography of violence, Jack remained standing, but now he was unarmed.

Amidst the tumultuous clash of bullets and chaos, Faye's attention remained singularly focused on the unfolding battle. She understood Jack's capabilities well enough to know he could handle himself in this dire situation. Jack, her 'highly decorated soldier, Olympic medal-winning, arrogant, commended police officer', had instincts and abilities to help him in the battle that was his to navigate; Faye was entrenched in her own struggle, a personal skirmish that demanded her immediate attention.

Determined to track down Dr. Brundle, Faye's resolve was unwavering. The doctor represented the sole source capable of birthing abominations like Delta 67-3, a thought that fueled her pursuit. Though her encounter with him had been fleeting during the firefight, she harbored the certainty that the next time her sights settled on him would also mark his last. She narrowed her inhuman eyes and with a decisive motion, squeezed the trigger. Her weapon delivered a concise three-round burst, the bullets unerring as they found their mark in the retreating back of the last guard, now dwindling into the distance.

Without hesitation, Faye surged forward, her genetically modified body granting her a speed reminiscent of a cheetah's grace. Swiftly navigating the corner, she ventured in pursuit of the elusive doctor. Even though he wasn't immediately visible in the hallway, this fact bore little consequence for her; it neither hindered her chase nor alleviated her simmering agitation. Her keen sense of smell came to her aid, guiding her through the intricate network of interconnecting corridors with unwavering precision.

Eventually, she found herself before a door that granted access to the very laboratory Dr. Brundle occupied. With one gun holstered, she pressed the panel embedded next to the door, causing it to retreat noiselessly into the recesses of the wall. Stepping inside cautiously, Faye meticulously scanned the room, her senses attuned to any lurking threats that might jeopardize her mission.

"Well, isn't this a surprise, Alpha 06 returning to the den," Dr. Brundle mused, his tone a curious blend of intrigue and apparent nonchalance. "Your data stream has abruptly halted. A self-imposed detachment, or was it another hand that intervened? Ah, it hardly matters now that you're back; the information I require can be extracted directly from your cells," he rambled, his words weaving through the air like an intricate tapestry of machinations.

"It doesn't matter who removed it and my name is not Alpha 06, it's Faye," she retorted with an unwavering calmness that belied the storm within.

"Very well, Faye it is then, a name to summon henceforth. But do indulge me, why this unexpected homecoming?" Dr. Brundle's inquiry hung in the air, his mental landscape an enigma she had struggled to decode for as long as she had known him. His thought patterns seemed an intricate dance of chaos.

"You know perfectly well why I'm here but I want to ask you a question of my own. Why are you doing this?" she asked

"Why, you ask? To restore the natural equilibrium, perhaps? The superior entities, they merit a station in this world befitting their essence. Far too lengthy has the reign of the inferior persisted. They necessitate guidance from a leader of refined sensibilities, a ruler driven by benevolence and contemplation," his speech flowed like a torrent, a torrent of convictions that he had long held.

Dr. Brundle's monologue, veering wildly into the realms of incoherence, felt like a jumble of words with no anchor in reality. His intentions seemed far from lucid; his claims of dominion over the world rang hollow. Faye had long seen through this facade. His obsession lay within the confines of genetic research, an obsession that had consumed him entirely. She saw past the veil of false motives, recognizing his motives were tainted, his visions skewed. World domination was but a smoke screen concealing his single-minded pursuit.

Faye couldn't help but find herself facing what appeared to be a deranged mind, a cacophony of thoughts that only amplified her determination to bring him to an end, once and for all.

"And you believe that person to be you? All those lives lost, the Shepherds slaughtered, just to seize control?" she pressed, her voice laced with a mix of incredulity and accusation.

In response, Dr. Brundle's laughter reverberated, a brittle sound devoid of mirth. "Their sacrifices were a crucial foundation for the emergence of a new world order. It's not for me to lead; I merely assume the role of a humble facilitator, nudging the evolution into existence. My influence, minuscule as it may be, shall only merit a passing mention, a mere footnote in the annals of transformation."

As Faye engaged in the exchange, she deftly orchestrated her movements, her steps guided by a dual purpose. Her words became a backdrop to her calculated repositioning within the confines of the lab. With strategic precision, she secured a vantage point that afforded her an unobstructed view of the doctor. Each movement was a chess piece skillfully placed on the board, an intricate dance with a deadly intent simmering just beneath the surface. She situated herself with discerning care, ensuring that when the opportune moment arose, her aim would be unhindered and her shot would be executed with utmost clarity.

Her voice dripping with contempt, Faye retorted, "Your delusions have driven you to madness and instability. The world doesn't thirst for your twisted brand of leadership."

A sinister amusement curved Dr. Brundle's lips as he responded, "Ah, but therein lies your misjudgment. Humanity craves it, hungers for the yoke of control. They yearn for dominion and willingly relinquish their autonomy to despots, to fascists, even to anarchists who promise upheaval as a conduit for change. They seek order—and we are poised to offer them the semblance of order they so desperately beg for in their lives."

With a voice weighted by the weight of history, Faye retorted, "Your words echo those of countless madmen who have embarked on similar paths in the past."

"Yes, yes, girl. But who cares about them." Dr. Brundle's hands waved around as he announced his brand of crazy to the world. "They are they and I am me. They are dust. What you say, that might be so but they do not have what I have," said Dr. Brundle.

Faye was becoming fed up with his nonsense.

"Ah, the masses, my dear, mere specks in the grand tapestry of existence," Dr. Brundle's hands gestured wildly, as if his crazed philosophy could be physically mapped out.

"Their concerns, their lives, they hold no relevance. They are as fleeting as dust, a truth that you profess. But amidst their insignificance, the crux lies in what sets me apart," he continued, his fingers delicately brushing a panel at his side.

With his touch, the once-opaque wall of the laboratory transformed into transparent clarity, revealing a vast chamber beyond. The sight within that chamber unfurled before Faye's eyes, painting a scene that shattered her prior assumptions. The realization dawned upon her with an unsettling weight—perhaps she had erred in confining Dr. Brundle's ambitions solely to genetic manipulation and engineering. The tableau before her now suggested a far more ominous intent: a plot of absolute domination conceived within the mind of a man driven by madness.

In the flickering light of the lab, the truth unfolded in stark clarity, jolting Faye's convictions. This unhinged individual wasn't merely content with genetic experiments; he aspired to reign supreme, and the menacing tableau before her served as a chilling testament to that disturbing reality.

"The arsenal I've crafted stands as a testament to my genius," he proclaimed, his voice laden with pride and conviction. "These creations of mine surpass all, wielding loyalty and obedience as their virtues. Their strength eclipses that of the feeble humans tenfold, their ability to mend wounds in moments unmatched. Not a force on this known Earth could challenge them. Once armed with the weaponry we've tailored to their capabilities, establishing dominion shall be as effortless as breathing."

Faye's retort was swift, a lash of skepticism driving her words, "No one is giving up their freedom willingly for this new world that you're talking about. It won't happen. They'll fight you with everything that they have before they bow down."

The desire to end his mad tirade surged within Faye, yet she remained immobile, her path obstructed by a partition impervious to bullets. Dr. Brundle, seemingly attuned to her intentions, had strategically sought refuge behind this protective barrier. His positioning was far from strategic or calculated, merely an embodiment of his deranged psyche that sought to prolong his verbal disarray. There was no grand strategy at play here, no dramatic unveiling of a masterstroke from the throes of defeat; there was just madness, and his compulsion to voice it.

"Foolish girl, who said we would accomplish these lofty goals through any use of force? These foolish humans will have the yoke of servitude about their neck of their own volition. The time will come and they will willingly hand us control, begging for it, and needing it before they even realize what they've done." In a fleeting lapse of lucidity, Dr. Brundle emerged from his haven behind the barricade, his actions driven by impulse rather than calculated consideration.

"You're a fool if you think I'm going to allow that to happen. I'll stop you here and now." Faye declared.

She trained her gun on the doctor. Briefly diverting her gaze from Dr. Brundle, Faye took in the new surroundings, a swift evaluation etched with the purpose of gathering intel. The lab's atmosphere carried a distinct hint of chemicals, a scent tingling at the edge of her senses. It was unmistakably reminiscent of the compound Dr. Brundle had previously introduced into the incubation pod systems—a sinister concoction that had facilitated the abrupt termination of clones in their early stages. Faye had been a reluctant witness to these macabre procedures, observing the transformation of nascent life into a grotesque mixture of cellular remnants and viscous matter, a haunting semblance of what once held human form.

Her heightened sense of smell drew her eyes to a vial containing the very substance that had caused such destruction. Curiously, it was the same vial Donovan Pike, an acquaintance from weeks past, had been inspecting. The interwoven threads of past and present were inescapable, converging in this very moment, within the confines of this unsettling lab. She reached over and picked it up.

"Your actions hold no leverage," Dr. Brundle retorted, comprehension dawning as he grasped the significance of Faye's chosen vial.

Faye's gaze shifted from the vial to the doctor, a steely resolve painting her expression. As if driven by an unspoken intention, she advanced further into the lab, her steps carrying a weighty determination. Her focus narrowed upon a vat, a nexus of tubes converging into the wall, leading to the incubation pods where the clones resided. It was the nutrient vat, the lifeline for the clone soldiers, and her gaze moved towards it with an unwavering sense of purpose. In her grasp, she held the conduit that, with a single decisive act, could terminate this legion of clone soldiers, erasing their existence in one swift stroke.

"Your actions won't deter us. Our course remains unchanged. Destiny is immutable, girl!" Dr. Brundle's voice soared in a cacophony of desperation, spittle flecking at the corners of his mouth.

Urgency fueled his movements as he lunged toward Faye, a fervent intent to halt her course of action. Yet, Faye's swift reaction was unflinching. In a heartbeat, her gun was aimed, and the trigger pulled. The doctor's body jerked violently, propelled backwards before collapsing onto the floor in a lifeless heap. A small hole punctuated his forehead, while the impact on the ground rendered the back of his head a shattered mass resembling a crushed pumpkin. With an air of detachment, Faye observed the aftermath for a moment, her gaze devoid of emotion. With an oath hanging on her lips, she cast the vial into the nutrient vat, the contents mingling with the once-vital essence that sustained the clone soldiers. Her attention then turned to the pods lining the wall, incubation chambers slowly transmuting from human-like forms to gelatinous remnants.

Turning her back on the grim spectacle, Faye moved towards a door opposite the wall. With deliberate steps, she entered a dimly lit room hosting another incubation pod chamber, distinct from the ones behind the wall. A separate nutrient vat fed this chamber, and its contents held a significance that eclipsed the rest. Her focus unwavering, Faye embarked on her task, the door closing softly behind her as she delved into her purpose within the shadows.

Jack's arm throbbed, a symphony of pins and needles that sang a promising tune. The sensation was a reassuring whisper from his body, a testament that the aftermath of that punch was receding, and life was trickling back into his fingers. It hadn't been an incapacitating blow, only a momentary nerve pinch, a stroke of luck that had saved him from the pitfall of vulnerability or worse—a knockout. Had the punch found his chin, he'd have found himself sprawled on the unforgiving corridor floor, senses scrambled.

Delta 67-3 was the owner of that punch, a punch laden with brute force that, if honed precisely, had the potential to shatter bones and cripple spirits. Jack could sense the weight of it in the very air that surrounded the towering figure. The aftermath of its impact echoed in Jack's arm, a harbinger of the devastation it could wreak. One thing was certain, a fraction of that punch, even a glancing blow, would leave him reeling.

His gaze flicked downward, resting on his discarded gun lying just out of reach. Retrieving it was a death wish he wasn't willing to indulge. A sense of impending doom whispered that he'd be a breath away from the abyss before he could even wrap his fingers around the weapon. He squared his stance, readying himself for the battle of flesh and grit.

Gradually, sensation flowed back into his arm, and he shifted his weight, subtly realigning himself. Delta 67-3 loomed opposite, his critical gaze dissecting Jack's every fiber. A single, odd sniff cut through the charged air, followed by a smile—eerily patient and revealing rows of incisive teeth that sent a shiver down Jack's spine.

A grin flirted with Jack's lips, a shard of dark humor in the face of danger. "Damn you're ugly. But that's least of your problems, you need a dentist."

The words seemed to slice through the tense atmosphere, settling around them with an audacity that couldn't be ignored. Delta 67-3, his eye concealed beneath a bandage, growled, his voice carrying the weight of accusation. The bandage was a symbol of the chaos that had followed their previous encounter, the trauma he'd inflicted. With a deliberate move, Delta removed the bandage, revealing a milky-white, partially healed eye—a canvas marked by past pain and healing efforts.

Jack's voice was tinged with an ironic sympathy. "Guess some things never quite go back to the way they were. That's too bad, I guess."

Delta 67-3's eye locked onto Jack's, their gaze locked in a standoff that transcended the physical. The tension was palpable, a mirror of their history of clashing wills and conflicting objectives. And yet, there was a mutual understanding here, buried beneath the layers of violence and hostility—a shared realization that they were players in a larger narrative, pawns in a relentless game.

In the stillness, a hint of the past lingered, the residue of actions and choices that had shaped their present. The corridor became a stage, their confrontation a choreography of danger, raw power, and quiet reflection. One man's dark humor met another's scarred resilience, and in that juxtaposition, the narrative unfolded, painting an intricate picture of conflict and nuance.

Jack was acutely aware that he had discharged an entire clip of potent .45 caliber hollow point rounds into the man standing right before him. The proximity was impossible to ignore; a mere five feet separated them at the moment of the shots. What Jack found even more astonishing was that all nine rounds had struck the man with uncanny precision, each finding its mark at or around center mass. It was a certainty etched into his mind.

However, as he observed the scene before him, Jack couldn't help but acknowledge the surreal truth: the man was now standing again, as if the barrage of bullets had never torn through the air and pierced his body.

Jack's certainty remained unwavering; there was no denying the stark reality of what had unfolded. The memories were etched vividly within him, a relentless reminder of the events that had transpired. He had been an active participant in that chaos, the one who had unflinchingly squeezed the trigger, unleashing that torrent of firepower. Thus, he found himself not grappling with disbelief, but grappling with a wholly different dilemma—how to confront this relentless behemoth once more, devoid of a firearm in hand. The futility of nine rounds failing to incapacitate the creature hung heavy over him, a bitter truth he couldn't escape.

As for the prospect of subduing the relentless Delta 67-3 once again, Jack harbored no illusions. Even if he managed to bring it to its knees, he knew beyond any doubt that its downfall would be a fleeting victory, a mere hiccup in its inexorable rise. Jack's shoulder lifted in a casual shrug, his inner musings spilling out into a muttered soliloquy, barely audible even to himself.

"Oh well, what the hell," Jack's voice carried a mixture of resignation and determination. "Guess I'll keep trying till I can't anymore," he declared, his words underscoring a spirit that refused to capitulate.

With that unwavering resolve, Jack swung back into action, ready to engage in a battle whose outcome seemed uncertain, yet he remained undeterred. Jack's movement was swift, a direct response to the unyielding presence of Delta 67-3. His fist, fueled by frustration and a grim determination, met the surface of the creature's jaw with a resounding thud. The sensation reverberated through Jack's hand, akin to striking a solid mass of concrete molded into the shape of a man. Pain radiated up his arm, but to his astonishment, Delta 67-3 remained unfazed, as though Jack had struck an immovable object.

Acknowledging the futility of his initial approach, Jack swiftly recalibrated his tactics. This time, his leg swung purposefully, delivering a calculated blow from the formidable steel-toed boots he wore. The anticipated satisfying crunch of bone meeting force didn't materialize, but there was a visceral connection as his boot connected with Delta 67-3's form. While it didn't yield the intended shattering impact, it left a mark—a cut along the creature's chin, a testament to Jack's resilience and resourcefulness.

Intriguingly, as the cut on Delta 67-3's chin started to bleed, Jack witnessed an inexplicable phenomenon. The flow of blood ceased almost as quickly as it began, as if the creature's very existence defied the laws of nature itself. In the recesses of his mind, a thought echoed—a bleak acknowledgment of the ordeal ahead. Jack muttered under his breath, his words dripping with a mixture of grim acceptance and unyielding spirit.

This fight is gonna hurt, and it ain't gonna be pleasant—not like fights are ever a pleasant thing for the victor or vanquished, Jack's self-directed commentary held an air of sagacious truth.

A testament to the raw reality of combat, where pain and struggle were intrinsic elements that transcended roles. As the confrontation continued, Jack's internal premonition stood vindicated—this encounter was shaping up to be an arduous and unrelenting trial, as he had foreseen.

With an instinctual surge of movement, Jack's arms darted upward, barely managing to intercept the oncoming strike from Delta 67-3. The force behind the creature's blow landed with a ferocious impact on Jack's left forearm, an explosive collision that fractured bone upon impact and forcefully propelled him several steps backward. Pain erupted within him, a raw and unrelenting agony that manifested itself in a primal scream, echoing his torment across the battleground.

His left arm, now rendered powerless, dangled uselessly at his side like a broken puppet's limb, a stark emblem of the ruthless power he was confronting. The shockwaves of the ordeal reverberated through his body, leaving him gasping for air as he grappled with the intensity of his suffering.

In the blink of an eye, Jack's world transformed. His breathless respite, a mere pause in the torrent of chaos, was shattered as Delta 67-3 capitalized on the smallest lapse of attention. The distance Jack had painfully created with his prior actions had vanished like a mirage, the initial six-foot gap closing as swiftly as it had opened. Delta 67-3 stood before him, an embodiment of impending doom, mere inches away and radiating an aura of chilling menace.

With a sinister intimacy, Delta 67-3's voice slithered into Jack's ear, a venomous whisper that carried a potent mixture of sadistic pleasure and impending torment.

"This is gonna hurt," the words, coming back at him, dripped like venom, "I'm gonna enjoy fucking you up." The utterance hung in the air, a declaration of suffering yet to unfold.

A sudden, open-handed shove landed squarely on Jack's chest, igniting an intense blaze of pain that surged outward like a spreading inferno. The sensation was akin to a searing brand pressed onto his sternum, leaving him reeling from the unexpected onslaught. The force of the impact reverberated through his body, a visceral reminder that he was entwined in a ferocious struggle that spared no mercy.

The reality of his battered state couldn't be ignored. An agonizing certainty gripped Jack as he grappled with the aftermath of that shove. Whether his ribs had fractured under the onslaught or merely bore the brunt of a bruising, the consequences were clear—his body had become a canvas of torment, painted with the hues of the ongoing battle.

Gasping for breath, Jack found himself in a state of perpetual exhalation, his body 'sucking wind' as he attempted to restore his oxygen-starved lungs. The fight had transformed into a grueling test of endurance, where each breath was a treasured commodity, snatched from the clutches of pain and exertion.

In a cruel twist, Jack's reputation as a formidable boxer, even in the twilight of his years, held no sway in this nightmarish encounter. Despite his years of honing the craft of combat, he found himself ensnared in a relentless dance where his strikes were thwarted by an adversary impervious to their impact. The futility of his efforts was palpable, a bitter acknowledgment that even if his blows landed, they would bear no consequence against the indomitable Delta 67-3.

With a deceptive gentleness that defied the strength behind it, Delta 67-3 delivered what could almost be mistaken for a playful tap to Jack's right side. A hint of restraint lingered in the gesture, a deliberate choice to withhold the full brunt of its power. Jack's reaction was a mix of grunted discomfort and a burgeoning certainty that rippled through his senses. He knew, deep in his gut, that this seemingly innocuous strike had a darker consequence. A kidney punch, expertly placed, had left an imprint that he was convinced would translate into days of blood-tinged urine. If, of course, he made it through this trial alive—a survival that remained uncertain at best.

In the ever-shifting landscape of their confrontation, Jack's perception had evolved. No longer did he view this as a mere fight; it had transformed into a macabre communication, a brutal conversation punctuated by blows and pain. The transition was stark, and as Jack found himself reduced to his knees, a new level of realization dawned upon him.

The prospect of turning the tide in his favor felt like an elusive dream slipping through his fingers. The realization that the odds were stacked against him, that a triumphant reversal was becoming increasingly improbable, weighed heavily on him. Amidst the anguish and doubt, Jack grappled with a surge of frustration and helplessness, emotions that cast a shadow over his spirit like an impending storm.

In the midst of his tumultuous thoughts, a stray query emerged with a belated urgency. Jack almost laughingly asked himself, *Where is Faye?*

Jack was teetering on the precipice of both exhaustion and a catalogue of past injuries that threatened to resurface with each demanding move. The relentless combat had consumed a mere fraction of time, not even spanning ten minutes, yet the toll on his body was monumental. To expect more from him in that very moment would have amounted to sheer discourtesy and lunacy, pushing the boundaries of human endurance beyond reason.

What remained of Jack's reserves was a scant offering, a dwindling gift to be presented in the face of his formidable adversary. Offensive maneuvers were now a luxury he couldn't afford, and even his defense had taken on an audacious and desperate form. Perched on one knee, the weight of his own body pulling at his energy, he fought to keep his head upright, to defy the mounting fatigue that threatened to claim him.

The rhythm of his breathing was a testament to the struggle, each inhalation a strained effort that resonated like a coin clattering within the hollow confines of an empty can. It was an image that mirrored his own waning strength, the reserves of air diminished and echoing through his chest.

As he grappled with his own limitations, a sense of despondency began to creep in, a shadow that threatened to engulf him. Hopelessness loomed, an ominous cloud that darkened his spirit. Yet, in an ironic twist, this feeling of vulnerability and helplessness roused his spirit to defiant heights. The venomous gasp of words emerged from his lips, a declaration not only to his adversary but also to himself.

"That... all... you've got?" Jack's voice was punctuated by gasps.

Delta 67-3 advanced with an unsettling nonchalance, a calculated stride that closed the distance between them. His form settled into a squat, positioning him at eye level with Jack, an intimate proximity that seemed to underline the predatory dynamics at play. The creature rose fluidly, his left hand extending towards Jack's shirt. Fingers curled around the fabric, the grip both assured and inexorable as Delta 67-3 effortlessly hoisted Jack off the ground. In the suspended space between them, Jack's feet dangled a mere two or three inches above the unforgiving ground.

A chilling declaration escaped Delta 67-3's lips, a macabre promise delivered with a twisted sense of poetic justice. The words hung heavily in the air, laden with a sense of foreboding. Delta 67-3's right hand ascended, poised in a posture that sent shivers down Jack's spine. The notion of retribution was embodied in that moment, a horrifying realization of the saying 'an eye for an eye'. The intention became shockingly clear as Delta 67-3 angled his fingers toward Jack's face, the intent to pluck out his eye an act of merciless violence. The narrative took a sudden turn, interrupted by an abrupt and almost ironic interruption. A klaxon's shrill blare pierced the tense atmosphere, its alarm announcing the presence of an intruder within the facility. The irony was stark—the alarm, belated and seemingly redundant, coincided with a moment where its purpose was moot. The firefight that had erupted earlier had already exposed the intruders, making the klaxon's cry an exercise in futility.

For Jack, the klaxon's sudden clamor was a small blessing, a fleeting distraction that temporarily diverted Delta 67-3's attention. It offered a momentary respite from the impending agony that awaited him, a reprieve from the certainty of impending pain. Within this whirlwind of chaos, a subtle collision against his left side shattered his momentary sanctuary.

The klaxon's blaring note reverberated through the tense air, pulling Delta 67-3's attention from his grim task. His irritation at the momentary lapse was palpable; frustration coiled like a serpent beneath his skin. With a swift return of focus, he sought out Jack's gaze, only to be met with an unexpected sight—a smile dancing upon Jack's lips. Simultaneously, a subtle movement caught his peripheral vision, an elusive hint partially concealed by his own raised arm. Intrigue overcame his irritation, prompting him to lower his arm.

In the fraction of a second, the unfolding tableau escalated from mere curiosity to a dire realization. Before Delta 67-3 could react, a gun's cold muzzle was aimed unyieldingly at his forehead. The words he likely intended to utter were stolen from him, a twist of fate that allowed Jack to voice them instead.

"Oh, shit," exclaimed Jack as a loud pop sounded too close to him.

Faye's extended arm was now visible due to Delta 67-3's lowered shoulder and focus on the movement he had seen in his peripheral vision. The gunshot that ensued cracked through the air, too close for comfort, punctuating Jack's exclamation with a lethal finality.

Delta 67-3's head jerked back, his gaze momentarily lost in the abyss. As swiftly as his head recoiled backwards, it snapped forward again, locking eyes with Faye. The center of his forehead bore a small, smoking cavity, the telltale mark of a gunshot wound. A momentary blink was all he managed before his fingers, once so unrelenting, released Jack's body, letting him fall to the ground in a lifeless heap. Death had claimed him, as sudden as the gunshot that had heralded his end.

Amidst the echoes of violence, Jack shook his head with a grimace, a futile attempt to dispel the dissonant ringing that reverberated through his ears. Amidst his pain and confusion, a question slipped from his lips, a query that held a glimmer of hope.

"Isn't he just gonna heal?" Jack's voice bore a mixture of incredulity and resignation, the notion of Delta 67-3's invincibility still embedded in his mind.

Faye's response was a solemn shake of the head, a gesture that carried the weight of somber truths. "Some injuries defy healing," she replied, her words laden with a tinge of sadness.

She elucidated further, painting a grim picture of irreversible damage that defied even the most formidable recuperative abilities. The details painted a stark contrast to the once seemingly indestructible force that had now been reduced to a lifeless heap, his reign of terror ended by a bullet that had forever silenced his menace.

"It's too bad that shot to his eye went out the side of his head instead of the back. He won't recover from a brain injury like this though. Even if he could, half his brains are on the wall behind him," Faye disclosed, her tone carrying a hint of melancholy.

"Injuries to neurological processes can't be healed from quickly, like his eye, if it has anything to do with severe trauma to sensitive nerve systems," Faye disclosed, her tone carrying a hint of finality at this point.

Her words painted a grim picture, an intricate puzzle of damage that was now irreversible. She elaborated on the how no room for recovery existed for brain damage. The description brought to life the profound impact that had ended Delta 67-3's existence.

Exhaling a deep breath he hadn't even realized he was holding, Jack felt the weight of tension lift from his shoulders. The specter of an unresolved threat had been extinguished, and he was now free to embrace the respite that his battered body so desperately needed. A sigh of relief escaped him, accompanied by the sense that he could finally surrender to the encroaching darkness, relinquishing consciousness and the persistent ache that had become his constant companion.

However, his inclination to descend into a pain-numbed coma was swiftly quashed by Faye's resolute determination. She positioned Jack's uninjured arm over her shoulder, her support a lifeline as they began the laborious process of navigating their way out of the facility. Jack's yearning for rest and escape was put on hold as he found himself propelled forward, each step a testament to his endurance.

Amidst the physical ordeal, an odd, almost surreal vision flickered in Jack's weary mind. A miniature version of Faye seemed to stand beside them, a mirage that defied explanation. Dismissing it as a byproduct of his injuries, Jack forged on, not realizing that he was grappling with shock, moments of consciousness slipping through his grasp even as he remained upright.

With little else to cling to, Jack allowed himself to surrender to the inexorable tide of fatigue. The boundaries between consciousness and unconsciousness blurred, a delicate balance that facilitated the beginning of his healing process. It was a surrender, not of defeat, but of the burdens he had carried. As they pressed on, the facility's corridors began fading into the background.

16

As dawn broke, its golden tendrils slipped through the parting curtains, precisely aimed to land a warm greeting directly on Jack's face. The sun's insistent caress roused him from slumber, coaxing open the eyes he was almost tempted to keep sealed against the world.

The initial sensation that danced across his consciousness was the persistent ache coursing through his body—a reminder of recent events that had left their mark in the form of relentless discomfort. That unwelcome sensation quickly found its counterpart in his awareness—a damn pain that had staked its claim within his being. After these twin revelations had made their mark, his attention was finally free to explore the other facets of his waking reality.

Slowly, meticulously, Jack began to take stock of his various body parts, cataloging their conditions, both in terms of pain and functionality. His chest was swathed in a bandage, an embrace that spoke of recent tribulations. The right side of his torso throbbed with a dull persistence, a reminder that it was far from pleased with recent events, yet still grateful for the continuation of life. He suspected his skin was painted in hues of blue and black, but verifying that visual truth would have to wait. For now, his concern shifted, focusing on two additional revelations that had found their place in the dawning morning.

The first was a visual proclamation of his current state—his left arm embraced by a cast, a modern emblem of childhood vigor and exuberance, which now marked his temporary fragility. The second discovery, and the one that breathed life into the rest of his morning,

was the delicate purring that emanated from the form of the woman
nestled by his side.

Jack allowed a soft smile to grace his lips as he absorbed the subtle
melody of contentment that radiated from Faye's presence. He drew
her closer, he felt her response—a joyful squeal that danced through
the air, bridging the space between them. There was a simple beauty
to the moment, in the curve of Faye's form against his, in the
interplay of their breaths and heartbeats.

"Good morning, Faye," Jack's voice, a gentle caress of sound, reached
out to the sleepy presence that had been nestled beside him in the
warmth of the bed.

Faye stirred, a graceful emergence from the bed's embrace, her form
guided by a languid stretch that mirrored the fluid grace of a cat
disturbed from a sun-soaked nap. Her movements, a symphony of
unhurried flexes, spoke of a tranquil connection with her body, a
harmony between slumber and wakefulness. As her gaze met his, her
lips curved into a smile, a silent exchange of unspoken camaraderie.

Jack found himself drawn to the sight before him, captivated by the
candid allure of her eyes, unadorned by the veil of contact lenses.
Her gaze, a masterpiece of nature's design, ensnared him, the vertical
slits of her greenish gold irises a magnetic invitation to peer into the
depths of her being.

With a grace that matched her earlier stretch, Faye leaned in, her lips
finding purchase on his cheek in a tender kiss. The fleeting touch
ignited a warmth that surged through his veins, a fusion of affection
and desire that stirred beneath his skin. Yet, as their proximity
heightened, another visual delight presented itself—a view down her
shirt, a tantalizing glimpse that heated his blood and quickened his
pulse.

Jack's good arm found its purpose, a protective embrace that drew
her closer to him, a gesture of intimacy that transcended the physical
realm. But as she pressed against his chest and side, his grimace of

pain betrayed the tender territory of his injuries, the echoes of their recent trials. These pains, however, carried a certain significance—a testament to survival, a reminder that life's adversities were worth the triumph of another day lived.

They shared a moment, amidst the quiet murmurs of morning, Jack and Faye found themselves entwined in the dance of their own narrative. The morning light, casting its benevolent glow upon them, was but a reflection of the luminosity they had discovered in each other's presence.

"I got you to the hospital, and they patched you up. Your sister played a crucial role in getting you back home. Leaving you in the hospital just didn't sit right with me when you could recover here with me," Faye's words, a soothing reassurance, flowed like a gentle current in the space between them. The weight of concern lingered in her tone, a testament to the depths of her commitment. "Though, I must admit, you've had quite the slumber—two full days, to be precise."

Jack's inquiry was laden with the echoes of their recent trials, a desire to comprehend the unspoken gaps in their shared narrative. "And everything that happened... How did we get past all of that?"

A sense of retrospection settled in Faye's gaze, her eyes like pools reflecting the journey they had undertaken. "The Foundation moved quickly. By the time your sister and I returned to the facility, it had already been locked down. Our entry required some finesse, but once inside, we discovered an empty canvas—every trace meticulously erased. Your sister worked her magic, alongside Jason, the coroner. They pieced together enough of a cover story to close the cases, even in the absence of a body. The explanation? The body was cremated, and the identity of the killer remains an enigma—no dental records, no health records, no identifiers. A perfect vanishing act."

Jack's nod acknowledged the neat resolution, the closure they had achieved amidst the chaos. "A rather seamless way to tie up loose ends. Now that the case is concluded, and your former employer is, let's say, retired, what's next for you?"

Faye's gaze shifted, a fleeting glimpse into the thoughts that swirled beneath her calm exterior. "Well, it turns out that Donovan Pike has embarked on a new career path as the state's governor. Unfortunately, there's little we can do about that."

"Wow," Jack managed, his weariness temporarily outweighing any immediate need to delve into the implications, allowing the statement to hang in the air unexplored.

Curiosity danced in the space between them, an unspoken question still lingering in the air. "So, what lies ahead for you?" Jack queried, his gaze locked onto hers.

A contemplative smile played on Faye's lips, an echo of the complexities that resided within her. "That, my dear detective, is an excellent question," she mused, her smile a subtle testament to the mysteries that still awaited them on the horizon.

Reclining once more, she rested her chin on folded hands, casting a coquettish gaze Jack's way. An internal alarm sounded for Jack—a sense of impending mischief. Yet, the prospect of having Faye nestled in his bed like this, even if it came with a dose of trouble, was a trade-off he was more than willing to accept.

"I thought I might suggest something a bit more intimate and adventurous than cuddling, provided you're feeling up to it," her words carried a teasing purr, a melody that echoed in the space between them.

As they stood on the precipice of a new experience, Jack contemplated Faye's proposition. This step would lead them beyond the bounds of platonic embraces. His physical state posed an obstacle, but the prospect of surrendering to his desires tugged insistently. However, practicality intervened—his injuries, his ribs protesting their participation.

Unbeknownst to Jack, this tender juncture held deeper significance for Faye. Their previous closeness had been tempered by the withholding of information, her identity shrouded in secrecy. What Jack didn't realize was that this was a first for Faye in more ways than one. Her unspoken truth was that she wasn't fully human and didn't know what that would mean for their budding relationship, an admission that trembled on the precipice of revelation.

For now, she refrained from words—instead, choosing to convey her intent through actions. Faye shifted onto her knees atop the bed, her gaze fixed on Jack. With tantalizing slowness, she began to undo the buttons of her shirt, the fabric yielding inch by inch. Only two buttons released their grip before the unexpected entrance of reality interrupted their intimate interlude.

The bedroom door swung open, shattering the atmosphere like a stone shattering glass. Jack's mind whirled, his confusion mounting as he tried to comprehend who would dare intrude uninvited. Faye's squeal cut through the air, her arms instinctively covering her exposed skin.

In the midst of this sudden disruption, a small voice piped up, breaking the silence that enveloped the room. As Jack struggled to sit up, his groan mingling with the sounds of surprise, his eyes locked onto an improbable sight. It was as if reality had bent itself to mirror his own disbelief—a miniature Faye, complete with the same mesmerizing vertical-slit irises, stood before him.

"Mommy, I heard you talking. Is the man awake?" inquired the miniature version of Faye, rubbing the remnants of sleep from her eyes with a childlike innocence.

In her small hand, she clutched a teddy bear that was typically found on the bed in the adjacent bedroom—the very room Jack's niece Brooke often occupied during her stays. Clad comfortably in one of Jack's button-down dress shirts, the little Faye replica stood before them, embodying an uncanny similarity.

With warmth and patience, Faye responded, "Yes, sweetie, the man is awake," her voice carrying a gentleness that bespoke the nurturing mother within her.

Inviting the child closer, she motioned for her to come near. "Come and say hello."

The little girl eagerly joined Faye on the bed, her youthful enthusiasm radiating in the room. As she settled in, Faye introduced her daughter to Jack, their worlds suddenly converging.

"Princess, this is Jack. Jack, this is Cadi, my daughter," Faye's words bore a mix of pride and tenderness.

Stunned, Jack stumbled over his words, "I didn't know that you had a daughter."

Faye's explanation flowed, revealing a complex truth. "Well, technically, I didn't give birth to her. She's a product of one of my eggs and the genetic manipulation conducted by that eccentric Shepherd scientist who created me and my brothers. They used Shepherd material to fertilize her egg, making her, like me, part Shepherd. Unfortunately, the implications for her future remain uncertain. Biologically, she's around eight years old. Chronologically, she's merely a month old, so her brain is still in the process of development. Yet, she's already operating at a high school level of intelligence, soaking up knowledge like a sponge."

Jack struggled to grasp the enormity of this revelation. "So, let me get this straight—you now have an eight-year-old daughter who's a genius, and she's expected to outlive us all. You, me, my sister and Brooke's lifespans all added together?"

Faye's smile held a touch of resignation as she offered a nod. "Yes, that sums it up."

Jack's astonishment found expression in a simple exclamation: "Wow."

Turning his attention towards Cadi, Jack extended his right hand, an unspoken invitation for connection. Her hand found his tentatively, and she graced him with a hesitant smile, the mixture of curiosity and shyness painting her expression. Jack's introduction was delivered with a genuine warmth that made her feel at ease.

"Hi, Cadi. I'm Jack. It's nice to meet you."

Her response held a genuine politeness, her voice a soft echo of her smile. "Hi, Jack."

Yet, as the conversation evolved, a mischievous glint danced in Cadi's eyes, hinting at the playful curiosity hidden beneath her childlike demeanor. With a pointed look at Jack, she addressed her mother, her question carrying layers of complexity that belied her young age.

"Mommy," she began, her gaze fixed on Jack, "do you love this man?"

The near-comical nature of the question almost prompted a chuckle from Jack, a reaction he managed to suppress just in time. Faye's measured response mirrored her attempt to discern the path of Cadi's inquiry.

"Yes," Faye answered, her voice deliberately steady as she gauged Cadi's intentions, "I do."

Cadi, unburdened by convention, pressed on with her questioning, her innocent demeanor belying the depth of her inquiry. "Then is this man here your mate?"

Jack had learned to peer beyond Cadi's youthful exterior, recognizing the wisdom that sparkled within her gaze. This wasn't just a simple question; it carried a weight that resonated with the unique dynamic between him and Faye.

"Yes, Cadi," Faye's tone was a blend of sincerity and vulnerability as she addressed her daughter, her eyes shifting between Jack and Cadi. "I do consider this man to be my mate," she confirmed, her gaze resting on Jack with hope and affection. "If he will have me."

Emotions surged within Jack, a mixture of joy and a sense of responsibility. He pulled Faye closer, pushing aside the discomfort from his bruised ribs to savor the closeness of the moment.

"I will have you for as long as both of us live and longer still," he declared, his commitment resolute.

With this declaration hanging in the air, Jack's attention turned to Cadi, his fingers playfully ruffling her hair in a gesture of acceptance and affection. The exchange between them was a silent conversation, a moment of connection that went beyond words.

Cadi gracefully descended from the bed, her youthful confidence exuding as she made her way toward the door, indicating her intent to leave the room. Her words carried a weight that seemed to mingle both with innocence and significance, as she addressed the newfound reality before her.

"I guess I'll have to call you daddy from now on," she commented, her tone imbued with a mixture of curiosity and acceptance.

With her declaration made, she exited the room, the door closing softly behind her. The room's atmosphere held a suspended moment after Cadi's departure, allowing Jack to process the implications of her words. He had only recently come to terms with one puzzling revelation—the real source of the constant purring he had been hearing was, in fact, Faye herself. Yet, this new development left him grappling with uncertainty once again, the doubts clouding his sense of reality in this ever-changing landscape.

Jack blinked, his eyes moving in a rapid succession as if trying to retrace the scene that had just unfolded. It was a reflexive reaction, a way to grapple with the profoundness of the moment. For all the experiences, knowledge, and revelations he had encountered, this instance managed to raise doubts within him yet again. The scene replayed in his mind, each blink bringing forth a series of fleeting images.

As Cadi exited the room, an almost imperceptible detail caught Jack's attention, triggering his disbelief. He could have sworn that, as she moved, a tail—covered in sleek black fur—flicked out from beneath the shirt she was wearing.

explicitus est liber

https://writingfortheworldpress.com